homestands

Chicago Wind
Book One

Sally Bradley

X

To Kerri

You read this book many times, when it was so far away from being ready for reader consumption. Thank you for being a kind and gentle fan way back then.

And by the way, your idea for the ending turned out to be the right one.

Louisburg Library
Bringing People and Information Together

Chapter One

The end came, as it nearly always did, when his thoughts were elsewhere, his focus on other things. When life seemed okay, if not good.

This time he was staring at the years-old picture he held of himself with Meg when he realized that someone had, several seconds ago, sat down beside him on the bed.

And that it could only be Sara.

It was too late to hide the picture.

But he did anyway.

Sara drew her eyes slowly to his, her lips pressed together. "This isn't working, is it?"

"I just found it. I was packing and—"

"Mike Connor." She laughed and eased to her feet with the same calm reaction she gave all of his jokes. "Who do you think you're lying to here?"

"No one. I'm not lying."

"Well, you're definitely not lying to me." She wandered across the room, then turned in front of the bathroom doorway and watched him.

He tried not to squirm.

Her crossed arms said control, not self-preservation. She pursed her lips. "I've seen this coming for a while, you know."

He played dumb. "Seen what coming?"

"The end of us."

"Sara." He forced all the emotion and love he could into her name. "I told you. I was packing and I found it."

"Why is it even here, Mike? You brought everything into this place six weeks ago when you came down for spring training. If this were your house, then maybe—maybe—I could see you stumbling across it."

He glanced around, his gaze finally landing on the black Samsonite peeking from the bottom of the open closet. "It must have already been in a suitcase."

"Right." She leaned against the doorjamb, sending him a sad smile. "You're not over her."

"Come on." He laughed. "Don't tell me you never think about past relationships."

"How often are we talking, Mike? Why do I get the feeling that every relationship you've had has ended this way? I know what I'm talking about—you're not over her. You need to see her."

"No. Nope." His pulse sped just a bit at the idea. He hadn't seen Meg in over six years. Six long years in which every relationship fizzled under the memory of what he'd thrown away.

But Sara was right about one thing—the two of them had been over for a while. Back in February he'd been eager to leave her in freezing Chicago and hightail it to sunny Arizona. Nothing to concentrate on but the team and baseball, until a week ago when she'd come down to stay with him over spring break. He rubbed his eyes, suddenly worn out and longing for sleep.

"Do you realize you're still sitting on the bed? That your hand is still on her picture? You haven't even bothered getting up to persuade me to stay."

Wow. He studied the pattern of the carpet. No rebuttal came to mind.

But the thought of going back to his massive home and finding it empty of everything Sara was depressing. He forced himself to stand, knees creaking, and walked across the bedroom to her.

She stayed where she was, eyes on him.

He pulled her into his arms, and she let him, even though her arms stayed folded in front of her.

They really were done.

His throat tightened. There was so much he should say, but his voice would betray him. And what was he really emotional about this time? Was he sorry to see Sara go? Or just sorry that he'd be alone?

Again.

Sara sighed as she moved out of his arms and stepped around him.

He turned, watched her walk to the nightstand.

Her straight brown hair hung down her back in a thick, soft ponytail. She loved her hair, and he'd lied and told her he thought it was beautiful too.

But it was always dark, honey-blonde hair he loved. Meg's long, wavy hair.

Sara pulled something from her planner and palmed it.

"What?" he asked. "You've got an ex-husband you're going to show me?"

"Stop it. I want you to go see her."

"This is dumb, Sara. I don't even know where she is or what—"

She held out her hand. A business card rested in her palm.

Mike stared at the card. She had to be kidding. "No."

"Take it, Mike."

He couldn't.

A moment later it was in his hands. *Meghan Connor Designs*. He read the raised lettering, his heart thudding inside him. This couldn't be.

"She's half an hour from you, Mike. From either home."

Half an hour.

"She's an interior designer. Another teacher recommended her when we looked into hiring someone. I hear she's good."

"She's very good."

"Yes." She cleared her throat. "Well."

Half an hour away? They'd been in Texas when they'd divorced, and she'd vanished so fast. He'd been traded to Chicago just over a year ago, fresh off another break-up, Meg on his mind.

For the last year she'd been half an hour away.

"I'll get into O'Hare around six tonight. By the time you get back to Chicago on Sunday, I'll be out of your place." Sara picked up her things as she talked—a perfume bottle, her iPad, her flat iron, and makeup bag. She shoved them one after another into her carry-on, the first sign that this hurt. "I'll mail you my keys. You'll get them next week."

Always on top of things. Always ready for anything. "Where will you go?"

"I guess I—" She stopped her stuffing and froze over the bag. Her ponytail slid over her shoulder and covered his view of her face.

He studied Meg's business card.

A moment later she sniffed and zipped her bag closed.

Mike looked up.

She was wiping her nose.

She jabbed a finger at him. "You go see her. You find out if there's anything left there. You hear me?"

"Sure." Not likely.

"And after all that, if there's nothing left between you two—"

Three quick steps, and she was in his arms.

He held her while she shook against him.

But just as quickly, it was over and she pushed herself back. "If it ever really ends between you two, then you call me. Okay?"

"Okay."

It wouldn't happen. Sara was already his past. There was no going back.

He looked beyond her at the picture lying on the bed. Not even Meg would take him back.

"I have to tell them about the foundation issues?"

Meg Connor laughed at Dana's horrified expression. It had been worth hiring an employee, just for this little perk. "It's best if you go there and show them exactly where the problem is. I'd send the general contractor, but he and his family should be landing in Florida about now."

"Did he plan that trip before or after he found out about the foundation?"

"Very funny." Meg slid her chair back to her desk. "They suspected there might be problems. Now that the basement is demoed, we know for sure. They won't be shocked."

Dana tipped her head back, her short blonde hair swinging away from her face. "Why can't you do it?"

"Because I have a date."

Dana straightened in her chair, her wide eyes saying, *Do tell.*

"With Jill. Girls' night out."

"Oh. You need a real date."

Meg rolled her eyes. "I'm fine, Dana. Be glad I actually get out every now and then, or I'd be a miserable boss."

"You're already making me tell these poor people that their foundation is sinking. Can it get worse than that?"

A knock at the office door drew Meg's gaze.

Jill Ashburn, her best friend, stood in the doorway, a grin on her face. "Time to go," Jill said. "Any work not done can wait for next week."

Meg closed her laptop. "More like tomorrow morning."

"Let's be honest, Meg." Dana pointed her pen at the computer. "That thing will be on five minutes after you get back tonight. Wear her out, Jill. Make her forget all about fabric and drywall and crumbling foundations."

"It's a lost cause, Dana. The woman loves her job. I'm hoping for a fifteen-minute reprieve before she starts talking shop."

"All right, all right." No one ganged up on her like these two did. "I'll try to not think about work. For a little while." She grabbed her purse from beneath her desk. "We're ready?"

"We're ready. The boys are with Clark, and we're free women."

She needed this night, more than Jill knew. As much as Meg loved her work, the schedule was killing her. She smoothed the front of her pants. "Lock my front door when you leave, Dana."

"Then you better have someone else give the news about the foundation."

Jill laughed.

Meg waved Dana's words away.

Outside, Jill's beige Camry sat in the driveway.

"Where are we headed?" Meg asked.

"Dinner and pedicures. I'm thinking Chinese sounds good."

It did. Meg opened the passenger door and climbed into the car. The last week had been so busy, there'd been no time for anything but food that cooked fast. Or could be picked up fast. Vegetables themselves sounded heavenly.

"So I've got two clients set up for April already—"

"Stop." Jill held up one hand as she backed out of the driveway. "No work talk, remember?"

Meg groaned. "But things are going so well. I might even hire another—"

"Nope. Not tonight. We're just going to have fun."

"Fine. What do you want to talk about?"

"Samuel started crawling today."

"He did? He's such a doll. Tell him not to grow up so fast. I loved that age."

"And…" Jill held up a finger as she stopped at a four-way stop sign. "Clark brought home a surprise."

"What's that?"

"Someone at church had tickets to the Wind's home opener. Right behind home plate. They can't use them so they gave them to him."

Meg's stomach seized.

"Four tickets. Me, Clark, you, and—"

"No." She shook her head, her hair swinging into her face. "No, Jill. We're not going."

"What do you mean you're not going? Terrell loves the Wind."

"It's too risky. It's too close."

"Meg, come on. There'll be forty thousand people there. Mike will never see you."

"You said the seats were behind home plate."

"Like twenty rows back."

What was Clark thinking? She hadn't been within eye sight of Mike in years. They couldn't go. It was way too risky.

"Relax, Meg. You've been saying for a month that you'd contact Mike. Think of this as a chance to warm up to it. A baby step. It'll be fine, I promise."

Would it?

"And it'll make Terrell's day. Think about that. He can wear his new jersey, watch Mike play. He'll love it."

Meg hid her face with a shaky hand. He would.

"We thought you'd be okay with this. You're still planning on talking to him, right?"

Eventually. From her death bed.

"No way." Jill shook a finger at her, eyes still on the road. "You're putting it off, aren't you?"

Meg moaned. "Jill, I can't."

"Meg, you *have* to. Go to the game. See that he's just a guy—"

"With a ton of money who can sue the daylights out of me."

Jill sighed.

Meg watched a strip mall fly by.

"You know what I think?" Jill asked.

"I don't want to know."

"I think you're working extra hard so you don't have time to deal with him."

Meg sank into her seat.

"You'll wear yourself out. It's not fair to you, and it's not fair to Terrell."

"Like life has been fair."

"Meg, you're the one who's not being fair. Terrell needs more from you than just a few minutes a night. Call Mike. Get it over with. Everything will be better after that."

Terrell… Meg stared blindly out her window. Almost done with kindergarten. Growing so fast.

And starting to ask more frequently about his father.

The father she didn't want to talk about.

Ever.

But that wasn't realistic. While she could ignore Terrell's questions now and shut them down, the day was coming when her little boy wouldn't be so little—and would *not* take no for an answer.

The tickets were a reality check. Far better to contact Mike now than years from now. If she waited too long, waited until Terrell forced her hand, she might lose her son because of her *own* choices.

Not because Mike had taken him from her.

"So are you going to the game?" Jill asked again.

Yes. No. Maybe? She closed her eyes in defeat. Baby steps, right? "We'll go."

Chapter Two

Ben Reynolds parked his Honda Civic in his driveway. Letting the engine idle, he rested his forehead against the steering wheel, knots of muscle burning at the base of his neck.

A shudder ran across his shoulder blades and down his back. He was safe, he reminded himself. The cop hadn't been following him after all.

Still, his heart beat faster than he liked. He hadn't had such a close call in months.

He lifted his head and looked up the driveway. Dana's Jeep Cherokee sat in front of the garage. She'd beat him home, all because of that annoying cop. He closed his eyes and exhaled a slow breath.

He hated not being in control.

When his heart rate returned to normal, Ben turned off the engine and pushed open the door. He checked the living room's picture window, but the glare of the late afternoon sun made it impossible to see in. Dana was probably in the kitchen making dinner.

His stomach rumbled.

He opened the car's back door and picked up the potted rosebush sitting on the floor, careful not to scratch himself on the thorns. With his other hand he grabbed the plastic Home Depot bag, then nudged the door shut with his knee.

There. He was ready.

Curly black hair fell across one of his eyes, and Ben tossed his head until the curl disappeared. Today their relationship moved forward. Or fell apart. He shook his head, that obnoxious curl falling again. He refused to imagine disaster. He wouldn't be taking this step if he wasn't sure of Dana's response. After a year together, he knew her as completely as he ever could.

He liked that feeling.

Ben walked up the driveway, between her Cherokee and the dining room's bay window and into the backyard where, as he'd expected, the kitchen door was propped open in honor of the day's breezes.

He stopped beneath the kitchen window. "Dana?"

Her face appeared, shadowed behind the screen.

"Come on out," he called.

Her forehead pushed the screen. "What is that?"

"Get out here and see."

She disappeared, and Ben walked the length of the back of the house, searching for the perfect spot to plant the rose. The slap of her flip-flops followed the bang of the screen door as she neared, but he didn't look up until her fingers settled on his shoulders.

Her smile warmed him. "Hey," she said.

"Hi." With one arm, he pulled her close and kissed her, refusing to stop when she drew back.

"Hello to you too," she said when the kiss ended. "Good day?"

Time would tell. He held the plant between them, tucking the bag behind his back. "This is for you."

Gold flickered in her hazel eyes. "What's this? A rosebush?" She bent to read the tag.

Ben's gaze traced the pale streaks in her short, blonde hair, her casual part, the strands tucked behind her little ears—and the sliver of green onion that clung to her cheek. He brushed it away. What was she was cooking?

"A climbing rose. How pretty." Dana stretched on tiptoes and kissed his cheek. "Thank you. Where should we put it?"

The mild reaction wasn't quite the one he wanted, but that didn't matter. There was more to come, and if there was anything Ben excelled at, it was getting his desired reaction. He thought of the cop again, this time with a smile. That cop would never have caught him. "I thought it would look nice outside our bedroom window." He set the plant in place and stepped back, draping his arm over her shoulders. "I can put some lattice around the window, and we'll have roses peeking in all summer."

"I like it." She flashed him a smile. "Will your landlord care if you build a trellis?"

"Not if he doesn't own the house."

"You're buying?"

"Don't you think a real estate agent should own his own home?"

Dana grabbed his arm, eyes shining. "We can remodel the kitchen."

Ben let out a laugh. Of course she'd say that, always the chef. As long as her incredible meals kept coming, he'd let her spend as much as she wanted building her dream kitchen. "Whatever you want, Dana."

She squealed and clapped her hands, bouncing like a blonde cheerleader. "I'll start designing tonight."

Not if he had anything to say about it. He nodded at the rosebush. "Can we plant this first?"

"I guess my dream kitchen can wait until after dinner. Where do you think, Ben? This side?" She slid the plant across the ground. "Or this side?"

"Back this way. There's more house for the flowers to cover."

She dragged the rose back and toyed with it until she was happy with its position.

"Here." He held out the Home Depot bag. "Put these gloves on while I get the shovel."

He counted his steps toward the garage, heart pounding again. *One, two, three, four.* Did she have the gloves on? He looked over his shoulder.

She knelt on the ground beneath the window, one glove already on. She reached for the second.

Ben held his breath as she put her hand in.

A frown covered her face, and she tipped the glove. "Something's in here—"

The ring spilled onto her gloved palm, the one carat solitaire sparkling in the sunlight.

She stared openmouthed, and Ben ran to her, falling to his knees beside her. *Say yes*, he begged silently.

Tears streamed down her cheeks.

His jaw locked, as tightly as when he'd seen the cop behind him. He'd been so sure this time. "Dana, listen—"

"Yes." The word was half sob, half laugh.

Ben stared at her until her meaning dawned on him, filling him with relief, then confidence. Yes, this was right. Dana understood him like no one else ever had. They were made for each other, for always. Ben slipped the ring on her finger.

What a relief that cop hadn't ruined the day.

Chapter Three

He'd lost the stupid card.

Mike froze on the top step of the Chicago Wind's dugout, ignored the fans yelling his name, and dug through his back pocket. Empty. He slipped his fingers into the other pocket. Was there a hole big enough for Meg's business card to slide through?

Memory returned. His shoulders slumped. After batting practice, he'd tucked the card into a dark corner of his locker so he could forget about it until after the game.

Lot of good that had done.

He jogged toward teammates doing last-minute stretches in shallow left field. The card had barely left his hands in the days since Sara had given it to him. He'd played with the top right corner so much that it had worn off a week ago. He'd even entered Meg's number into his phone.

Then deleted it.

The only thing he hadn't done was drive past her office. He drew the line at that. There was no point in contacting Meg. None at all. She was probably married and had five kids.

How ironic would that be?

Slowing to a walk, he glanced around the packed stadium, at the fans wearing short sleeves due to an unusually warm April day. Their hopeful faces told him they actually thought this team might make the playoffs.

If only he believed it. Better yet, if only he could get another opening day on life. Maybe a rainout with a chance to replay his thirty years rested and prepared after learning from all of his mistakes.

Another chance to do right by Meg, by himself.

There was no point, though, in dwelling on the impossible. Hope might spring eternal for this franchise, but for him? He focused on the thick green grass beneath his feet and breathed in the scent of spring on Lake Michigan's shore—clean, fresh, unspoiled. He scowled. Clean and unspoiled—that hadn't described him in years.

So what?

Mike stopped walking, squared his shoulders.

So what was right. What was wrong with him? He didn't need to see Meg to get a fresh start on life. He could make his own opening day right here, right now.

He nodded to himself. Fine. As of today, Mike Connor— centerfield for the Chicago Wind, Triple Crown winner last season, a man thoroughly confused and disgusted with himself—would live life properly. No mistakes, no regrets, no looking—

Shouts from the crowd broke into his vow.

Might as well start with a few autographs. Giving back to the fans and all that. He veered toward a section of the wall packed with people waving pens and baseballs and hats. A little fan love wouldn't hurt, either. And if everything he signed ended up on ebay, well, today he didn't care.

"Mr. Connor!" a child called.

Someone had manners. He searched the crowd. Had to reward that.

"Mr. Connor!" A blond kid waved a baseball at him. "Will you sign this please?"

Please? "Sure." He took the boy's ball and pen and scribbled his signature.

"I'm Terrell," the kid said. "Mommy says my name means powerful."

Well, that was wonderful. Mike handed back the ball and pen. What made someone pick a name like—

Behind the boy, a woman with honey-gold, wavy hair and green eyes pushed through the crowd and grabbed the kid's shirt. "Terrell, don't you run off like that." Her eyes met his. She froze.

Mike blinked. She had to be a hallucination. That's all. Just his frustrated conscience morphing her face with…

She remained real, just feet in front of him.

He swallowed. "Meg?"

"That's my mom," the kid said.

She grabbed the arm of a man beside her. Spoke to the guy. "We shouldn't have—we need to go."

Mike couldn't lose her a second time, not on his own opening day. He lunged forward, his knees banging into the brick wall of the stands. "Meg, wait!"

She pushed against the people behind her, and she and the boy vanished into the crowd.

The man she'd spoken to—the man she'd grabbed—hesitated. A sad smile covered his mouth, and his eyes… There was no victorious arrogance in them. No swagger, no puffed-out chest.

Who was this guy?

Who was he to Meg?

The man slipped into the crowd, and the sounds of fans crying for attention rushed into Mike's ears. Someone waved a baseball card in his face. Blindly he scribbled his name on it, searching the stands above him. Someone shoved a ball at him, and he took it and a Sharpie. Signed his name. Handed them back. Took another ball while he scoured every honeyed head above him.

After a minute, he gave up.

Meg had disappeared. Again.

His teammates walked by, and Mike followed them to the dugout. So much for his personal opening day. Meg was a mother—a mother of a little boy who wore a miniature of his own jersey.

How ironic that his ex-wife's son had chosen him as his hero.

Chapter Four

Somewhere in the seventh inning, between his second and third strikeout, Mike decided he would go see Meg right after the game.

The drive to her office took over an hour, thanks to rush-hour traffic. Mike exited the highway for her suburb where condominiums and townhouses gave way to large, older, single-family homes with tall, mature trees lining the road.

Evidently she worked from home.

He found her house and parked along the curb in front of her yard.

For several minutes, he didn't move. He took in the large brick house, a two-story with five windows across the upper level and two on either side of the wooden door, its front step covered by a small overhang. A chimney extended from each end of the house, and a well-manicured lawn curved up from the street, the bushes that lined her yard flaunting spring colors.

A small weight lifted. At least she hadn't been hurting. She must have met that dude right after their divorce, judging by the age of her son.

What was the kid's name?

Her business card sat in his cup holder. Stifling a yawn, he picked it up and ran his fingers over the raised lettering.

Meghan Connor.

Whoa—Connor? She still went by his name?

How had he missed that detail? And what did it mean? Was she dating that guy?

Then who was the boy's dad?

Mike glanced at her house. Maybe he belonged to the man.

No, the kid had called her his mom.

Maybe his stepmom?

He tucked the card safely into the cup holder, remembering her panicked face when her eyes had met his. What had she thought about during the game? Did she wish they could try again? His years with Meg, despite their problems, had been the best of his life, and even though his career had soared after the divorce, he longed to go back to those happy days with her, back to that first year in the majors and even back to the minors.

He snorted at the thought. "I *am* tired."

Silence answered him.

It had been two weeks since Sara had left. Two very silent, silent weeks. His parents had asked about her when he'd had lunch with them in Anaheim during last week's season opening road trip, and he'd told them they'd broken up during spring training. That she'd been gone by the time he got back.

He hadn't told his parents about Sara finding Meg, though. His marriage was still a touchy subject. After the divorce, a couple years had passed before he could look them in the eye without feeling like they were fuming.

No way was he resurrecting that whole issue.

Because Meg was probably with someone else. He was just here to… say hi. To make sure she was okay because she'd seemed upset, maybe, at the ballpark.

We shouldn't have—we need to go.

What had she meant?

He looked back at her house. Lights shone on each floor.

Someone was home, probably Meg if she worked here.

What about that man? What if he opened the door?

"I'm Mike Connor," he practiced. "Meg's first husband. And you are?"

The guy would punch him in the nose if Meg had told him anything.

So he'd punch him back.

He climbed out of his Range Rover, slammed the door, and started up the sidewalk. His heart beat faster, and he matched his stride to it until he reached her door.

What would she do when she saw him?

He pushed the doorbell and listened to its faint ring. Maybe he'd imagined she looked the same as he'd remembered. Maybe the sparkle in her green eyes had faded and she'd turned gray.

What did that matter? He needed to see her, if only to say he was sorry and ask for forgiveness. Then he could tell the guilt goodbye and move on with life, wherever that took him.

He lifted his hand to press the bell again, but the knob rattled. Mike squared his shoulders.

The door swung open.

Framed in the doorway Meg—his Meg—froze, her small smile slipping away. She wore jeans and a red sweater that gave color to her pale skin. Her long, wavy hair framed her face in dark gold layers, and her green eyes glazed as she stared at him.

Despite her less-than-welcoming expression, she looked better then he'd remembered.

He forced a smile, hands stuffed in his pockets. "Hi."

Still she stared.

"May I come in?"

She blinked, did not move, did not speak.

Gently he nudged the door farther open.

She shifted out of its way.

He doubted she knew she'd moved, but he'd take it as a yes. He stepped into a foyer, warm light reflecting off dark wood floors and subtle yellow walls. A wide staircase stood on the left, and a doorway on the right led to a living room done in some soothing orange color.

He smiled. Only Meg could make orange soothing.

Behind him the door clicked shut, and he turned to find her watching him, her face unreadable.

"Sorry to drop in," he said, "but I had to come by."

She said nothing, the silence blaring.

"I haven't stopped thinking about you since I saw you." He tried to joke. "You made me play awful."

"Oh." She looked sideways at the stairs and then at his feet.

He'd have to save the humor for later. "I hope this isn't a bad time. If your husband or boyfriend is here and you want me to leave, I'll go."

She looked up. "My husband?"

"You're not married?" Mike cleared his throat, fought to control his sudden smile. "I saw you with someone, and I assumed—" He rubbed the back of his neck. Why had he said that?

"Why are you here, Mike?"

This wasn't what he'd expected. "I wanted to make sure you were okay, doing fine." He glanced around the foyer again, noting the side tables, mirrors, and odds and ends that gave the room an expensive, designer look. "Your place is great."

"Thank you. I did it myself—my own design business."

He opened his mouth to congratulate her, but she cut him off. "If you've soothed your conscience making sure I'm fine after all these years—"

Footsteps sounded on the stairs.

Mike looked up as Meg's little boy appeared.

The blond kid halted when their eyes met. "Wow! Mr. Connor!" He raced down the rest of the stairs.

Mike braced for the kid to fling himself at him.

Instead, the boy skidded to a stop and lifted his hand for a handshake. "Nice to see you again."

The manners just kept coming with this kid, didn't they? Mike raised his eyebrows at Meg as he shook her son's hand.

She didn't seem amused. "Terrell—"

"Mr. Connor, do you think we could play baseball sometime?"

Mike couldn't help his laugh. What would this kid think if he knew his history with his mother? "That's up to your mom. If she says it's fine, we'll do it. How's that?"

Terrell nodded. "Can we, Mommy?"

Her smile was grim. "We'll see. Right now you need to go to Jill's."

Terrell's lower lip protruded, but the sideways glance he sent Mike said he didn't want to embarrass himself in front of his baseball hero. "Can't I stay?"

"No, Terrell. You need to go. Now."

"But I want to tell him something."

She relented, as Mike knew she would. "Quickly, Terrell."

Terrell beamed at him, a grimace-like grin splitting his face. "We have the same name."

Chapter Five

Mike looked at Meg. "Same name?"

Meg's face blanched, and the panic he'd seen at the stadium flashed in her eyes. "Terrell! Go. Now!"

Terrell ignored her, smiling around Meg's frantic push deeper into the house. "Connor. Me and you. See you later, Mr. Connor." He managed a wave before Meg forced him out the back of the foyer with her.

Mike's breath left him. *Same name. Connor.* He sagged against the wall. She hadn't. She had *not*—

The truth rushed in.

Mike swore and pushed off from the wall. The foyer was empty. Where was she?

Fury propelled him after the way they'd gone and into Meg's kitchen, his angry breath coming faster. Meg was shutting her back door and leaned against it as he entered. "Why does he have my name, Meg? What are you pulling?"

"Me? You're the one who shows up unannounced." She shouldered past him.

Mike stormed after her to the living room.

She sank onto a couch and buried her face in her hands.

He squeezed the back of a chair, but his anger boiled. "Terrell is mine?"

Her hands formed fists over her eyes.

He had no time for sympathy. "Answer me!"

A moan escaped her. She nodded her head once.

"You've kept me from my own son?" His throat felt as if it might explode. "You signed divorce papers saying you weren't pregnant. How dare you lie about *that!*"

"And how dare you run out on your wife! Don't condemn me for what I did."

Her words stung, but he narrowed his eyes and glared at her. He could cut deep too. "You didn't look pregnant."

"Nice, Mike."

"What am I supposed to think?"

"Obviously your mind thinks the worst." She leaned back on the couch, arms crossed. "I was a month along."

"Then you should have told me!"

"Why? So you could take him too?"

"It wasn't that way."

"Yes, it was," she snapped.

No, it wasn't.

Well…

Okay, but he didn't want to face what he'd been. Why, now that he had something to be truly angry at Meg for, did the memory of all he'd done sting so much? What mattered was her horrible deception.

He clenched his teeth and forced himself to sit on the opposite couch. Bitter, condemning words pushed for release. He squeezed his fingers into fists until the veins in his wrists felt they might pop.

Meg had lied. Worse, she'd stolen what she knew he'd find most valuable.

She glared at an invisible spot on the coffee table. He glared at it as well, as if the table were at fault. He blew out a deep breath and then another before dragging his eyes to her face.

Her mouth stretched in a tight line, and she looked ready to attack as soon as he spoke.

Well, let her.

But his angry words refused to come. Their past and his wrongs stretched before him. Suddenly drained, Mike gripped his head with both hands. His child, the child she hadn't yet wanted, was alive. He had to respect that. He rubbed his eyes with his fingers. "He looks like my dad as a kid."

Meg said nothing.

"What's his birthday?"

"He'll be six July twenty-fourth."

"And his name?"

"His name?"

"His full name?"

"Terrell Jason Connor."

Mike repeated the name. "Why Terrell?"

She studied her hands. "I liked it."

Her body language said otherwise. "What's it mean, Meg?"

"Jason means healer."

Was that supposed to hurt? He scowled at her. "And Terrell?"

Meg glared again. "Look it up."

So she was playing games. Fine.

He leaned back on the couch, eyes closed. How could this have happened? Shouldn't he have known, somehow, that he had a child? Shouldn't there have been a feeling or suspicion that some incredible part of his life was missing?

But there'd been nothing. *Nothing!* He'd missed his son's first six years—because of Meg. It was her fault. She'd kept him from naming his son. He would never have chosen Terrell.

"Do you realize the only things I know about my kid are his name and his birthday?"

"And I'm supposed to feel sorry for you?"

"You don't see what you've done wrong?"

She laughed incredulously at him. "Me?"

He stood, relishing the way he towered over her. "I should sue you for everything you're worth."

"Got to take it all, don't you?"

They weren't rehashing that. He waved her words away. "Where's Terrell?"

"What?"

"I want my son. Where is he?"

"You're not taking him. He doesn't know you're his dad."

Mike snorted. "That was obvious, wasn't it?" He stormed to her front door and jerked it open, pained as he remembered his little boy calling him Mr. Connor. "You can't keep Terrell from me, Meg. You'll hear from my lawyer."

Chapter Six

Where is Margo?

In the kitchen, Ben stared at his open soda can. Not again. He should be allowed a few months reprieve. Wasn't that the pattern?

Is Margo okay?

If Dana hadn't been sitting at the dining room table perusing design books, Ben would have answered out loud, just to chase the thought away. Instead, he swigged his Pepsi, answering silently while he swallowed. He wished he knew where Margo was. How she was. How life had gone for her these last two years.

The question was not unusual. For two years it had popped up at the strangest times, like two months ago when he'd shown a client the playhouse in a backyard and last night when he'd caught a rerun of Cal Ripken tying Lou Gehrig's consecutive game streak.

Ben walked past Dana to the recliner in front of the TV showing the White Sox and Royals game. Baseball had once distracted him from everything wrong with his life. Maybe it could again.

He stretched out in the chair. Ah, the White Sox had broken up the shutout. He wasn't a fan of either team, but he refused to watch that other team in town.

What about Margo?

He pulled a green plastic binder from beneath a stack of comps and arranged it on his lap so Dana couldn't see it. After Mom left,

Ben had endured three years with his silent, morose father. Then Margo swept Dad off his feet. Ben drained his Pepsi at the thought of her. Tall, blonde, beautiful. She'd made Dad happy again, and as a result, she'd made Ben happy too.

And nothing against Mom, but Margo was way more of a mother than Mom had ever been. Margo had tucked him into bed at night, played catch in the backyard, washed and folded his clothes, thrown birthday parties, and planned vacations. Not that they ever went. In high school, she cooked sausage and scrambled eggs and pancakes with fresh fruit and milk and orange juice and sometimes even real hash browns—all at five-thirty in the morning so he'd have stamina for 6:30 AM baseball practice plus a whole morning of school, and she *never* laughed at his dream like Dad did.

And when Mom killed herself, Margo had let him vent.

His thumb rubbed the spine of the binder. The day he'd packed his bedroom and left Baltimore, he'd told Margo with all the solemnity of a six-foot-one-inch, two-hundred pound eighteen-year-old who knew the world awaited him that if she ever needed anything, she should let him know.

Eighteen years and one reality check later, Ben still meant every word of it, never mind that Margo had no idea where he was. If she found him, he'd risk his fragile security for her.

The thought turned his head to where Dana sat at the dining room table, hair tucked behind her ears.

She flipped some pages, then paused to jot something down.

"Dana."

She kept writing. "Hmm."

"Dana."

This time she lifted her head. "What?"

"I—" His throat turned thick. He swallowed once, twice. Pushed himself from the recliner and crossed the room.

Dana straightened.

He knelt beside her, wrapping one arm around her slim shoulders. He'd failed far more than he'd succeeded. Was that the way his life was to be?

She tilted her head against his forehead, and Ben shut his eyes, willing himself to be weak, to say what she wanted to hear. "I'm sorry," he whispered.

"Me too." Her fingers grazed her cheek, a subconscious gesture. "Me too, Ben."

He nodded, his throat still tight with regret and fear. The regret he understood, but the fear—the fear scared him more than he'd ever admit.

He drew in a shaky breath, his smile forced. "Thank you."

Dana nodded, and he returned to his recliner and the game, knowing she must still watch him. He picked up the binder and the empty soda can and pretended to drink, pretended everything was fine.

But his mind refused to play along. As the Sox game continued, one question echoed in his head.

Was Margo okay?

Chapter Seven

Soft showers clouded Saturday, their sound a steady patter against Meg's tears.

With Terrell asleep in his own room, Meg sat by the window in her dark bedroom and traced the rivulets of rain down the glass. The lightning had started minutes ago, and each flash illuminated her room before returning it to deep darkness.

All week she'd been immobilized by fear and anger and pain. Jill had tried to help by researching child custody laws, but Meg found little comfort knowing she'd face no jail time. A big-name star like Mike? He'd find a way to take Terrell.

At least Terrell had stopped asking why Mike Connor, baseball superstar, had been at his house, but her head ached and her shoulders throbbed from deflecting his questions. She'd refused to lie. No, it wasn't that. She was too tired. Even if she'd wanted to, she couldn't have come up with a lie.

The way Mike had.

She followed a single raindrop down her window. Their marriage had been like that—high hopes that slid lower and lower until there was nothing left.

But the beginning had been so wonderful.

She was still amazed at how easily Mike had convinced her to marry him. They'd had other plans—for Mike to work his way through the minors while Meg got her degree in interior design. And then marriage.

But Mike's reasons made sense. A top draft pick, he was playing in the Virginia minor league club and doing better than expected. Two months apart had felt like forever. And four more years? He was a millionaire, he'd reminded her. His signing bonus could easily pay for her education. Why wait?

Three weeks later they were married in a small wedding in Pulaski, Virginia, that their families, nine high school friends, and some of Mike's teammates attended. At eighteen and a half, they were husband and wife.

So young and naïve.

Those first months flew in a blur of games, college classes, and hours decorating their home. The months turned into a year, and while they struggled with her classes conflicting with Mike's mornings off, their individual dreams kept them going. Mike continued his advance through the minors, each step resulting in a physical move to a new city, and Meg practiced what she'd learned on each house. When Mike made his major league debut a week before their third anniversary, she was as excited as he was. When he won the centerfielder position the next season, she knew Mike had realized his dream. Only a long, happy future together remained.

Where had they gone wrong?

In the distance, thunder rumbled. A car splashed through the watery street, the quiet slipping back while taillights disappeared.

The night her marriage gave way hadn't been much different than this one. The rain had started after Mike's home game ended. Meg watched it from home and went to bed as soon as the last out was made, but the thunder kept her awake, so she painted her nails and waited up for him. After all, his next road trip started after tomorrow's game. Maybe he'd come home early and they could talk, something they seemed to have little time for lately.

But now the clock neared 2:30.

She'd been kidding herself.

Since late spring, Mike's behavior had changed, his return from games growing later and later and his goodbyes increasingly early. When she asked why, he'd said he needed extra batting practice. That he had errands to run. That he was going out with some of the guys.

She didn't buy it anymore. Not that she ever had. She just hadn't wanted to face it—whatever *it* was—hoping the problem would go away.

But it hadn't. And there she sat in the living room of her dark house, watching raindrops run in silver streams down the windows, admitting the truth at last.

She was losing Mike.

The clock passed three before headlights flashed across the wall. Meg turned on a small lamp beside the couch and sat with legs crossed Indian-style, waiting.

His key fumbled in the lock, but she made no move to help him. The door opened, and Mike stumbled over the one step from the garage. He swore softly, then looked at the light.

And then at her.

Jaw set, he glanced away as he stepped inside and tossed his keys on the table. "Why are you up?" he asked, moving out of sight into the kitchen.

She heard the refrigerator open. "Waiting for you."

He said nothing, so she stood and walked to the kitchen.

He was opening a bottled water.

He dropped onto a kitchen chair, stretched his long legs, and kicked his shoes off. He tugged his white shirt loose beneath him and crossed his ankles before taking a drink.

Meg waited for him to speak. How did one started a conversation like this?

But he kept silent.

"Where have you been?" she asked at last.

Mike studied the water. "Out."

"With who?"

He pushed his chair back and moved around her toward the stairs.

He was *not* going to blow her off. Not tonight. "Are you going to answer me?"

His voice rang with irritation. "Answer what?"

"Who were you with?"

Mike stood with his hand on the wall, one foot on a step. When their eyes met, he looked away. "Nothing I say will make you happy, so why bother?" He started up the stairs, his voice drifting to her. "I'm taking a shower."

Another shower. Over the summer, he'd fallen into the habit of taking a shower when he got home, waking her first at two and lately three in the morning with his less-than-stealthy entrance. Did he think she hadn't noticed? And why wouldn't he answer her? Why didn't he say he was with the guys?

Because he wasn't.

The thought twisted her stomach until she sat on the kitchen table and doubled over, arms around her waist.

It couldn't be true.

She listened to the shower run in their master bath. She couldn't deal with this now. It was too late. Or maybe too early. The clock moved from 3:20 to 3:30, Meg growing more and more numb as the shower ran on.

Finally she slid off the table and trudged upstairs. The shower noise increased as she neared.

But when she entered their bedroom, Mike lay on his back across the bed, knees hanging over the edge, still dressed except for his socks which lay in balls at the base of the wall six feet away.

Dazed, she walked into the steamy bathroom and turned off the shower.

Let him sleep in his clothes.

She returned to him, silent on the thick carpet.

He didn't stir.

She reached a hand to the stubble on his face, the scraggly goatee he'd decided to grow, but at the last second pulled back. Had someone else suggested he grow it? The idea had not been hers.

She rubbed her forehead. Maybe in the morning things would make sense. She clung to that thought as she slipped between the sheets, for once thankful for their king-sized bed. She turned her back on her husband and slept.

When she woke, Mike lay curled beneath the covers, only his forehead and nose showing. Meg squinted at the clock. Eleven-thirty.

She tiptoed out of their room and showered in the guest bath, not wanting the sound of water to wake him and force them together.

Not yet.

She dressed and slipped downstairs, making herself a cheese omelet filled with tomatoes and green onions. As she slid the omelet onto her plate, Mike appeared at the bottom of the stairs, wearing shorts, his chest bare, his hair sticking up.

"Hi," he said after the tiniest pause.

Meg turned back to the stove, throat tightening. "Morning." She shut off the burner and scrubbed the stovetop before she felt ready to face him. When she did, she found him sitting at the table, reading something on his phone.

And eating her omelet.

Something inside her hardened.

He took a bite and texted something—someone. He took another bite, the omelet over half gone.

What did the omelet matter? Their marriage was farther gone than that. Meg swallowed. "Who is she?"

He stared at the phone for several seconds before lowering it and squinting at her. "What?"

"I want to know her name."

"Who?"

She turned her back, shook her head. He could pretend all he wanted, but she refused to listen while he denied it.

She walked into the laundry room down the hall and closed the door behind her, heart swollen in her chest, her vision blurring. Stacks of fresh laundry, evidence of an evening's work, sat in piles on the dryer. Mike's clothes, everything he needed for the next eleven days, the longest road trip of the year starting tonight. She grabbed a white golf shirt by the throat and crumpled it against her face. Why now?

When her tears dried, Meg returned to the kitchen, but Mike was gone, the plate empty, his fork lying on the table amid egg residue.

Upstairs, the shower ran.

She gathered his clean clothes and climbed the stairs, lungs thick and heavy. Mike's bag lay on the unmade bed, a few items in the bottom. She put each pile of clothes away and left as the shower turned off.

In the kitchen she started a second omelet.

Mike would be down soon, bags in hand, heading out the door for tonight's game and then the airport. Almost two weeks would pass before he'd walk through that door again. What would he say before he left? Would he tell her he loved her? Would he mumble it? Or would there be a ring of truth to it?

A stair creaked.

So he was coming. Fine. She'd keep silent, concentrate on the omelet. Keep that, at least, from ruin.

Behind her, his shoes hit the tile. Bags thudded against the floor, and keys jingled as he picked them up.

And then silenced.

She stared at cheese that oozed out of the omelet and sizzled. *Keep quiet. Make him talk.*

"Her name's Brooke."

Meg's gaze lifted to the stove's digital clock. 1:03. As she watched, it turned to 1:04.

1:04. She would never forget that moment of change.

She forced herself to turn toward Mike's voice.

He stood in front of the door to the garage.

"Whose name?" she asked.

"Brooke." He studied his keys. "You asked me her name. Her name's Brooke."

"Who, Mike? Your new agent? A new GM? A new bat girl? Who is Brooke?" She swallowed, stunned at the volume she'd finished with. She'd make him say the awful truth, make him hear his own disgusting words.

Instead he motioned to the door behind him. "I'll be gone awhile. Tuesday—I get back on a Tuesday, real early. We'll talk."

He wouldn't call? Yes, the phone calls had come less frequently, their length shorter and shorter, but eleven days? Nothing?

He started out the door, and this time she couldn't hold back. "Mike—"

He shook his head and closed the door, leaving red-hot pain behind him.

⌒⌒⊙⌒⌒

The ringing of her phone jarred Meg from the past. Disoriented, she scanned her dark bedroom, focusing on the digital clock. 9:30. The phone rang again, and she hurried to her nightstand to answer it.

"Hello?" The word came out a whisper. She cleared her throat.

"Meg? We need to talk."

She closed her eyes at Mike's voice, remembering the disaster that had followed the last time he'd said that.

"Are you there?" he asked.

"Yes." No more cowering. It was time to take charge—for herself and for Terrell. She opened her eyes and forcefully repeated herself. "Yes."

"I want you to meet me after tomorrow's game."

She eased onto her bed and pushed her hair back with a shaky hand. "I'm not meeting you, Mike. You're not taking Terrell—"

"Will you listen?" He lowered his voice. "I think we can work this out."

Men talked and laughed in the background. Tonight's storm must have rained out his game if he was calling from the stadium.

A door closed, muffling background sounds of conversation. "Tomorrow, Meg, let's go out for dinner and talk everything over, just you and me."

How could he make a call like this from the clubhouse? And did he really think she'd discuss their son in public? "I'm not going anywhere with you."

"If you say no, then I hang up and call my lawyer. And I won't go easy on you."

As if he ever had.

She squeezed her eyes shut. *Lord, help. What do I do?*

"Come on, Meg. This isn't that hard."

"Just a minute. I'm thinking."

"I don't have time—"

"Come here then, after your game. I'll make dinner."

Where had that come from?

"Your house?" He paused. "Only if Terrell's there. I want to see him."

"Then no lawyers, nothing. Just you and me, like you said."

"Done."

"You promise? I can trust you?"

"Meg…" Mike's voice sounded a mix of concern and confusion. Someone called him, and he muffled the phone, responded quickly. "I have a one-oh-five start tomorrow. I'll be there when the game's over."

"Fine." She ended the call without a goodbye.

Sat motionless on her bed.

The phone's screen blended into the room's darkness.

The nightmare she'd dreaded for six years had begun. Mike would take Terrell away.

Her shoulders slumped.

No. *No!*

She would not be weak. She would *not*.

Instead, she'd be ready for everything he threw at her, for every promise he'd just made to be broken.

When he came, she'd be ready.

Chapter Eight

How was she going to tell Terrell about his dad?

The red numbers on her clock marked the night's slow progress. Meg forced her eyes closed, but Mike's deadline kept sleep away. How would she tell Terrell? And when?

When she finally slept, she dreamed that she and Terrell pulled up in front of her old Texas townhouse. The door was shut and the curtains ominously closed, but, like a fool, Meg led him up the sidewalk and knocked.

The door creaked open, revealing a woman's silhouette.

Brooke.

In the room behind her, Mike sprawled across a couch and watched a baseball game on television. He lifted a hand in greeting before returning to the game.

Before Meg could react, Terrell fell through the doorway, and the heavy door slammed in her face.

She was alone.

Throughout the Sunday morning service, Meg argued with God. Why had he allowed Mike to find her? Why hadn't he kept Terrell from speaking? What horrible wrongs had she done? Mike was the one who'd forgotten his wedding vows, not her.

Over lunch Meg tried to bring up Mike's name, but it stuck in her throat.

Afterward Terrell planted himself in front of the Wind game. Meg hid in her bedroom's walk-in closet, immersing herself in the box of high school yearbooks, hers and Mike's, that held all the good she needed to remember about him before she introduced her son to whatever kind of man Mike had become. She flipped through the scrapbook she'd made of newspaper articles covering his minor league games and that first month in the majors. Old memories taunted her, marking the end of anything positive between herself and Mike.

How many negatives would tonight bring?

In the kitchen, she began dinner, dishes she hoped were still Mike's favorites. While she washing fingerling potatoes, she focused on Terrell who colored at the kitchen table. The clock's constant ticking meant that at any moment Mike would start his drive to her house.

And Terrell still didn't know.

"Look, Mommy." Terrell lifted his coloring book, his cocky grin reminiscent of his dad's. "My giraffe is green and orange. And has a sword. Isn't that crazy?"

"Absolutely crazy." As was she for meeting Mike before she'd talked to a lawyer. She washed and dried her hands. The secrets she was about to reveal—sitting at her table with a warrior giraffe as witness was not how she'd envisioned it.

She walked to Terrell and planted a kiss in his hair. "Terrell, I need to talk to you."

He eyed her, crayon in hand. "Is something wrong?"

Everything. How she wanted to take him and run, but that wouldn't work anymore. She eased into the chair beside him and held his hand. Her fingers shook, and she swung their joined hands so he wouldn't notice. "Nothing's wrong. But I need to talk to you about your dad."

Surprise passed over his face. "My dad?"

"Do you remember that your dad and I got a divorce?"

"Yes."

"That happened before you were born. A long time ago."

He nodded.

"I moved far away from him, up here, and then you were born. But now—" She stumbled over the word. "Now your dad has moved near us."

"Can he come see me?" Terrell interrupted.

"Yes, he will. Soon." Too soon. She ignored his growing grin. "Terrell, I want you to know… It's my fault you've never met him."

He cocked his head. "What do you mean?"

How do I tell him, Lord? She closed her eyes for a moment, taking in much-needed air. Maybe he wouldn't understand what she'd done. "Your dad didn't know I was going to have a baby—that I was going to have you. And after you were born… I never told him."

The severity of her words seemed to strike him. His gaze fell to the floor, and he studied his feet for a moment before looking up, forehead furrowed as if trying to grasp the concept. "You never told him about me?"

He *did* understand. She sucked in a quivering breath, her lower lip catching on her teeth. "I did what I thought was best—for you and me." A tear streaked down her cheek. She swiped at it.

Terrell stared.

"I'm sorry you've never known your dad." Her chest shook, but she choked out her apology. "Will you forgive me?"

"Oh, Mommy." He wrapped his arms around her neck. His fingers patted her shoulder as if he was the adult.

Meg squeezed her eyes shut. She couldn't fall apart on him.

"It's okay," he breathed in her ear. "But you can tell him now, right?"

"I already have." She sent him a brave smile as they pulled apart. "He's coming to dinner tonight so you can get to know each other."

"Really?" Terrell's eyes popped. "Will I like him?"

"I think so. You've met him twice already."

"I have?"

She forged ahead before she had time to think this through. "Do you remember Mike Connor, the baseball player?"

Terrell nodded, then understanding dawned. "Mike Connor is my dad?" He tossed a handful of crayons into the air. "Yippee!"

"Terrell!" Meg grabbed his hands to keep him from flinging more crayons. *Yippee?*

"Now I have someone to play baseball with. I hope he brings his glove."

"Terrell, he's not coming here to live."

Silence reigned. "He's not?"

Her poor boy. She shook her head.

"Why not?"

"Because we're not married anymore. That's what a divorce does."

"It un-marries you?"

"Yes."

"Oh." He folded the corner of his coloring book. "Can't you get re-married?"

"Terrell, it's not that simple." She ran her fingers over his soft hair, praying he'd understand and that the temper he'd honed wouldn't make an appearance. "I know this is hard to understand, but there are lots of reasons why we can't get married again."

He scowled at the bent cover. "Tell me one."

"Your dad isn't a Christian. He doesn't love Jesus. So I can't marry him."

"We'll have to tell him about Jesus."

"Sure. We'll do that." As if Mike would listen.

"If he's not going to live here, when will I see him?"

"Well, your dad and I will talk about that."

He nodded, silent for several seconds until his bottom lip began to quiver. "Mommy, will I have to live with him? Will I move away from you?"

"No!" She pulled him close. His fingers dug into her shirt, and she squeezed him as tightly as he could handle. "No, Terrell. This is your home. No one's taking you away."

What if she were wrong?

"Mommy, do you think—" He pulled back, fear in his eyes. "What if he doesn't like me?"

"He will, Terrell." She blinked back her tears. How much pain she'd caused him. "He will. Daddies always love their little boys."

CRADLE

For the next hour, Terrell shadowed her.

Meg put him to work. She gave him plates and silverware to set around the table and had him folding napkins like an exclusive restaurant would while she peeked out the foyer window.

A black Range Rover sat in her driveway.

She waited for the driver's door to open, but nothing happened.

What was he doing? Was his lawyer coming after all? Or the police?

He's nervous.

The thought surprised her, and she stepped back, colliding with Terrell who had raced into the foyer. He bounced off her and dashed up the stairs. "Sorry, Mommy. I have to go potty."

I guess we're all nervous.

The doorbell sounded.

Meg's stomach rolled. This was it. No matter how things went tonight—and she'd imagined a dozen endings—life would never be the same.

Mike was back.

Chapter Nine

Meg flicked on the foyer light before taking a deep breath and opening the door.

Outside, Mike stood alone, dressed in a blue-and-white checked, button-down shirt tucked into jeans.

"Hi," he said.

"Hi." She moved aside.

Mike entered the foyer, sending her a tight smile. He looked around. "Is Terrell here?"

"Bathroom."

"Oh."

They waited silently until the toilet flushed and the bathroom door banged open. Running footsteps headed their way.

Meg leaned up the staircase. "Wash your hands."

The footsteps retreated, followed by a splash of water.

Meg looked at Mike.

He was smiling.

Her stomach's churning slowed.

As Terrell's footsteps approached, Mike's smile faded. "Did you tell him why I haven't come before? I don't want him thinking I don't care."

That was good. "He knows," she said and looked up as Terrell appeared on the stairs.

He took his time walking down, and on the bottom step he stopped and smiled shyly at her, then Mike.

How did she introduce a father and son? Meg opened her mouth to say something yet unthought of, but Terrell jumped in. "Mommy says you're my dad. Are you?"

Mike let out a laugh, his eyes taking in Terrell like a man uncovering treasure. "Yeah, I am," he said.

Terrell nodded.

"Here." Mike held out his hand, a baseball in his palm. "I brought you something."

Terrell took the ball and rolled it over.

"It's got the autographs of everyone on the Wind. Look." Mike pointed to a name. "That's Brett Burkholder. He's a pitcher—"

"Your closer. I know." Terrell searched the ball. "Where's your name?"

"Right here. See? Mike Connor."

"Wow." Terrell beamed at Mike.

Mike grinned back. "You like baseball?"

Terrell nodded, eyes glued to the ball. "I watch every game Mom lets me." He held the ball close. "Thanks, Mr.—"

They looked at her, then each other.

"What do I call you?" Terrell asked.

Mike sent her a stunned look.

She shrugged. Let him figure it out.

"Whatever you want, I guess. Except Mr. Connor." He made a face. "I'm not mature enough for that."

"Me, either." Terrell studied his ball again, missing the melting look in Mike's eyes.

Meg squeezed her own shut. Mike had every right to hate her.

And yet he'd come alone. With no lawyer. No police. No threats. Why was he being nice?

She spoke, but no sound came. Clearing her throat, she tried again. "I'll be in the kitchen." She hurried past them.

"Mommy, can I show him our house?" Terrell called.

She nodded without looking back.

While she regained control of her emotions, she listened to the conversation drifting from upstairs—Terrell showing Mike his bathroom and Mike's comments on Terrell's baseball-themed room.

By the time dinner was ready, Mike had seen everything. Meg seated him at the head of the kitchen table with Terrell to his right and herself at Mike's left so she wouldn't have to look at him. Too much. "Terrell, would you pray?" she asked. From the corner of her eye, she caught Mike's head shift in her direction. Meg closed her eyes, and, while Terrell prayed a simple prayer, she pleaded for help.

How long since she'd eaten a meal with Mike?

When Terrell's prayer ended, she waited for Mike to attack her for what she'd done, but he didn't, instead talking to Terrell about baseball and kindergarten and his hobbies and favorite things which led them back to baseball. They talked until the food grew cold and the wall of windows behind Terrell changed from blue to periwinkle, hinting at the night to come. Meg began cleaning, peaking at them while she stacked the dishwasher. The well-lit room made the scene cozy, more like nine-to-five suburbia than a divorced couple about to *talk*. So far she hadn't seen legal papers, but maybe Mike had left them in that Range Rover.

She cleaned the kitchen, stacked leftovers in the fridge, and started the dishwasher. She was wiping the table when Mike thumped open palms against it. She jumped, flushing when he crooked an eyebrow at her.

"Time to play in your room, Terrell," he said. "Your mom and I need to talk."

"About how often I'll get to see you?"

"That's part of it."

"Why can't I stay?" Terrell dropped his chin onto his fist.

Meg straightened, ready for a tantrum.

"Come on, junior." Mike pretended to struggle while pulling Terrell off his chair. "We've got stuff to discuss. We'll tell you about it later."

Standing at Mike's feet, Terrell craned his neck and looked up. "Yes, sir," he said and saluted stiffly, looking for a moment as if he might topple backward. "I'll report back soon."

"No, you won't," Meg told him as he goose-stepped past. "We'll get you when we're done."

His marching turned to shuffling. "Aye, aye," he mumbled, then left the room.

Mike sat down with a laugh. "I'm surprised he listened to me."

They were alone. And Mike was smiling. She squeezed the dishcloth in her hand and turned her back on him, scrubbing the peninsula. "This is all a dream to him. Imagine if you were his age and found out your dad was…"

"Frank Thomas?"

His boyhood hero. "Well, something like that."

"He seems like a good kid, Meg."

"He is. Thank you." She spread the dishcloth over the sink's edge and looked around. What else could she do?

"Will you sit down? It's hard to talk when you're working."

That was the point, but he was right. She couldn't postpone their conversation any longer. She pulled a chair as far from him as she could without being ridiculous and sat down, arms crossed.

"Thanks for dinner." Mike leaned forward, elbows on knees, fingers intertwined. "You hit most of my favorites."

She acknowledged his compliment with a nod, waiting for Monday's wrath to return. "Thank you for being civil in front of Terrell."

He studied her, his mouth forming a half-smile. "Actually—" He gave a small laugh. "I've been thinking about you for a long time.

I've wanted to see you."

She blinked away her surprise, forcing a fake smile. "Should I feel flattered?"

"Feel however you want. I guess that doesn't impress you, though."

"Not when you walked out on me." Where was he going with this? "Why are you here, Mike? I thought this was about you taking me to court."

"We're not going to court—unless we can't work this out."

He was crazy if he thought she'd hand over any part of Terrell's custody. "What are you expecting?"

"I want to spend time with Terrell. Lots of time."

"So you want weekends or…" She dragged out the last word, hoping he'd catch her sarcasm. It was awfully hard for a guy to parent when he traveled half the year.

"Meg." He straightened. "I'm not trying to take custody from you. He's lived without me for six years, he looks happy and healthy here, and as much as I hate to admit it, I can't take care of him by myself. Between my games and travel, he'd be living with a nanny half the time."

"Three fourths of the time."

Mike held up a hand. "Whatever."

Silence fell between them. Mike sat still, watching her.

Meg eyed him back. What was behind this sudden change? "Did your lawyer tell you that you wouldn't win custody?"

"I didn't talk to a lawyer. When I thought it through, I knew it wouldn't be right. Having a dad all of a sudden has got to be a shock to him. I can't shake up his life any more than that."

Interesting. Mike Connor with a conscience. Well, she'd take it, whatever his true motive. "How do you plan on this working?"

"I can call when I have free time and we can get together, hang out, do whatever six-year-old boys do."

"Terrell would like that."

"Good. During the off-season I can watch him while you're working, keep him at my place every now and then."

She gave a non-committal shrug. Until she knew Mike's character—if he had any—she wouldn't agree to a thing.

"Who watches him when you're working?" he asked.

"My neighbor, Jill. Her husband's been—" She paused, embarrassed at what she'd almost said. Well, Mike might as well know. "Clark's been like a father to Terrell."

Mike nodded, but his mouth twisted and he toyed with the rim of his cup. "Jill keeps him at her house? Nearby?"

She nodded. "Next door. Jill and Clark are good friends. They have a little boy too. Samuel, after Samuel in the Bible."

Mike stared blankly.

What was she thinking? Mike wouldn't know that story. It was new to her too. "It's a story in the Bible. A woman who couldn't have kids." She waved her hand between them. "Never mind."

He raised his eyebrows. "Since when do you read the Bible?"

It didn't sound like a real question, but after a moment, she answered. "I became a Christian over a year ago."

His mouth twitched. "Good for you."

"We go to church Sundays and Wednesday nights."

"Wednesday? Why do you go to Mass twice a week?"

"It's—it's not Mass, Mike."

He sat up, expression serious. "What kind of church is it? I don't want my son picking up weird ideas."

"We follow the Bible. Is that weird?"

He shrugged as if that were up for debate. "And your parents?" A smirk covered his face. "I can't picture them happy with this."

The words stung like a sudden paper cut. "My parents are dead."

His grin vanished. He pulled back, eyes closing. "Meg, I'm sorry. I didn't know."

She studied her hands, angry that with no warning he'd resurrected her pain. "They died in a car accident awhile back. Bad snowstorm, white-out conditions."

"I'm really sorry."

Silence covered the room. The enormity of all the divorce had taken shook her still. She'd visited her parents in Dixon, Illinois, her childhood home, on rare occasions, afraid a mutual friend from high school would see Terrell, guess, and tell Mike. She'd never imagined that she'd lose her parents or that she'd be forced to sell the family farm she loved—because of him.

Mike blew out a deep breath, then tapped the tabletop. "My parents had been wondering. They'd lost touch with your parents and were afraid they were upset with them over… us."

Us.

Meg met his eyes. How could he be so calm? "Mom and Dad were never angry at them."

"If it's any comfort, my parents were pretty peeved at me."

"It's not."

"Yeah, I guess not." He glanced around the room, lips pressed together as if he was thinking things over.

What had he expected tonight? What was it with all this niceness?

Her mind traveled back to the months following their separation and the way she'd asked him to come back every chance she got. Had he expected that?

She lifted her chin and waited for him to look back. When he did, she held his gaze. Did he see how strong she was? Had he noticed she'd said nothing about them?

"Meg, I've missed you."

She caught her breath and turned away.

Mike leaned in front of her. "Do you ever wonder if we were too quick to—"

"*We* were too quick?"

He dragged a hand over his mouth. "Okay. Me. Sorry."

How could he twist what had happened? If he even accused her of being the one who was unfaithful…

"You're right." His words seemed to pain him. "You're right. I was the idiot. I can't tell you how sorry I am. I've spent years wishing I could change everything."

Too late for that. Too late to take back his words and smirks and humiliations. "What good does that do me now, Mike? What am I supposed to do with that?"

"I mean—I messed up. Okay? I wanted to make things right, but nobody knew where you were. When I saw you at the game, I had to come see you. You can't think us running into each other doesn't mean something."

"Stop. Just stop." She stood up, heart pounding, tears threatening. He'd looked for her? "I expect to fend off you and your lawyers, and instead—"

Thudding footsteps sounded in the foyer.

Terrell—what had he heard?

Meg sat, folded her arms and crossed her legs in an effort to calm herself.

A moment later Terrell's voice sounded behind her. "Mommy?" His bare feet padded across the floor. "Is everything okay? You guys were talking loud."

He leaned his head against her shoulder, and Meg forced a smile, wrapping an arm around his waist. "Everything's fine, Terrell. Mike was about to leave."

"Actually, I can stick around."

Wasn't he being helpful? "Not tonight."

Terrell moaned.

Meg shot him a look. "It's getting late, and you still need a bath. You have school tomorrow." She stood, avoiding Mike's eyes, and headed for the foyer.

Terrell followed. "But you said you'd tell me what you talked about."

Meg listened for Mike's footsteps behind her. There they were. "Later, Terrell."

"Everything's fine, Terrell. Your mom will explain it to you."

His voice quivered. "I'm not moving away, am I?"

Her anger at Mike melted. How could she have forgotten Terrell's fear?

She turned, finding Mike kneeling before him, his hands gripping Terrell's forearms.

"You're staying right here," Mike said. "Whenever your mom and I say it's okay, you can visit me, but this is your home. I don't think it'd be right to take you away. Do you?"

Who *was* this thoughtful man?

Relief covered Terrell's face. "When will I get to see you, then?"

"I'm not sure. Tomorrow the team starts a road trip, but when I get back we'll plan something."

Terrell's lower lip protruded.

"I'm sorry, Terrell, but that's the way it is when you play baseball. I travel a lot. When the season's over, things will be different."

Meg closed her eyes at the heartbreak on Terrell's face. She should have prepared him.

"I got it." Mike snapped his fingers. "Let's make up a sign I can give you when I'm at bat. I'll rub my chin, like this." He dragged his thumb once beneath his chin, as if absentmindedly wiping something away. "That'll be my way of saying, 'Hi, Terrell. Looking forward to coming home and seeing you.' What do you think?" Mike rubbed Terrell's chin.

Terrell laughed. "I like that."

With a grin, Mike stood to his feet. He rubbed Terrell's chin again, then bent over for Terrell to rub his own.

Once they finished, uncomfortable silence returned.

Mike looked around, patting his pocket for his wallet. His eyes finally met hers. "I can't go, Meg."

"You can't—what?"

"I need more time. Another half hour. We can get ice cream, play a game, something."

She didn't want another second with him, not after everything he'd dropped on her.

But he had her in a bind, and he knew it. A refusal would have him calling his lawyer.

He wasn't playing fair.

"Fine. Ice cream." She could hear the chill in her voice. "But he has school tomorrow."

"Then half an hour." Terrell's cheers almost drowned out Mike's voice. "Thanks, Meg."

She ignored him as she headed for her purse. She hadn't done it to be nice.

Chapter Ten

Twilight lingered over the ice cream shop, its crowded parking lot lit by brightness spilling from the shop's windows.

Mike pulled into the last parking spot, disappointed to see so many people.

Two teenage boys walked in front of his car. One nudged the other with his elbow and pointed Mike's way.

Not good, not tonight when he needed privacy.

Meg's voice cut into his thoughts. "Something wrong?"

"No." He smiled at her as he shifted into reverse, ignoring the way she sat with arms crossed. "We'll go through the drive-through."

Terrell ordered a caramel sundae and Meg a cup of frozen strawberry yogurt, the same thing she'd ordered the last time they'd eaten ice cream together. However long ago that was. She must live in ruts—fifteen years ordering the same frozen yogurt, six years hating his guts.

They waited silently while the sleepy teen, clearly not a baseball fan, filled their order.

So far the night had been a roller coaster. Getting to know Terrell had been the climb, followed by the deep plunge of rejection. When was the last time a woman told him no? He searched his memory. Seemed he was the one telling them no.

Their order finally ready, Mike handed his sundae to Meg, who directed him to a park at the end of her block. He parked on the street and followed her and Terrell to an isolated picnic table.

Two kids and a woman, who ignored him, played on the swing set.

This was better than he'd hoped. Privacy *and* setting.

Terrell scarfed his ice cream before Mike was halfway done and ran for the swing set.

The silence in his absence drew Mike's gaze to Meg.

She played with her melting yogurt.

What did he say, now that their common bond was gone? He glanced Terrell's way. "Having Terrell—and seeing you again—we're like our own little family."

She smiled as if humoring him. "We're not a family, Mike."

"I know." He scraped hot fudge from the side of his bowl as he waited for the sting of her words to fade. It didn't. "But it'll be nice to look forward to seeing someone when I come home from a road trip."

"What about your parents? Your sisters?"

"Mom and Dad live near LA now. Betsy's up in Lake Forest, but I really don't see her unless her boys want tickets to a game. They're still White Sox fans. Go figure."

Terrell waved from atop a plastic slide.

Meg waved back. "How are Betsy and Linda?"

"All right." No, Meg had missed the bombshell that had rocked his family. "Actually, Betsy was getting beat up."

The confusion in Meg's eyes changed to shock. "Doug? He beat her?"

"From the moment they got married."

She stared at him, the longest gaze she'd given him yet. "I never knew."

"Neither did we. A couple years after you"—he swallowed, rephrasing his words—"after we divorced, he almost killed her. I was up here, playing the Sox, I think. My parents called, said Betsy had phoned them, was incoherent, and wouldn't answer when they called back. They asked me to go check." He tapped his fingers against the wood. "I found her."

"Oh, Mike."

"Yeah." His voice shook at the memory of his sister lying unconscious on her kitchen floor, bruised, bleeding, looking as if she were dead already.

"Is she okay?"

"Other than permanent back problems, I think so." He forced fisted hands beneath the picnic table. "I wanted to pound the guy. If he'd been there—" Mike breathed deeply. Closed his eyes. Later he'd been shaken by the insanity of what he'd longed to do.

Sometimes that still shook him.

Meg lowered her eyes to her yogurt and pushed it around with her spoon. Sorrow covered her features.

He gave her a minute. The news was a downer, but he'd had time to deal with it, time to celebrate Doug's prison sentence, time to make sure his sister was back on her feet. Betsy was stronger than anyone had expected.

"Please tell me you have better news about Linda."

"I do. She's in San Diego, and she and Chris are grandparents. My niece Heather had a baby girl in January, so I'm a great uncle. And at such a young age." He pointed his spoon at her, willing her to smile. "My new purpose in life is to live long enough to be a great-great-great uncle."

"I thought it was grand uncle. Great-great grand uncle."

"Whatever. It's a goal."

Meg smiled into her yogurt.

Score one for him.

When she lifted her head, he looked away at Terrell, who swung from the monkey bars. Strong kid. "I haven't told my parents about Terrell yet."

Meg went still.

Evidently she'd not thought about his parents' reaction to a birth announcement six years late.

Her voice trembled. "When will you tell them?"

"I don't know. When we're ready to face them." What would his parents say? Finding out about Terrell would revive all their anger over his affair and divorce.

What would they say to Meg?

"I'm sorry, Mike. I shouldn't have done what I did."

No joke. "It's in the past, Meg."

She stared beyond him.

He shifted in his seat. He'd been gracious there. Super gracious—which she did *not* deserve. Had she heard him? Was she listening? "You ever think about us getting back together?"

Her gaze shifted to his.

Guess she was listening. He inhaled before taking the plunge. "I was serious when I said I've missed you."

"I take it there's no one else in the picture—no, wait, that wouldn't follow the pattern, would it?"

Her words smacked him in the chest.

She sighed and plopped her cup onto the table. "I'm sorry. I shouldn't have said that."

"No, it's fine." Not really, but…

She withdrew again, her gaze lingering on the street as if some deep thought were revealed there.

She needed to listen.

"The girl—Brooke—you know, the one I was with…" He waved his hand in the air, filling in the ugly blanks. At least he hadn't been a wife beater. "We weren't together long—"

"I don't want to hear it."

"Meg, I'm trying to—"

"Mike. Like you said, it's in the past."

Head lowered, she attacked her yogurt, stabbing and slicing. A small glob flew from her cup and landed on his wrist. "Sorry," she said again.

He shrugged and wiped it off. What would make her listen—and consider his words? He whacked his plastic spoon against the table top, the spoon making a thwacking noise.

Meg looked pointedly at him.

He quit, and she returned to her yogurt.

"I've been doing well," she told the pink slush. "I've got my own business. I work my own hours. I'm not rolling in money, but I make a good living. And I'm happy."

That last one sounded like an afterthought. Mike reached for her hand, his fingertips skimming her nails as she pulled away. "Are you?"

Her hand fluttered to her hair, pulling strands over her shoulder in a familiar gesture he'd forgotten. "It's late," she said. "Terrell needs a bath." She fumbled for her purse, knocking it beneath the picnic table.

Mike snagged it before she could. "We were good together, Meg. Now we've got Terrell. We can't just quit."

She stared at him as if he'd lost his mind. "I didn't quit."

"Let's go out then, you and me."

She leaned for her purse, but he pulled it out of reach. She huffed at him, hands fisted. "Why would I do that, Mike?"

Never had words hurt so much. "Have you forgotten how much fun we had?"

"No, *you* had that problem."

He ground his teeth into a closed-mouth smile. In case she'd forgotten… "Neither one of us was perfect."

Her eyes flashed. "*I* wasn't the one who had an affair!"

"So it's all my fault we got divorced?"

Meg picked up her cup, half-full of strawberry yogurt, and hurled it at him.

Chapter Eleven

Her yogurt landed with a slosh on his chest. Mike leaped from the table, stunned by the sudden cold.

The cup fell to the ground but not before most of the yogurt, a freezing mush, spilled across his shirt and soaked through the cotton fabric and T-shirt underneath. He bent at the waist, trying to shake off the cold mess sliding down his skin.

"Say goodbye to your father, Terrell."

Where was she going? Mike straightened to see Meg tugging a forlorn Terrell toward the sidewalk. The icy cloth burned his skin again, and he jerked the shirt from his stomach. "Meg!"

They disappeared past a house.

Her yogurt cup lay upside down on the grass. Gritting his teeth, Mike smashed it with his foot and ground it into the dirt.

Pink squirted up around the sides of his shoes.

"Perfect," he snarled. He snatched the flattened paper cup and hurled it into a trash can. The remainder of his sundae joined it.

Nice of Meg to throw the blame on him. Literally. He swiped a layer of pink off his shirt. So much for tonight. He shook his hand until most of the yogurt fell to the ground, then flexed his fingers, the yogurt sticky on his skin.

He stormed for his Range Rover, then backtracked to wipe his hands in a thick patch of grass. His jeans would have to do for the rest. He yanked his front pocket linings inside out and rubbed them between his fingers until his skin felt cleaner.

What now? He jerked open the driver's door and climbed in.

No way was he going home yet. He drummed his fingers—his cleanish fingers—on the steering wheel. If he could get her to laugh, she'd thaw a little.

Thaw. Nice choice of words. He started his car, his mind racing.

By the time Mike parked in her driveway, night had chased the last bits of dusk away. Warmth had vanished, as well. At Meg's front door, he hunched his shoulders, only to feel the sticky, half-frozen yogurt cling to his chest.

Remember, he reminded himself, *humor. Smile. Make her laugh*. He pushed the doorbell and rested his hand high on the door frame while he waited for her to answer.

The foyer window remained dark. He tilted his head to listen for footsteps, but none sounded. He pushed the doorbell again. Waited some more. No sound. No light. Nothing—

Lights flicked on.

Mike plastered on a smile.

The door opened, and Meg stood silent, welcoming light reflecting off the wood and walls behind her. He waited for her to say something—hello would be fine—but she didn't.

He raised his eyebrows. "That was cold, Meg."

She'd never been able to stay hurt. One joke, and a smile, however faint, would force its way onto her face. He watched for that hint of amusement, for anything that would tell him he was forgiven.

Instead she remained unmoved, her face empty.

Not good. Tears would have been better than this.

"Where's Terrell?" he asked.

"In the tub. Do you need something?"

"A washcloth, perhaps?" He motioned to his shirt.

She stared him down, arms crossed.

"You're right," he said. "We need to talk. May I come in?"

"No. But you can leave."

"How about you talk, and I'll listen. You can get things off your chest while I get this stuff off mine."

"I have nothing to say."

She moved to close the door, but Mike caught the edge and held it open. "It's a good thing I didn't take you out for coffee," he joked.

"Go away, Mike."

Go away? He dropped his hand from the door.

"I'm tired," she said, "and I don't—I don't want to argue. Can we just—" She looked away. "Thanks for the ice cream."

She moved the door, and, numbed by her words, he let it go.

The door clicked shut and the locks turned. The foyer window darkened.

Go away.

Had she just told him to get lost? He stared at the carved door shut in his face. She'd better not if she wanted to keep Terrell. He raised a fist, ready to order her to open up, but Terrell's face, marred by fear, stopped him. He lowered his hand. He couldn't do that to Terrell. He'd already done enough.

Tonight, just tonight, he'd leave.

He glanced at her house before climbing into his Range Rover.

The Meg he remembered had not been home tonight. But if he was patient, maybe in time she'd make an appearance. Then he'd get that elusive second chance that haunted him.

Mike backed out of her driveway, spirits rising. She'd have a couple weeks to cool off before he returned. And when he did, he'd have a plan.

Next time everything would be different.

Chapter Twelve

"What are you watching?"

Ben stiffened at Dana's soft voice hovering above the recliner. Her arms circled his neck, and he held himself still instead of pushing her away. "Baseball reruns," he said.

"I thought it looked old." She slid onto the arm of the chair, blocking the light. "Do people really watch these games?"

"There's a whole channel for it." He should tell her to go away. The last thing he wanted was her asking lots of questions—and then feeling sorry for him.

"Who's playing?"

"Boston, Oakland." The teams had gone into the final game of the year tied for the last playoff spot. The winner of the game had moved on to the post season. The loser had gone home.

"What's the score?"

It was right there in the corner, for Pete's sake. "Four to three, Boston." He added more to keep her quiet. "Two on, no outs, bottom of the ninth, Oakland's batting."

If she couldn't find the score, maybe she wouldn't notice who was pitching.

"Is that *you?*"

Ben closed his eyes. "Yes."

"Why didn't you tell me you played in the major leagues?"

"Watch," he growled.

Dana's body turned rigid, but at least she was silent.

Ben covered his mouth with a fist, watching himself—eleven years younger and thirty pounds lighter—nod at Reddick's pitch choice. What had it been, a fastball?

The Oakland batter swung late.

Yep, fastball.

His best pitch. On rare days, almost a hundred miles an hour.

The picture changed to Reddick signaling slider.

That call still made no sense. Ben's slider had been unreliable that last month. The whole pitching staff knew it, Reddick included.

Shake him off.

Instead Ben watched himself check the runners on first and third. He started his windup, the runner on first going a moment before the ball left Ben's hand for home plate.

"Miss," he hissed into his fist.

But the Oakland batter connected with Ben's pitch, the ball zipping by the first baseman. The runner on third trotted home.

Tie game.

Dana sucked in a breath.

The third base coach waved the oncoming runner home. The camera flipped to the right fielder scooping up the ball.

The television picture faded, and Ben watched the play from where he'd backed up Reddick behind home plate. He saw umpire Edwin Byrd move into position, felt the cool air swirling around him, followed the ball sailing in from the outfield as the thunder grew from the Oakland crowd, all standing, all watching the ball in flight. And then the ball disappeared into Reddick's glove. The slide, the tag, the dust—all at once. So close—

Byrd's arms stretched horizontally, and Reddick, already on his knees, fell backward, glove over his face. Oakland players streamed from the dugout, and in the corner of the TV, behind the mad pile of men celebrating their success, Ben watched himself, the losing pitcher, lunge at Byrd.

"Oh, Ben—"

He slammed his fist against the armrest. He should have shook Reddick off. The idiot couldn't call a decent game. And Byrd?

Ben shot out of the chair and down the hall, ignoring Dana's voice. He kept going until the hallway ended, then, at a loss, veered into his office and slammed the door behind him. An autographed Greg Maddux photo fell to the carpet, but tonight he didn't care. He dropped into his desk chair and stared at the blackness of his computer screen.

This was where he'd ended up, eleven years later. A has-been.

No, a never-was. One of those pitchers that drove a team's fans mad.

He turned on his computer, forcing open his clenched fist. What now?

Margo.

Ben rolled his eyes. Not again. He yanked open a file drawer and pulled out the green binder. He spread it open on the desk, but tonight the contents did not console him. Instead the longer he sat there, his failure consuming him, the more appealing calling Margo seemed. Forget the risk.

Maybe Margo could help him forget his last pitch in the majors.

Chapter Thirteen

Mike's words disturbed Meg's sleep.

I'm sorry. I've missed you.

Do you wonder if we were too quick?

I've spent years wishing—

She kicked the comforter to the foot of her bed. Her clock read 1:30, and she glared at it. "He's too late," she told it. "Years too late."

Why couldn't he have said those things when they mattered?

Like after that eleven-day road trip?

Meg flopped onto her back and tried to sleep, but her eyes refused to close. She stared at the ceiling, reliving those lonely days after Mike dropped the Brooke bomb and left to play baseball.

On the night he was to return, Meg had gone to bed early, knowing that when she woke sometime in the day's first hours Mike would be there, back from Kansas City. She needed to be rested and alert in case he was ready to talk.

They could overcome whatever had gone wrong in their marriage, even Mike's betrayal. She had adjusted the pillow beneath her, pulled the covers over her shoulders, and forced her eyes shut. Everything would be better, in time.

When she woke, sunlight poked around the drapes. She rolled over and looked at Mike's side of the bed.

Empty. Untouched.

She grabbed her clock. Eight-thirty. Was that right?

The light edging the curtains said it was.

Where was Mike? Had something happened? Had the team's plane gone down?

She flung back the covers, jumped from her bed.

No, someone would have called.

Where was he?

The guest room.

She grabbed her hair and yanked it into a ponytail, then hurried down the hall, but the room was empty. So was the other bedroom and the couch in the living room and family room. In the garage, her Lexus sat alone.

Okay. Okay. Calm down. She dragged her hands down her cheeks and fell onto a chair at the kitchen table. *Think, Meg.*

She turned on ESPN. The sports ticker streamed across the bottom of SportsCenter. There was last night's score. Texas, three, and Kansas City, seven. And nothing else. No plane crash, no extended game, nothing out of the ordinary.

Pain flared in her stomach, a low flame that burned hotter and higher. Meg shoved it aside. For eleven days she'd faced the truth and survived. This wouldn't kill her, either.

He was with Brooke.

She forced saliva so she could swallow. He'd always come home. After all, she did his laundry, kept his favorite beer in the fridge, cooked his favorite meals. Brooke hadn't kept him yet. He'd be back. In a couple hours maybe—

Tears rolled down her cheeks and onto her fists. How could Mike do this?

Hours wore on. Mike did not appear, did not answer her calls. At 6:30, she turned on the team's pre-game show. If he so much as smiled—

The pre-game showed him sitting in the dugout, talking to two players, the three of them laughing at whatever story they shared.

Her pain vanished.

When the game was almost over, Meg drove to the stadium and waited in the concourse outside the clubhouse. If Mike didn't like it, he could blame himself.

Marty, one of the security guards, walked to where she leaned against the wall. "Any reason you're out here, Meg?"

She kept her focus on the clubhouse doors. "Pink eye. I'm contagious."

He nodded as if he'd seen it all before and returned to his chair.

Meg waited twenty minutes before the first player walked out. As Mike's teammates emerged alone or in groups, she realized she could tell who knew and who did not.

Cliff, Jeff, and Juan waved, smiled, said hello.

Aaron wouldn't look at her, although Lindsey, his wife, stopped to talk.

Dante and Mariah gave weak smiles and hurried past.

Maury, Eve, and their twin daughters asked why she was out here. Maury backed away at her excuse.

Adam Destin, one of Mike's closest friends, took three steps outside the clubhouse before he saw her and turned back.

"Adam," she called.

His shoulders slumped. Reluctantly he came over.

She prayed her voice would hold. "Please don't tell him I'm here."

He looked all around her before meeting her eyes, his own heavy. "I'm sorry."

She shrugged—it was that or bawl on his shoulder—and he left.

Two more players appeared before Mike walked out alone, a grin on his face. It vanished when he saw her, but he walked to her without missing a step, as if he'd expected her to be there.

"What are you doing here?" he asked.

"Waiting for my husband."

"Ah." He adjusted his collar and looked around, nodding and smiling at someone down the concourse.

Couldn't he pay attention for more than two seconds?

She fought to keep her voice calm and firm. "When are you coming home?"

"I don't know." He looked down, and she followed his gaze, watching him rock up and then down on his toes.

"I thought we were going to talk."

"Yeah."

"When?"

Noise from the clubhouse entrance distracted them, and Mike called goodnight to two more close friends, teammates who had to know this conversation wasn't a good one.

She didn't want to do this here. "Mike, come home. We can start over."

"I have." He took a step back, calling his friends. They stopped and turned. "Don't come here again."

"Mike, what am I supposed to—"

He held his arms out from his sides before turning and jogging away.

For the rest of the week, Meg stayed home, unable to end the nightmare.

By Saturday, she had to escape. She left home midmorning and drove to a decorating store to think. Just after one o'clock, she returned to the empty garage and carried her bags and Subway meal into the townhouse. At least Mike hadn't cancelled their credit cards.

The moment she stepped inside, a familiar scent met her.

Mike's cologne lingered in the air.

"Mike?" She dropped her bags on the table and ran through the first floor. "Mike?"

Maybe he was upstairs.

She rushed to the second floor, calling his name.

No answer.

In her bedroom, she stopped in the doorway, studying Mike's side of the room.

His dresser—

Her hand clutched her throat. "No." She stepped closer to Mike's dresser. All of his drawers were open slightly, the way he left them that annoyed her so much. Only this time no socks stuck out. No T-shirt corners hung over the drawer's edge. She tugged at his top drawer, knowing before it flew open that it would be empty.

They were all empty. So was his half of the closet. And his side of the bathroom.

Even his pillow was gone.

An ache spread through Meg, down her arms and legs, into her head and fingers. She sat on the edge of the bed and ran her hand over the empty spot, ignoring the tears that trickled down her face. "Why?"

He'd left without warning, without reason. Why was he doing this?

Downstairs, the doorbell rang. Hope rose within her that it was Mike, but reality gripped her. Of course it wasn't him. If he'd forgotten something, he'd walk in and take it.

She wiped her cheeks with her hands and rubbed them dry on her shorts before taking her time down the stairs. She didn't want to talk. Maybe by the time she got to the door, whoever it was would be gone.

But when she looked through the peephole, a man not much older than Mike still stood on the doorstep.

She shook her hair, took a deep breath, and opened the door.

"Meghan Connor?" he asked.

"Yes?"

He held out a manila envelope. "This is for you." He waited

while she opened the screen, but as soon as the envelope was in her hands, he darted for his car at the curb.

Her hands shook. She seated herself on the couch and forced herself to open the envelope.

Divorce papers.

The tears returned, building from a steady stream to sobs that sucked air from her lungs. Her stomach lurched and Meg ran to the bathroom, crying beside the toilet until she threw up.

An hour later, eyes swollen, nose plugged, and legs trembling, Meg walked from room to room, laying each picture of Mike face down in its place.

That scum.

In the living room she turned the eight-by-ten picture of them walking down the aisle, hand in hand as they grinned at each other, to the wall before sitting on the couch beneath it and calling a locksmith.

Next time he'd face her.

Chapter Fourteen

Mike could hear and feel the music before the doors to the Cleveland club opened. Eager for warmth, he trailed three teammates inside, Travis Benes, Will Hamrick, and Brett Burkholder, all as bored as he was.

Pressure built below his eyes, and Mike bit off a sneeze, then another as he looked around. A crowd packed the place—a good thing, he tried to convince himself. A crowd meant he'd be harder to notice.

Or was it more people to hassle him?

Some of the guys joked that he'd turned into a hermit, but he had his reasons. Wherever he went, people hounded him, men wanting autographs and women wanting… numerous things. Even now three women at a nearby table made no attempt to hide their availability.

He detoured away from them. Wait until they found out about his personal life. That'd send them running. "What am I doing here?" he asked.

Travis made a face. "What?"

Mike shook his head.

Brett picked a corner table, and Mike seated himself across from Will, his back to the crowd. This wasn't so bad, a night out instead of room service. Mike flipped through the menu, even though he'd filled up on the post-game meal.

A new song started, the music pounding against him. Mike ordered a drink and leaned back in his chair. What was Meg up to tonight? Had she and Terrell seen his signal? He'd debated calling on pretense of making sure but decided not to. No telling how Meg would react.

At least she couldn't throw frozen yogurt through a satellite.

Someone nudged him. "Connor. Wake up."

"Hmm?" He looked up at his friends and then at the waitress standing beside their table.

She set his drink and another in front of him. "This is from one of the women at the bar."

Without thinking, Mike looked over his shoulder.

The three women had moved to the bar and watched him. One smiled, her dark, silky hair falling over her shoulder. She crossed her legs, raising the glass in her hand.

Will chuckled and kicked him under the table, but Mike turned his back on the woman. He felt sick. "No. Thanks." He shook his head and watched the drink disappear, leaving an incomplete wet ring on the table.

Another reason to stay close to his hotel. Like he needed reminders of Brooke. Mike rubbed his hand over his eyes and forehead. What an ugly year that had been. Life had taken on a grimy, sandy feel since then.

"What was that?" Will leaned across the table. "Did you *see* her?"

"Not interested."

"Really." Will pushed his chair back, the legs scraping the floor. "Maybe I'll buy her a drink. Someone has to apologize for your behavior."

Mike shrugged. "It's your life," he said as Will disappeared past him.

"You all right?" Brett asked.

"I'm sick." He toyed with his drink, realizing how true that was. He was sick of relationships that failed one after the other, sick of his thoughts returning to Meg like a magnet, sick of the way his conscience hounded him. And now that he knew where Meg was and that they had a son—

Suing for custody flashed again in his mind.

Mike sucked in a slow breath. No, he couldn't go that route. If he forgave Meg, maybe she'd forgive him. And maybe then he'd feel okay again.

Maybe.

The waitress returned with their appetizers. Mike dragged triangle-cut French bread through Will's spinach and artichoke dip. What was it about Meg that drew him? Even during his relationships after Brooke, he'd never been able to completely shake his feelings for Meg, and he'd often wondered how long it would take before her memory no longer haunted him.

And Sara… She'd seen the truth he hadn't. That it would never happen. Fifteen years from the first time he saw Meg, and he could still replay the moment. Even here, in a loud, crowded club. He pictured her walking into biology class seconds before the bell, approaching him, and sliding into the empty seat in front of him. Her long, wavy hair whirled out around her, and Mike fought the urge to lean into it.

He'd never seen her before. Was she new? As roll call began, Mike listened for her name.

Meghan Caldwell.

Meghan. What a perfect name. Unique, gorgeous. Like her.

He had to meet her.

By the time Mike heard his name, Coach Patterson was glaring at him and emphasizing each syllable. "Michael Connor?"

Around him kids snickered.

"Are you here or not?" Coach Patterson asked.

"Here," he'd said. "Very glad to be here."

Brett's voice broke into his thoughts. "What are you smiling at?"

Mike moved his eyes from the wall behind Will's chair to his teammates, feeling the dopey expression on his face. "What?"

"What's up with you?" Travis asked.

"Nothing." Standing, he pulled out his wallet, grabbed some money, and dropped it on the table. "Will you take care of this?"

"Sure. Where you going?"

"To the hotel." Where he could reminisce in peace.

Mike shouldered through the crowd, past pens and autograph pleas, past Will who punched him in the arm before returning to the dark-haired woman, and past the front doors.

What was Meg doing tonight?

Once he was inside his hotel room, he pulled her business card from his wallet. He called her number, then stretched out on the bed, channel surfing while he waited for her to answer.

Instead, voicemail picked up.

He tossed his phone aside, still flipping channels. A news station caught his attention, and he listened to the update on Sunday's earthquake in Japan. He hadn't known there'd been one.

Meg could probably tell him all about it though, if she was still a news junkie.

He pictured her early in his baseball career lying on the couch with the TV on, some textbook pressed against her knees, her bare toes playing with pillow fringe.

"What are you watching?" he'd ask.

"The news," she'd say, then greet him with a hug and a kiss and an update on the most recent political scandal or international tension or natural disaster. He'd tease her about being addicted and needing help and she'd smack his chest, pretending to be hurt...

He closed his eyes. He hit the off button, and silence filled the room.

Better.

What was it he wanted from Meg? Her grace, her looks, and her demeanor intrigued him, just as they had when she'd so regally walked into biology class and ignored him. Was that it? Because she didn't fall all over him, he was interested in her again?

He clicked his tongue against the roof of his mouth. No. Meg had been his first love, and although he'd wandered, no one had compared to her. He and Meg had been right for each other, right in a way that couldn't be matched by anyone else.

After all these years, could they get that back?

The silence would not answer.

Mike flipped the TV back on, surfing for something loud enough to overpower Meg's grip on him.

For something—anything—that would make him happy again.

Chapter Fifteen

She could not be weak when Mike returned.

Would not be weak.

Across the room someone called Meg's name, but the voice barely registered. She must not cave in to Mike like she had that first time he'd returned so many years ago. Of course then she'd wanted their marriage to work. But now—

"Meg. I've got it."

The words broke through her thoughts, and she looked across her office to where Dana tapped a pencil against the computer screen. "Come see this. I've figured it out."

Bless Dana. Meg pushed her chair away from her desk and crossed the room. Wasting precious work hours on Mike was the last thing she should be doing. She leaned over Dana's shoulder. The layout for the Layton's kitchen remodel filled the screen.

Dana tapped one side of the island in the center of the large room. "What if you put the stove in the island? Pot and pan storage would join it. Then this part of the wall"—her pencil moved across the screen—"could be converted to an entryway into the pantry from the kitchen."

The finished product flashed in Meg's mind. The pantry doors would be the same buttery cream as the upper cabinets with a bit of French blue glass set in the top of the doors. Yes, it was perfect. "I love it."

Dana grinned at her. "I'll take my own kitchen remodel whenever you're ready."

"Keep refining my designs, and you'll get it." Maybe it was time to schedule her in since May wasn't looking too busy. "Take a look at their great room next, and I'll pencil you into my calendar."

Dana turned back to the computer. "I'm on it."

If only she could hire a dozen Danas. She'd be the most sought-after designer in Chicagoland. She'd have more clients than—

Probably than she could handle. Meg dropped onto her chair and fingered her to-do list forty-some things long. Maybe it was good there was only one Dana.

Meg's high school dreams of interior design had never included twelve-hour days or clients who fought every technique she'd studied. The decorating she'd done in Texas had been rejuvenating—a day spent with the girls picking paint chips and fabrics, visiting showrooms and furniture stores, interrupted by leisurely lunch and conversation.

In this real world, though, her job threatened every minute in her day. Too often Terrell spent his afternoons at Jill's house and his evenings watching part of a Wind game while Meg crunched numbers beside him. Jill hadn't been exaggerating about giving Terrell a few minutes a night. And that scenario was only becoming more common. More than once Terrell had spent the night at Jill's when a project required her presence from early morning until late in the evening.

Mike would have a heyday with that.

Sadly the Mike who'd encouraged her dreams in high school hadn't shown up for the marriage. He didn't understand that she hated their conflicting schedules as much as he did or that once she had her degree, she could schedule clients around spring training in order to be with him. So he'd had to spend seven weeks in Arizona without her a couple times. It wouldn't have been that way forever.

Meg shook old justifications away. She should not be thinking about him. She could not afford even a minute—

Against her will, memories of Mike's first return, a night over six years old, filled her mind.

She could picture everything from that Thursday in mid-October. The sun had vanished, and a sliver of moon hung in the sky. Meg had returned from three days visiting her parents in Dixon and folded laundry in front of the television when the knock sounded.

Two months had passed since Mike had left. She'd spent her nights alone, watching him on TV, searching for any trace that his relationship with Brooke might be ending. She'd wanted to leave Texas forever, but her lawyer and parents convinced her to stay until things were settled. Perhaps Mike would have a change of heart, Mom had said.

Now, looking through her peephole, she found him standing on her doorstep, head down, shoulders drooping. Was he coming back? Was this whole nightmare about to end?

She held a hand against her stomach, somersaulting inside her, and ran the other through her hair before opening the door.

Mike lifted his head, his eyes flat and empty.

Meg reached for him anyway and pulled him inside.

In the living room, he looked around as if reacquainting himself with the house. When he saw the picture above the couch turned to the wall, his face crumpled. He dropped into a chair, one broad hand covering his eyes.

Meg waited a minute, then handed him a box of Kleenex, amazed that she had no tears.

"Thanks," he croaked.

Thanks. It was the first word he'd spoken to her in a month.

He rested his head against the chair back and stared at the ceiling.

Meg returned to her laundry, her insides queasy, and waited for him to speak first.

"You're quiet," he said at last.

She stared at the towel she'd finished folding. "What do you want me to say?"

"I thought you'd ask why I'm here."

"You'll tell me when you're ready." She pulled another towel out of the basket and smoothed it over the couch cushions.

"I can't. I don't know why I'm here."

Meg looked up.

He stared at the television, his chin cupped in his palm. "I got in the car and drove, and here I am."

So nothing was over. Yet. She ran her hand over the towel, swallowing. "Why did you get in your car?"

He didn't answer, wouldn't look her in the eye. Instead he slid to the edge of his chair and reached for her hand. "Where's your ring?"

Was he joking? "Where's yours?"

He stood abruptly, as if she'd yelled at him, and crossed the room to the kitchen table. His shoulders shook once as he leaned over it.

Why all the tears? Did he finally realize what he'd done to them?

Before she knew it, she was behind him, her arms wrapped around his waist, her cheek pressed to his back.

Mike turned and pulled her to him. Her tears joined his, and Meg closed her eyes in a vain attempt to hold them back.

"Can I stay?" he whispered above her. "For tonight?"

How could she say no? If he stayed one night, maybe he'd stay for another, and before long those empty drawers would be full again.

But in the morning, Mike left.

He had no reason to. Texas had already lost their playoff series, and she knew he would spend the next few weeks relaxing before preparing for the next season. Still, he hurried down the stairs, refusing her offer of breakfast, refusing to look her in the eye.

Had he gone back to Brooke?

Would he return?

Her hope faded as November arrived, and Mike's callused ways reappeared. Meg visited her lawyer a week before Thanksgiving. "I want to take my half and end this," she told him.

He looked at her in surprise. "Meg, that's ridiculous. We're making our case. Be patient, and you'll get everything you want."

Not everything. "Some things are worth more than money."

"Like what?"

She swallowed and lifted her chin. "Like moving on."

"Meg—"

"I want to be home for Christmas."

"You're not thinking straight. Take a few days—"

"A few days? I've had months! Call his lawyer."

He studied her before speaking. "You're that sure?"

"I can't drag this on anymore." Her hand covered her stomach. "I want to go home."

"All right." He motioned for her to sit.

The truth was all over Mike's hardened face. He was never coming back. Despite their history and years of friendship, their marriage was over and Mike wanted to take every crumb he could, just to rub it in her face.

Well, she'd one-up him.

This child, hers and Mike's, was worth more than their money and cars and furnishings. Because that was how Mike would view their baby.

When he'd been called up to the majors, he'd asked her to get rid of the birth control.

But they were only twenty-one.

Mike reasoned that by the time the baby was born, they'd be twenty-two. If it took awhile, maybe twenty-three or -four. That wasn't so young, was it?

Meg had won the battle, but there'd been others, a few times each year. Mike would mention having kids, and the argument began all over again.

"Why do we have to have kids now?" she'd ask in frustration.

He'd answered, but she hadn't listened. Mike was better than the average player. What if he played ball well into his thirties? He could. He probably *would*. Then they'd have kids about to drive, and she'd be the only one home with them from February to October.

A few more years, she'd told him. *Maybe when we're close to thirty.*

He'd thrown up his hands and walked away.

Just as he walked away now.

Funny, wasn't it, that his walking away had resulted in this pregnancy. She'd stopped using birth control a month after he'd left, and look what had come of it.

Mike would be a dad. She would be a mom.

They just wouldn't be those things together.

And Mike couldn't know. At first she'd thought she could use the baby to bring him back. But he'd want proof she was pregnant. He'd accuse her of being unfaithful.

And what about custody? No matter how unexpected this baby was, she couldn't let a groupie raise her child. Not two days a week. Not one day a week.

Not at all.

The decision came easily. She'd take the ultimate revenge. Even if Mike never found out, she would always know that, in the end, he'd been the true loser.

Dana's faint voice called again.

Sometimes she couldn't live with what she'd done, even though God had forgiven her. She hadn't known him then, she reminded herself. She hadn't known that revenge only poisoned herself. She hadn't known there was any other way to live.

But she did now.

And she'd still refused to tell Mike.

"Well, he and Terrell are together," she whispered into her hands. "Just please—please don't let me hurt so much."

"Meg?" Dana repeated.

"Just a minute." She lifted a finger and pretended to take notes while she gathered control.

And then the truth hit her. Mike was not the only loser. Terrell had lost. So had she.

And maybe they were all still losing.

When would it end?

Chapter Sixteen

He'd found Margo.

Ben sat frozen before his computer, the pictures and phrases burning into his brain.

Five days had passed since he'd watched himself fail on TV, five days filled with memories of what should have been. Over and over he'd debated calling home. Two years had passed since he'd been home, since he'd had to run. Two years—surely contacting Margo would be safe.

Today he'd given in when a client cancelled an afternoon showing. He dashed home and called the number from memory, trying to slow his breathing as the phone rang. Would his dad recognize his voice?

The phone was picked up mid-ring. "Hello," an old man snapped, voice gravelly and cantankerous.

Ben frowned as the voice registered. Uncle Pete, Dad's brother.

"I said hello," Pete growled in his ear. "If you're calling about the house for rent, speak up."

What house was he renting? Ben lowered his voice, counting on his uncle's poor hearing. "I'm trying to find the people who used to live here."

"Why?"

"I'm a friend of Margo's."

"Really? Who is this?" Pete snapped.

"I told you—a friend of Margo's."

"Not much of a friend if you're looking for her here."

"What's that mean?"

"Don't you read the papers?"

"I'm not from the area."

"Where then?"

The man could still irritate the daylights out of him. "Pete, I'm trying to get in touch with Margo—"

Too late he realized his slip.

"Who is this?"

Ben dropped his forehead into his hand. Pete wouldn't turn him in, not unless he'd changed in two years. All the Raines men were alike.

Himself, included.

"Pete, it's *me*."

In the background, the doorbell Ben had grown up with rang. Pete lowered his voice to a whisper. "You coming back?"

"No. Where's Margo?"

Faint voices, a woman's and a man's, neared his uncle. "Pete?" he prodded.

"Check the paper, two years ago. You know the date."

The paper?

He pulled up the *Baltimore Sun's* archives, wondering what might have happened after his own troubles started.

His search took three minutes. The headlines of the article almost two years old told the story. "Local Woman Dead; Husband Accused of Murder."

Ben read the article again, numbed by the smiling photo of Margo beside his father's mug shot, both beneath the horrible headline.

Margo was dead.

Dad had killed her.

Articles covering the trial spread across the next year and a half, detailing the lives of a woman who'd lived thirty years with abuse, a son who'd become a fugitive, and a father who'd refused to take the blame, coming home drunk one night and beating her, resulting in her death.

Ben closed his eyes, the awfulness washing over him in an icy rush. Margo was dead, killed by his own father, who lived in prison and would for the rest of his sorry life.

His stomach heaved, and Ben lunged for the trash can just in time.

When the cramps ended, he wiped his mouth and returned to his desk chair, guilt descending with its mind-numbing cold.

"Ben?"

He jolted at Dana's distant voice. The door to his office was closed, and he kept still, praying she wouldn't search the house for him.

"Ben, could you give me a hand with these groceries?"

He closed his eyes. Those who'd gotten in the way of his career were just as culpable for Margo's death as his dad was. They were murderers, every one of them.

They'd pay for her death.

Something thudded in the kitchen. "Ben, I know you're here. Your car's blocking the garage."

Go away.

Her footsteps sounded across the kitchen, then vanished where the carpet began.

Leave me alone, Dana.

Her voice sounded in the hall outside his office. "Ben, I've had a long day. Help me carry food in."

She'd had a long day?

The doorknob turned.

What had Margo said about him to his dad? That had to be what it was about. What words of defense had she offered that drove his dad to murder? *Margo, I'm sorry—*

"I've been calling you." Dana stood in the doorway, irritation creasing her features. She sniffed, the lines in her forehead deepening. "What is that smell?"

Anger poured through him. What did she know about bad days, about being the root of someone's murder?

She huffed at him. "Can't you leave your computer for a minute and help me?"

Dana was in his hands before he could think.

Chapter Seventeen

Mike hadn't meant his hiding spot on the couch to be that good.

He lay curled in a ball beneath the chenille throw, bare feet and ankles poking beyond the cream fringe, but Katie and Nate Destin had run past him three times already.

"Hurry up! I'm hot under here!" he hollered.

"Daddy, where is he?" Katie called from the dining room.

Adam Destin, his closest friend from his ball-playing years in Texas, laughed in the overstuffed chair beside him. "I told you not to play hide-and-seek with them. They're clueless."

This four-game series against his former team was the second time Mike had returned since Texas had traded him. And, as before, he was staying at Adam's home instead of at the team hotel, enjoying the company of Adam, Shauni, and their three-year-old twins.

Mike pulled the blanket off his head, neither kid in sight. "I'm putting an end to this. I'm in the living room!" he yelled before ducking under the blanket.

Squeals and laughter answered, but they came no closer.

Unbelievable. "Nobody can be this bad at hide-and-seek."

"Yeah, they can."

"You should be embarrassed, Adam."

"I'm humiliated. So. Dude. Someone's been asking about you."

Mike listened for Katie and Nate, but their voices were muffled as if they'd gone upstairs. "Who?"

"Brooke."

He snorted beneath the blanket, regretting it when he inhaled small fibers. Too bad that wasn't the only thing he regretted about her.

"Just so you know, man, she's hoping to see you while you're in town."

Mike sat upright, the blanket falling off his chest. "You tell her I don't want to be in the same building as her."

Adam held up a hand. "I'm just giving you the head's up."

The thought of Brooke lurking nearby made his head pound. "She'd better not be coming here."

"I think she's gonna call you at the clubhouse."

"I won't talk to her. And if she waits outside the clubhouse, I'll walk right by her."

"That's it, huh?"

"Are you kidding?" Meg flashed through his mind, but Mike refused to compare the situations. "I plan on never seeing her again, and you can tell her that at your next family reunion—"

"Connor!" Nate stood in the living room doorway, feet spread, finger pointing.

Mike dove beneath the blanket as Nate raced for him, Katie on his heels. Their small bodies flopped on top of him. Mike pulled his legs to his chest and covered his head as the blanket slid to the floor.

"Connor! Connor!" Nate jumped up and down. "We found you!"

"And all by yourself too, didn't you?" Mike pulled the twins close, tickling each with one hand while they laughed and pushed him away in vain.

Shauni appeared in the doorway, eyebrows raised. "Mike, you wouldn't be riling up my children, would you?"

Nate whacked Mike with a throw pillow.

It caught him across the chin, and he grimaced. "You think your kids are angels?"

"Hardly." She pulled the pillow from Nate's grasp. "Lunchtime, guys."

The twins ignored her, tickling Mike instead.

He shrugged and held his hands out, waiting for them to discover he wasn't ticklish.

Shauni grabbed each twin by a shoulder. "Give Mike a break, you two. He's not here for your entertainment."

"Now she tells me." Mike picked up Nate, who'd lunged for him again. Did the kid ever quit?

Katie darted into the dining room. "I want to sit by Mike!" she yelled.

"No, me!" Nate slithered out of Mike's grip as if made of liquid and ran after Katie who defended her spot beside Mike's chair with her lungs.

Mike trailed after them, raising his voice above theirs. "I'll sit between you."

Silence and innocent smiles answered him, the two looking as incapable of arguing as they were capable of winning hide-and-go-seek by themselves.

Adam followed Mike. "Want to take one home for a month?"

"I heard that." Shauni moved a chair between the twins' booster seats. "You're too good with kids, Mike. You should have some."

"I do." Mike grinned as Adam sent him a confused look. "I have a son."

"Since when?"

A platter of barbeque-slathered ribs filled the center of the table. Ribs and three-year-olds? What was Shauni thinking? "Long time ago," he said, sitting between the twins, anyway. "Terrell's going on six."

"Get real, Connor. I'd know if you had a kid that old."

"Only if I knew too."

Adam's eyes widened. "Was it that singer after Brooke? I thought—"

"No! Not her." Every muscle in his face tightened. The fun in stringing Adam along fled. "It was Meg. We have a son."

Shauni passed a bowl of corn on the cob to Mike. "Who's Meg?"

"His ex-wife."

"I didn't know you'd been married," she said. "What happened?"

"Your husband introduced me to his cousin."

Shauni sent Adam a disgusted look.

Adam passed the look on to Mike. "Thanks a lot, Connor. She's not my cousin, she's my cousin's wife's cousin," he told Shauni. "And I just introduced her to Mike and a few others during spring training. I had no idea she had a crush on Mike."

But Mike had known. Within a minute of meeting her, when she'd laughed at all his comments, when she'd flashed that wide smile, when she'd slid away from Adam to sit across from him, he'd known. And the knowledge had been a mental anesthetic, easing his conscience enough for him to lean across the table and lose himself in conversation with her.

As the night had progressed and the others left, Mike and Brooke stayed. He could claim that he'd said nothing to make her think he was interested, but all these years later, he knew that sitting with her, listening to her, talking and sharing some of his dreams had been the same as if he'd egged her on. After all, Brooke had followed him back to Texas, a real ego boost. And since she and Adam were almost family, Mike told himself there was nothing wrong with her presence in the group he hung out with.

If only he'd admitted where things were headed.

Shauni's voice broke into his self-recriminations. "I cannot believe you'd do that, Mike." She flung a pat of butter on her corn, then pointed the knife at him. "I hope you've changed."

He raised his hands. "I have. Really." He waited, jokingly, until she lowered the knife. "I'm trying to convince Meg to give us another shot."

"Good luck."

"I'll need it."

Nate wiped his barbeque-covered mouth with his hand then held it up, fingers spread, and eyed it as if someone had just used him as a personal napkin.

"Need some help, bud?" Mike wiped Nate's arm and face until the napkin looked more red than white. Shauni handed him a stack of napkins, and Mike stashed them all beside Nate's plate.

Maybe he'd make it through lunch stain-free after all.

Katie's voice sounded beside him. "Me too."

Mike turned to find her red, sticky hand reaching for him, and he grabbed her wrist before she could share the stains. He swiped a few of Nate's napkins, pausing at the sight of Adam with his hands behind his head, chair tipped back, face covered with a grin. Mike smirked back. "You could have warned me."

The doorbell rang before Adam could say anything. He started to lower his chair, but Shauni waved him back. "I'll get it. If Adam answers the door, he ends up signing autographs and talking baseball with the UPS man."

"If you'd stop ordering stuff, there'd be no UPS man to talk to," Adam teased.

Shauni, already out of sight, didn't answer.

"Are you serious about Meg?" Adam asked. "After she keeps your own kid from you?"

"I can't blame everything on her." Mike released Katie's hand, but a glance at Nate showed his face covered in sauce already. Mike sighed, making a mental note to change shirts after lunch. "I've thought about Meg off and on for years, and I've regretted what I did since before Brooke and I split up. If I can forgive what she did with Terrell, maybe she can forgive me."

"If that's what you want, then I hope it works."

Shauni appeared in the doorway, halting their conversation, but she made no move to enter.

"Who was it?" Adam asked.

Something in the way she avoided Mike's face turned his stomach.

"It's Brooke." Shauni dragged her gaze from Adam to him. "Mike, she wants to see you."

Chapter Eighteen

Dana, I'm lost without—

The pen in Ben's hand left inkless marks on the card. Another one dead. He shook it, but it refused to work.

"You got another pen?" he asked the blonde toothpick behind the florist counter. "This one's out of ink."

"Sure."

She handed him his third pen since he'd walked in. He ignored her flirty smile and held out his hand. "And another card?"

She slid him a second pale pink card, and Ben rewrote the message for this last bouquet. *Dana, I'm lost without you. Forgive me? Ben*

Mushy, yet to the point. Just like the other four bouquets. He slipped the card into the envelope, wrote Dana's name across it, and tossed the pen toward the cash register.

There had to be an easier way.

"All done?" the girl asked.

"Yes." He held out the card. "This goes with the tulips."

She added the envelope to the pile, writing a note on the order form. Ben scanned the pictures of the arrangements he'd chosen. Besides the pink tulips, he'd picked some exotic purple flower, a pink-and-cream vase with matching flowers, the ivy topiary thingy, and a massive red bouquet with chocolates. Ben couldn't remember the names of all the flowers, and he didn't care to. As long as they were delivered at the right time, each an hour apart. Maybe by the time he finished work, all would be forgiven.

"What'd you forget?" the girl asked. "An anniversary?"

Ben scrawled his name across the sales receipt, not looking at the total. He didn't want to know. "Birthday," he lied.

"Ouch." She made a face, then smiled again. "Well, if these don't do it, nothing will."

She wasn't blonde for nothing. He handed her the signed receipt and stuck his credit card in his wallet.

"Good luck," she called when he turned to leave.

He jerked his chin in goodbye. He didn't do luck.

Chapter Nineteen

On Monday night, Meg opened her door to find Mike standing on her front step. Before she could speak, he stepped into her foyer as if he belonged there.

Which he definitely did *not*.

He flashed her that warm, enveloping smile. "It's good to see you."

It was? After the way they'd left each other? She forced a grim smile back at him. "You too." What had happened during their years apart to turn Mike into such a gentle, forgetful giant?

She hadn't forgotten. Couldn't. She closed the door and motioned to the kitchen, resisting the urge to offer him ice cream. "Would you like something to drink?"

"That'd be great."

Terrell interrupted from the top of the stairs. "You're back!" He thudded down the stairs and leaped into Mike's arms.

Mike pretended to drop him, and Terrell squealed and grabbed his arms. Mike leaned back and squinted at Terrell's chest. "What's that on your PJs?"

"Baseball players." Terrell yanked at the stomach of his shirt. "This guy's pitching, this one's hitting, and this one's the centerfielder. Like you."

"Like me?"

Mike seemed to give Terrell every bit of his attention, his wide smile and happy eyes showing how much connecting with her son—his son—meant to him. And seeing Terrell happy with his dad and still living with her... she'd never dreamed that could be possible. *Thank you, God,* she breathed. If every visit with Mike went like this, maybe she could bear it.

And it was only for an hour. Terrell would go to bed, and Mike would leave. She watched the man she'd feared cuddle with her son like a big teddy bear. Yes, this she could handle just fine.

Her offered drink forgotten, Mike and Terrell sprawled across the family room floor, playing board games she'd bought for Terrell but never had time for. She paid bills from her favorite recliner and listened to Terrell beat Mike at Chutes and Ladders then lose over and over at Connect Four. A chuckle escaped. She'd always known Mike would make his kids earn every victory, no matter how young they were.

At precisely eight-fifteen, Meg closed her computer. "Bedtime, Terrell. Go brush your teeth and use the bathroom."

"Nooooo." The tantrum began. "I don't want to go to bed—"

"Whoa, whoa, whoa." Mike held up his hands, and Terrell froze mid-wail, looking as stunned as Meg felt. "Tell me you don't do that every time your mom tells you to do something."

Terrell blinked.

"I don't want to hear that coming from you again, bud." Mike lowered his head, his eyes drilling into Terrell. "You got it?"

Evidently Terrell did. Tears filled his eyes until Mike growled like a bear about to pounce. Terrell ran for the stairs, squealing all the way, with Mike right behind him.

Wow.

Maybe having Mike around wasn't such a horrible thing.

She put away Chutes and Ladders and the Connect Four game and followed the sounds of water splashing in Terrell's bathroom.

Terrell stood before the sink and brushed his teeth, Mike beside him, while the faucet ran.

There went her hard-earned money.

She pointed to the running water.

After a blank look, Mike got it. He turned the water off, winking at her as he did.

Okay, the winking could go.

In her office next to Terrell's bathroom, she straightened her desk, leaving the room as Terrell turned off the bathroom light from his perch on Mike's back. "All done, Mommy," Terrell called. "I brushed every tooth—twice."

And she hadn't had to be the enforcer. Who was this Mike Connor look-alike?

She followed him into Terrell's room, where he dumped Terrell onto his bed.

Terrell bounced a few times before sliding to the floor and kneeling. "It's time to pray, Dad." He craned his neck back as far as it would go. "You have to get down."

This she had to see. Meg leaned on the doorjamb, watching Mike bend his tall frame and fold his hands on the bed.

Terrell waved her over. "You too, Mommy."

She knelt beside Mike, who gave her a wry smile before looking at Terrell for direction.

"We have to close our eyes," Terrell said. "We're talking to Jesus."

Good for Terrell.

Meg bowed her head and listened while he prayed for his friends at school who were sick, for Jill and Clark, for his friends at church, and for his mom and dad. "And thank you, Jesus," he said, "that Daddy could be here to say goodnight. Please fix everything so he can live with us. Amen."

Meg caught her breath, her eyes opening to Mike's grin.

He laughed, linking his fingers and stretching his long arms over his head. "What an interesting prayer."

Her face burned. "Don't count on an answer to that."

Mike shrugged, still chuckling.

She tucked Terrell into bed and kissed him goodnight, then left so the two could have the last few minutes together, although whether they deserved it was now debatable. Wait till she got Terrell alone. She peeked in the bathroom, expecting to find his hand towel on the floor and toothpaste globs in the pedestal sink, but the towel hung over the rod and the toothpaste cap was snapped shut, the sink damp but glob free.

So very nice.

As she left the bathroom, Mike met her and followed her to the stairs.

She spoke before he could bring up Terrell's prayer, her skin heating at the thought of it. "Terrell's kindergarten graduation is coming up. He wants you to come, but I told him I didn't know how that fit with your schedule."

"When is it?"

"June first, a Saturday."

"What time?"

"Morning. I can find the exact time for you."

"I've got a night game that day. Tell Terrell I'll be there."

"Thanks. And lunch afterward, if you can." She stopped at the front door, hand on the knob. The next step was simple—open door, say goodbye, lock door behind ex-husband, then find something else to do besides wringing child's neck.

But Mike's eyes twinkled. "Are you kicking me out?"

She opened the door in answer. "Terrell's in bed, Mike."

"I know." He wiggled his eyebrows and let his gaze roam the room. "Isn't this alone time nice."

If he liked talking to himself. "Goodbye, Mike."

"Stop it. Come sit with me." He closed the door and started for the living room, grabbing her hand when she didn't move.

His fingers felt warm and familiar—no. She yanked her hand from his. "Mike!"

He huffed his frustration. "What is wrong with two adults enjoying conversation?"

Nothing, unless that conversation included a certain ex-husband.

"You're scared," he said.

Maybe that too. She flipped her hair over her shoulder, gaze locking onto the dark floor behind him. "That's silly."

"So what we went through—that's over and done for you? No unresolved issues?"

He had to mention that.

His hand tipped her chin up.

Meg jerked away. What right did he have to touch her?

"Some night, Meg, we need to talk."

No, they didn't. What he'd done, what he'd said—he'd hurt her enough. Filling in the *why*s and *how*s wouldn't heal anything.

What she needed to do was change the topic. She forced her eyes to his. "I have something for you. Wait here." She tried not to run up the stairs. Maybe giving him his yearbooks and baseball scrapbook would end wherever Mike expected their conversation to go.

Being alone with him terrified her.

She ransacked her walk-in closet in her search, not caring that she messed up perfectly organized shelves. The sooner Mike left her house, the better.

Her eyes welled up, and Meg cleared them with her palms. She would not cry in front of Mike. She would not let him know how much she still hurt.

She clamped a hand over her mouth, muffling the sob that shook her. She hated what he'd done to her. With one decision, he'd changed how she thought and acted and how she viewed everything and everyone.

And now he was back, acting as if they could actually forget the wounds they'd inflicted on each other. Was he really that crazy? That insensitive?

Sniffing, she pulled her yearbooks from the box and dropped them on the floor. She'd deal with her closet later. She lifted the awkward box and started down the hall.

Right now, Mike had to go.

He stood waiting at the bottom of the stairs and took the box from her arms. "I was about to come after you." He looked from the box to her, eyes narrow. "What's this?"

"Some things of yours I didn't realize I had."

"Like?"

He set the box on the floor, bent to open it.

"Mike, no!" He couldn't look at them here. One bittersweet memory and she'd lose control again.

"No, what?"

He needed to take them home. He needed to leave. Her vision blurred. Maybe her tears would scare him away. "Please go."

He took a step back and ran a hand through his hair, his mouth tight in a frustrated smile. The muscles along his jaw clenched. "Fine." He nodded her way, then picked up the box as if it were full of cotton candy and tucked it beneath an arm. "After everything I did, I understand why you'd want nothing to do with me." He blew out a breath, fingering a frayed corner of the box. "But someday, Meg, we have to talk. We don't have a choice."

No choice?

He opened the door, said goodbye, and left.

No, he was wrong. She might share Terrell with him and listen to their baseball conversations, but never again would she relive the death throes of her marriage.

Somehow she would move on.

Chapter Twenty

So Monday night had not gone as planned. Fine. This morning would be different.

Outside Meg's house, Mike slammed his Range Rover door and locked the vehicle. He started up her sidewalk, bag of fresh cinnamon rolls in hand.

His refusal to see or speak to Brooke had convinced Shauni that he was committed to making up with Meg, and Shauni had spent a full morning brainstorming with him on how to rebuild the connection between them. Recreating good memories was one idea, and cinnamon rolls dated back to their first month of marriage. They'd sat in bed the morning after he returned from a road trip and caught up with each other while they ate their gooey rolls.

What he wouldn't give to do that again.

He halted at the sight of two cars parked in her driveway. It figured she'd have people over just when he thought he'd catch her alone. What would Shauni tell him to do?

Probably to think like a woman.

He sighed and squeezed his eyes shut, listening to the birds chirp in Meg's bushes and the dog across the street yap away.

Nothing entered his mind.

Of course not. If he could think like a woman, he wouldn't be in this situation. He sighed and continued up her sidewalk. All he could think about were the dozen fans he'd fought off at the restaurant just to get these rolls. Meg was going to eat them, and she was going to enjoy them. Clients, friends, whatever—he didn't have a day to lose because in less than two weeks he'd leave for another road trip. By then, he needed to be back in her good graces.

He rang her doorbell. One of the Wind's charities, a childhood cancer foundation, was hosting a black-tie fundraiser next Friday. He'd already bought two tickets, one for himself and one for Meg. He pictured her in an evening dress, silver earrings dangling with that thick, golden hair piled on her head. He'd introduce her to his teammates and to local celebrities—actors and musicians—who came to the event. After the dinner, they'd spend the rest of the night enjoying downtown Chicago at its best, and by the time the city began to stir—

First, he had to find some alone time with her.

Without warning, her door swung open. Meg stood there, lips downturned, eyes narrowed.

Yeah, good thing he couldn't think like a woman. He looked around her, but the house seemed silent and empty. "Hi," he said. "You got a minute?"

She tilted her head, lips squished together as she debated. "I can spare that."

Just like always, giving him crumbs. He held up the brown bag, forcing a smile he didn't feel anymore. "I've had a taste for cinnamon rolls. Thought you might like to share them with me."

Her mouth twitched, but she stepped back enough to let him enter. "I guess I can take a short break."

"Don't worry. I've got to leave for the stadium in an hour." She could go back to her precious job then.

She led the way to the kitchen.

Mike glanced in the living room and family room and, when he entered the kitchen, the formal dining room. There didn't seem to be anyone around.

"What are you looking for?" Meg asked, pulling two plates from an upper cabinet.

"I thought you had a client here. The cars."

"Oh."

She stepped around him, seeming to take care not to brush against him.

He followed her to the table and sat down, waiting for the explanation.

Instead, she opened the bag and put one massive roll on each plate, pausing to suck warm icing from her thumb.

"Good?" he asked.

She nodded, seating herself to his left. She unwrapped her roll with her fingers, just like she always had.

Had she forgotten he didn't believe in getting sticky? And where was her explanation of the cars? He leaned back in his chair, fingers linked across his stomach. "You're way too helpful."

She glanced at him, swallowed her mouthful, and looked down at his roll. "What?"

"Got a fork?"

"Oh. Right." She pushed her chair back and took her time getting his fork. Had she forgotten the way he'd teased her about getting icing all over her fingers? Or how she'd claimed it tasted better that way? Those memories were instant replay in his mind. If she'd forgotten—

"Here you go." She handed him the fork and sat down, digging into her roll once again. "Terrell will be sorry he missed you."

Probably her way of telling him not to bother coming if Terrell wasn't home. Whatever. With his fork he cut a piece of the roll and stabbed it. "Do you remember how often we did this?"

"Too often." Her eyes darted to his plate, his hands, his shoulders, never reaching his face before returning to her roll.

He leaned forward, willing her to look at him. "Why did we quit?"

Her hand fell against the tabletop, and she sent him an exasperated look. "Because I was gaining weight."

"Oh." So he'd forgotten that detail.

He ate the bite on his fork, his gaze never leaving her profile. Somehow she wasn't enjoying this as much as he'd hoped she would. No reminiscing, no *remember when*. She seemed cold, aloof, as if she didn't want to talk to him. As if he'd done something wrong.

Shauni would tell him to ask. "Meg, did I say something wrong last night?"

Her shoulders slumped, but she kept on unrolling the sticky layers.

"You clammed up and kicked me out. I want to know what I did. So I won't do it again." There. He'd taken the blame. That had to work.

She glanced at him.

He met her gaze, smiling his encouragement. If she'd just talk to him—

"It isn't you, Mike."

What? "It's not you. It's me," he joked.

She smiled at her roll. "No, really. You caught me off guard." She shoved her chair back and walked around the peninsula to the sink.

Mike waited while she washed her hands, but again she didn't speak. He filled in the silence. "How'd I catch you off guard?"

From the stairs in the foyer came sounds of a conversation. A man's and woman's voices neared.

No. Not now. "Clients?"

Meg leaned against the counter. She looked relieved. "My assistant. Her fiancé."

"I didn't know you had someone working for you." Mike joined her as a tall, slim blonde walked into the room followed by a dark, big-muscled man. Talk about opposites.

The man's eyes settled on him. And narrowed.

What was this?

The blonde quickstepped her way to Meg and grabbed her shoulder, eyes glued to Mike as she stage-whispered in Meg's ear. "Tell me that's not Mike Connor."

A fan? This, he could handle. He forced seriousness into his expression. "I'm not Mike Connor." When confused belief registered on her face, he broke into a laugh. He held out his hand, and slowly she took it. "Hi," he said. "Mike Connor."

"Dana. Jarvis," she added, hazel eyes big. "Meg's assistant."

"Nice to meet you." He reached a hand to the man. "I hear you're the fiancé."

The man hesitated before gripping his hand. His fingers squeezed Mike's to the point of pain. "Ben Reynolds," he said, jaw tight.

Mike tightened his own grip before releasing Ben's hand, resisting the urge to see if his own bore finger marks. What was up with this guy?

"How do you know Meg?" Dana asked.

Meg's head lolled toward one shoulder. "Mike's my ex-husband."

So *no one* knew about him. Not Terrell, not her own assistant. Huh.

"No kidding." Dana's eyes went wide. "You're Terrell's dad?"

"In the flesh."

"No kidding," she said again.

Her eyes were still wide. Ben's were still narrowed. Meg's were closing in irritation.

Time to change the subject. Mike focused on Dana. "How long have you worked for Meg?"

"Nine, ten months now?" she asked, her head slanted toward Meg.

Meg nodded. "She'll be taking over my business before long."

"Don't believe her. She's taught me everything."

"Then you're a pro." From the corner of his eye, Mike caught Ben cross thick arms over his chest. "What about you?" Mike asked him.

"I'm a real estate agent."

"Cool. Next time I need a house, I'll know who to call."

Ben glared.

Well, that went over well. This guy was as rude as his fiancée was nice. Mike opened his mouth to ask Dana when the wedding was, but Ben spoke. "You gonna' tell us what you do?"

Dana shot Ben a startled look.

Mike's face heated. There he went, assuming the guy knew who he was just because his girl did. Nothing quite like coming across as an arrogant jerk. "Sorry. I play baseball."

"Right. For the Wind." Ben lifted his chin as if in challenge. "You're quite an athlete, aren't you?"

Did the guy know who he was or not? Mike straightened and tipped his shoulders back, his smile frozen in place. "Thanks. I enjoy what I do."

"I bet. Nine years in the majors. A few All-Star Games and Gold Gloves. Not bad."

Mike fought the urge to laugh. Most people who followed his career asked for an autograph instead of listing his achievements as if he were on trial. Whatever this guy's problem, Mike refused to let it goad him. "Who's your team? Wait. Let me guess." He held up a hand. "You like that other team in town."

Ben ignored the joke. "I played in the majors."

An ex-ballplayer? Mike studied his face. Was that the problem?

Ben seemed to have read his thoughts. "We played each other."

He'd only hit one guy in the few bench clearers he'd been a part of, and this guy wasn't him. So that couldn't be it. But now that he thought about it, something about Reynolds did look a little familiar. "Sorry, I can't place you."

"It was in the minors."

"No wonder. That was ten years ago."

His words seemed to fuel Ben's heated calm. "Let me help. I was a pitcher. Triple-A. Remember? Your first Triple-A game? Your first at bat?"

"I hit a home run my first—" He froze, suddenly remembering everything about that particular at bat. "You were the pitcher."

Ben continued his stare-down. "Once you crossed home plate, I got pulled."

Well, what were the odds of that? Mike clamped his mouth shut over those words. "That's baseball," he said.

"No, pulled for good."

The guy blamed *him* for his career ending? What an idiot. The urge to teach Ben a lesson swarmed over him. No, Meg would hate him for sure if he started a brawl in her kitchen. "Sorry, man."

Dana laid a hand on the guy's arm. "Ben," she whispered

He shot her a dirty look.

She flinched, pulled her hand back.

Ben returned his hardened stare to Mike. "You have a good day," he said, his tone contradicting his words. He turned and left, footsteps clomping across the foyer. The front door opened and then slammed.

Silence followed.

"Well." Mike's shoulders sagged a bit, but he held his smile for Meg and Dana, both wide-eyed. "That's a first."

"Mike, I'm so sorry—" Dana began.

"Don't apologize for him."

"Ben's sensitive about baseball. I'm sure he doesn't blame you." She toyed with her fingernails. "A couple weeks ago I caught him watching one of those classic ballgames. He gave up the hit that cost his team the playoffs."

"Oh, wow." How awful that had to be, watching himself blow it all over again, knowing that a game termed classic and played over and over was one in which he'd been the goat. His irritation with Ben faded some, and he glanced at Dana, at the worried expression on her face.

Something around her eye caught his attention. He squinted. "Is that a black eye?"

Her hand flew to her face, covering part of her left eye and cheek. "It's old. It's almost better now."

So what? "How'd that happen?"

Dana fingered the make-up covered bruise. "I got hit with a softball."

And it only left a bruise? He knew what a ball to the face could do.

"She got a concussion too," Meg said. "She stayed home all last week. She couldn't drive."

He offered Dana a smile, even as he took another look at the faded bruise. He wished he'd noticed it earlier. He'd liked to have heard Ben's response.

Knock it off, Connor. There he went, finding domestic abuse in every relationship. She got hit with a ball that maybe wasn't moving too fast. It left a bruise. That could happen.

Still, Mike couldn't force away the image of his sister Betsy sprawled across her kitchen floor.

His eyes lingered on Dana's shiner. However she got that, it had to have hurt.

Chapter Twenty-One

The dream was reality, every bit of it hard fact.

Beneath an overheated sun, Ben wiped his upper arm across the sweat on his forehead and replaced his cap. At home plate a hot wind stirred dirt into a dust devil that made the minor-league umpire step back and wipe one eye. Ben wrapped his fingers around the ball in his glove and squeezed till it felt as if his knuckles might pop.

How had he come to this?

Once he'd been the number four draft pick, a future star pitcher and a wealthy man fresh from high school. Now—after a number of call-ups followed one month, one week, or one day later by a ticket back to the minors, he was close to becoming a former minor leaguer who'd only tasted big league life, never big league success.

It was enough to make him crazy.

He kicked the dirt on the pitcher's mound, trying to forget the closed looks he'd seen on his manager's face. Sure, he'd given up a few runs the last three times out, but he had only one loss to show for it.

He glanced around the infield. One out. Runners on first and second. No biggie. The next batter would be out number two, maybe even a double play.

While the batter was announced, Ben glanced at the kid's stats on the scoreboard.

Michael Connor, just called up from Double-A, batting .325 with sixteen homers and forty-one RBIs this year.

Already?

Ben shook himself. None of that mattered. This was a different level, and this punk was now facing a guy who'd pitched in the majors. Some. He returned to the rubber and studied the batter digging in at the plate. Good gravy, could Mikey even drive?

Javier signaled for a curveball away.

Ben shook his head. No one fresh from Double-A was going to get a hit off him. He shook off the sign for his change-up. *Come on. Fastball.* This kid was getting nothing but heat. Three pitches, and the guy could go sit. Maybe then it would be clear to everyone where Ben Raines belonged.

After a long look into the dugout, Javier called fastball.

Ben checked the runners and started his windup. Let Connor try and hit this.

Connor did.

The ball sailed over Ben's head and disappeared behind the centerfield wall.

A three-run bomb of a homer.

Ben jammed his glove onto his hip, barely containing the urge to throw a tantrum, and glared at the kid rounding the bases. Let him try that a second time.

Connor reached home, tapped the base, and high-fived his waiting teammates.

Ben caught the ball Javier threw him and turned his back on the high-fiving in the home team's dugout. *Come on, breathe. Calm down.* He walked around the mound, smoothing dirt with his foot until he could relax his jaw. He shook his head, rotated his neck. Ready. He blew out a long slow breath.

Bring on the next loser.

He faced home plate.

But Javier was standing, watching the manager cross the baseline.

He was getting yanked again? So what if he'd faced four guys and retired one? They were still up by three. Why wouldn't anyone let him work out of a jam?

He glared at his approaching manager. No way he was going calmly, not this time. Ben hurled the ball toward center field, then chucked his glove at home.

The packed stadium erupted in a mix of hoots, boos, and cheers.

He stormed past his manager, head throbbing. He snatched his cap and threw it down the dugout steps.

The guys in the dugout ignored him.

Not for long.

He kicked a cooler and, when it didn't topple, pushed it over with his hands, leaving it leaking on the floor behind him.

Still, no one paid attention.

Too bad he couldn't take a bat to—

He halted and backtracked to the bat rack.

The pitching coach glanced his way.

About time. Ben grabbed a handful of bats and tossed them out of the dugout and into foul territory.

Heads turned.

He grabbed helmets and flung them as far as he could. More helmets, another bat—

Voices buzzed in his ears.

Aiming at the field, he launched a bat like a javelin.

It whizzed past an approaching umpire's head, an umpire who immediately threw him out of the game.

Ben laughed, his fingers curling around a baseball. Too bad the bat had missed.

"Knock it off, Raines," someone farther down the dugout yelled.

Ben spun. He flung the ball at the concrete wall at the far end of the dugout, watching in satisfaction as players hit the floor, hands covering their heads. The ball popped off the wall and into someone's ribs.

Who cared?

Ben gave a few fallen bats and helmets one last kick before storming down the runway, slamming the sides of his fists against the walls.

No one ignored him now, did they?

He stomped into the clubhouse, eager to create another mess, but what he saw when he entered stopped him short.

Some employee emptying Ben's locker. Fast.

His nameplate gone.

And Arnie, the ex-wrestler security guard, standing nearby. Taser drawn. Looking right at him.

⁂

Ben sucked in air, bolting upright in bed.

Over the soft hiss of the shower, Dana's alarm clock was going off.

He knocked it over with his fist.

Still it buzzed.

He left it and stumbled to the kitchen, made himself a cup of coffee. He leaned against the counter as he drank it.

His dream returned.

Each detail remained clear—the way Arnie and another security guard had taken him out of the stadium, the anger he'd felt that his coaches had given up on him, and then rage when he'd discovered how bad his reputation had become.

A head case.

Damaging to team chemistry.

No self-control.

Over and over he told his agent it wasn't true, but every team believed it.

No team, at any level, would touch him.

When he returned home, Dad had laughed and said *I told you so* before leaving to play pool, but Margo had cooked him a huge meal and, with damp eyes, sat across the table, listening to him rant while he devoured three helpings. Someday, he'd told her, he'd set things right with everyone who'd trashed his career.

And he was keeping his word, although too late to do her any good. He set his coffee down as his arms twitched, remembering the way he'd been forced to shake hands with a man who'd helped murder Margo. He'd ached to beat him senseless right there. To be that close—

Ben shot his fist into an upper cabinet.

He'd go nuts if he thought about it any longer. He shadowboxed his way to the front door, imagining Connor taking every blow. On the chin and jaw, in the stomach and the teeth followed by a knockout punch to the nose. He shook himself like Muhammad Ali and opened the door. The paper lay on the steps. He picked it up, proud of his self-control. He'd changed, hadn't he? If any other team had given him a chance, they would have been celebrated as geniuses.

And Margo would still be alive.

He plopped onto his recliner and searched the paper for the sports section. He pulled it out, his gaze landing on the article covering the bottom half of the front page. "'Umpire Accused of Throwing Games,'" he read out loud and skimmed the story. Edwin Byrd, forty-nine, major league umpire for fourteen years with an untarnished record—until the FBI talked to a low-life with mob connections who, in addition to giving up a crime boss, also let slip this interesting bit of information.

Ben held his fingertips to his mouth. "Whoops."

And, oh look, Byrd was suspended pending an investigation. Well, anyone knew an ump didn't accept money to call one team's strike zone larger than the other.

"What were you thinking, Byrd?" Ben carried the paper to the kitchen and rummaged through a drawer until he found scissors. He cut across the page, then down the fold. Byrd's somber face stared at him from the article. "You threw that game to Oakland. You called my fastball a ball when everyone knew it caught the outside corner. You walked in the go-ahead run, and you sent me to the minors." He held up the cut-out article. "Now it's your turn."

Ben tossed the remainder of the paper onto the recliner as he headed for the hallway. He walked past the bathroom, where the shower still ran and into his office, locking the door behind him before sitting at his desk and pulling the green binder from the file drawer.

His fingers caressed the pages inside. Newspaper articles from various papers and of various lengths were taped to plain white paper. Ben flipped through them slowly, smiling at the different memories each story brought.

Marc Hollowell, a former All-Star pitcher and pitching coach indicted for insider trading.

Aaron Ramirez, a former ballplayer and arena football team owner who committed suicide earlier in the year. The guy had chosen death instead of facing his family when they learned what he did when he traveled.

Two more articles followed, two more heart-rending tales of men whose careers—whose family lives—were no more.

He laid the latest article sideways across an empty sheet of paper and taped it carefully in place. After snagging a pen from the pen holder, he flipped to the last page of the notebook and crossed off Edwin Byrd. Chills ran down his shoulder blades as his gaze lingered on the next name.

Very soon another man would fall. Two in one month? He was making incredible time.

Ben closed the binder and returned it to the back of the file drawer. It was good he hadn't flattened Connor. Waiting for the perfect moment would be much, much sweeter.

Because Connor deserved something bigger, something better than Ben had originally planned. And, just like the rest, Connor would never see it coming.

Chapter Twenty-Two

Mike's visits continued.

After his game ended Thursday afternoon, he brought dinner over—potato salad, Hawaiian sweet rolls, salad, and ribs he grilled to perfection. After they'd eaten, he stayed long enough to play three games of Uno and two games of Operation with Terrell.

On Saturday evening Mike stopped by again, playing a lazy game of catch in the backyard, tossing the ball to Terrell while talking to her. Always including her.

Anyone listening would never guess they shared a past, one happy and heartbreaking. There were no jabs at each other, no tactless hints that they should date, no rehashing their broken marriage. Just talk about her current design project, Terrell's first year in school, Mike's rising batting average, the shocking success the team was having, and some charity dinner that Mike and other teammates were attending.

As Mike chased Terrell's errant throw, Meg realized that the man she'd loved was a much larger part of this older Mike than she'd thought possible. His humor, his easy laugh, his positive personality that had made him so much fun to be around—none of that had changed. Despite his betrayal, there was still something safe about him, something kind and gentle. He played with Terrell as if there was nothing better in the world. He thanked her for the drinks she brought him and smiled whenever he looked her way.

Meg relaxed her armor, returning his kindness with civility. But she couldn't help examining the year when cruel Mike appeared. Had it been some bizarre blip in his personality that she'd bailed out on too quickly?

When Saturday's light faded, the three of them moved inside and watched a kids' movie with Terrell. For the first time in years, Meg found herself laughing with Mike and sharing a bowl of her favorite popcorn, an act that felt too intimate. When he finally left, she leaned against the closed front door, pleased with the peacefulness of the evening—until she caught herself smiling at the thought of him.

Why was Mike being so attentive? He should concentrate on Terrell and leave her out of their relationship. Wasn't that the way it was done?

She called Jill, sharing her confusion on how to handle Mike. Should she treat him as a friend? As someone she didn't care to be around? One exhausting week of navigating the happy, the bittersweet, and the excruciating—suddenly Meg felt worn out.

Sunday and the church services she craved were hours away. What would Mike say about her attending church so faithfully? Would they see him tomorrow, or would he drop by after they'd left for the evening service? Would he try to stop her from going to church? Would he make jokes? Would cruel Mike reappear and prove there was no blip in his character?

Mike's Sunday afternoon game ended two hours before the evening service started. Every few minutes after that, Meg glanced at the clock, calculating what he might be doing— talking to reporters, eating, working out. If he didn't hurry, they'd be at church before he ever knocked on her door.

No, she was thinking that all wrong. If she and Terrell didn't leave early for church, he'd catch them at home.

They would leave early.

But Terrell couldn't find one of his shoes, and the doorbell rang five minutes after Meg had hoped to leave. She straightened her shoulders and raised her chin, then opened the door to find Mike wearing his familiar grin.

This was… bad. Yes, bad. Not good.

"Hey there." He entered the foyer, surveying her. "Going somewhere?"

She glanced down at her spring-green sheath. "We're on our way to church." She pulled her hair over her shoulder, feeling the flutter in her hands. "Terrell's looking for his shoe."

"I found it, Mommy."

She turned toward him at the top of the stairs, glad she didn't have to see Mike's reaction.

Terrell ran down the rest of the stairs, missing shoe in hand. "Hi, Dad." He raised his hand for a high-five, and Mike slapped his palm. "That was a big home run."

"Thanks. Those are fun." Mike's gaze returned to her, brown eyes smiling as if he knew something. "Can I talk you out of your plans? I made reservations at a French restaurant downtown." He soft-punched Terrell's shoulder. "You can eat snails."

"Yuck!" Terrell grinned and launched into authentic gagging noises.

"Stop that, Terrell." She hungered for church, especially with Mike's presence wearing on her. "Thanks, but not this time."

"We're going to church," Terrell said. "You could come with us."

What?

Terrell tugged on Mike's hands. "If you came, you could meet my friends."

And have her whole church whispering about her? Of course, Mike would never set foot in—

"Why not." He shrugged at her. "Then I can see what kind of outfit your mom's joined." He pulled his phone from his pants' pocket. "Let me cancel those reservations." He disappeared into the living room.

Meg slumped against the half-wall of the stairs. *He can't come.* She covered her cheeks with her palms. *God, please. He can't come.*

"Mommy?" Terrell tugged at her arms. "What's the matter?"

"Nothing." She moved out of his grasp, ducking into the powder room beneath the stairs. She stared at her face in the mirror. "I can't be seen with him. Not at church." Having Jill and Clark and even Dana know about Mike was one thing, but for her whole messed-up past to be paraded in front of her church—

"Meg?" Mike knocked on the door. "Are you all right?"

"Just a minute." She couldn't tell him he couldn't come. How would she explain that to Terrell? And Terrell was what mattered, she told her reflection, not her reputation.

The thought didn't help.

She forced herself to leave the safety of her powder room and followed Mike and Terrell outside, pausing to make sure her door was locked. Terrell ran for the Range Rover, but Meg took her time climbing into the front seat.

"Don't you have a church you go to?" Terrell asked as she buckled her seatbelt.

Mike backed out of her driveway. "I don't think I've been to church since I moved here." He lowered his voice to a stage whisper. "I always feel like I'm in trouble. Don't you?"

Terrell shrugged. "Maybe you are."

Leave it to Terrell. Hiding her amusement, Meg turned away, but not before catching Mike's surprised look.

"What do you mean maybe I am?"

"People who don't know Jesus are in trouble because they can't go to heaven."

Between Meg's directions, Mike asked, "And I suppose you know Jesus?"

"Yes. Mommy does too."

"Really?"

Why did he poke fun at his own child? "Don't make this a joke, Mike."

He raised his eyebrows, a smile tugging at his mouth.

"Yeah, Dad. You have to believe Jesus paid for your sins and tell him you're sorry for all the bad things you did. And when you die some day, you'll go to heaven and live with him."

"You don't say. So Jesus forgave all those horrible things you've done?"

His words tipped off Terrell to his amusement. "I've done bad things. Ask Mommy."

Mike sent her a smirk, eyebrows raised.

"Mike," she warned.

"And your mom did this too?"

"Yeah, but she had more bad things to confess because she's older."

Mike laughed, grinning at her. "Oh, I know all about those."

Wasn't he hilarious? She flashed him an insincere smile, then glanced out her window, leaving him to chuckle to himself.

Mercifully, the subject died, and the drive was soon over. But as Meg stepped out of the Range Rover, she debated snatching Mike's keys and driving away. How would she be able to come back once people found out who her ex-husband was?

She dragged her feet to the church's main doors, pleading for time to freeze, for the door to seal shut—

Mike reached around her and swung the glass door open before she could scream at him not to touch it, which was probably a good thing. She walked through the door and nodded a hello at the greeters. Nothing like a scream to ensure attention.

Inside, she scoped out the fastest route to the auditorium, but people stood in groups throughout the foyer while others weaved around them.

She speed-walked for the nearest entrance, only to tangle with members heading to the nursery or bathrooms or… someplace that slowed her progress. Those she knew paused to say hello and touch her arm before doing a double-take, their eyes above and behind her.

Wonderful. He was still there.

More heads turned. Eyes widened. People whispered, staring at Mike, then Meg and Terrell, then Mike again.

Her vision blurred. Already the speculating had begun.

Somehow she lifted her chin and marched the last few yards into the auditorium, stalking into a row near the back. Terrell and Mike slid in beside her, and she relaxed a little. Now if the service would just start already—

Two single men stopped to shake Mike's hand.

Meg clenched her teeth. She shouldn't have let him sit on the aisle. Now there'd be autographs and—

A small crowd had already formed beside Mike, all wanting to know how he knew Meg and Terrell. Meg glared at them, but no one seemed to notice as they listened, fascinated, to Mike explain that Meg was his ex-wife and Terrell was his son.

Unbelievable. The story would spread before church even started. Those who met Mike would tell friends and family about the baseball star in the back and how he was Meg Connor's ex, and were they getting back together? She crossed her arms and legs, her eyes straight ahead. Her toes tapped the seat in front of her. There'd be fakes coming out of the woodwork, people cozying up to her in order to meet Mike, rumors as convoluted as a soap opera. She clenched her teeth at the thought.

"Meg?"

She looked past Terrell and Mike to the aisle, where Jill waved before pointing at the empty space beyond her. "May we join you?" Jill asked.

Amazingly Clark, who was talking with Mike, and Jill were the only people in the aisle currently.

Where had everyone gone?

Mike waved his hand at her. "Scoot down, Meg."

The Ashburns wanted to sit by Mike? Terrell slid against her, leaving her no option but to make room for two more. How could they? Were the only two people who knew what had happened between her and Mike swayed by his fame too? Was that why they'd befriended her?

Throughout the service, Meg stared at the blonde highlights of the woman in front of her. She stood when the woman did, sang songs without hearing the words, closed her eyes during prayer, and managed to open her Bible during the pastor's message, all the while sitting in her own anger-heated space, brain buzzing as she planned a fast departure.

At last, people around her stood for the closing prayer.

She squeezed the back of the chair in front of her. If she could rush Mike and Terrell out of here, maybe she'd make it home before imploding.

But when the service ended, Mike and Clark stood there, talking.

Jill squeezed past the men and Terrell while Meg, ignoring her, grabbed her Bible and purse for a quick exit.

"What a surprise, huh?" Jill said in her ear.

Meg shot her a dark look. "Let's hope it doesn't happen again." She held up a hand when Jill opened her mouth. "Sorry, Jill, but I have to get out of here."

"I understand…"

Did she? Jill's words faded, replaced by the betrayal of Jill and Clark buddying up to Mike, making her scoot down so they could sit by *him*—

Jill's words broke through her irritation. "…what do you think?"

She didn't want to talk. She wanted to leave. "Sure. Whatever. Tell *Mike*," she said, emphasizing his name in sarcasm Jill either missed or chose to ignore, "that I'll be at his car."

Meg slid her purse strap onto her shoulder as she eyed a way out of the middle of the row. Mike and Clark still stood at one end, ignoring the people who filed past, whispered, and pointed at Mike and then her. She glared at a few of them, smiling when they flushed. *Gossips.* She turned her back on all of them and escaped out the row's other end.

In the foyer she returned the hellos and calls with a tight smile. She held herself to a fast walk across the parking lot until she reached Mike's Range Rover, alone in the farthest row.

Safe, at last. She pulled the handle to open the door, but it was locked. Of course. She resisted the urge to smack the hood. That would probably set off an alarm. She slumped against the passenger door, the heat from the black surface warming her back and head. The ache in her shoulders spread down her spine.

It was over. She'd survived it all going public, although she knew now who her true friends were.

Or weren't.

For a few more minutes, Meg leaned against the Range Rover, darkening her already bleak mood, until the sudden beep of the locks jarred her. She looked across the hood to find Mike opening a door for Terrell. Without a word, she climbed inside and buckled her seatbelt.

Mike seated himself behind the wheel. "You sure took off," he said over his door slamming.

"I'm tired. Just ready to go home." None of that was a lie.

He turned the key in the ignition. "Clark and Jill—they're your neighbors?"

She nodded.

"They invited us over for dinner tomorrow. I've got an off day."

"*Us?* We are not an *us.* They should have talked to me."

"Jill said you okayed it."

She had? Was that what Jill had been talking about?

Mike glanced her way, lips tilted as if he were annoyed. Or confused. Or both.

Yes, she was being a bit of a baby. But who could blame her? She rubbed her hand over her face, wanting to go straight to bed. If anything good had come from this night, it was that her eyes were wide open. If these people and her own friends acted starstruck over Mike, how much worse was his everyday life? And if he'd had an affair when he was a much lesser known ballplayer, what made her think he'd handle magnified attention any better?

Beneath crossed arms, she squeezed her hands into fists. Never, she promised, would she let anything happen between herself and Mike. *Never.* She'd do whatever it took to make Mike realize that he was a part of Terrell's life only.

Mike chuckled. "I thought Clark was your husband."

Her husband? Meg frowned at him. "What?"

"I saw Clark with you and Terrell on opening day." His agreeable smile was back. "I thought you two were married."

"No. Obviously. We're not."

She should be so lucky.

Chapter Twenty-Three

Despite Meg's best wishing, Monday's work hours passed with no news of a cancellation from either Jill or Mike. Meg worked feverishly on the Layton design, using that as her way out of spending the entire day with Mike like he'd suggested Sunday night. He'd accepted her excuse, promising to see her Monday evening.

As Terrell would say, yippee.

Jill called three times. Meg didn't answer, and Jill finally texted for Meg to bring a side dish. Now, with six o'clock nearing, Meg put the finishing touches on a taffy-apple salad. How she dreaded being with Mike and her supposed friends.

Her clock inched past the hour, and still Mike did not ring her doorbell. Maybe something had come up, some team golf outing he'd forgotten about. Or maybe during his off-day workout, he'd dropped some huge weight on his toe.

One could hope.

Terrell ran into the kitchen as she washed her hands. "When are we going next door? I'm hungry."

"You're always hungry." She dried her hands and tossed him a leftover apple cube. "We'll go when your dad gets here."

Your dad. How long until those words felt normal?

"But he's been here. His car's in Clark's driveway."

She clenched her teeth, irritated over her unconscious

expectations. Of course he'd go straight to the Ashburns' house. Why did she think he'd stop by her place first, as if they were family?

Salad in hand, she locked her back door and followed Terrell through the gap in the side bushes to the Ashburns' yard. From the back of their two-story white house, a red brick patio extended, home to deck chairs and a round glass table with an open umbrella in soft yellow and white.

Beyond the furniture Clark stood at the grill, turning what smelled like steaks. Mike, dressed in an aqua-blue T-shirt, tan shorts, and sandals, stood with his back to her, a can of Coke in one hand.

Well. At least there were steaks.

When Terrell's sneakers thumped on the patio, Mike turned.

Clark looked up too, a smile spreading over his face. "Here they are. Better late than never."

"Mommy was waiting for Dad to meet us at our house."

Her face burned. Did Terrell have to tell everything?

"Sorry." Mike set down his drink and reached for her salad. "I assumed we'd meet here."

Meg let him take the bowl.

Jill stepped through the sliding glass doors and onto the deck, holding Samuel in one arm and an ExerSaucer in the other.

Meg faked a smile and crossed the deck to meet her. "I'll take Samuel." She lifted him from Jill's arm. She'd spend the evening with his cute, diapery self, since he was the only one who hadn't betrayed her.

Then again, Samuel would probably reach for Mike the second he walked by.

"Thanks for bringing the salad." Jill stacked the plastic plates on top of the napkins to keep them from blowing away. "I wasn't sure if you'd gotten my message or not."

Meg snagged a potato chip from a bowl and snapped it between her teeth. She focused on the wavy air over the grill. "I was working."

"Really. Meg, if we upset you, I wish you'd tell us instead of ignoring us."

"*If* you upset me?" She struggled to keep her voice low enough so the men wouldn't hear. "What do you expect when you plop down beside Mike and invite him over for dinner?"

"We're not allowed to talk to him?"

Jill knew what she meant. "I told you everything he did to me. But evidently Mike's more important."

Oh, did that sound petty.

"Clark saw how upset you were with people swarming him. Didn't you see him shoo everyone away?"

Samuel dropped his caterpillar rattle. Meg picked it up and wiped it off on her shorts. Clark was a pastor—he would want Mike left alone so he'd enjoy the service.

Ugh. That sounded petty too.

"We thought if Mike got to know us, your next-door neighbors, you wouldn't be alone with him as much. He comes over, and we all get together, take some pressure off you."

Bitter words slipped away. What a wonderful idea—if it worked.

"Believe me, I'd never put him above our friendship." Jill wrapped her arm around Meg's shoulders. "You're the one who's going to redecorate my kitchen, right?"

Meg leaned into her friend. How was it possible to feel relieved and horrible at the same time? "I'm an idiot, Jill."

"Aren't we all every now and then?"

"I should have known better."

"Don't worry about it."

Samuel reached for Jill, and Meg released him to his mom.

Jill rubbed her nose against his cheek, smiling when Samuel laughed. "I'm so hungry, I can't remember—were we talking about something?"

With friendship restored, Meg relaxed enough to enjoy the

evening, Mike's presence included. And as she sat across the table from him, Jill and Clark opposite each other, she had to admit that their plan of befriending Mike for her sanity's sake looked to be working. Mike seemed to like Clark, and the relaxed conversation eased the tension that had built in Meg's shoulders and neck.

The meal over, Meg and Jill cleaned up the small mess while Clark, Mike, and Terrell played catch in the backyard. Later Jill brought out a half-full bag of marshmallows, and everyone gathered around the small fire pit, toasting and burning marshmallows.

The hot coals faded with the sun, coaxing the cooling evening to an end.

Terrell licked sticky marshmallow bits from his fingers before waving goodbye to the Ashburns and leading the way through the bushes to their yard.

This time Mike joined them on the way back.

"That was fun." Terrell watched his fingers cling to each other. "I want to do that again."

"You just like burning marshmallows." Mike grabbed Terrell by the waist and slung him around his shoulders. "You pyro."

Terrell shrieked, and Meg ducked out of the way of his feet. They'd been more hands on today, playing like boys probably, since it was nothing she understood. She watched them wrestle and tackle each other until they fell to the ground.

Grass stains.

"Bath time, Terrell," she said. "You've got school tomorrow."

He moaned and flopped onto his back, arms and legs spread.

Mike pretended to sucker-punch him, and Terrell curled into a ball, shielding his stomach while he laughed.

Meg smiled as she unlocked her kitchen door.

"Get up, bath boy." Mike grabbed Terrell's hands and hauled him to his feet.

"What's *pyro*?" Terrell asked.

"Nothing you need to know about." Meg gave him a playful swat. "Go take that bath."

Terrell shuffled for the back door.

"Hey, where's my goodnight?" Mike asked.

Terrell hugged him, his voice muffled in Mike's stomach. "You're leaving?"

"I've got a day game tomorrow. Got to get up early like you."

"Will you come over?"

"Can't. I've got a full day. But I should see you Thursday or Friday, definitely Saturday for your graduation, okay?"

"I guess." Terrell wiped his chin at Mike, and Mike lunged as if to chase him. Terrell squealed and ran through the kitchen into the foyer.

Mike chuckled. "He's crazy."

Somehow that was a fitting compliment. "Thanks for all the time you've spent with him." A breeze flung hair across her mouth, and she tucked the strand behind her ear, pausing to study this man who'd changed far less than she'd imagined. She should have known how good he'd be with kids—how he'd play with them yet at the same time demand respect.

Kids had meant everything to him. And she'd taken that away.

The smile in his brown eyes faded. His expression turned serious as if he had something to say.

Her stomach clenched, and she turned for the screen door Terrell had slammed. Whatever it was, she didn't want to hear it. Not now, when she felt weak. "Goodnight, Mike."

"Meg, wait."

Mike's hand on her arm—his fingers long, gentle, familiar— turned her back around. She eased out of his grasp as she faced him.

The light Terrell had turned on in the kitchen highlighted his mouth and jaw. He moved into the shadows, and his eyes became dark, almost black.

Meg swallowed. If only she could lean into her door and slip right through it.

"Tonight was fun," he said. "Your friends are great."

She nodded, searching his face.

"There's something I've been wanting to ask you." He rubbed his palms together, shifting his weight to his other foot. "Do you have plans for Friday night?"

He stood so close. "Friday?" She'd forgotten how tall he was, how muscled and lean his arms and chest were, how very masculine he was. She cleared her throat as if the sound could clear her mind as well. What had he asked? Friday? "No. I'll be here. With Terrell. Working. The Layton project."

"Oh." His gaze drifted past her. He caught his lip in his teeth. "I've got that charity dinner."

"What was it? Some children's..."

"...Cancer foundation. A couple of other guys are going. Plus some Bulls and Bears players. Chicago actors, musicians. The mayor. The governor. Although that might not be a selling point."

A smile slipped past her. "True."

He broke into a grin, exhaling as if relieved about something. "Yeah. Well." He nodded at the ground.

He still had those deep, long dimples around his mouth when he smiled like that. She'd forgotten—

He raised his gaze to hers, his smile and dimples gone. "Meg." His voice lowered. "Would you go with me? As my date?"

Time spun backwards to her junior year in high school, to that freezing April day where she'd sat through every inning of Mike's blowout game, hoping he'd understand that she was there because of him. She could still picture him trailing his teammates after the game ended, his head tilted so his eyes were on her. She could hear his spikes on the metal bleachers as he'd climbed them, could replay his fast "Hi, how are you?" and the words she'd wanted to hear—

would she like to go out after he'd cleaned up?

She'd thought him sweet in his nervousness, cute and such a gentleman.

Callused hands touched her wrists.

Meg flinched, face to face with Mike again, but this time a man, strong and built, no longer cute but handsome, attractive. And still tied to her life.

"Meg," he whispered. He drew her close. Bent his head to hers, his lips brushing hers in a slow, light kiss.

Her eyes drifted shut, and Meg let him kiss her again, overwhelmed in memories and feelings. Hadn't she lived on these for a time, wondering if they'd ever recover the beauty of what they'd lost? If Mike would ever look for her? He'd found her, hadn't he? He'd come back—

She jerked her arms from around his neck, her head down, her eyes on her hands. How could she have let one sentence, one touch, melt her like that?

How could she have kissed him?

Mike reached for her.

She stepped back. "You shouldn't have kissed me."

His chuckle was low and intimate. "Says the woman who was enjoying that kiss."

She had. She *had*. How horrible that he knew. "Don't kiss me, Mike. We can't kiss."

"Why not?"

Good question. She held a hand to her suddenly throbbing forehead. "We're not married."

"So? You don't have to be married to kiss."

His words cleared her head. "And you don't have to be married at all, do you?"

"Wow." He huffed his surprise, took a step back. "Did not see that coming. Really nice, Meg. That was low." He set his hands on his hips.

"I know what I did was wrong—"

"But you did it anyway."

"Our marriage was a wreck—"

"And that makes it okay?"

"Can I finish a sentence?" He lowered his voice. "I *know* what I did, and I hate what I did. I'd give anything to go back and undo it, but I can't. I've apologized, and I meant it. What else do you want?"

"Apologizing doesn't change the fact that I can't trust you."

"So you want to trust me?"

She met his gaze. "I didn't say that."

He took a step back, his tongue pushing against his cheek, his eyes focusing somewhere above the roof.

He would be angry now, his voice raised, his words blaming her.

But when he spoke, his tone was flat. "Are you coming? On Friday?"

Wouldn't this feel good. "No."

He shrugged immediately, as if he'd known she'd never say yes. "Then I'll take someone else."

He disappeared around the corner of the house.

Meg stood in the faint light and waited for the good feeling to come.

Waited.

Waited.

After several more seconds, she gave up. She walked inside her quiet, empty kitchen and closed and locked the door behind her.

The faint sound of the running shower met her.

She leaned against her door, wrapped her arms around herself, and closed her eyes. Why did she feel like she'd lost when she'd been so certain she had won?

Chapter Twenty-Four

Midnight passed before Mike calmed down. He lay in bed and stared at the tray ceiling, replaying the evening.

Tonight he hadn't felt anger but something he couldn't yet name. Yes, going to her church had upset her, and, yes, they'd experienced friction, but she'd softened so much in the past week. How many times had she laughed while he played with Terrell and listened while he talked about mundane, everyday things?

And tonight kissed him back.

Mixed signals—that didn't begin to describe what she was doing.

He rolled onto his side and studied the picture on his nightstand. He and Meg stood in front of the dugout, he in workout shirt and shorts, his arm around her shoulder and his glove dangling from his other hand. Meg's arms circled his waist, and she laughed at the camera, at a joke someone had cracked. He'd found the picture when he moved into the house over a year ago, but he hadn't set it out until Sara left.

Sara...

With a disgusted snort, he turned onto his back. He couldn't believe he'd called her.

They had talked awkwardly for a minute before Mike asked her to attend Friday's fundraiser with him. She said yes. They hung up.

Mike hadn't been home five minutes.

"Why did I call her?" He covered his face with the crook of his arm. He didn't want to go with Sara. He didn't want to go with anyone but Meg. The right thing to do would be to call Sara back and cancel.

And the right thing for Meg to do would be to forgive him.

Since that didn't seem to be happening any time this millennium, who cared whom he took to the fundraiser?

He blew out a breath and propped his head on his hands, fought against the tightness in his throat. That's what he felt—pain. Hurt. How he wished there was some way to make Meg forget, some way to tear down this wall she'd built.

How else could he get rid of the pain and guilt of what he'd done?

Chapter Twenty-Five

Meg could not forget Mike's kiss.

Although the next four days were slow and quiet without him, Meg's skin warmed each time she relived him asking her to be his date and kissing her.

More than once she reminded herself that saying yes would have given him the wrong impression. He would think their past forgiven and forgotten, and there would be more drop-ins, more dinner reservations, more Mike.

Still, the kiss replayed itself.

As she and Terrell watched Friday afternoon's Wind game, she tried not to wonder about Mike's plans. Maybe he'd said he'd take someone else out of anger.

But what if he'd meant it?

What kind of a woman would catch his attention? Some celebrity he'd been introduced to? A pretty fan who'd asked for an autograph? Or worse, one of those women who hung out in the lobby of the team's hotel?

But she didn't care. Right? She'd told *him* no. Let him take someone else.

And good luck to the unfortunate woman.

But the thickness in her throat refused to leave. Meg ate little at dinner, opting instead for popcorn after Terrell was in bed.

She added extra butter to drown her misery and carried the bowl into the family room, where she curled up in front of the news, ready to let the problems of the world minimize her frustrations.

Her plan worked. Meg munched popcorn as she listened to the latest on the Middle East, the flooding in Texas, and the twin gorillas born at Brookfield Zoo.

Terrell would have loved that one.

The broadcast was half over when coverage changed to the evening's charity event.

Great—just when she'd forgotten, a reminder. She should have realized the event might make the news.

While the blonde anchorwoman talked, footage rolled of Chicago celebrities milling in a packed chandelier-lit lobby. The mayor and his wife, the governor talking with an aging Chicago-born actress, a tuxedo-clad Mike navigating the crowd with a tall, dark-haired woman—

Meg sat up.

The woman's hair was pulled back in a French twist, her indigo gown reflected in her eyes. But worse than her sophisticated looks was the fact that Mike enveloped her slim hand in his.

They looked perfect together. He, the handsome baseball star, and she, the beautiful whatever-she-was. How could he? Was Mike so shallow that he could jump from one woman to another in four days? How dare he!

Tears stung her eyes, and she flung her handful of popcorn at the television. The kernels pinged against the screen, one leaving a buttery smudge, before falling soundlessly to the carpet. To think that she'd actually started to believe he was sorry—

"Mommy?" Terrell stared at her from the doorway.

"Why are you up?" She jumped from her chair, flicking the television off before snatching tell-tale kernels from the floor. How much had he seen? She tossed the kernels into the trash can beside the desk, her appetite gone. "What do you want?"

"I'm thirsty." He looked from the silent television to her. "Why did you throw popcorn?"

"I don't know." She pressed her hand to her forehead, too weary to make up a story. "Let's get you some water."

"Can I have popcorn too?"

"Why not?"

In the kitchen she turned on the light. Terrell hopped onto a chair and dug his hand into the popcorn bowl. "Did you and Daddy fight?" he asked before stuffing his mouth.

"What makes you think we had a fight?"

"He didn't come over like he said he would."

She set a glass of water in front of him. "He said he *might* stop by."

"But now he's with another lady on TV."

So he'd seen it. Her heart sank, and she reached for his hand. His fingers were coated with butter, but she squeezed them, anyway. "Terrell, your dad and I don't agree on everything. But that doesn't mean you won't see him."

"What about that lady?"

"She's a friend of your dad's."

"Oh." Terrell scowled at his water. "I don't like him having other girls for friends."

Neither did she.

"What's her name?"

"I don't know."

"Can I ask him?"

"If you want." She fought back the urge to have him pass on the information. What good would knowing do? "Finish your water, Terrell. You need to get to sleep."

"Is Daddy still coming to my graduation?"

"He said he'd be there."

"And I can talk to him then?"

Someone in this house probably should. Meg gave him her best fake smile. "Talk to him all you want."

Chapter Twenty-Six

Saturday arrived via steam bath. Approaching thunderstorms raised humidity levels, and the sun radiated until the temperature passed ninety degrees. En route to Terrell's graduation, Mike turned the AC on full blast.

The past three days had been lonely and miserable, Friday night being the worst. He'd picked up Sara at the last possible second and spent the twenty-minute drive trying to sound interested in her conversation. What had he seen in her, other than another attractive shot at forgetting Meg?

Conversation around their table kept them from private moments. And each time he found himself alone with Sara, someone stopped to talk to him. Mike welcomed each interruption, drawing them out as long as possible.

By evening's end, his jaw ached from endless smiles and forced laughter, but when he parked in front of Sara's home, he had to fight back the urge to grin as he announced their arrival.

She asked him to come in.

He said no.

Never again would he see Sarah—or any other woman. Maybe he hadn't made much progress in his Win-Meg-Over campaign, but she had kissed him back. Some kind of feeling still lived inside her.

And a whole lot of feelings for her, despite her coldness, still burned in him.

He'd hold onto the few, memorable seconds of that kiss.

In a week and a half he'd be back from his road trip, and with school out, he'd take advantage of the mornings. Maybe he'd even go back to that church with her. It hadn't been too bad. The Father, reverend, whatever, had read from somewhere near the back of the Bible about a guy—Paul, was it?—who'd talked about what a horrible person he'd been. Despite his claim to be a murderer, he didn't seem to suffer guilt.

How had he gotten rid of that load?

Mike pulled into the school's lot with three minutes to spare. He parked, locked his Range Rover, and jogged to the entrance where Meg had promised to meet him.

The school lobby appeared empty.

No, there she was—standing far to the right, arms crossed as she waited, her lips firm.

Well. Didn't look like she'd softened toward him at all. He forced a carefree smile. "Are we in the front row?"

"Close enough." She turned for the gymnasium door, not waiting for him.

Mike stretched his steps to catch up. No wonder she wasn't dating anybody. Who could get close?

She led the way to two empty seats on the aisle. Clark and Jill were already sitting beside the seats, and Mike nodded in their direction, glad he'd chosen to arrive at the last moment. Already whispers buzzed through the crowd. Arriving would probably prove much simpler than leaving.

When the program ended, Terrell ran straight for Mike. "I'm glad you came," he said, arms tight around Mike's waist. "You're staying for lunch, right?"

"Wouldn't miss it."

For whatever reason, Terrell looked relieved.

Meg left to start Terrell's graduation dinner. Clark and Jill said their goodbyes too, explaining that a church emergency had come up and they would not be eating at Meg's.

Mike tried to look sorry. Now he could figure out what had her so ticked off.

It couldn't be that kiss.

Terrell dragged Mike around to meet his friends, which translated into meeting parents too. Mike signed autographs and posed for way too many pictures, his smile painful again.

Finally they escaped. Terrell jabbered away from his seat behind Mike in the Range Rover, and Mike contented himself to listen to this little boy who, miraculously, belonged to him.

Mike pulled into Meg's drive, and he and Terrell entered the kitchen through the back door, near where Meg stood at the peninsula, shredding lettuce as if it had offended her.

He waited for her to look up, but she didn't.

Great.

Terrell snatched a piece of lettuce from the cutting board. "Nachos are my favorite," he said. Meg flicked his hand, and he grinned at her as he chewed the lettuce. "Mom made them special because today's a special occasion. Right, Mommy?"

She favored Terrell with a smile. "You only graduate from kindergarten once."

Mike eyed the food spread across the counter—black olives, shredded cheese, guacamole, sour cream, diced tomatoes, green onions, even his favorite, jalapenos. His stomach rumbled at the smells. "Looks good," he translated.

Meg said nothing.

Well. Good thing he had to leave for the ballpark in less than an hour.

"Mommy, are we eating in the dining room?" Terrell turned to Mike. "Mom says that's for special occasions too."

He glanced at the kitchen table, already set. "I can move things, Meg."

"No. Thank you. I'll do it." She wiped her hands on a dishtowel and walked by without looking at him. "You stay with the graduate."

Happy to. 'Cause the graduate was tons more likable than his mother right now.

Terrell offered him a tortilla chip, and while Mike ate it and listened to Terrell's chatter, Meg smoothed a tablecloth over the rustic table. Mike took in the palest green walls above white wainscoting, the fireplace, antique sideboard, and a rectangular chandelier that was all bling.

Nice.

How would she decorate his downtown condo? Or his ginormous, empty place in the suburbs?

Meg worked fast, and in moments they sat in the dining room, passing nacho toppings. Once they filled their plates, though, silence reigned.

Mike tried to come up with some conversation, but Meg's coldness chased his words away and flamed his own irritation.

Even Terrell noticed the tension.

What a bust this party had turned out to be.

When they'd finished, Meg carried plates to the kitchen, again rejecting Mike's offer to help. "I can take care of it myself," she told him.

Good. Let her.

"Mom made me a cake," Terrell said while Meg banged dessert plates in the kitchen. "My favorite. Chocolate with lots and lots of frosting. And a million colored sprinkles."

"A million, huh?" Mike glanced into the kitchen where Meg seemed to be slicing the cake as if it were him. Enough of the pretending. Maybe Terrell knew something. "I think your mom's mad at me," he whispered.

Terrell nodded. "Yeah. She threw popcorn at you."

"Popcorn?"

"Last night, when you were on TV with that lady. She threw popcorn at you."

"Oh." Mike coughed, hiding a smile behind his fist. So he and Sara had made the news.

Meg was jealous.

"Are you going to marry her?" Terrell asked.

"Who?"

"That lady. You were holding her hand."

His smile froze. *That* had been on TV? He'd offered Sara his arm on their way through the packed entry, and she'd slid her hand down to his. *She'd* been the one holding his hand, and it had lasted only seconds. After that, he'd let her forge her own way through the crowd.

"Well, are you?"

He couldn't believe they'd chosen those few seconds to play. "No, Terrell. She's just someone I know." No wonder Meg wouldn't look at him. "She held my hand so she could get through the crowd. It's called being polite."

Meg would never believe him.

"Then you don't like her?"

He leaned over the table, his voice low. "Not at all."

"But you like my mom, right?"

Meg's footsteps sounded. Mike winked at Terrell and gave him a thumbs-up. At least one person in this house knew what was going on.

Meg placed large triangles of cake, half of it sprinkle-covered frosting, before them. Terrell devoured his and begged for another piece. Meg agreed, blaming her leniency on the special day, but Mike knew better. With Terrell at the table, there would be no chance for the two of them to talk.

When the cake was gone and Meg was back in the kitchen, Mike sent Terrell outside with a promise to join him soon. He carried their forks and plates to the sink, where Meg rinsed dishes.

She glanced over her shoulder at him, face pinched. "Go outside with Terrell," she said, scrubbing a plate harder than seemed necessary. "I'll clean up."

"I told him I'd be out in a bit." Mike set the dishes next to the sink. He leaned backward against the counter. "I missed you last night."

She kept quiet, intent on the dirty dishes.

"They put me at a table with some Bears players. Nice guys. Big, though. The mayor was at the next table over. My friend Travis got stuck with a bunch of highbrows, but knowing him, he probably enjoyed it."

She dropped silverware into the water, the clatter a slap to his dying patience.

"Felt like I talked to everybody there. People stopped by my table all night." He gave her a sideways glance, but she didn't seem to be listening. "Of course, I would have told them to get lost if you'd been there."

Still no reaction.

"You can't be mad at me for this, Meg. I wanted to take you. It stunk going with someone else."

"Didn't look like it," she snapped.

This woman... "I paid for two tickets. I had to take someone. So stop making judgments based on what you think you've seen."

She faced him, her jaw clenched, anger blazing in her eyes. "What I think I've seen? What about what I *know* happened?"

"I'm not talking about the past, Meg! I'm talking about last night. You saw... what? Half a second of us with our hands together? I wasn't holding her hand. She held mine, and I got out of it as fast as I could."

This wasn't worth it. This was *not* worth it. If only he liked Sara; then he'd call her back like she wanted.

But he didn't like her.

Not that he liked Meg at the moment, either. He bit down on his tongue and forced himself to stay. To wait for her to speak.

She rinsed one dish after another, the dishwasher slowly filling.

She was gonna drive him crazy.

He leaned back to catch her eye and force her to acknowledge him.

Her cheeks looked damp.

"Are you crying?"

"No." She swiped her cheeks with her wrist. "I splashed water on my face."

He'd never meant to hurt her. At least, not this time. Why were they suddenly so bad for each other? "Meg, you can't jump to conclusions." He reached for her shoulder.

She backed away, sudsy hands in front of her. "Don't touch me," she spat, tear tracks continuing down her face.

His temper snapped. "Believe me. It's not even tempting right now."

Her eyes hardened. Flickered.

Good.

He swallowed. No, not good. He'd just hurt her worse.

But she'd pushed him to it. What woman turned a guy down, then got upset when he took someone else? Did Meg not get her own insanity?

She returned to the sink. "Go outside with Terrell."

Might as well. "I'm taking him with me. He can play on the field, hit in the batting cage. A kind of graduation present. You good with that?" Not that he cared. He *was* taking Terrell.

She shrugged. "Whatever, Mike. Just go."

He headed for the back yard.

How had this week gone so wrong?

Chapter Twenty-Seven

The view through her office window reflected her emotions perfectly. Dark treetops across the street bounced beneath the wind and pounding rain, their movements backlit by flashes of lightning. The storm hadn't started until Mike's game ended, but her clock showed it was after eleven, and Mike and Terrell still weren't back from the stadium.

She flipped her pen end-over-end between her fingers. Her anger from Friday had morphed into cold numbness. And why not? Mike had forced her to relive the old pain of his betrayal. For all she knew, the woman he'd been with had been Brooke.

Meg gave up trying to distract herself with work and shut off her computer before trudging downstairs. The kitchen was spotless, but anger always did that to her. Their Texas townhouse had been spotless, too, when she turned in her key to her lawyer and returned alone to her parents and the soothing smells of the farm.

She stood before the bank of kitchen windows, staring at the Ashburns' house. A single light shone from their living room. What would Jill's advice be?

The light went out.

So much for that idea. Looked like she was on her own.

Jill, of course, would say Meg was not. She had God. The Bible. But the pain of desertion still craved human comfort.

And tonight even Terrell was gone. With the one who'd deserted her.

A car door's slam drew her to the living room. She peeked between closed curtains.

Mike lifted a sleeping Terrell from the Range Rover. He held him against his chest and hunched over him to protect him from the downpour before darting up her sidewalk.

Meg let the curtain fall. If only someone would shield her like that.

She could already hear Jill saying that God *did* care for her like that, and, while Meg knew it was true, she was afraid to let her hurt go and be limp—like Terrell—in her heavenly Father's arms.

Doing that would require her to forgive all that Mike had done.

Chapter Twenty-Eight

Mike was sick of rain.

Sunday evening the team arrived in Kansas City with storm clouds towering in the west. At the airport, wind whipped his suit coat and pants against him as he boarded the team bus. By the time they reached the hotel, blowing rain drenched everything, and the sound of wind and water beating his window kept him from a deep sleep.

That and Meg.

More storms rolled in Monday, twice halting the night's game while the grounds crew spread the tarp over the infield. Mike spent the rain delays with his teammates in the clubhouse, but he escaped once and jogged up the runway to look at the field. Sheets of rain blew across the stadium. He leaned against the cement wall, wondering if Meg's stormy coldness had passed.

In the morning, the sun peeked around the clouds, but the rain came and went all afternoon. By game time, the outfield was soaked again. Mike dove for a ball in the first inning, only to catch a faceful of grass and water.

Before the inning ended, the light rain turned into a downpour, starting another rain delay.

Mike ran across the field to the dugout, water splatting up around each footfall. Once inside the clubhouse, he paced. Rain delays were the worst, but two straight nights of them?

Again he jogged down the runway and stared through the dugout.

Fine droplets blew in toward him.

He needed something to distract himself, something to relieve this stress that seemed to build with every minute. He stepped farther into the dugout, letting rain touch him. Like he could get any wetter after his hydroplaning act.

The tarp caught his attention.

He ran up the dugout steps and onto the grass. In a few strides he reached the edge of the rain-covered tarp and dove head first. The cool water shocked him, but he held himself straight as he slid, water piling on either side of his body. He'd hear about it, for sure, but a guy could only stand so much rain and time and angry ex-wives. He slid once more, feeling better. The few fans left cheered him, but he gave them only a token nod as he returned to the dugout. He hadn't done it for them.

Like a dog, he shook his head, water flying from his hair.

In the clubhouse, teammates laughed at something on the television.

Mike joined them and watched himself dive onto the tarp.

Will Hamrick tossed him a towel. "You look like you might need this."

Mike ran the towel over his face, hair, and neck. "Think they'll call it?"

"They just did. No sense wasting the night. Let's go out."

Not in this mood.

But by the time he'd showered and dressed, Will had talked a third of the team into hitting a club.

Mike caved and joined them.

He, Will, and Travis shared an Uber ride. Mike dug out his phone, tempted—for some bizarre reason—to call Meg.

Why? To irritate her more? To mend fences?

Hard to fix them when she'd demolished them.

But his phone showed that she'd called him. During the game. He smiled his surprise. His relief. *She'd* called *him*.

Wait. She knew he wouldn't be able to answer his phone.

Was something wrong?

Or had she wanted to tell him off when she knew he couldn't say anything back?

There was no message.

Okay. He pocketed the phone. He'd find someplace private at the club to call her back.

By the time the car stopped in front of the club, the downpour had lessened, but the sidewalks were still empty. Mike slid across the seat and out the door after Travis, pausing to tip the driver before catching up to Will and Travis.

The double doors of the club opened, and a couple ran out with a shared coat over their heads. Neither noticed him, which was fine. He caught the door, following his friends inside.

Voices and laughter mingled with the band that played on one side. The smell of burgers and fries suddenly called him, waking hunger he thought he'd already satisfied. He worked his way through the crowd to the opposite side where Will, Travis, and five other teammates surrounded two tables. He'd place an order, then call Meg.

With food coming, he headed for the exit. Outside he'd be able to hear her better, even with the rain.

Which had slowed to a soft gentle shower.

"Where've you been for the past three days?" he muttered as he found Meg on his phone. He stayed under the building's overhang, tucked into the corner, and listened as her phone rang.

The doors opened, a lone man filing out, the band's noise exiting with him.

Mike turned his head into the corner and stuck a finger in his ear in time to hear Meg say hello.

"Meg, it's Mike. I'm returning your call."

"My call?" She sounded confused. "From when?"

"Tonight, eightish?"

"I didn't call you. I was cleaning Terrell's—" She halted, and when she spoke again, a smile colored her words. "Terrell called you. I was coming downstairs from my office and caught him acting funny. I must have walked in on him."

"Sorry I missed him." Their Saturday at the stadium had been a blast, despite how the day had begun. "Is he awake?"

"No."

"Bummer. Well, tell him he can call me anytime."

A noise distracted him, and he looked over his shoulder as someone walked by, head down in the rain. He turned back to the brick corner. "How are you?"

"I'm all right." She didn't elaborate. "I should go. I've got laundry to fold."

"That can't wait?"

"It's been waiting. We're digging through it each morning."

"Got it. Then I guess I'll talk to you later."

"I'll tell Terrell you called."

"Thanks. Meg, wait." He pressed his lips together. He shouldn't say this. He shouldn't start it all over again— "She isn't anybody, Meg." But Sara had been, he remembered after the words were out. "I don't want you to think... I'm not seeing anyone. I don't have my eye on anyone but you."

She said nothing.

He took in a deep breath. Why did he keep putting himself out there? He forced his voice to be light. "What about you? Have your eye on anyone?"

Her voice, this time, was gentle. "Mike, I don't want to talk about this."

"Then *what*, Meg? Tell me what to talk about."

She kept quiet for a moment. "We enjoyed your slide. It looked fun."

She watched his games? Even after their fight Saturday? "It was a decent stress reliever."

"Well, good, I guess."

"Yeah."

"Mike, I'm—I hope your stress isn't from me."

How did he answer that?

She sighed. "I'll take that as a yes."

"No, Meg. Don't—just—" He stumbled over his words and swallowed before trying again. "I don't want us handing out fault every time we turn around. Yeah, I'm a little stressed, but so are a lot of guys on the team. I hear that's life."

"Maybe."

The silence returned. Mike held his breath.

"Well, thanks, Mike. I should go. Our clothes are still waiting."

"Sure." He pushed off the wall with his shoulder. "Go have fun with your laundry."

She gave him the light chuckle he'd almost forgotten. "I will. Goodnight, Mike."

"Night." He'd made her laugh. They'd actually had a conversation that went... well? Was that the right word? No one was mad, she wasn't crying... Hope rose—flooded—through him. This was good. This was really—

"Mike Connor?"

He turned toward the male voice behind him. "That's me."

A hooded figure stood with arms upraised. Mike looked up as the arms began their downward swing.

They held a crowbar.

Mike threw an arm up over his head.

The crowbar smashed against his forearm.

White-hot pain knifed through him, the blow knocking him

backward into the brick. He clutched his arm to his chest as he fell to the ground, the burning on the side of his head minor compared to the agony in his arm.

A clank sounded.

Mike braced for another blow.

But the man was gone, already a distant figure down the street.

A woman dashed into view, almost toppling over his feet.

Reflexes jerked his body into a ball, his elbow banging the brick. Pain flashed up his arm. Mike let out a gush of air, not recognizing his own cry of pain.

Because he'd never felt pain like this before.

The woman pointed down the street. "Did that guy hit you?"

Awareness registered. Someone had attacked him.

Another woman dropped beside him, brown hair sliding over her shoulder. "Are you okay? Did you see who did that?" She looked from his arm to his face, then sat back on her heels. "You're—"

Pain sent dark shapes across his vision. He closed his eyes and clenched his teeth. His shoulders shook. "Just call the police."

Seconds later she spoke into her phone.

But the words didn't register. He pressed his lips together, barely holding back the agony that pushed from the pit of his stomach.

Breathe, man. Deep breath. Breathe.

He opened his eyes to find the other woman kneeling at his feet, focused on his arm.

Mike followed her gaze.

Red drops dotted his hand and arm.

Was that blood?

He stared at the specks of red. He could feel them now on his face, see them on his shirt. Whose blood was that? He shifted for a better look, but pain flooded him again, and he slammed his fist against the sidewalk.

Spots flashed before his eyes.

Passing out sounded wonderful.

"Don't do that," one of the women said. "You'll make it worse."

He breathed through his mouth until his eyes cleared and the nausea passed. "I've got friends inside." He ran through their names until the brunette nodded at Brett Burkholder's name and dashed in to find him.

The blonde stayed with him.

Slowly, he tried to cradle his arm against his chest. But the slightest movement shot torture through his arm, and he tried not to sniff, tried not to blink, tried not to breathe.

The club doors crashed open. His teammates surrounded him, but Mike ignored their questions. All he wanted to know was where that blood had come from.

Chapter Twenty-Nine

The sky hinted of dawn when Ben woke. Dana slept, so he slowly slid out of bed. He pulled a gray Air Force T-shirt over his head, then watched her to make sure her sleep was deep.

She was out.

He slipped through the partially open door and crept down the hallway, avoiding the areas that creaked, until he reached the living room. He unlocked the front door and opened it.

The paper wasn't there yet.

He heaved a sigh as he closed the door. No, he was in control. He could wait.

In the kitchen, he flipped the light switch, squinting against the fluorescent's glare. The Keurig sat silent and empty on the counter. He placed a pod inside, set a cup beneath it, and started it. With a sigh, he dropped onto a dining room chair to wait.

Yesterday had been exhausting. He'd started showing homes at eight in the morning and didn't stop until after nine that night. Dana had reheated her homemade focaccia bread for him, and he'd stayed up until eleven, nibbling it while he watched SportsCenter. Like the previous two nights, he'd found the show uneventful.

Maybe today.

If not today, there was always later in the season. He could wait. He'd waited years already.

Coffee gurgled quietly into his cup.

Ben eyed the clock on the stove. In five minutes SportsCenter would start all over again, giving him enough time to get comfortable in the recliner. Until the paper arrived, that would have to do. When the show's familiar intro began, he'd get the same thrill he got from opening the paper, a rush he was beginning to look forward to.

He pushed himself up from his chair, giving in to a yawn. The mug was half full, and he leaned against the countertop, tapping his fingers on the fake granite.

Patience, Ben. He smiled. Funny how difficult it was to wait for coffee when waiting for revenge could be so easy.

Chapter Thirty

From the first-class seat behind him, an air-conditioning unit hissed as the passenger redirected the flow of air. Mike shifted in his window seat, his back muscles tight from the weight of a cast that ran from the bottom of his fingers to halfway up his biceps. The sling's strap pulled against his neck, and for the third time since he'd walked onto the plane, Mike ran a finger beneath it in hopes of finding some comfort.

At least his painkillers were helping. He'd suffered an open fracture, and the Royals' surgeon had attached a plate to... some bone. Yep, he'd be setting off metal detectors for years to come.

The Kansas City police, though, had come up with zilch. Elizabeth and Kerri, the women who'd witnessed the attack, didn't see anything he hadn't seen himself—some guy had whaled on him once and run.

But why? He'd received no threatening mail, and despite turning down the usual number of autograph requests, no one had stood out as being that angry about it. He'd even considered Meg's assistant's fiancé, but Meg had carefully asked Dana who said Ben had been showing homes all day.

Mike stared out the window for the hour-long flight. There were no clouds, ironic after almost a full week of rain. Green squares of farmland gave way to suburbs butting up to each other until Lake

Michigan, dotted with boats, appeared. Nice—a beautiful day to be absolutely miserable.

Inside O'Hare, Mitch Wilcox, the team's General Manager, met him. So did a mob of reporters. Mitch deflected their questions as he and Mike walked, surrounded, down the concourse. Once they escaped, Mitch drove him home, talking about the investigation and trying to weed out any clues Mike might have forgotten.

As if he hadn't spent his time in the hospital doing the same thing.

To his relief, Mitch dropped him off at the front door of his off-season, suburban home—his current home now that he was on the disabled list—and left. Few things were more humiliating than getting beat up. Listening to another man talk it over was worse. "I'd rather get beat up again," he mumbled as he wandered into the kitchen. He set his wallet, phone, and keys on the counter. Might as well let Meg know he was back.

His call went to voicemail. "Hey, Meg. It's Mike. I'm home." He fiddled with the strap of his sling, reminded why he was home before the rest of the team. Suddenly he was glad she hadn't answered. She'd probably want to know how he was, and he didn't want to talk about it. "Guess you're busy. Bye."

He ended the call.

His phone beeped, reminding him that his dad had called while Mitch had been driving him home. He put the phone on speaker and set it on the counter, then headed to the fridge to see if Maria, his mom-like housekeeper and assistant, had gotten the fridge stocked like he'd asked.

One shelf was completely filled with bottled water. Mike grabbed one and managed to twist off the lid.

"Hi, Mike," Dad's gravelly voice sounded. "Give us a call when you're home. Thought we'd come see you for a few days since you're laid up. Mom wants to do some cooking for you."

Mike stopped guzzling the water and glanced at the phone. And? "Also decided this might be a good time to meet Terrell."

There it was. Meg would love hearing this bit of news.

In his bedroom, he unpacked quickly and, once his bag was empty, tossed it into a corner of his closet, kicking it in farther. With this arm, he wasn't going anywhere.

He ordered a deep-dish spinach pizza in a half-hearted attempt to eat healthy. With dinner on the way, he wandered into the great room and turned on the TV. He was rarely home this time of day. What was even on? He surfed for a minute. Looked like he wasn't missing a thing.

The afternoon news caught his attention, only because of Meg's old habits. And what timing—the sports segment was showing highlights from last night's White Sox game. He watched with envy as pinstriped players crossed home plate and an infielder snagged a line drive.

Nice.

The news program played two clips from yesterday's make-up game in Kansas City, where the Wind had been blown out. No pitching, no hitting, and a bullpen that made the starting pitcher look good. Thank goodness the newscast didn't play any more of that ugliness.

Except now he was seeing… himself. In the airport. Pushing through reporters and their microphones, eyes drooping, mouth a tight line, and stubble all over his face. He sank lower on the couch, squinting in mental pain as the clip continued. He should have smiled, should have said something beyond his annoyed, "I'm fine."

He looked anything but fine.

The broadcast moved on, and when the local news began all over again, Mike tried to find interest in the top story, a manufacturing plant leaving the city.

If Meg found this stuff interesting, so could he.

But after two minutes of angry workers followed by the most recent name-calling between men running in the fall's election, Mike gave up. News junkie he was not.

Baseball player extraordinaire... Well, for the next couple months, he wasn't that, either.

Hurting, angry, and humiliated... Sadly, that description *did* fit.

With a growl, he pushed himself up from the couch. He glared across the wide, sunlit room. So some cowardly man had injured him with his back half-turned. There had to be something he could do to pass time until he started rehabbing.

His gaze landed on the coffee table. Meg's blue scrapbook, the one she'd returned with his yearbooks, sat on it. He picked it up and plopped back onto the couch.

Ow. He sucked in a breath. When would every little movement quit causing pain?

Once the sting faded, he flipped the book open to years of forgotten memories.

There was his first minor-league home run, a solo shot over the left-field wall. He remembered that one. A few articles later was his first four-for-four game followed by the game in which he'd made two costly errors.

He smiled. Meg had not censored his career.

Page after page detailed his time in the minors. The year in Double-A and his first game in Triple-A. Playing in the Futures All-Star Game. He read the names of the other players, noting those who were stars now and those whose careers had flopped.

There was the article from the Dixon paper the day after his major league debut, with Meg's memories written beside it—her pride when he was announced for his first at bat, his command of veteran players in the outfield, and his first big-league hit, a two-out single in the seventh that led to Texas's come-from-behind win.

Mike added his own dusty memories to hers, major league fans asking for his autographs, getting a hit off Baltimore's ace, and stealing second for the first time. He'd stood, brushed himself off, and taken in the view from second base in a packed big league park.

The articles went on until the album's last page. He eased the book shut and stared at the cover. The articles beckoned him, a link to the healthy ballplayer he'd been three days ago, and he returned to the front, flipping back to his favorite memories.

Halfway through, he stopped.

Hadn't his first homer in Triple-A been off Dana's fiancé?

He flipped pages until he came to the article and read the few lines that mentioned his at bat. "Pinch-hitting in his first game, twenty-year-old Michael Connor belted a three-run homer, knocking reliever Ben Raines out of the game."

Mike read the sentence again. Something felt wrong.

He read it a third time, feeling like he was waiting for a sneeze that wouldn't come.

The doorbell rang.

Dinner. He set the scrapbook aside and headed for the front door. Whatever felt odd would come to him later.

Chapter Thirty-One

On Monday evening Mike sat at Meg's kitchen table, fiddling with his fork while Meg cleared the table around him.

A very different Mike had returned from Kansas City. He'd yet to give his usual smile and spoke only in response to Terrell's questions until Terrell probed too close to Mike's attack. Already she'd learned not to mention that.

Yesterday he'd shown up at church, halfway through Clark's Sunday school class. From across the room Mike had nodded at her before pulling a spare folding chair from the wall. She took in the bags beneath his eyes, his sling, and the cast that covered most of his arm. He looked less than thrilled to be there.

"I'm bored," he told her afterward as the three of them walked into the auditorium. "I've been home less than two days, and I'm going crazy."

Terrell couldn't keep his fingers off the cast. "Can you eat with one arm?"

"The doctors aren't sure, Terrell. If I get thin, tell your mom to have me over for dinner."

Wow. He was quick.

Terrell, lips pursed, had studied Mike's long, muscular frame. "Let's not wait."

Now Mike twirled his fork. The tines snagged on his fingers, and the fork clattered to the table and then the floor. Mike grunted as he reached for it.

"I'll get it." She picked up the fork before he could fold himself over his cast.

"I'm not an invalid," he snapped.

"No, just a crab." She turned her back on him, heading for the dishwasher. "Terrell's still waiting for you to watch the game with him."

"Like I want to torture myself watching baseball."

"So you're taking it out on Terrell?"

"Enough, Meg. I know I'm a jerk."

She couldn't stop her tongue. "Admitting it is the first step."

He scowled at her. "I'm starting to wonder where you were last Tuesday."

"Right here, watching the news, I think."

"Got an alibi?" He walked to the peninsula that separated them. Sighed deeply. "I'm not enjoying my company, either. All this free time, and I can't do a thing. Stupid arm hurts every time it gets bumped. And try sleeping with brick burn on one side of your head." He rested his sling on the countertop, his weight on his right arm. "Did I tell you my parents are flying in Wednesday?"

"Yes." Now there was a topic she didn't want to talk about.

"Don't know what we'll do for six days."

"You'll talk, go downtown, go to a game—"

"Thrilling."

"You'll eat out a lot, and your mom will pack your freezer with all your favorite foods."

His scowl lessened. "True. And they'll want to spend time with Terrell. Don't forget."

"I won't." She swallowed at the thought of seeing Davis and Patty Connor. Six days? How would they treat her? "I'm sure they'd like to avoid me."

He pushed himself away from the peninsula. "I'll make sure they don't give you grief."

Her one-armed hero. She started the dishwasher and followed him out of the kitchen. "Would you mind staying here with Terrell tonight? I need to meet a client in forty minutes, and Jill can't watch him."

"Sure. Where are you going?"

"Dana's house. She and Ben are redoing their kitchen."

Mike stopped in the family room doorway and turned.

Behind him, Terrell looked their way before returning to the television.

"You're going there?" Mike asked.

How else was she supposed to meet them? "Yes."

With two fingers, he motioned for her to come with him.

She followed him back into the kitchen.

"I don't like you going to that guy's house," he said.

"What?" She stared at him. "You're kidding, right?"

"No. Something about Ben's sketchy. I don't like you being around him."

"They're my clients, Mike. You can't tell me to stop working because you don't like him."

The words—almost verbatim from arguments seven, eight, nine years old—dropped like a boulder between them. Meg's eyes widened.

Even Mike blinked and took a step back.

She opened her mouth. She had to say something—anything— to move past the resurrection of so many problems. But she couldn't. She brushed her hair over her shoulder. Why couldn't she find anything to say?

Mike's voice, soft and low, rang accusing in her ears. "So we're back to that."

How like him to blame her for what he'd done. "It's not the same. This is how I support myself and Terrell."

"Does it have to be that way?"

"We're not getting back together—"

"Child support, Meg."

"No." He'd brought it up before. Once. She'd shut him down. "Just stay here with Terrell."

He ignored her, his smile sardonic. "Has anything changed?"

She looked away from eyes that knew so well what she had been—and what he believed her to still be. But this time things *were* different. Weren't they?

"I thought all this church stuff was supposed to make you different, better."

What did he know about how much she'd changed? "Who says what I am is wrong? If you don't like it, move on."

A smile grew on his face. "Step on your toes?"

She turned her back on him. "Like you said, Mike, you're a jerk."

"You're still not going to Reynolds' house alone."

"Watch me." She swung her purse strap over her shoulder and grabbed her keys, jangling them at him—

Mike stood in the kitchen doorway, mouth open, eyes staring past her.

She looked behind herself.

There was nothing there but the front door.

"What now?" she huffed.

His focus shifted to her, and something in his expression sent a shiver through her.

"Mike? What is it?"

"I'm not sure." He stared at her for several more seconds. "Terrell," he finally called. "Get your shoes on."

"Mike, he can't come."

He grabbed his wallet from the console and shoved it into his back pocket. "Here's the deal. I'll drive you so Ben knows I know you're there. We'll pop in, say hi. Then I'll pick you up when you're done."

This was dumb. "But will Ben know that *you* know that he knows—"

"Knock it off."

Terrell entered the room, holding his sandals. "Where are we going?"

"We're dropping your mom off at a client's home."

She closed her eyes. "This is embarrassing."

"Trust me, Meg."

She met his eyes.

Something in them underlined his concern.

Still… "Just for tonight," she snapped.

Pain flickered across his face.

Nicely done, Meg. Way to be mean.

She marched upstairs to her office to gather her things.

Chapter Thirty-Two

The drive to Ben and Dana's home took half an hour. Mike parked his Range Rover, out of place in an older neighborhood of starter homes, on the cracked concrete drive.

As Meg stepped out of the vehicle, Ben appeared in the front doorway. He opened the screen. "Look who it is." He nodded at Mike's arm. "How are you enjoying the cast?"

"Loving every minute." Mike turned his back on him to open Terrell's door and help him climb down. His low voice reached her. "Moron." He slammed the door, then started up the sidewalk with Terrell in tow.

"Be nice," Meg whispered behind him.

"I called him a moron, didn't I?" he hissed over his shoulder.

At the front door, Ben extended his hand, and Mike gripped it. Even with Ben's grin, Meg felt the tension. She offered Ben what she hoped was a calming smile and followed Mike and Terrell into the living room.

Ben let the screen slam behind him. "I suppose this isn't much compared to what you're used to, Connor, but it's home to us."

Meg surveyed the room, the furniture older but laid out well.

"Actually," Mike said, "this is nicer than mine. More color, cozier."

Ben snorted, shouldering past them to the dining room. "Cozy is how agents describe tiny houses no one wants to buy."

Mike rolled his eyes.

In the kitchen Dana was drying dishes. The room smelled of cheese and herbs, and Meg inhaled the lingering aromas.

"Wow. What did you have for dinner?" Mike asked.

Ben smirked as if he'd cooked the meal. "One of Dana's specialties. Four cheese chicken pizza with white sauce. Out of this world."

"Smells like it," Meg said. The men were like snarling animals fighting over territory. If she ignored them, maybe they'd both go away. "Dana, may I put my things on your table?"

"I just wiped it. Make sure it's dry." Dana held out a hand for Terrell to give her a high-five. "Did you come along for the ride, or do you have ideas for fixing up the place?"

Meg tugged her bags from Mike's hand as she answered for him. "They're leaving." Right this second if she could help it.

"We're just dropping Meg off." Mike's gaze moved from Dana to Ben. "Terrell and I are hanging out tonight, but we'll be back when she's ready to go."

"Yes, and I'll text you when we're done." Meg tugged on his arm until he moved for the front door, he and Ben still in a stare-down.

"You've got my number, right?" Mike asked.

"Yes. Got it." *Go already,* she pleaded with her eyes.

He did.

Ben locked the door behind them, then raised his eyebrows at her. "A little controlling, isn't he?"

Protective, yes. But controlling? The words she'd thrown at him in her kitchen resurfaced. Meg chased them away with a smile. "He just wants to make sure I'm safe, I guess."

"I think it's sweet." Dana pulled out a chair and motioned for Meg to sit. "Ben, are you going to join us?"

Meg settled herself at the table before looking at Ben.

His coal-like eyes were trained on her.

She held them a moment before reaching for one of her bags. A small shiver slid over her as she unzipped it, considering for the first time that perhaps Mike wasn't overreacting.

⁂

Two hours later Meg stashed the last of her things in her bag as Mike's headlights flashed through the living room window.

Ben didn't move from his seat in the recliner. "Your guardian's here," he called.

The night had not gone well. She'd hoped to leave with a final budget along with their wants and ideas, but after a few minutes, it was obvious they were dreaming up completely opposite kitchens.

And sitting there while the two of them tried to hash it out—Dana not listening, Ben… bullying—had been uncomfortable.

Horribly uncomfortable.

Meg hurried through her goodbyes and jogged down the sidewalk, despite her bags.

Mike met her halfway and stowed her things beside Terrell while she climbed in the Range Rover. "How'd it go?" he asked as he backed out of the driveway.

"Terrible. They don't agree on anything. Dana has this dream kitchen that will cost ten times their budget."

"So what now?"

"She has to give in to Ben. He's right, but she doesn't see it." Why was she talking to him? She was mad at him. "She wants to knock out half of the back of their house and triple the kitchen size. It'd be twice as big as their living room."

Mike raised an eyebrow. "Can you do that?"

"Do what?"

"A remodel like that."

"Sure. I've got a contractor I work with. He's really good."

"He?"

"Forty-nine, happily married, grandchild on the way."

"Glad to hear it."

She shook her head and looked into the back of the Range Rover. Terrell slept, his head bobbing with the ride.

"Looks like you wore him out."

"Too much ski ball."

"Where'd you go?"

"Chuck E. Cheese's. Which was a mistake—an obnoxious amount of autographs and pictures." He raised his eyebrows, puffed out his cheeks. "Then we found a park with those remote control boats."

"Sounds fun."

"It was. And I didn't have to see the guys get blown out in New York."

"They lost?"

He nodded, melancholy in the motion.

"They haven't won a game since you got hurt."

He shrugged. Weariness clung to his features, dragging his mouth down. He looked so different without his usual smile.

Poor Mike.

Poor Mike—what was she thinking? When he'd actually blamed *her* tonight for their messed-up marriage? A hard thing to do when he'd had the affair, left, and filed for divorce.

What could he fault her for? She closed her eyes. He'd been busy, loving life in the big leagues. She'd filled his days away with design classes and friends, with decorating her home and her friends' homes. He'd spent hours hitting in the cage, hours working on defensive skills, hours working out—and that was the off-season. What was wrong with finding her own interests?

Meg opened her eyes.

They sat at a red light.

Mike was watching her.

He turned back to the stoplight, silence filling the air between them.

She closed her eyes again and pretended to doze.

But the emptiness that had been on his face was hard to ignore.

When the Range Rover stilled, Meg looked up to find her dark house before them.

She'd forgotten to leave a light on. As usual.

"I'll get Terrell." Mike opened his door, light filling the interior.

Meg reached for her purse.

It wasn't beside her feet or her seat. Mike must have put it with her bags.

But it wasn't there, either.

She'd left it at Dana's house.

"Mike, I forgot my purse."

He looked up from where he was about to lift a still-sleeping Terrell from his carseat. He sent her a blank look.

"My keys. I'm locked out."

"Don't you have a spare somewhere?"

He'd be mad. "I've been meaning to do that."

He rested his good arm on the doorframe, eyes closing.

"I was in a hurry to get out of there…" Why was she apologizing?

"It's fine." Lips pinched, he fumbled with Terrell's seat belt. "We'll just go back. Like I've got anything to do tomorrow, anyway." He shut Terrell's door before returning to his seat. He tossed her his cell. "Let them know we're coming."

Meg called, but no one answered.

How could she have forgotten her purse? If she'd gone alone, this would not have happened. The next time Mike pulled this stunt, she'd bring that up.

The Range Rover's clock read 10:13 when Mike pulled into Ben and Dana's driveway. The front of the house was dark.

Mike sent her a look of pure frustration.

"They could still be up," she said.

"Right. I'll wait here."

"Thanks a bunch." She stepped out of the Range Rover, planning to walk to the front door, but as she rounded the Range Rover, light spilling into the backyard caught her attention. She walked the length of the drive and crossed the grass to the back stairs.

Kitchen light rested on the lawn in a golden rectangle.

The interior door must be open. Someone was up.

Meg took one step up the stairs and screamed Mike's name.

Chapter Thirty-Three

Mike lurched at Meg's scream. He pressed the gas, raced up the driveway, almost bumping the garage. He slammed the vehicle into Park and jumped out, leaving his door open.

Meg stood on the bottom stair, hands covering her mouth.

Mike grabbed her around the waist and tugged her aside, his gaze darting to the doorway.

A woman—his sister, Betsy—lay on the kitchen floor, motionless, bruises darkening on her face, the one eye he could see swollen. Blood trickled from a small cut at the corner of her mouth, but far worse was the blood beneath her head.

Mike gasped for air, reaching for the top step. Not Betsy, not again.

Someone pulled him back. "Don't go in!"

He turned.

Meg? Why was she here?

Her hand on his arm shook. "Don't, Mike!" she begged.

A neighbor's porch light flashed on, and a man in a Bears T-shirt looked out.

"Call 911!" Mike hollered. "Someone's hurt!"

The man scurried back inside.

Mike looked at Betsy, but it was Dana lying there—alive or dead? He squeezed his eyes shut, opened them, mentally shook himself.

"Get in the Range Rover," he said, "and lock the doors. I'll check her."

"Mike! What if whoever did that—"

"Ben did this." He clenched his shaking fingers into a fist. The guy deserved a beating of his own. "Get in the car. If you see him, lay on the horn."

Meg ran.

Mike waited until the Range Rover's door slammed, then stepped into the kitchen. The screen fell shut behind him. So what? If Ben were in the house, he'd already heard them, already knew they were there.

He knelt beside Dana and felt her wrist.

Nothing.

He held his lip between his teeth. That didn't mean anything. He wasn't an EMT. What did he know? He sat back and slowed his breathing. He couldn't do anything anyway—

Her chest rose.

Mike slumped against a cabinet. She was alive, at least. Alive but in bad shape.

He surveyed her again, but the only other bleeding he could see was beneath her head. The puddle was small, and he knew better than to move her to see what had caused the damage. Probably couldn't stomach it, anyway. He looked around the room, halting when he found a smear of blood on the counter's edge above her.

Anger leapt up inside him. Fresh. Fierce.

"Ben!" He rose to his feet. A knife block sat beside the coffee maker. Mike pulled out the largest knife, just in case. "Ben!" he shouted again, the rage in his voice not lost on himself. "Where are you?"

Silence met him.

He slid down the refrigerator and watched Dana's chest rise and fall. The least he could do was stay and defend her if Ben showed his cowardly self.

A minute passed, then another.

Still Dana breathed, and Mike kept his eyes on her, as if watching kept her alive.

"Sir?"

He jumped at the voice at the kitchen door.

Three police officers stood at the bottom of the steps, the first one training a gun on him. "Sir," the cop repeated, "I want you to set the knife down."

Knife? Mike stared at his hand, startled to see his knuckles white around the handle. They thought—

"No, it's not me." He laid the knife on the ground and slid it toward the back door. "It was her fiancé. I got the knife in case—"

"Keep that hand up, sir. We're going to come in and take a look, okay?"

"Fine."

Two of the officers entered the room, their eyes on him. "Mike Connor?" one asked.

"Yes."

"You and your wife found her?"

"Yes, my ex-wife. This woman—Dana... her fiancé did this."

"Why don't you go outside. Officer Rowand will take your statement."

"Sure." He pushed himself to his feet, one leg tingling. He glanced Dana's way again as he left the kitchen.

How much had this woman endured? And for how long?

Outside, Officer Rowand led him to a squad car parked in the street.

Mike followed and leaned against the vehicle's hood, his legs shaky. After Betsy, he knew the routine.

Chapter Thirty-Four

Ben turned off Northwest Highway and into his subdivision.

The moon was bright, the neighborhood quiet and still. He drove slowly, just in case—

No. He couldn't think that way. Things would be fine. He'd panicked, that's all. When Dana had fallen against the countertop and slumped to the floor, he'd experienced the same gush of fear he'd felt two years ago. And he'd gone through the same motions, the frantic packing of his clothes and stash of money before leaving.

But the hour of driving had calmed him. By the time he reached the town of Aurora, he'd finally separated the two incidents—no matter how uncannily alike they were—and knew that Dana was not dead. He'd return and take her to the ER if needed. Then he'd spend whatever time it took repairing the damage he'd done.

Dana would come around.

Ben flicked on the turn signal as he approached his street.

Police lights flashed halfway down the block. Four cruisers sat in the street. Right outside his house.

Ben turned off the signal. Slowed the car to a crawl. It was a coincidence. It had to be.

The headlights of a police car dimmed as an officer walked from the driver's side toward…

Ben craned his neck.

The cop opened Ben's front door, inside light illuminating the front steps.

They were at *his* house. Which meant… Dana had called the cops.

He pounded the steering wheel. She'd called the cops? She'd destroy everything he'd rebuilt. Everything! How could she? How could she be such a traitor?

He pulled over where he could watch undetected, then turned off the engine and lights, waited for his breathing to slow. In another day or two, he'd call Dana. She'd change her mind about pressing charges, and if the cops hadn't found out about—

A large SUV backed out of Ben's driveway. The vehicle turned toward him, its lights sweeping across houses and lawns and curb.

Ben fell flat across the front seats and held still as the headlights swept over his car window. The lights grew brighter, closer, then passed.

Ben sat up. Turned. Looked.

That wasn't just an SUV. That was a Range Rover, a big, black Range Rover.

Dana hadn't called the cops—he knew she wouldn't.

But Connor would. Connor was the problem, again.

And if the police found out the truth, Connor would regret he'd ever returned to Ben's house.

Chapter Thirty-Five

Mike spent the night at Meg's house.

She fought him on it, as he'd expected, but he'd been right about Ben. Plus, after what Meg had seen, she might have nightmares.

He still did.

He lay across one of her living room sofas—the color was pumpkin, she'd told him, not orange—while night shadows faded in and out as clouds drifted past the moon. Sleeping upstairs in the guest bedroom she'd finally offered didn't seem right. For some reason he needed to sleep here, as if he were on guard.

He flopped around, trying to find a comfortable position. He couldn't lie flat since he'd discovered, too late, that he was a few inches longer than the couch. He'd already tried lying on his side with his legs bent, but then his knees hung off the edge. Between their weight and his casted arm trying to balance on a pillow, gravity threatened to go into effect.

He gave up and stretched out on the floor between the coffee table and the couch. Meg needed a recliner, a giant La-Z-Boy he could get comfortable in.

He stretched the blanket over his legs and, lifting himself to adjust the pillow, banged his head on the edge of the coffee table.

He bit back words of pain until the throbbing faded. "I'm dying down here," he muttered, rubbing his skull with his good hand.

He'd never be able to sleep like this. The floorboards beneath the area rug pressed into his stomach. The upstairs bed was becoming more and more—

Something creaked in the foyer.

Mike jerked still, eyes trained on the small square of the living room doorway that he could see.

Some guard he was.

There it was again, definitely someone creeping through the foyer.

Slowly he pulled himself up and, in his bare feet, tiptoed to the other end of the living room where the kitchen, family room, and living room doorways converged. If this person was going toward the stairs, he'd catch them from behind. If he was headed Mike's way—

A floorboard creaked on the other side of the wall, and he pressed himself against it, almost missing the soft intake of breath. Was that— He flicked on the lamp beside him. "Meg?"

With a yelp, Meg flattened herself against the foyer wall. "What are you scaring me for?" she hissed.

"Keep it down," he hissed back. "What are you doing, sneaking around your own house?"

"Since someone refuses to sleep upstairs in a bed, I have no choice but to sneak around *my* house." She marched past him into the kitchen, pulled open the refrigerator, and grabbed a pitcher of orange juice from the door. She set it down hard on the counter.

Juice surged from the spout, splashing onto the counter and floor.

Mike hid his smile.

She sent him a side glance before jerking a towel from the refrigerator handle and wiping the counter, then bending to clean the floor. She pulled the lapel of her cream robe closed with one fist—

He stilled. Looked away, even though she was plenty covered up with the robe over pale blue pajama pants. It had been a long, long time since he'd seen her… like this. At night. In her home.

He sucked in a slow breath.

And here he stood, shirtless, wearing only the shorts he'd worn that day. He had to go… somewhere. Or this would not end well.

Mike turned for the living room.

"Where are you going?"

"Nowhere."

In the living room he pulled his T-shirt over his head and fought his cast through the stretched-out armhole, then stood there and stared blankly at a wall. She hadn't asked him to stay; she'd fought against it. She wouldn't welcome his advances. Nope, not at all, not like other women had.

Meg might be in pajamas—and yes, they might be the most modest pajama-and-robe combo known to mankind—but that didn't matter. She didn't want him here. Didn't want… *him*. Instead, he'd talked her into letting him stay.

For all the right reasons.

He nodded, agreeing with himself. Yes, his reasons had been purely honorable then. But right now…

She'd been his wife. His high school sweetheart. His first love. He'd fallen in serious like with her before he could even drive. Long before he'd gotten up the nerve to ask her for a date.

Any asking he'd do now would get him nothing but a slap to the face.

She doesn't want you here, Connor. She doesn't want you.

"So now what?" he whispered to himself.

"Mike?" Meg called softly.

He blew out a breath, ran a hand over his hair, swallowed, and traced his steps back to the kitchen.

Meg sat in his usual spot at the table, drinking from a coffee cup.

She'd left a second coffee cup by the orange juice pitcher, a vague invitation to join her that he refused to let himself read into.

But a coffee cup? For orange juice? He glanced around her upper cabinets.

"What do you need?"

"A glass."

"Cabinet above the dishwasher."

He grabbed a tall glass and filled it, then joined her at the table. He eyed her mug. "You drink OJ from a coffee cup?"

She shrugged.

"Couldn't sleep, huh?"

"No." She set the mug down and stared at it. "I keep seeing her, lying there all—all beat up like that."

"Not an image you forget."

She toyed with the mug's handle. "You still see Betsy?"

"Yep." He drank long and slow from his glass, watching the window frame's silhouette on her kitchen table fade to nothing as the moon passed behind another cloud.

Too bad the clear image of his sister didn't fade away too.

Meg's voice broke through the memory. "How does something like that happen?" Darkness covered her face, but when she looked up, tear tracts glistened on her cheeks. She shook her head, tangled strands of hair falling across her shoulder. "How does that happen to Dana? I feel so stupid. That dumb softball story—"

"Don't, Meg. I suspected. I should have said something." It had been the same with Betsy, the signs that had dawned on him later, so obvious after he'd found her.

"I've thought of a handful of times I should have known something wasn't right." She dragged her thumb and forefinger across her eyes. "But she seemed happy. She talked about him all the time, about how great he was. I never imagined…"

"I know."

Meg's shiny eyes locked onto him.

He watched her right back, ready to comfort her if she asked.

"Well. Get some sleep, Mike."

"You too."

"You'll never sleep on that couch."

Probably not. "I want to make sure you're safe."

Her mouth curved. "No one's coming here." She pushed her chair back. "And if they do, God's here."

She moved past him, out of sight. He listened to her cup clank against the sink, to her soft footsteps fading away, to a lone creak in the foyer. To the silence that Meg's parting words filled.

Words that disturbed and appealed at the same time.

She trusted God more than she did him.

Was God really that strong?

He watched the silhouetted frame fade away again.

The night dragged on.

Somewhere before dawn, Mike managed to doze with his head propped on the couch's armrest, but when he woke to sunlight streaming in the windows, his neck stung and his arm throbbed.

He stumbled into the kitchen, expecting to find Meg and Terrell, but a quick walk through the downstairs found no one there but himself.

He returned to the kitchen. The microwave clock greeted him.

Not even six-thirty.

"When was the last time I was up this early?" he asked the refrigerator's contents.

After five more silent minutes, Mike left Meg a note saying he'd gone home. He needed a shower and clean clothes and ibuprofen. He couldn't find hers.

Not until he'd showered and dressed and felt the Advil kicking in did the previous evening's thought return to him, the one that had made him drive Meg to Ben's place. There'd been something about the guy's name—hadn't it been different in the article covering his first Triple-A game?

Holding his arm close to his chest, he jogged downstairs where the scrapbook lay open on the coffee table. He flipped through it until he found the article and ran his finger down the yellowing page. There it was—Ben Raines.

Was it a typo? What was his real name? Raines or Reynolds?

He stared out the French doors at the lawn sloping down to the pond. Would Dana know if Ben had ever gone by a different name?

Maybe someone who'd played with Ben.

The thought barely entered his mind before Adam Destin's face flashed before him. Adam's time in the minors corresponded to Mike's years there. And if he remembered right, Adam and Reynolds—Raines, whatever—had played for the same organization.

Had Adam ever crossed paths with Ben?

Mike called Adam, who answered on the fifth ring, his hello groggy and irritated. "Do you know what time it is?" Adam asked.

"You mean your kids aren't bouncing on your bed? Like they did to me when I was there?"

"They know better. Why are you up?"

"Long story."

"Then I don't want to hear it. Too tired."

"Then give me information, and I'll let you go back to bed."

"Fine." Mike heard him flop against his pillows. "Hurry up."

"Did you ever play ball with a Ben Reynolds, probably in the minors?"

Adam repeated the name, then yawned loudly. "Don't think so. I played with a couple of Bens, but not—"

"Who?"

"It's too early for this." Adam blew out a sigh. "I played with Benji Humbrecht before he retired."

Mike remembered Humbrecht enough to eliminate him. "Not him."

"The only other one I can remember was that head case Ben Raines."

Despite that name being in the article, Mike hadn't expected to hear it from Adam. "Who?"

"Ben Raines. He was a pitcher when I was in Triple-A."

"What'd he look like?"

"I don't know—six foot, dark skin, curly hair."

"What color hair?"

"Dark. Black, I think."

"Do you remember his age?"

"Sheesh, Connor. Hold on while I look that up in my diary."

Mike grinned. "I always suspected you of that."

"Yeah, right. Why are you asking this stuff?"

"I thought you didn't have time for it."

"We got in from a road trip last night. I didn't get to bed till three."

"Then you've had more sleep than me. Come on, Adam. How old was he?"

Adam groaned, then was silent for several seconds. "I think he was twenty-six or seven when I knew him."

"You sure about the name?"

"Of course I'm sure—"

"It wasn't Reynolds?"

"Dude. We all made jokes off his last name. When it Raines… Yeah, it was definitely Raines."

Okay then. "Why'd you call him a head case?"

"Because he *was*. I saw him during my first spring training, and I remember hoping he was the best pitcher in the league or I was in trouble. The guy could throw almost a hundred miles an hour, and he had four good pitches. But it didn't take a thing to get in his head. Guys would yell stuff from the dugout, and he'd get rattled. He'd hit batters on purpose, then he'd throw harder and miss his spots. After that, it'd be like batting practice."

"What else?"

"He had a temper like nothing I've ever seen. A few of us used to hang out where he did just to watch him act like an idiot. We thought it was funny until he threw a chair that about took my head off." Adam talked through a yawn. "I think he got arrested after that one. Actually, it was kind of sad. He could have been winning Cy Youngs, you know? But he couldn't control himself. A few times we'd hear that he'd taken things out on his girlfriend, and we'd watch the stands, and she'd be gone."

"Did she press charges?"

"You know, Mike, I forgot to ask him. What's going on?"

"Long story," he repeated.

"Well, I'm awake now."

If Raines had changed his name to Reynolds, there had to be darker secrets in his past than domestic abuse and failed baseball dreams. "It looks like this guy changed his last name, Adam. Can you think of any reason why?"

"No. I only played with him part of a year, and I think halfway through the next season, he was out of baseball."

Mike's home run, most likely.

A whole decade had passed from his and Adam's last memories of Ben. What had happened during that time? "Thanks, Adam. Sorry I woke you."

"You're not gonna fill me in?"

"Later. I've got to make another call."

In the kitchen he flipped through his wallet for the police officer's business card, then stood there, fingering the card. Either he was about to make a fool of himself or he was on to something the police needed to know.

He pictured Betsy. Pictured Dana.

And called the officer's number.

Chapter Thirty-Six

Meg unlocked her kitchen door and walked inside. Somewhere in the house, Terrell's laughter mingled with Samuel's coos, and Meg leaned against her door, soaking in their innocence.

"Meg?" Jill's voice sounded in the family room. She popped her head into the kitchen. "I thought I heard you. How's Dana?"

"Awake. Alert." Meg tossed her purse onto the table and sank into a chair. Amazingly Dana's injuries had consisted of a concussion, some facial bruising, and stitches to the gash on the back of her head. The physical trauma had resulted in no life-threatening injuries.

The emotional damage Dana had yet to deal with.

"Any idea how long she'll be in the hospital?"

"No." Meg closed her eyes at the image of Ben pummeling Dana with those big fists. Why hadn't she left him?

"Is she pressing charges?"

"I hope so. When she gets out, she's staying with family in the city."

"That's a start."

But would it last? A yawn split her face. Five hours of sleep wasn't enough. Thankfully Terrell had slept through everything, waking only as they pulled out of Ben's drive sometime before midnight. Nothing of what she'd seen and experienced would scar him. "Has Mike stopped by?"

"No. He still isn't answering his phone?"

"He's probably got it off so he can sleep." Meg pictured him at the table, the moonlight bright on his face, concern in his eyes. The memory warmed her. He'd been silly to stay at her house, but honestly? She was thankful he'd done it.

Samuel fussed in the family room, and Jill returned there to take care of him.

Meg yawned her way to the front door. She opened it and scanned the quiet, serene neighborhood. Who really knew what went on in their neighbors' homes? Had Dana's neighbors known? If a woman here lived through what Dana had, would Meg be able to spot it?

Mike's black Range Rover turned into her drive.

A smile relaxed her mouth. Even her shoulders eased, and for once Meg didn't fight it. Mike had been safe and strong last night, exactly when she'd needed him.

She jogged down the sidewalk and grabbed his good arm as he closed the Range Rover's door. "Hey."

He flashed her the grin she hadn't seen since his injury. "What's this?"

"Stop it," she said, trying—and failing—to bite back her smile. His eyelids hung low over bloodshot eyes. "You look exhausted."

His nod was weary. "Did you get some sleep?"

"Yes." It hadn't taken long after the orange juice to fall asleep, and she'd slept until Terrell woke her. "I thought you went home and went to bed."

"No. I've been—busy." He looked at the open front door. "Where's Terrell?"

"Inside with Jill. I'll get him."

"No. I don't want him around."

"Why?"

He held up a finger and walked to the front door and closed it quietly. He jerked his head at the side yard and started in that direction.

Meg jogged to catch up.

When she fell into step beside him, he sent her a vacant smile and wrapped his muscled arm around her shoulders, pulling her snugly to him.

Meg caught her breath and, after the briefest hesitation, leaned against him. If she regretted it later, she could always blame it on the day. "Are you okay?"

His voice above her was husky. "I called my sister."

"Betsy?"

"Yeah."

"How is she?"

"She's good."

He removed his arm, lifted his hand to his face. He faked a yawn and rubbed his eyes, but he couldn't fool her. The temptation to reach around his waist and pull him to her was strong. *I know you, Mike.*

And he knew her. Despite their mistakes, they understood each other as well as anyone else on earth did. Divorce couldn't take away the good that had come before the bad.

He stopped her between the house and the bushes separating the Ashburns' lawn.

"What's going on?" she asked.

The muscles in his jaw tensed. "I called the police this morning. At some point, Ben changed his last name, and half an hour ago I found out why. He's wanted for murder."

Chapter Thirty-Seven

Sunlight was fading, but warmth still fell on Mike's face. He adjusted his position in one of the Ashburns' deck chairs and closed his eyes. He could fall asleep and not wake up until the sun went down tomorrow.

Jill's and Meg's faint laughs reached him from the kitchen. After a day like this, laughter was a welcome sound.

Behind him the deck door slid open. Meg spoke, voice soft as if she smiled. "Do you want anything to drink, Mike?"

"No. I'm good." He crossed his ankles and let his head slump to his shoulder. Five minutes, and he'd be out.

The door closed.

His breathing slowed. His whole body relaxed. Make that two minutes.

"You awake?"

He flinched at Clark's voice beside him. "Barely." With one squinted eye he watched Clark lower himself onto another deck chair and stretch out, hands propped behind his head. Mike closed his eyes again. "Is Samuel asleep?"

"Just about." Clark's chair squeaked. "What a day, huh?"

Mike grunted.

"So what'd this guy do? Jill didn't have the details when she called me."

"He killed a former girlfriend's best friend."

"Wow. Do they know why?"

"She talked his girlfriend into leaving him. I guess he told someone he was going to convince the friend to talk his girlfriend into giving him another chance. Doesn't sound like it was premeditated, but no one saw her alive again."

"What about Ben?"

"He emptied his bank accounts before anyone found her. I guess he got himself a new identity and came out here."

Clark's chair creaked again. "You worry about him coming after you or Meg?"

"He doesn't know we found Dana." Knowing Ben Raines, murderer, was loose wasn't going to keep him awake tonight, but he'd enjoy his sleep more when the man was found. He pictured Ben standing on the front step, that smirk on his face. *How are you enjoying the cast?*

"Is your finding Dana all over the news?"

Mike glanced at Clark. "Evidently you don't listen to sports radio."

"I'm a working man."

"Yeah, rub *that* in."

Clark chuckled. "How's the arm?"

"Bearable. I haven't noticed as much pain since this morning. I'm starting cardio workouts tomorrow. Only a week, and I'm turning flabby."

"If you're flabby, I don't want to know what I am."

Mike eyed him as if debating. "Lard ball?"

"Dude."

Mike laughed, then glanced at Clark to make sure he hadn't offended him.

Clark grinned.

Who'd have thought he'd become friends with a pastor?

"So," Clark said, "now that a week's gone by since you were atta—"

"Since my injury." The word *attacked* was not allowed.

"Right. Injury. Do you look at anything differently?"

That was an odd question. "Well." What did he say? "I guess the first thing I've learned is to keep my back to a wall. And that I really need to find a hobby, something one-armed-men-who-don't-want-to-move-because-of-the-pain-it-might-cause-them can do."

"Good luck with that."

"Thank you. What else?" Beyond the trees edging Clark's lawn, an airplane approaching O'Hare Airport lowered its landing gear. The sound of its engines grew after it passed overhead. "I've learned my son doesn't think I can eat with one hand and that it's good for invitations to Meg's."

"I bet you're milking that one."

"She's a better cook than I am."

"Didn't say I blamed you. Anything else?"

Anything else? What difference had this week made on him? He'd been attacked, operated on, and knocked out of his career. Had found a woman beaten by a guy already wanted for murder. And all in less than seven days.

But had he learned anything? "Was there anything I *should* have learned?"

"I don't know. I wonder if living through a week like you've had makes a person examine his life."

"A week like this? You mean this isn't normal?" He dropped his head against the deck chair. "What a relief."

"Do you take anything seriously?"

The words were couched with a grin, but the message was clear. "It's a minor character flaw." Mike smirked. "When things get rough, I turn into Mike Connor, super smart aleck."

Another plane descended with its wheels down.

Mike waited for the sound of its engines to fade before speaking again. "I was like this when I left Meg. For the rest of the season, I was the clubhouse comedian."

"How come?"

Why *did* he gloss over the rough areas in his life? He pictured his first dinner at Meg's house, the way he'd laughed and smiled and pretended her coldness didn't hurt when instead he ached to hold her and tell her how sorry he was. Of course, he'd said he was sorry, but maybe the way he'd said it had not conveyed the remorse he'd felt for years. His life might be completely different had he gone home after that road trip so many years ago.

His throat felt swollen. He cleared it and turned his head toward the bushes that separated Meg's yard from her neighbors'.

Clark shifted. "You okay?"

A comical retort formed on his lips, but this time Mike bit it back. Was he?

No.

"My life stinks."

His chest felt as if it were caving in. Sure, his baseball career was as great as he'd imagined, and the money was crazy. He owned two dream houses, undecorated shells that they were, and sweet cars most men only dreamed of.

But after that, beneath the smile and the jokes, lay the truth that the life he longed for, the life he'd once lived, lay torn apart. And despite reuniting with Meg, despite his growing relationship with his son, he saw no hope for that life to be restored.

What were his options? Start over with another woman?

He'd tried that, had already made the same mistakes, but after all this time with Meg, nothing seemed to be changing there, either. Sure, she'd cuddled up to him this morning, but would she have done that twenty-four hours earlier? No. Would she do it tomorrow? Next week?

The truth was that something was deeply wrong—with him. He could trace every problem in his life back to his own hands. He swallowed. "I wish I could have the last ten years back."

"You'd change something?"

"Try everything. The way I treated Meg—"

"What difference would that make?"

Mike blinked at him. How did Clark—had he said something to make Clark believe Meg was at fault? "How did you know?"

"Know what?"

"About—" He held out his hand, but the action explained nothing. "About Meg. About us."

"I'm not sure I know what you mean, but I do know that anytime we look to people for happiness, they fail us."

"Meaning?"

"Meaning what if you could redo the last ten years? What if you went back to that first day and did everything right? Would that have been enough?"

Ten years ago? Maybe. But what about the next year and the next? Meg had been slipping away. What if he'd been everything she'd wanted? Done everything she'd wanted? Would the outcome have changed?

He pictured himself telling Brooke no, imagined the rest of that year home with Meg, on the road alone, at home alone.

Flat out alone.

Something would still have been wrong.

"You've got a charmed life, Clark."

"Charmed?"

Please. Couldn't the guy see how good he had it? "Yes. Charmed." He scowled at Clark. "I'm jealous, all right?"

"Of what?"

Of everything. A happy home and marriage, a baby boy—

"You want my house, my mortgage, my income? My wife's

kitchen with nineties wallpaper? Maybe the seven years of college bills we had? Or the years of infertility we struggled through? You want that?"

"No."

"Then what?"

His lips tightened over the words. "You're happy."

"What would you do to be happy, Mike?"

Not again. "You're big on the deep questions, aren't you?"

"How do you think I found my happiness?"

Deflecting came too easily. "Don't tell me you sell Amway." He slapped the arm of his chair. "I *knew* it."

"I'm not selling anything, Mike."

Sure he was. Someone was always selling him something. "Go ahead. I don't mind."

Clark eyed him before settling back in his chair. "No, that's all. Just don't turn in easy answers to the hard questions."

Mike waited for more.

There was none.

Instead, Clark tipped his face to the sunset and closed his eyes, hands over his stomach. A glimmer of a smile rested on his mouth. This pastor with the nineties kitchen, the dated home and tight budget—this pastor was happy.

Clark Ashburn had found something that multi-millionaire Mike Connor had yet to find.

Mike tilted his face upward and watched another airplane cross salmon-colored skies. Fine then. From now on, he wouldn't blow off the deep questions.

Chapter Thirty-Eight

Thursday morning Meg sat on the stairs in the foyer, her Bible open to Psalms.

Because Mike had called ten minutes ago. He was on his way with his parents.

O Lord my God, in You I have taken refuge; Save me from all those who pursue me, and deliver me, Or he will tear my soul like a lion, Dragging me away, while there is none to deliver.

Well. Hmm.

Davis and Patty might not tear her soul like a lion or drag her away, but their words probably wouldn't be very pretty.

O Lord my God, if I have done this, If there is injustice in my hands—

The comfort vanished. She dropped her head onto her Bible, groaning. She didn't deserve protection. There was injustice in her hands. She *was* guilty.

She'd kept Davis and Patty from their grandson.

She'd kept Mike from his child.

She'd lived life for herself.

The words she'd thrown at Mike before heading to Ben and Dana's home had replayed steadily in her head. The familiarity of her challenge to their battles in Texas had shocked her and brought her face to face with herself.

And selfishness, for the first time, reflected clearly in her mirror. She'd tended her own desires, had made her own schedule, had not cared about the constant conflict with Mike's job or his frustration with her all-consuming goals. When he'd asked her to slow down and make time for him, she'd told him no. He could wait until her class ended or the project was completed.

But there'd always been another project. Another class.

She'd even used him to fulfill her dreams. Meg groaned, burying her face in her hands. Yes, she'd loved him. Of course she had. But part of her decision to marry him was based on his signing bonus. He could afford her school bills while her parents could not. He could afford her decorating dreams—

Had she really gone into marriage with the sole purpose of taking?

Meg set her Bible aside and rubbed icy hands over her cheeks. How had she never seen this? For years she'd known—*known!*—that Mike had been the problem. He was the one who'd broken their vows.

Now it was hard to ignore that her selfish neglect might have driven him away.

Not that it excused what he'd done. She sniffed. Wiped her nose. No man could justify having an affair on his wife. Abandoning a wife like Mike had.

Still, she felt hollow inside. She wedged her trembling hands between her knees. Was this why God had allowed Mike to find her? So she would finally admit her sin?

Fine. She'd admit it. She'd sinned. Against God, against Mike—

She pictured him grilling ribs, tucking Terrell into bed, and sitting in her kitchen that horrible night, on guard. She closed her eyes, shoulders sagging, grief rising up—

No. Meg shook her head. Forcefully. No, she couldn't allow his kindness to touch her emotions. And she could never tell him what she'd realized about her role in their marriage. Somehow Mike could still weave a magic that captivated her, and if she came to him, sorry about what she'd done...

She straightened her shoulders. Dried her eyes. She couldn't let him get to her. She had to be strong. She had to be tough when Mike and his parents came. She'd show his parents that she and Mike had moved past their hurt and that they should too. She'd treat Mike like a family member, just not a husband. He'd be the man in her life without any attachments and requirements and commitments.

Picking up her Bible, she stood and forced a deep breath. She could do this. She could pretend that those long-ago feelings for Mike weren't ever so slowly coming back to life.

⚬⚭ʘ⚮⚬

Across the coffee table from Meg, Patty and Davis Connor laughed at Terrell's story.

Meg sat on the opposite couch, jaw tight with a feigned smile. How much longer would they stay? They could take Terrell with them if they wanted to. Were they trying to make her uncomfortable?

If so, they were doing a fabulous job of it.

Just out of arm's reach, Mike smiled her way, his look one of conspiratorial companionship. As if she should be enjoying Terrell's time with his grandparents as much as Mike did.

Nope. Not with the coldness they'd shown her when she'd opened her door, their greeting icier than her sidewalk in February.

Of course once Terrell entered the room, they'd became all smiles—the real ones for him, the fake ones for her.

Mike was his usual self, as if he didn't notice the tension. His only unusual action was the brief, one-armed hug he'd given her when he'd entered the foyer.

She'd tried to keep from melting into him.

Especially with his parents watching.

Across the room Davis laughed the hearty laugh Meg had once enjoyed and started on another knock-knock joke that would be new to Terrell only. Mike's parents had aged, moving from their mid-sixties into their early seventies. Davis's hair was a thick white, his fingers gnarled with arthritis Meg didn't remember him having, and Patty, who used to dye her steel-gray hair, had given up coloring it.

Meg peeked at Mike. How would he look with time? She could imagine lines worn into his face, his dark hair changing to salt-and-pepper. He'd be one of those men who still drew attention as he aged, perhaps even more so, with his grin and athletic build, his laughter and friendliness. She imagined his brown eyes turning to hers. How would he look at her twenty years from now? Or forty years, when they were his parents' age?

Or, with Terrell all grown up, would they even know each other?

Meg looked back at Terrell and his grandparents.

Patty watched her.

Meg swallowed. How long had she been looking at Mike?

Patty looked pointedly at Mike and then back.

Too long, evidently.

Heat flashed across Meg's cheeks. "Would anyone like a refill?"

Patty looked at Davis, who was still caught up in telling a joke.

Meg picked up Mike's glass from the coffee table. "More Coke?"

"Yes, thank you." He flashed her a smile, the kind he'd sent her in high school when they approached each other in the hall, the kind that filled his eyes with a glimmer he'd sent no one but her.

Meg's breath caught. Did Mike know what he was doing to her?

In the kitchen, she placed his glass on the peninsula, opened the refrigerator, and pulled the two-liter from the door. She set it on the counter.

Muted voices floated to her.

How much longer could she last? She grabbed the edge of the counter with both hands and closed her eyes. She'd give in to tears if it didn't mean her nose would turn red and expose her.

Another glass clacked on the counter.

Meg jumped. Looked up.

Patty stood beside her, her hands on the base of an empty glass. "Davis would like some coffee," she said, "if you have it."

She should have remembered how much coffee he drank. "Of course." She moved to an upper cabinet, grateful for a reason to keep her back to Patty. Her fingers fumbled through her selection of K-Cups. "I'll bring it when it's ready."

"Thank you."

The click of Patty's heeled shoes approached.

Meg pressed her lips together. How had she missed the woman's entrance?

She forced herself through the motions of making coffee, waiting for harsh words.

Not until the coffee began to drip did Patty speak. "I'd like to know your feelings for my son."

The brown liquid splashed into the mug, not moving fast enough to end this painful conversation. What was she supposed to say? That she was still angry at Mike for what he'd done? That sometimes she imagined them together? That she was falling for his charm all over again?

"I don't know," she finally whispered and knew it was the truth.

Patty stepped beside her. Those dark eyes, so like Mike's, studied her. "Mike says you've done a good job with Terrell."

"Thank you."

Patty shrugged. "They're his words, not mine."

Her manicured nails tapped the countertop.

Did Patty enjoy drawing this out? Why didn't she speak her mind so the rest of their visit could go on without pretense?

"Mike says you go to church a lot."

"Yes."

"Good."

Meg looked up.

Patty stared through the window at the backyard. She tucked a shiny strand of hair behind her ear, running her fingers down its length. "I'd like you to talk with Mike."

"About…"

"About what happened."

Oh no. Meg shook her head, backing away a step. "I can't."

"I would hope you'd try—for Terrell, at least." Patty's gaze was direct, her expression hard. "You were always good for Mike." She tucked more hair behind her ear before turning on her heel. "I'll take a cup too."

Meg leaned against the counter as her former mother-in-law left. What Patty asked her to do terrified her.

Except… Didn't she want to know what had happened to make him leave her the way he had? Didn't she want to know what had changed Mike during those lonely years apart?

Didn't she long to prove to herself that she really wasn't at fault for their divorce? That she hadn't driven Mike away after all?

Meg set the full mug aside and reached for another one. Maybe Patty was right. Maybe talking would heal.

Chapter Thirty-Nine

Thursday afternoon Ben called Ronnie DaVannon from outside a Buffalo Grove Pizza Hut.

He and DaVannon went way back to when Ben was a can't-miss prospect and DaVannon was just figuring out what everyone else knew—that he'd never make it to the majors. DaVannon had leeched onto Ben, the one everyone predicted to be filthy rich in ten years, and Ben allowed it after DaVannon bailed him out of trouble one summer night, his connections invaluable. Even when baseball turned on Ben, he'd kept the guy close, knowing someday he'd need his friend's less-than-savory connections.

Those contacts had been coming in handy.

DaVannon answered on the fifth ring, music blaring in the background. Ben forced friendliness into his voice. "What's up, Big D?"

The music quieted. "You calling on a safe phone?"

"A new cell. Don't worry." Ben glanced around to make sure no one was within earshot.

A handful of cars filled the parking spaces.

He turned his back to the street. "Find anything?"

"Maybe. Same first name or just initials?"

He hated to change his name again, but what choice did he have? And going by another Ben alias might be too obvious. "Initials."

"Okay. Got one—"

"Don't say it."

"Chill, bro. I'm smarter than that. You're nervous—get a drink."

Not until everything was taken care of. A car door slammed behind him, but Ben resisted the urge to turn around. His nerves were on edge, and he was seeing cops in every shadow. "When can I pick it up?"

"When can you get here?" DaVannon's voice turned flippant. "Where you want to be from?"

"Something by you."

"So you're moving to KC?"

"I don't know. Maybe." Only if his life here was over. "I've got some things in the area to tie up." Maybe Dana hadn't pressed charges. Maybe Connor's presence hadn't caused any damage.

"I'll look for you, buddy." The music blared suddenly. "By the way, congrats on the ump, huh?"

"Yeah. Nice job." Who cared about that when his freedom was in jeopardy? "Later."

Ben ended the call, tucked the phone into his pocket. This was the last time he'd change his name. After this he'd be even more careful, even more in control. He'd deal with problems himself, tying off loose ends before they even became loose ends. This was his life, and he was sick of others pulling the strings.

He turned for his car.

A police officer approached from the front of the building, his vehicle big and white behind him.

Ben kept his expression to a passing glance as he walked toward his car.

The footsteps followed. "Benjamin Raines?"

Instinct kicked in.

Ben dashed past his car and around the building, ignoring the officer's shout and pounding footsteps. No way was this cop taking him. He'd fight as hard as he had to, but he wasn't going to jail.

He vaulted a chain-link fence and raced across an overgrown backyard. He crossed an empty residential street, ran into another yard, and climbed over a picket fence into some gardener's paradise. He cut across the grass, keeping himself below the thick shrubs. He slid over a solid wood fence and stumbled through another backyard filled with children's toys.

He kept moving—running, ducking, climbing fences and criss-crossing whenever he could, wondering as he went how they'd known his name.

Connor.

It had to be. He berated himself for telling Connor their connection. No one else knew.

He sucked in air, ignoring the dagger-like pain in his side. Connor was toast.

Chapter Forty

Mike and his parents showed up at church Sunday morning.

Meg forced herself to be pleasant, but having already spent three days around people who were more frigid than dry ice made her eyelids twitch.

And why did Mike continue his church appearances? Sure, Patty and Davis had attended church more often than not, and Mike's lack of church attendance had bothered them. Maybe that was it—he was doing it for them. Maybe once they left he would quit coming.

The thought stopped the eyelid twitch.

On Monday Meg turned her attention to another project, Jill and Clark's kitchen. Late last week they'd received a large gift of money from someone in the church, the accompanying letter telling them to use it on their home in whatever way they wanted. The money was more than enough to gut and remodel Jill's kitchen.

Clark had Monday off, and he, Jill, and Meg spent the afternoon brainstorming on the remodel. Jill had already picked out her dream cabinets, and a trip to a kitchen showroom confirmed that the cabinets fit the budget.

The planning continued through a dinner of Meg's homemade alfredo sauce over fettuccine, garlic bread, and a salad drenched in balsamic vinaigrette. Clark left for a deacons' meeting as soon as they finished eating, but while Samuel sat in his Exersaucer and watched Terrell play with his remote control Range Rover—his latest gift from Mike—Meg and Jill spread out paint chips and fabric swatches at one end of the kitchen table.

They'd narrowed the color scheme to two subtle shades of bluish gray when Terrell drove his Range Rover into the kitchen.

Meg glanced his way. "What do you need, Terrell?"

"Daddy just drove up. Can I open the door for him?"

Surely Mike wasn't bringing his parents over again. "Go ahead. I'll be there in a minute."

Jill watched him leave the room. "Don't look too thrilled," she teased Meg when he was gone.

"It's not Mike. It's his parents. They aren't fond of me."

The front door opened. Mike's and Terrell's voices floated through the kitchen doorway.

"Go on," Jill said. "I'll wait."

"What, no moral support?"

Jill tossed up her hands in fake frustration. "All right."

In the foyer, Terrell spun donuts with the Range Rover while Mike laughed approval, a thick, ribbon-wrapped bouquet of white rosebuds in his hand. He looked up at their approach. "Hey, Jill." His eyes turned to Meg's, warming. He held out the flowers. "These are for you."

When was the last time he'd given her flowers?

She took them, careful not to brush his fingers, and pretended interest in their aroma. The silky buds brushed her nose, her cheeks warming. "Thank you."

"You're welcome." He smiled at her again, then at Jill. "She's been putting up with my parents. They weren't easy on her." He turned his gaze back to Meg. "Thanks."

"No problem." She examined the flowers some more, not daring to look at her friend. Jill was probably giving Mike a thumbs up. "I think I'll put these in water." Meg fled to the kitchen.

Three sets of footsteps followed.

Mike sniffed. "Whatever you had for dinner smells great."

From beneath the sink she grabbed a short, wide glass vase and set it beneath the faucet. "Leftovers are in the fridge. Help yourself."

Mike opened the drawer beside her and pulled out a knife and fork before opening a cabinet and taking out a plate and glass.

"Hmm," Jill said. "I think you've eaten here before."

Meg flashed her a look.

Jill raised her eyebrows in innocence.

Mike opened the fridge. "Like I told Clark, she cooks better than I do. In fact, I should buy her groceries. Speaking of which, can I get your Wi-Fi password, Meg? I do need to order some things."

She gave him her password, fingers floating over the perfect white buds.

He set his full plate in the microwave and started it, then pulled out his phone and tapped away on it.

"You really buy groceries online?" Jill asked. "Don't you want to squeeze all those tomatoes and cantaloupes yourself?"

"And sign autographs and pose for pictures every few feet? No thanks." He wandered to the table where the paint chips, swatches, and sketch of Jill's kitchen lay. "What's this?"

"Meg's designing me a trademark Meghan Connor Designs kitchen."

"Lucky you. When does work begin?"

"We're just starting. It'll be awhile."

"Then Terrell and I will get out of your way." He pulled his plate from the microwave, grabbed his milk-filled glass, and left the room with Terrell.

Jill grinned. "Flowers, Meg?"

Meg flashed her a dirty look. "He was being nice. It was difficult being around his parents. Can we get back to work?"

"You don't want to smell your roses again?"

She did not hear that. Meg seated herself at the table, and Jill joined her, serious at last while they discussed design elements for several more minutes.

Still, Meg found her eyes drawn repeatedly to the cluster of white roses.

He'd remembered that these were her favorite.

What did she do with a man who did all these nice things—when she wasn't innocent in their hurt and rebuffed every kindness?

Why did he keep being so good to her?

Jill left when Samuel's bedtime approached, and Meg packed up the Ashburns' file before cleaning her kitchen.

The last bowl had just gone into the dishwasher and the last counter wiped down when Mike entered with a dirty plate, glass, and silverware.

Oh, did that bring back memories.

"Jill left?" he asked.

"A few minutes ago."

"Hope I didn't mess up your evening." Oblivious, he set the dirty dishes on the counter.

"Did your parents leave?"

He leaned against the counter while she rinsed his dishes. "I dropped them off at O'Hare before coming here. Which means I'm back to cooking on my own again. Well, tomorrow I am."

Somehow she knew he'd end up at her table. She squeezed dishwasher liquid into the machine. "Did you have a good visit?"

"I guess. Actually, can we sit in the living room? I need to prop my arm."

Meg started the dishwasher and followed him out of the kitchen. In the living room, he piled throw pillows at one end of the couch and sat next to them, removing his sling. "Much better," he breathed. His broad shoulders relaxed. "This thing gets heavy."

She sat across from him. "Where's Terrell?"

"Upstairs. I told him to take a bath."

"You—sent him to take a bath?"

"He usually takes his bath now. Right?"

Meg listened for the sound of running water. There it was. "He does." What was the point in reminding him that this was her house? Not his?

He stretched his legs under the coffee table. "Thanks for being nice to Mom and Dad. I tried explaining that this isn't all your fault, but I guess they're still spoiling me."

His words rankled. "They do know you had the affair?"

"Yes, but they don't understand why you couldn't have told them, at least, about Terrell."

She let out a laugh. If only it had been that simple.

"Mom and Dad liked your church, by the way. Mostly."

"Mostly?"

He shrugged. "Too informal, just not what they're used to."

"Ah."

"You've never told me why you've gotten into church so much."

"You think it's too much?"

"Twice on Sundays and again on Wednesdays? What's so thrilling that you'd go that often?"

"Well, sometimes we have jugglers, sometimes comedians, sometimes—"

He smirked.

She smirked back. "It's important because it's a chance to learn more about God."

"You know about God. You grew up in a church."

"No, I didn't know anything. Not really. What I've learned about God here…"

He stared at her, his expression one of confusion.

"It's just different at this church, Mike. You wouldn't understand."

"Try me."

And have him make fun? Like he'd done before? "It's not something you'd understand unless you wanted to."

He leaned forward. "Maybe I do. Maybe I'm ready for a change."

"This isn't something you do when you're bored. It's a way of life. It changes your life."

"Then how's it changed your life?"

How did she sum it up? "It's filled a void, something that's always been missing. I liked our church growing up, but it never satisfied me."

"And this does."

"Yes, but not in a way that works just for me. This is what everyone needs. We're all made to worship God. We can't find our own way—this *is* the way."

"You mean going to church—"

Frustration crept into her voice. "No. Not church."

"Then what? You're talking in circles."

She gritted her teeth, irritated with her inability to communicate. "I'm new at this, all right?"

"Fine. Take your time."

She exhaled. "I go because each service is an hour where I can focus on God, when I can learn more about the Bible and living as a Christian. I know so little compared to most people there. And that's why I want Terrell to go too. Some of those kids have grown up in church. They've memorized the books of the Bible as children."

He wrinkled his forehead. "Impressive."

"See? I knew you wouldn't understand."

"So what if they can memorize the books of the Bible. Do you have to recite that to get into heaven?"

There he went again—everything was a joke. "Forget it, Mike. I'm not going to sit here and let you make fun of something that's important to me."

His eyes widened. "I'm not making fun. I don't understand. Explain."

"No." Mike would never see his need for God, and it would be his own fault. "You mock what I believe every time it comes up."

"I wasn't mocking." He gritted his teeth. "It's a bad habit. I'm sorry. I'm trying—"

The running water stopped.

Meg looked at the stairs. Had Terrell's bathwater been running all this time?

"What do you bet that water is one millimeter from overflowing?" Mike asked.

"Let's hope that's with Terrell in the tub." She jogged for the stairs, grateful for the interruption.

Mike was a hopeless cause. Men like him didn't think they needed anything or anybody. He was faking interest for her.

For the first time Meg felt sorry for him.

Chapter Forty-One

After the near flood in the bathroom, there was no more talk of church, but when Meg entered the auditorium Wednesday night and saw Mike sitting in her usual row, her stomach sank. What was he doing, looking for new material for his jokes?

"There you are," he said, smile bright, when she seated herself in the empty space beside him. "Where's Terrell?"

"He has his own kids' program."

"What's that like?"

"They play games, learn verses and Bible stories."

"And memorize the books of the Bible?"

That did not deserve a reply. Something on the other side of him caught her eye. "What is that?"

"Um, a Bible." He held it up for her to see. It was burgundy and simple, one of those cheap Bibles available in almost every bookstore.

Why had he bought it?

He spoke before she could ask. "How's work going on Jill's kitchen?"

"We're still laying it out." He'd asked that for three days straight. "Why the curiosity?"

His shrug seemed overly careless. "Just want to see it done. That kitchen is bad."

It wasn't that awful—Meg caught her breath. "You sent the money!"

"Shh." Mike shot her a fierce look, then slouched in his seat, glancing around the filling auditorium. No one seemed to be listening. He leaned toward her. "It's not a big deal. I make more than that in one at bat."

True, but he'd never been so generous during their marriage. "That was very nice, Mike."

"Well, I try. And you should let me do something for you too."

Admiration faded to suspicion. "Like what?"

"Expect groceries tomorrow morning."

No problem there.

"And let me watch Terrell at my place while you work. I'm only good for a couple weeks until I start serious rehab, but you might as well use me while you can."

She'd dreaded this next step. "I don't know, Mike."

"What's not to know? I'm his dad, right? And no one takes care of your kid like yourself, no offense to Jill. I can pick him up and drop him off. He'll keep me company while I ride the bike and do other self-imposed torture."

"But I don't know what your house is like."

He stared at her. "It's got four walls and a roof. I insisted."

That wasn't what she'd meant. Sending Terrell to be alone with Mike was a big step. What would he expose Terrell to? What might he do or watch that she wouldn't like?

"Come over tomorrow," he said. "I'll pick you two up and make dinner."

She looked at his cast, then at him. "Dinner?"

"I can grill ribs and—well, I'll figure it out, but there'll be plenty to eat. I'll also give you a tour of my place, after which you may voice your concerns."

"I'm not concerned—"

"Don't lie in church, Meg. Even I know that's got to be wrong."

The drive to Mike's home took twenty minutes, thanks to empty afternoon highways. Mike lived in a town known for its exclusive homes, but the grandeur of the neighborhood he drove through was more than she'd expected. Two- and three-story houses with multiple chimneys and garage doors dotted wide, manicured lawns with manmade ponds in the distance.

"Aren't you a little far from the ballpark?" Meg asked, spotting another six-car garage. The house attached to it looked like a small castle behind its dramatic iron gate and fountain centered in the cobblestone drive.

"This is my off-season place. I've got a condo in Lincoln Park for the season. Since I'm not able to play for a few weeks, I decided to move back here for a while. It's a little closer to you."

He wanted to be closer to her? Why was she touched by that?

He pulled into an S-shaped drive in front of a sprawling mocha-colored brick house built in French Provincial style. Four chimneys rose above the multi-pitched roof, and a massive two-story entryway sat in the home's center, an elaborate chandelier filling the curved window above the double front doors.

Mike parked in front of the four-car garage.

Meg stepped from the Range Rover, imagining what the inside of this amazing house must look like—ornate hardwood floors, marble countertops, vaulted ceilings, at least five bathrooms and bedrooms, and fifteen or more rooms with custom everything. She followed Mike and Terrell, his eyes wide and mouth hanging open, up the landscaped front walk.

She understood Terrell's reaction completely. The house dwarfed even the Layton's McMansion.

He unlocked the double front doors and pushed one open.

Terrell darted inside, halting almost immediately. "Whoa. You could fit ten houses in here."

"I don't know about ten." Mike flashed her a grin and motioned for her to enter.

She did, stepping onto a polished marble floor. Before her, a grand staircase curved up to a second-floor landing supported by matching marble pillars. The opposite wall, other than an ornate carved door which she assumed hid a coat closet, stood bare and empty. Beyond the foyer lay a wide living room.

Mike passed her and tossed his keys onto a side table. "Want a tour?"

"Sure."

He stood beside her and held out his good arm. "This is the living room."

She eyed its sparse décor, a black leather couch and matching chairs surrounding a glass coffee table that disappeared into the expensive but bland winter-white carpet. Even the fireplace faded into the white wall.

"Back here's the kitchen."

Meg followed Terrell and Mike past a staircase tucked behind the living room's fireplace and into another white room, saved by dark-stained cabinets. More marble countertops blended into the walls and tile floor, but the deck doors at the far end of the room let the view of the pond and green outdoors invade the stark interior.

Mike led them through a barrel-ceilinged butler's pantry that connected the kitchen to the formal dining room and from there to the two-story family room with more views of the pond in the distance. French doors on the other side of the living room led to a library with polished oak bookshelves lining the walls. Most of the shelves were bare, but the lack of white walls made her label this room the most welcoming so far, despite the room giving the impression that Mike was about to move.

No wonder he spent so much time at her house.

She followed him downstairs to a walk-out basement, one wall filled with paned windows and French doors. But the room lacked appeal with the massive television screen and white built-ins, filled as they were with Mike's baseball awards, framed photos, and memorabilia. Mike's exercise equipment at the other end of the room did nothing to warm the space.

The second floor was more of the same. Meg had seen many well-designed houses buried beneath furnishings. But this one—anorexic described it best.

And, surprisingly, she'd seen none of the furnishings they'd fought over in the divorce. Maybe all of that was at his Lincoln Park condo?

"Is this the first single-family home you've owned?" she asked as they returned to the first floor.

"Yeah. After the townhouse, I lived in a high rise, but I decided I wanted something where I could walk in and out without having to say hi to anyone if I didn't want to." He stopped at the edge of the living room and looked around.

Did he see the same white-out she did?

Mike turned. "Let me get the grill going."

Meg followed him and Terrell through the kitchen to the deck. Jewel-green grass spread before her, the backs of other massive homes dotting it, the sky above a brilliant blue with little lamb clouds floating past.

Mike opened the door to a storage space built into the house and, with one hand, lifted a large, unopened charcoal bag as if it were nothing, his T-shirt stretching across his chest.

Meg caught her breath. Looked away.

He'd been strong back when they'd been newlyweds. But he'd still been a kid, basically. An eighteen, nineteen, twenty-year-old kid.

Not anymore. Not even close.

She peeked at him.

He frowned, concentrating as, with one hand, he tugged the opening strip off the top of the charcoal bag. His dark hair was getting long across his forehead, the stubble he'd returned from Kansas City with thickening into a rather appealing beard he kept short.

What would that feel like beneath her hand?

Stop it, Meg.

Swallowing, she focused on Terrell, running the length of the deck. "You use a charcoal grill?"

"Not usually." He dumped briquettes into the grill. "But I like ribs best over charcoal."

"What else are we eating?" There. She was fine. Back in control of herself again. "Or should I fill up on ribs?"

He grinned, piling the briquettes. "No need. I picked up a broccoli salad, Jell-O for Terrell—"

She stuck out her lower lip, mimicking Terrell. "I like Jell-O too."

"I'll let you have some if you're nice to me."

"Forget it."

Mike jerked his gaze up from the grill. "What?"

She laughed, waving a hand at him. "I'm kidding. Continue."

"Oh." He lit the mound of charcoal. "So the Jell-O is still just for Terrell, and I also bought corn on the cob and cornbread."

"No dessert?"

"I'm getting there." He stepped back as flames leaped from the grill. "How's strawberry pie sound?"

"Perfect. You know, for having one arm"—*one very strong arm*—"you throw together a pretty good meal."

"Thank you." He raised his eyebrows at her, his smile bringing back a dimple and carving those attractive lines around his mouth. "Maybe we should do this again sometime. Just you and me."

The idea appealed. *He* appealed. Meg shrugged, then smiled at him, ready to stop fighting his pull. "Maybe."

Chapter Forty-Two

When Mike came in after the fire died down, he found Terrell spinning in circles and Meg standing before one of the family room windows.

Terrell staggered toward him. "Dad, can I watch something on that big TV downstairs?"

Mmm, alone with Meg. "Go ahead, but don't touch anything else down there."

"I won't." He tripped off in the general direction of the stairs.

"What are you going to watch?" Meg called.

"There's a ballgame on MLB Network," Mike said.

Terrell nodded, still stumbling over his feet.

"Are you sure he'll be all right?" she asked.

He seated himself on the blue sectional where he could see the grill through a window. "Baseball on a TV that big? He'll be entertained for hours."

She stood silently until Terrell's footsteps faded. "You have a beautiful view."

"You should see it with a layer of snow."

"You really live here during the off season? No home in Arizona where you can golf every day?"

"I don't want to go to Arizona until I have to."

"Why not?"

That's right—she didn't know. He swallowed and made a play at nonchalance. "I guess the northern boy in me needed seasons. I grew up here—before we moved to Dixon, you know? The suburbs, the winter, the snow… I missed it."

She sat on the other end of the couch, giving him a view of her profile.

Mike rested his ankle on his knee and sat back, content to watch her for as long as she let him. She seemed different somehow. Softer, gentler.

"How long have you lived here, then?"

"Bought it the November after I was traded."

"You must have paid a fortune."

He was still paying a fortune. "Let's just say I have a mortgage."

"Ouch."

"Yeah. It's a custom build I bought from a guy who got transferred to New York partway through construction. That's why it's all white—that, and I've been too busy to get it decorated."

"It's an impressive house. My home must look paltry to you."

Was that what she thought? "Meg, your house is beautiful. My place looks great on the outside, but the inside—I don't have a clue what to do." But she would. If he asked, would she decorate this beast for him? This, and the one downtown?

"Mike, I have to ask." She studied him, curiosity and apprehension mixing in her eyes. "I haven't seen a single thing I recognize."

"Like what?"

"Everything you took in the divorce—none of our things are here."

No. Panic raced through his chest. *Oh, no, no, no.* Why hadn't he thought of that? Of course she'd look for items she'd chosen for her home.

"Mike?"

His foot slid from his knee. He leaned forward, rubbing his forehead. He'd treated her terribly. And now, when she seemed more receptive, he would ruin it.

He clenched his jaw. He did *not* want to talk about this. She'd be mad. Worse, she'd be hurt. The truth would destroy them.

Again.

"Mike." Tension pinched her voice. "Tell me."

"You won't understand."

"Give me a chance."

What chance did he have? If he refused, she'd be angry. If he told her, she'd be angry. He'd lose every bit of momentum, no matter what he did.

He ground his teeth together. This was unfair—to both of them. His hand formed into a fist, and he knocked it against his cast. "They're... I don't have them anymore."

Her eyes showed surprise.

She had to be remembering the way he'd fought her over every table, chair, lamp, and rug. And then she'd agreed to a money settlement and left. He should have known something wasn't right, but he'd been too busy laughing her out of the state.

"Where are they?"

"Meg, this was so long ago—"

"What did you do with *our things*?"

He stared at the wooden beams of the ceiling. Hard to believe that a month ago he'd wanted to rehash all this with her. He knew now nothing good could come of it. "After the divorce—" He cleared his throat. "Brooke wanted to get rid of it, said we needed a fresh start. So we bought all this ridiculously expensive stuff that never looked half as good as what you picked out."

She stared at him, her face as hard as a boulder. "You got rid of it."

His neck muscles tightened. "I sold some of it." He'd never tell her he'd curbed a portion, watching from the window as rain ruined her chaise lounge.

"You fought me for things that meant nothing to you? You took them just to hurt me?"

"Meg, we're not the same people anymore."

She sniffed as if that were up for debate and leaned back on the couch, arms and legs crossed. Her toes tapped the tufted ottoman, then stilled. She pulled her foot back from the ottoman as if it were contaminated.

He read her thoughts. "None of this is from Brooke."

Her green eyes sparked. "You get rid of her things too?"

"No."

She raised an eyebrow, her head cocked.

"She wanted everything, and I wanted to be done with her so—" He shrugged. "I let her take it. Good riddance."

"Good riddance? Is that how you view people?" She gave a half-hearted laugh. "Everyone's here to serve you, and when you tire of them, you throw them away."

What did she know? "Get your facts straight, Meg. Brooke dumped me."

Meg glared at him.

"And just so you know, I got a big dose of what I did to you. Hope that makes you feel better." The clichés kept coming, but he couldn't help himself. "You don't have to say it—I'm sure it was what I deserved."

"Must have been horrible then," she snapped.

"The worst break-up I've been through. Happy?"

She stared at him. Then slowly she unfolded herself from the couch. Arms across her chest, chin up, she walked to the window, body straight as a pole.

Mike rolled his eyes. Warm and flirting one minute, cold and angry the next. What had her ticked off this time?

When she spoke, her hand muffled her words. "How many break-ups have you been through?"

"I don't keep track. Do you?"

She faced him, her jaw tight. "I was your first girlfriend, Mike. And then your wife. *You* dumped *me*. Of course Brooke dumping you would be worse. Unless Brooke wasn't the last woman. Was she?"

"Of course not. When did I say I never dated after Brooke?"

Her mouth shook.

"You thought I'd been alone for six years?"

"Like I have?"

In six years, she'd never dated?

"I'm curious, Mike. Have you even lived here alone?"

His chest ached. His throat burned. He couldn't tell her. He forced himself to stand, his knees fighting him as if he'd aged suddenly. "Meg—"

She dashed into the kitchen.

"Meg!" Mike ran after her, holding his cast against his chest. He caught up with her halfway through the living room, grabbing her upper arm. She tried to pull free, but he held her close, cradling her against him. "Stop it!"

She did, every bit of fight leaving her. Tears streamed down her cheeks, and she lowered her head until he couldn't see her face.

He hunched before her, hoping she would look at him.

She turned away.

He fought to keep his voice calm. "You can't run off, Meg. What will you tell Terrell?"

"I don't care anymore." She wiped her eyes, but more tears flowed. She pushed at his hand, her fingertips damp. "Let me go."

"Only if you sit down."

"Why? There's more?"

"No." Nothing he wanted to relive. "I want to know why you've been alone."

He loosened his grip, and she jerked away, crossed the room, and dropped onto the couch. Her eyes fell to her lap where she toyed with her fingers. "I just have," she said at last.

"So in six years no one's asked?"

She didn't answer.

That's what he thought. He seated himself across from her. "Why'd you say no?"

"Why would I say yes, Mike?"

Her words jabbed at his conscience. "You can't judge every guy by me."

She shrugged. "I learned I couldn't judge a man at all. I never thought—" She shook her head. "I can't risk that again. It was too…"

The damage he'd laughingly inflicted had cut deeper than he'd imagined. Mike saw himself sitting across from her in a conference room, tipping his chair back while their lawyers talked. Back then he'd almost laughed at the emotions playing across her face. The more he'd hurt her, the better.

He wished he could grab that Mike by the throat.

But he *was* that Mike. Just as Meg couldn't separate him from the past, he couldn't separate that Mike from himself. He rubbed the back of his neck. Meg was right. How could she trust him? Why should she?

"No answer? No excuse?" She spoke without looking up. "You actually surprise me."

"Do you know how many times I thought about looking for you but were sure you'd be married?"

"I thought you did look for me."

How many feet could he put in his mouth? "I asked around."

"Around?"

"The other guys' wives, girlfriends, people I thought you'd keep in touch with. When no one knew where you were… I figured nothing I could say would bring you back."

"What about people in Dixon?"

He pinched the bridge of his nose. "I didn't want to face your parents."

Her gaze returned to her lap. Her shoulders slumped.

She couldn't have looked any more defeated when she'd buried her mom and dad.

"Meg, I can't explain the way I acted." He prayed she'd have mercy and listen. "I was horrible to you. I was wrong, and every day I live with my guilt. Nothing I do makes it go away."

She wiped more tears, gaze never leaving her lap.

Was there no end to the mess he'd started? His nose tingled, and he rubbed his eyes, forcing his emotion inside. "More than anything, Meg, I want to make up for what I did."

He waited.

Nothing.

"I've tried everything I know of to show you I'm different. I need you, Meg. I've known that for years. I've tried to move past you, but I can't."

She sniffed. "How did you find me? After that day at the stadium? How did you find me so fast?"

She wasn't listening. And she knew so little. What would happen if she knew it all?

He forced himself to his feet, one foot moving ahead of the other until he reached the kitchen. His wallet lay on the island, and he picked it up and pulled her business card from it, pausing to read the words across the back. *She's incredible. You'll love her.* He tossed the wallet onto the countertop and retraced his steps to the living room.

He had loved her. He *did* love her.

Now he'd killed any love she'd had for him.

He handed her the card, then crossed to the recliner and sat. He propped his ankle on his knee and toyed with the sole of his sandal, willing himself to stay together.

"Where did you get this?"

"From a friend."

"Who?"

He gave the name immediately, hoping she wouldn't guess at the relationship. "Sara Rolen."

She flipped the card and read the handwriting on the back.

"If I'd never seen you at the stadium, that card would have led me to you eventually."

She ignored his words. "Your friend Sara hasn't been gone that long, has she?"

He dropped his head into his hand. What was the use? He'd charmed her before, but Meg wasn't sixteen anymore. She didn't need him—just when he'd realized how very much he needed her.

Wasn't there some way he could open himself up so she could see?

"I'm sorry, Meg." He stared through the coffee table at the white carpet below. "I can't even tell you how sorry I am."

Chapter Forty-Three

On Sunday, Meg stood outside Clark's Sunday school classroom, almost oblivious to kids running past her and adults greeting each other.

Mike sat inside the room. For the moment he was alone, head bent over the morning's handout. Last week, with his parents in town, he'd only come for the worship service. But here he was again, and people would expect her to sit beside him, all smiles and goodness.

After what she'd learned, how could she?

The realization that Mike had not truly looked for her stung. There'd been no money sacrificed to find the wife he'd thrown away, no pride set aside. He'd moved on—with other women.

And she'd talked to one of them. Liked her, even. Just before Valentine's Day, Sara Rolen had called. She'd asked about Meg's decorating strengths and philosophy, and they'd talked for thirty minutes. Meg had actually *enjoyed* the conversation. Sara had seemed to enjoy it too.

As much as Thursday's revelation hurt, Meg was better for it. She had a clear idea now of the life Mike had lived, and while she acknowledged her part in the failed marriage, she still placed the brunt of the blame on him. She might have driven him away, but he'd been too eager to go.

And so the fault fell to him.

Today marked Mike's fifth time in church in four weeks, easily a decade-best, despite the off-season when three Texas teammates, Adam included, got married. Mike sipped home-style orange juice while the classroom filled. He'd first attended to make sure Meg hadn't fallen into a cult. Instead, the things he'd heard left him thinking.

Did he believe in God? Of course. Mom and Dad had taken him to church often enough to establish that, but he'd never seen God have an impact on how people lived like he saw in Clark and Jill. Even Meg. It only made sense, though. If God were real, shouldn't he have an effect on the people who believed in him? And wouldn't that mean there were guidelines to live by?

All he knew was that the way he'd lived these last ten years had not brought him peace. With baseball success came a never-ending, nightmarish pressure to keep performing, to stay ahead of every upcoming centerfielder in the team's system. The pay provided luxuries, but more than one relationship had been based on his wealth.

Everything he'd dreamed of in high school and the minors failed to create the satisfaction he'd expected. The money, the endorsements, his homes, his cars, the fame—how could so much feel so little?

He rolled up the handout and smacked his palm with it.

Then there was Meg, whom he couldn't seem to fix anything with. She'd withdrawn after their argument, as timid as if he'd struck her and she could not believe it.

He closed his eyes, shocked at his comparison. Was he any better than his sister's ex?

He ran his hand through his hair. Meg had barely spoken to him over the weekend. Whenever she'd caught him watching her, she'd busied herself with something else or gone into another room. More than once he'd walked into her kitchen to find her standing before the bank of windows, arms wrapped around herself, staring in the direction of the Ashburns' backyard.

What was she thinking about?

During each relationship after Brooke, Mike had not considered himself betraying Meg again, but evidently she did. She acted as if he'd left her not once but—

A heavy sigh came from the aisle.

He looked up to see Meg.

"Morning," she said.

Had she dropped the *good* to keep from lying?

Her green eyes sat heavy in her face as if she wasn't sleeping. She nodded at the empty seat beside him. "May I sit here?"

"Sure." He fumbled for his Bible and slid over.

She seated herself and crossed her legs, arranging the folds in her dress.

He hadn't expected this. He hadn't even come to see her, not today. But it was nice to sit beside her, even if she was ignoring him. He leaned closer, her perfume filling his senses. "Meg, you don't have to sit with me if you don't want to."

She spoke to hands folded in her lap. "People would ask why."

And she didn't want to explain.

Fine. As long as she sat beside him, he'd enjoy it. She looked great. Her honey-blonde hair curled across her shoulders and down her back. And her reddish-pinkish dress—no, Meg would come up with some unique name for it. He pursed his lips. She'd call it raspberry or something like that. Whatever it was, the color brought out the pink in her skin and left her looking soft and feminine. He clasped his hands together, remembering how good it used to feel to put his arm around her and tell people she was his wife.

He cleared his throat.

Her gaze flicked toward him and then away as the class started.

After a short prayer, Clark began with a Bible reference he asked everyone to look up.

Mike flipped pages, annoyed with the crackling of his new Bible. And with his slowness in finding the reference.

A man in the back read the verse, and Mike gave up looking. Showoff. He'd have found it himself. Eventually.

"Let's review last week's lesson," Clark said from his stool behind a small podium. "What did we say meekness was? Being a wimp?"

The class remained silent.

"No. Let's take Mike for example."

Mike jerked his head up from somewhere in Isaiah.

"I think we all know what Mike does for a living." Clark sent him a smile as the class chuckled. "If Mike had walked into church this morning wearing his uniform with a glove tucked under his arm and an award or two in his hands, we could say he was not exhibiting meekness. Why? Because he would be flaunting his success as a baseball player. And that's a very modern way to define meekness—if you've got it, *don't* flaunt it." Clark's gaze swept the room. "We defined meekness as a spirit not occupied with itself but fully committed and subordinate to Christ."

Why wouldn't he flaunt what he had? Mike glanced at Meg who wrote the definition on her handout. Of course, look what had happened when he'd shown off his house.

Clark asked the class to turn to another verse, and Mike fumbled through the pages before giving up and searching the Table of Contents for Colossians. Maybe there *was* something to being able to recite the books of the Bible in order.

Not that he'd admit that to Meg.

Clark moved to love, the day's topic, but it was not what Mike expected. Instead Clark talked about different types of love. "Agape love is a love that comes from your head," Clark said, writing the foreign word on the white board. "Sometimes it goes counter to your emotions. You may not feel like it, but you love anyway. It's a choice. In fact, this is the way a husband is told to love his wife. He makes that conscious decision to do it, no matter how he feels."

The Bible told him *how* to love his wife? Strike two then. Mike glanced at Meg, who stared unseeing at her handout. She must be thinking how horribly he'd failed. Everything here made him look completely flawed.

Clark asked the class to turn to another verse, but Mike didn't bother. He flipped through the surrounding pages. If the Bible could point out where he'd blown it, maybe it could show him how to fix it.

It was a thought.

Chapter Forty-Four

The last week of June felt like Chicago's dog-days of summer had arrived early. High heat and humidity left Mike's injured arm damp and aromatic. The old pain was gone, but the new pain of fatigued muscles replaced it as each day he worked out with Carter, one of the team's strength and conditioning coaches.

The work gave him time to think, and recent threatening letters filled his mind. After the first one, a photocopied article about his separated shoulder four years ago, he'd assumed some joker thought reminding him of his past injuries was funny.

But that type of mail usually came with a moronic message from someone who didn't know which end of the bat to hold. The more he thought about it, the more the absence of an in-your-face message made him uneasy. And when the second envelope arrived with a blown-up copy of the photo showing him writhing on the ground seconds after the injury had happened, his unease increased.

Was Ben sending these? A week ago, a police detective had called about a binder they'd found in Ben's house, a binder containing an alphabetized list of former ballplayers, managers, coaches, and himself. His name was crossed off—as were a few others whose lives had recently gone through upheaval, some even death. Should he feel relieved that he lived? Or worried that Ben might not be done with him?

The timing of the letters could be a coincidence.

Either way, it would not ruin his day. Other things demanded his thoughts.

Like Meg.

Nothing had changed in the week since she'd visited his house. Like the thunderstorm building in the west, there had to be some storm brewing in her. Meg couldn't go on like this. Something would give.

Another scenario he shouldn't think about unless it happened.

On Thursday morning, his long cast was removed and replaced with a short one. Most of his forearm was still encased, but with his elbow exposed, he could begin rehabbing that joint, regaining strength and movement there before the rest of the cast came off in three weeks. Carter wasted no time working the elbow muscles, and before Mike left for Meg's house, he downed a few Advil, praying it'd take the edge off.

Rehab stunk.

The medicine had yet to help by the time he pulled into Meg's drive. He walked to her back door, studying the distant western sky where gray clouds massed. The predicted storm was on its way.

Through her screen door, he could see Meg seated at the kitchen table, papers spread around her, head bent low and her hair about to drag a magazine clipping to the floor.

At his knock, she jumped, the clipping beginning its lazy freefall.

She sighed when she saw him. "I thought you weren't coming till later."

Oh no, the pleasure was all his. He swallowed his irritation while she let him in. "The weather's so nice I thought we should enjoy it." He forced a smile. "How about a couple of hours at the lake?"

"Lake Michigan?" She looked at him as if he was crazy. "It's supposed to storm."

"Yeah, but for now it's nice, and I want a break."

She picked up the clipping. "Fine. But you've got to keep Terrell busy tonight. I have to finish this layout."

"Is that for the Ashburns?"

"No. You'll keep him busy?"

He gritted his teeth at her brusqueness. "Whatever you want, Meg."

She took his sarcasm at face value and disappeared into the foyer. She called up the stairs and moments later returned with Terrell tripping on her heels.

"Hi, Dad," Terrell called, flinging himself against Mike's legs.

Mike wrapped his good arm around Terrell's chest and tipped him up over his shoulder.

Terrell squealed and pounded his back.

Now here was a welcome.

"Where's your sling?" Terrell asked once his feet were back on the floor. "And your cast. Did you get a new one?"

"Yep. Got it this morning." Mike squatted so Terrell could reach it easily. "I'll keep getting a new one every few days until I'm better."

"How come?"

"Because I'm working out a lot, and all that sweat stays in the cast since I can't clean my arm. Gets kinda raunchy."

Terrell's jaw dropped. "You don't have to take a bath?"

"Terrell, I shower a few times a day."

"Oh." His face fell. "That's a bummer, huh?"

"It's real rough."

Terrell ran his hand up and down the blue cast. "Why is this cast smaller?"

"So I can exercise my elbow. They took an X-ray of my arm and saw that I'd healed enough for me to start moving my arm."

"When do you start rehab?" Meg asked.

He looked up, allowing himself to find concern on her face. "Already did. Carter said we were starting light, but he lied."

"Are you all right? Terrell, stop that." She flicked Terrell's hand from Mike's upper arm, where his fingers rubbed Mike's skin.

"That's fine. My arms look different, don't they?"

"This one's thinner."

"That's because it's been lazy. Now I have to make it work so my arms match and I don't look like a freak."

Terrell laughed. "You're a freak."

Mike grinned. "No. You're a freak."

"No, you are." Terrell poked his chest. "You're the freak."

"Hey, dude. You're the freak."

Terrell's laugh drowned out Meg's groan.

Within minutes, they were in the Range Rover. Mike backed out of Meg's drive and started east. Dark clouds built in his rearview mirror, and through his open window Mike felt the breeze increase. They'd be lucky to have an hour at the lake, but he'd take it.

He wove around light traffic on the highway and through the forest of downtown skyscrapers until they opened up to Grant Park. He turned south on Lake Shore Drive and drove toward one of the quieter beaches, praying it would be even emptier with the coming storm.

It was.

As they stepped from the Range Rover, the wind whipped Meg's hair. She pulled a ponytail holder from her wrist and secured her hair in a casual knot. A handful of shorter strands escaped, flinging themselves toward her emotionless face.

What on earth was the woman thinking?

Terrell raced across the beach, a purple Frisbee in one hand.

Mike put on dark sunglasses and an old John Deere hat that Meg's father had given him years ago as a joke. Between the hat and the sunglasses, no one should give him a second look.

"Dad! Catch!"

Terrell launched the Frisbee toward Mike, but the wind caught it and pulled it toward the water. Mike sprinted after it. Between Terrell's skill level and the wind, he'd get another workout.

Mike picked up the Frisbee and flipped it at Terrell before glancing up the beach.

Meg sat on a beige blanket, arms wrapped around her legs. She stared straight ahead.

Mike followed her gaze. Nothing but water.

"Dad!" Terrell hollered.

Mike looked back to find the Frisbee magically on course. It caught an updraft, and he leaped and nabbed it with his fingertips, pulling it in to his palm.

Terrell whooped and applauded.

Meg woke from her trance to glance their way.

This time he purposely tossed the Frisbee beyond Terrell, and while Terrell chased it down, Mike watched her. He couldn't leave her sitting alone, not when her depression was partly his fault. He had to fix it. "What do I say?" he asked, then frowned when he realized whom he'd turned to.

Why not? None of his own ideas worked.

What do I do, God?

Last Sunday he'd discovered the concordance in the back of his Bible and searched it for verses dealing with husbands and wives. A handful pointed out what he should have done the first time around. One verse even said a man was to love his wife as Christ loved the church, which had been to the point of dying for it. Having to die for Meg was unlikely. But loving her selflessly, serving and protecting her—he was willing to try.

The Frisbee crashed yards to his left. Mike jogged to it and dusted it off. "God, I'm sorry."

The simple words weren't enough. Was God even listening?

I didn't know what would happen. I didn't know how much I would hurt Meg and Terrell and myself. Help me.

Please.

By the time Terrell tired of the Frisbee, dark clouds hovered behind the downtown skyline. Terrell decided to build a sand fort, and Mike walked to Meg, the sand dry between his toes. She didn't move, and with sunglasses covering her eyes, he couldn't tell where she was looking or what mood she was in.

Although he could probably guess.

He sank down beside her and tossed his hat and sunglasses at his feet. "How are you?"

"Fine." She nodded at the hat. "That's not—"

"The hat from your dad. Comes in handy. People here don't pay attention to anyone wearing John Deere hats."

She nudged it with her flip-flop. "Looks like you've used it a lot."

"That, and it's how many years old?"

He left silence for her to fill, but she kept her face on Terrell and the water.

"Meg." He leaned back on his elbow, waiting until she turned her head. "How long has it been since your parents—since the accident?"

"Four years in November."

"How often do you visit the farm?"

"Never. I sold it."

She'd sold it? She loved that farm. In Texas, she'd talked about it so much that he'd used it as one of his excuses when he left her—he wanted someone who appreciated civilization, not the smell of manure or a stroll through cornfields. "Who bought it?"

"I don't remember. I had a lawyer out there deal with it."

"You didn't go yourself?"

She pulled in a deep breath. "I didn't want someone we both knew to see me."

Her words punched him. She'd been alone for six years because of him. She'd sold her childhood home because of him. What else had she endured? Because of him?

He didn't want to think about the damage his actions had caused her, but now he couldn't stop. What he'd thought would be an innocent flirtation had destroyed her marriage, kept her from her family, forced her to carry the weight of single parenthood, and left her leery of him and men in general. Guilt stacked on top of guilt, and the weight seemed as real as the weights he'd used that morning.

He had to *do* something.

He sat up. "Meg, I'm sorry about last week."

A long chunk of hair fell from the top of her head and flapped in the wind.

"I assumed you knew I'd dated other women—"

Her head whipped in his direction. "You want to talk about it? Didn't you say a few weeks ago that you wanted to tell me everything?" She held out her palm. "Spill away. I'm ready."

No, she wasn't. She'd never be ready.

"Go ahead. Tell me what life's been like. Tell me how much fun it was."

"It wasn't." His voice was hoarse, and though he cleared his throat, nothing changed. He rested his arms and forehead on his knees. "I don't want to talk about it."

"I don't care, Mike. You owe me the truth."

She'd hate the truth.

"I want to know if you ever remarried."

That wasn't a question he'd expected. "No."

"Did you come close?"

She was digging deep. Resignation settled over him. "Yes."

A wind gust swept the beach.

Mike closed his eyes too late.

"What happened?"

He blinked repeatedly, his eyes watering at the grains of sand lodged there. He'd willingly rub handfuls of the stuff in his eyes if she'd stop asking questions. "She broke it off."

"Why?"

"I don't want to talk about this."

"I don't care what you want!" She faced him again. "You never told me why you left, and I want to know. I've lived all these years thinking I was a failure somehow. I don't care how much I'll be hurt. I want the truth."

She was right. He couldn't leave her guessing. "Fine." His agreement lodged in his throat. "Ask your questions."

"Where did you meet Brooke?"

He covered his head with his hands and spoke to his knees. "At a bar during spring training. You were back in Texas."

She seemed to ignore his last sentence. "Why her?"

"You want the truth, Meg? No matter what?"

"Yes."

"I was lonely. She paid attention."

He waited for a reaction—anger that he'd blame her or denial that she'd neglected him—but none came.

Only the wind reacted, a gust whipping his shirt against his back.

"When did it end?"

"March, I think."

"Why?"

"Because she found someone else. From what I've heard, she's made a living off dating professional athletes. I was the first."

"What about the one you almost married?"

He gritted his teeth, hating the direction of her questions. "What about her?"

"How did you meet her?"

"During my last rehab."

She turned her head to him, but Mike could see nothing behind the glasses. He resisted the urge to pull them off.

"Are you sorry you're not with her?" she asked.

"No."

She kept her face to his, obviously waiting for more, but he kept silent. She was asking the questions. He wouldn't volunteer anything.

"Why not?"

"Why not what?"

Her mouth tightened. "Why don't you regret that breakup?"

"Because we weren't right for each other."

She looked back at the lake. Swallowed once, twice. When she looked down at her legs and rubbed her hands on her shorts, it signaled some disastrous question was coming. He licked his lips, blurting whatever came to mind. "Do you know I can still picture the first time I saw you?"

She pulled the elastic from her hair and busied herself finger-combing her hair.

"I saw you the second you walked into biology class. You walked across the room and up the aisle and sat right in front of me."

"It was the only seat left."

"I couldn't take my eyes off you." He touched the hair ponytailed in her hands, ignoring how she leaned away, elbows out to ward him off. "Your hair was so long, so pretty. You had some fake, hot-pink flower pinned in your hair. The way you walked, the way you held yourself—I never thought I'd get someone like you to notice me."

"I wish I hadn't."

Her words closed his eyes. She was sorry she'd married him.

He was sorry he'd let her go.

"Mike, how many—how many women?"

His fingers clenched. "Aww, Meg."

"I want to know. How many?"

Didn't she understand all of *that* was over? He toyed with his thumb, tugging at a hangnail until it bled. The pain gave him a mental excuse for the moisture in his eyes. "Not—it's not like you think."

"How many?"

"Not that many."

She gave a soft laugh. "That's relative, isn't it?"

He couldn't look at her. He wiped the blood across his knee and stared at the water crashing against the dark sand. "After Brooke, there were five."

"Five," she repeated. "So six total."

Six. He nodded, unable to speak. Such a small number—Will would laugh—yet it sickened him.

She heaved a sigh. "I guess… considering—I mean, all week I've wondered…"

Blood pooled along his thumbnail and skin. He watched the blood turn at the base. Whatever wrath she unleashed was less than he deserved. He tilted his thumb and watched blood slide beneath his nail.

"For all I knew," she said, "you could have had another child somewhere, but I told myself you'd—"

His spine locked at her words, his back rigid, breath on hold. The pain slashed through him as torturous as that first time. A guttural moan fought past his lips, and Mike covered his mouth with his hand.

"Oh no. You do."

He closed his eyes as heat seeped out and down his face. He wiped it with the back of his fist, and when he looked down, the blood on his thumb had transferred to the inside of his fingers.

Beside him, the wind carried Meg's aching voice away. "You have another child."

"Not on this earth." He swallowed the sting the words brought. "It was after Brooke left. Another woman. Just a stupid, meaningless…" Anguish choked him. "I called after a road trip. Her sister was there—said she wasn't well."

Twenty feet away, Terrell smoothed the crumbling mound of sand.

Mike pictured another child hunched beside him. "I went to see her. She was a mess. I had to take her to the hospital. They told me she was suffering complications after the—after—"

A sob shook him. "She did it while I was gone. Never told me. Never gave me a choice. I wanted to kill her."

The familiar burn flooded him again. He'd done so much wrong. He'd hurt so many people, had caused so much irreversible harm to so many. Raindrops pelted his back, but Mike let them. He was worthless. All he'd ever done was ruin things.

Beside him, Meg struggled to her feet. She tugged one corner of the blanket. "Get up." Tears choked her words. "Get off my blanket."

Chapter Forty-Five

Severe storms pounded the northwest suburbs until midnight, but when Meg woke Friday morning, the sun shone in a brilliant blue sky.

Meg moved through the day as if yesterday's clouds still surrounded her. Even preparing for an afternoon design pitch could not force away memories of the awful beach conversation.

By the time she returned home with the go-ahead on a basement remodel, her neck and back ached. Terrell had spent the day at Jill's, and Meg called to let her know she was back.

"Come on over," Jill said. "Clark's gone, Samuel's napping, and Terrell's in the middle of *Monsters, Inc.* Bring whatever you've got for a salad, and we'll eat here."

The plan appealed. Meg scrounged up a bag of lettuce, croutons, and two dressings before wandering to Jill's house. Anything more required brain cells.

Jill emptied her hands at the back door. "Lettuce and stale bread isn't going to cut it. Let's see what else I've got."

Meg leaned against Jill's chipped laminate countertop as Jill added the food to bowls of cherry tomatoes, freshly cooked bacon, and pungent blue cheese, Jill's salad staple. Meg dropped her cheek into her palm and closed her eyes. "Sorry. I'm on zombie mode."

"How'd your meeting go?"

"They hired me."

"Congratulations. What are you doing?"

She opened her eyes. "A basement in Barrington."

With no warning, Jill tossed her an egg, then another.

Meg caught them against her chest, relieved that they didn't crack down her front.

Jill laughed at her. "They're hard-boiled. Peel them, and I'll chop them up."

She sniffed. Yes, they were hard-boiled. She tapped the first egg against the counter's edge, and for a minute the only sounds in the kitchen were the running faucet and eggshell cracking.

"Are you making it without Dana?"

Was she? "For now, I guess. I wish she'd come back, but I get it. She doesn't want to be anywhere where Ben might look for her."

"Poor girl. At least she isn't going back to him." Jill rinsed a piece of lettuce. "Where's Mike tonight?"

"At the stadium. The team's back in town." She handed the peeled eggs to Jill without looking at her and busied herself collecting eggshell. Just the mention of Mike, and her eyes were full.

"You okay?"

No. Every part of her wanted to drop to the floor and give up.

"Meg?"

She opened the cabinet beneath the sink and shook the damp shells into the trash. One triangular piece stuck to her palm. She slid her nail beneath it and flicked it into the garbage. "Sorry. I'm fine."

"Liar."

She closed the cabinet door with a bang, softening the action with a smile. "Sometimes I hate how well you know me." She washed her hands. "I don't want to talk about it."

Great. She sounded like Mike.

"I understand. You and Mike are going through a lot. We pray for you two every day."

Words that comforted in the past now grated. "You pray for Mike?"

"Yes," Jill said, dragging out the word. "Don't you?"

"He doesn't deserve it." She shrugged. "Neither of us deserves it. You should stop." She picked up the crouton bag, a salad dressing, and the bowl of tomatoes and walked past Jill to set them on the table.

"What happened?"

"Nothing. I've just decided I don't like Mike." She slid into a chair and folded her hands on the tabletop, meeting Jill's eyes at last.

"That's a change, isn't it?"

"Well…" she hedged. "Maybe it was up in the air before, but now I know. I know I don't." His answers flashed through her mind—the women, their relationships, the role she'd played.

"You found something out, didn't you?"

"I can't talk about it."

Jill sat down opposite her. "As long as you're talking with God."

Talking to God wasn't possible. How could he listen to her? Had he ever listened to her?

Tears threatened, and as she'd done all day, she forced them back. "I'm hungry, and my blood sugar's low. I promise I'll smile after we eat."

"All right. Why don't you pray?"

Not tonight. "You pray."

Jill did, including in her prayer a request for wisdom for Meg and Mike.

Meg's tears escaped. Cascaded down her face.

Jill flew around the table and wrapped Meg in her arms.

Meg rested her head on Jill's shoulder and let the sobs take over.

Everything she'd learned was too much. The fault in their marriage lay at her feet. She'd driven Mike away, and he'd never looked back. He'd turned to other women, and one of them—

"Jill, it's my fault."

"What is?"

"I was so caught up with myself, and I lost him. Because of *me*, he had that affair. Because of *me*, one of them—" The truth gagged her, but she opened her mouth for air, forcing out the horrible words. "She had an abortion."

Her hands were coated with her tears, coated with a child's blood.

"Who, Meg?"

"One of his girlfriends—" The rawness of her words tore through her. From behind her, she heard Terrell run across the linoleum, but she couldn't stop. "Because of me, a baby died."

"Terrell, go back to your movie." Jill's voice was firm. "Your mom will be fine."

What a lie. She'd never be fine.

Terrell must have obeyed because Jill turned back to her. "That's not your fault, Meg."

"Yes, it is! If I had loved Mike, he wouldn't have left. He wouldn't have... have *slept* with that woman. She wouldn't have gotten pregnant, and that baby wouldn't have been killed. How is that not my fault?"

Jill left her chair, returning seconds later with a Kleenex box.

Meg took a handful. "What do I do?" Hopelessness seeped into her words. "How do I talk to Mike? Half of me wants to tell him how sorry I am, and the other half is so mad at him."

"Meg, you did not kill that baby. There's another woman who will answer for that."

"But I started everything."

"You are responsible for your actions, and that's what you need to deal with."

"My selfishness." She wiped her cheeks and nose, her foundation smearing on the Kleenex. "It sounds petty, but that selfishness has done so much."

"That's the way sin works. What starts out tiny grows until it brings consequences. My mom used to say that sin, no matter how little, brings pain."

"But for how long? When does it stop?"

"Some of that depends on you, Meg."

Sounds of Samuel waking came from the baby monitor on the counter. Jill glanced at it. "I've got thirty seconds before he drowns us out so I'll make this quick."

"Okay."

"Mike's not dating other women."

"Okay," Meg repeated.

"What I'm saying is—he's trying to reconcile. With you."

Her meaning sunk in. Meg sank in her chair, letting go of Jill's hand. "You're telling me to marry him, just like that?"

"No, I'm not—"

"He's not a Christian, Jill!"

"I know that. Meg, listen before you get mad at me."

How could her best friend say these things? "You don't know how much hurt he's caused me. Forgive him, after everything he's told me? You don't know what I know."

"You're right, Meg. I don't. But Mike is trying to make up for everything he's done. Clark thinks he's sincerely sorry."

"Mike should be sorry."

"But what about you?"

Meg clenched her teeth, her hands, her toes.

"You have to forgive him."

"I don't have to do anything."

"Then you'll be continuing the consequences. God tells us to forgive, Meg. When someone asks for forgiveness, we forgive. If you continue like this, you'll be sinning. First it was selfishness with its results. This time it will be anger, and its results will follow. Who will they hurt? You? Mike? Terrell?"

On the monitor, Samuel reached a full roar.

Meg covered her face with her hands. No one understood. Jill's marriage was too simple for her to understand how badly she hurt.

"Meg." Jill gripped her arms. "I know this is hard, but I'm telling you this because I don't want to see you live with pain. Forgiving Mike will be freeing, and while there will still be hurt from the past, you won't be entertaining hurt in the future."

"I can't, Jill." She asked too much. For that matter, so did God.

"I have to get Samuel. Think about it. If you want to talk some more, we'll talk."

Not today, they wouldn't. Meg would eat dinner and take Terrell home. After a week like this, she wanted to do nothing but sit alone in silence.

Chapter Forty-Six

The Wind's weekend home games were against the cross-town White Sox. Mike took Terrell and Clark to Saturday's afternoon game and gave Clark a tour of the Wind's stadium, introducing him to some of the team.

As on Friday, the White Sox won. Mike tried to let another Wind loss roll off him just like he tried to avoid the division's standings.

After the game, Clark grilled a late dinner of burgers and brats. Meg sat across the table from Mike, staring at nothing while she toyed with her food. When the meal was over, she and Jill vanished to her office to work on the kitchen design. Terrell and his toys took a bath.

The sun dipped behind the trees, and chunks of gold and gaudy orange peeked between the leaves. Mike stretched out on his usual deck chair. Beside him, Clark turned up the baby monitor that sat between them.

Samuel, in bed for the night, jabbered to himself.

"I heard Meg say you're watching Terrell," Clark said. "When's that?"

"Monday. She's working with a client out my way."

Clark hid a yawn with one hand, then tucked it behind his head. "That's a good sign."

"You'd think." More like her way of giving him time with Terrell without having to see him herself.

"You don't sound sure."

"No, I'm sure. It's not a good sign."

"Why not?"

Mike shrugged. Another conversation he didn't want to have. "She found out what a jerk I've been." He lowered his eyes to the hangnail that had yet to heal. "So did I."

"What's that mean?"

"That I understand why she hates me." He shrugged again, feeling his heart's pain in every joint. "I've hurt her pretty badly."

"But that doesn't mean Meg hates you."

He shot Clark a look. "Then you haven't been paying attention."

Above the trees, an airplane followed the now-familiar path to the airport, its wheels lowering before it disappeared. Mike looked to his right, waiting for the next plane to appear in the sky.

"So Meg hates you. Is she being unreasonable?"

"Nope." He spotted the plane, a distant silver speck.

"Hmm."

The plane grew to bullet size, the logo visible on the tail. "You wouldn't understand, Clark. You're one of those guys who'd never—"

"Stop it." Clark held up a hand. "Pastors are men too. I get tired of people thinking we're above everyone else."

"You're capable of murder?"

The shock Mike expected did not register on Clark's face. "We all are."

"Really. Well, not everyone does it."

"You murder someone?"

There went the landing gear. Here came the sound of the engines. The plane disappeared behind the trees. Mike took a deep breath. "Not exactly."

Clark said nothing.

Mike waited for the next plane to appear, watched it grow until it crossed in front of them, lowered its wheels, and descended out of sight.

Still, Clark said nothing.

Mike's thoughts tumbled from his mouth. "Have you ever hurt so badly you wanted to give up?"

"Is that how you feel?"

"Worse lately." He tugged on the hangnail, ignoring the sharp jump of pain. "Actually, worse since I started going to your church."

Clark chuckled.

"Oh, real funny."

"Sorry." He swung his legs to the deck and faced Mike. "Why are you feeling worse?"

"It's this guilt. I've hurt Meg, I've hurt Terrell, I've hurt a child I'll never know. I see Meg react to what I've done to her, and…" He dropped his head against the chair. "I look over the last decade of my life, and I think what have I done? I've hit homers, I've stolen bases, I've made money." He shrugged. "But inside, I—" He stopped at the tremor in his voice and took a deep breath. "I wish I could change everything."

This time the deep breath did not help. He pinched the bridge of his nose.

"Mike, you don't have to live with guilt."

What a joke that was. "I've had six years to forget about Meg and five years to forget about my child, and it hasn't happened. And I don't see it happening. You know what I see? Meg hating me for the rest of my life. I see Terrell growing up to realize what a loser he has for a dad."

"You don't know the future."

"You're right. It could be worse." He yanked again at the stubborn hangnail. He deserved the pain. "You know what I've learned about myself?"

"What?"

"That I'm a horrible person. All those people who asked for my autograph today—I wanted to tell them they were crazy. There isn't anything good about me."

"You're right."

Mike squinted at Clark. "You don't have to agree so quickly."

Clark ignored him. "Everything you've said is the first step toward changing."

"Please don't tell me there are eleven more." There he went, making jokes. Mike let his hands fall onto the armrests. "Sorry. Go on. I think."

"You've told me you believe in God."

He nodded. God seemed pretty obvious.

"Do you know that God says there is no one who's done good, that all of our good works are like dirty rags? Not just you, Mike. Everyone. Me, Jill, Meg, Terrell."

"Can't say that I see that in you, but we've established that I'm not perfect."

"No one is. We've all fallen short of God's glory. It's like this. Let's say you and I go to your stadium. We each have to hit a ball out of the park."

"Okay."

"You go first. You hit a ball that lands on the warning track. Almost a home run. Pretty good. Then I get to bat."

"If I can hit a ball to the warning track," Mike joked, gesturing to his cast, "you can hit a home run."

"Let's say I do. It lands in the bleachers, back row. I got farther than you, but I still failed to hit the ball out of the park. So what does it matter who did better? We both fell short of the goal."

The image made him think. "You're saying it doesn't matter how good you are."

"It's not what I say, Mike. It's what the Bible says. We all fall short. Are there people who live better lives than others? Sure. But the sin we *all* have keeps us *all* from God."

Inside, sin coated Mike. Every day he lived with its weight. But how did he get rid of it? "You're not making me feel better."

"I'm not trying to make you feel better. I want you to see the truth. The truth is what changes you."

Could he change? "Clark, I understand enough to know that if I believed what you believe, I'd have to completely change my life."

Clark held his gaze. "Is the way you're living that great?"

Mike opened his mouth, closed it.

"All these things you're realizing about yourself, all the sin you've done—that keeps you from God. He's holy, Mike. Perfect. He created a perfect world, and we destroyed it and each other. God has every right to let us go on in the mess we made. To face the consequences of our sin. But he loves us. He made a way for us to be free of the guilt. Free to have a second chance."

A second chance. Mike sat up in his chair. "I'm listening."

Chapter Forty-Seven

Somehow Mike made it to the Sunday evening service.

Meg had not expected him—the Wind's afternoon game had gone into extra innings—but he must have left as soon as the game ended. He pulled into the church parking lot just as she and Terrell reached the main doors.

It had been nice, sitting alone with Terrell in the morning service. Mike had been at the stadium, working out with the trainers, then with the team during the game. Now he sat beside her, fidgeting as if his seat were upholstered with steel wool. He leaned forward and rubbed his face with his palm, blowing another deep breath from puffed-out cheeks. What was the matter with him?

Every movement was characteristic of Mike on edge. He'd acted the same on draft day while they'd waited for a major league team to call. He'd been like this in the Virginia Burger King when he'd asked her to marry him.

Mike sat back hard, and Meg's seat jiggled.

Why was he nervous?

The piano began the closing song, and Meg stood with everyone else. The head pastor gave his usual invitation.

Mike pulled his hand from his pocket and ran his fingers through his hair, his eyes squeezed shut.

Around her people began to sing, but Meg could not. Surely Mike wasn't—

A laugh welled up in her throat, but she held it back at the misery on his face. She had to be mistaken. Mike wouldn't—

No. This couldn't be.

She gripped the seatback until her knuckles turned white. If Mike became a Christian, everything would change. Terrell, Jill, Clark—they'd all expect her to marry him and would never understand why she didn't. Mike would end up the good guy, and she'd be labeled a bitter, unforgiving—

He shifted in place.

She caught her breath, holding it until she was sure he wasn't going anywhere.

Still, his fingers drummed the top of the chair in front of him.

The song played on, and Meg held herself motionless, watching his fingers fight to release his tension.

The song finally ended. Pastor prayed, said amen. People turned, gathering their things. Conversations built around them.

It was over, and Mike still stood beside her.

Maybe she'd read him wrong. She bent to pick up her purse and Bible. Of course she'd read him wrong. Mike would never—

"Meg."

His voice startled her, and she straightened, cracking her head against his chin. "Ow." She held a hand to the top of her head. "What?"

"I need to talk to someone."

"Why?"

"I've got to find Clark." He looked past her, searching the wide auditorium. "Do you see him?" His eyes halted on a spot beyond her. "There he is."

Mike strode up the aisle, his focus glued to the far wall where Clark laughed and talked with a young couple. He hurried along the back wall, giving a distracted smile and nod to the many who said hello before honing in on Clark.

She couldn't stand to watch. Not when everything was about to change. She clutched her Bible to her chest. "Let's go home, Terrell."

⚜

An hour later, Mike's Range Rover pulled into her drive. Clark stepped out of the passenger's side and walked with Mike to her front door, the two of them smiling, laughing, as they talked.

Meg's heart sank.

Which was horrible. How could she be upset about this?

Yet there it was. She did *not* want to talk to him. Not right now.

She opened her front door, a smile pasted on her face, and the men stepped inside.

Meg studied Mike. All the tension from earlier was gone, and his eyes—even his eyes smiled.

Clark broke the silence. "Meg, we've been talking with Pastor. Mike wants to tell you what's happened."

He didn't need to tell her; she already knew.

But Mike ducked his head, a smile filling his face. "I've been struggling with guilt—for a long time. Guilt over you, over everything we've talked about." He glanced at Clark. "Clark and I have been talking. I stayed up last night, reading some verses he showed me, and I had to admit that the things I've heard at your church are the truth. The things you and Terrell believe, the things Clark teaches—" His smile increased. "I know they're true, and I've given myself, such as I am, to God. I'm gonna follow him."

She looked at him, waiting for more.

But they were waiting for a reaction from her.

She drew in a slow breath. "Wow," she managed.

"Yeah. Hearing me say things like this—it'll shock a ton of

people. But I know I've made the right decision. Already I feel like—like I have hope again." He swallowed and looked away. Cleared his throat. When he turned back, his eyes were damp. "Thank you for telling me what you believed, even when I made fun. I'm sorry for that."

Meg couldn't look away from him. "It's all right." How she wished she felt like that again, full of hope and laughter at what the future might hold.

"Where's Terrell?" Mike moved farther into the foyer, peering into the living room. "I want to tell him too."

"He's in bed."

"I'll be right back." Mike took the stairs two at a time.

When he reached the top, Meg turned to find Clark studying her. "You okay?" he asked.

"Yes," she lied.

"You want to talk about it? Want to talk to Jill?"

Did she? "I don't know what I want, Clark. I don't know what to do about this. Or even think about this."

"You don't have to *do* anything, Meg. Just be happy for him."

"Right." Except being happy for Mike was the last thing she wanted to do.

And she hated herself for it.

Chapter Forty-Eight

The clock in her car read 6:28 when Meg parked in Mike's driveway Monday night. She rang his doorbell, her stomach growling as she waited for the turn of the doorknob. Tonight, the first drive-through she passed was cooking her dinner. Mike had probably fed Terrell.

The day had gone better than expected. In the morning, she'd dropped Terrell off at Mike's and escaped with a wave before peeling out of his driveway. At the client's home, things ran smoothly, a rare occurrence. Now if she could get home and eat, she'd relax for the night.

When Mike didn't answer after two more rings and didn't answer his phone, she walked around the massive house to the stone terrace outside the basement level. On the lawn beyond the terrace, Mike crouched like a catcher, his back to her, while several yards away Terrell, ball glove on his hand, looked over his shoulder as if there was a runner on first.

So today he was a pitcher.

Terrell went through his wind-up, looking like a right-handed Chris Sale with his crazy delivery.

The ball sailed to Mike, thumping against what sounded like a glove.

On his right hand? His throwing hand? Meg frowned. "What are you catching with?"

Mike turned at her words and lost his balance, falling backwards onto the grass. Terrell laughed and ran to his dad who shaded his eyes with the catcher's mitt on his right hand.

"We bought it this morning." Mike lifted his gloved hand to her, a flirtatious grin on his face. "Help me up?"

No, thanks.

But that grin…

"Here, Dad." Terrell grabbed Mike's good arm, planted his feet, and pulled.

"Ow." Mike hauled himself to his feet. "A little less skin there, but thanks." He tucked the glove between his side and upper arm and pulled his hand free, then set the glove on Terrell like a hat.

Terrell shook his head, and the glove slid to the ground.

"How'd work go?" Mike asked.

She kept her eyes on Terrell, who shoved half his forearm into the adult-sized mitt. "Fine. Thank you for watching him. Terrell, time to go."

Terrell's face fell. "Not yet."

"Stay, Meg," Mike added. "We can order Chinese."

"You haven't eaten?"

"We were having too much fun playing baseball."

Mike ruffled Terrell's hair, and Terrell grinned at her. "Dad says I could be the next Cy Young."

"Do you even know who that is?"

Terrell shot Mike a confident look. "No. But Dad says he was pretty good." He clutched his glove beneath his throat. "Pleeeease can we stay?"

Mike cocked an eyebrow. "Sweet and sour pork, Meg?"

That wasn't playing fair. "All right. Chinese it is." They'd eat and leave.

But the night didn't end with dinner. Their food arrived as a game between Pittsburgh and St. Louis began, and Terrell talked her into staying a little longer so he could talk pitching with his dad.

Meg gave in and followed them downstairs to eat in front of the big-screen TV.

The game turned into a pitchers' duel. Terrell hung on every word as Mike explained the catcher's role in the game. Meg curled up in one of the side chairs—what it lacked in looks it made up for in comfort—and felt the day's exhaustion seep from her. Even when the clock passed Terrell's bedtime, Meg said nothing. Mike was pouring all of his attention into him. This was one of those nights Terrell would never forget. If he managed to stay awake on the drive home, he'd be begging for a catcher's mitt.

"Look at that," Mike said on the replay of a St. Louis player's home run. "The pitcher missed his spot. See where the catcher wanted it?"

The picture changed to the back-slapping in the dugout. "Has he hit more homers than you, Dad?" Terrell asked.

"Only 'cause I broke my arm."

Meg cocked an eyebrow. Seriously?

"You'll catch him once you're back—" Terrell broke off as Mike's name sounded on the TV. "They're talking about you!"

Mike held up a hand, and Terrell's mouth fell open as they listened to the commentator.

"—despite being out for the past three weeks, Connor still has the most National League All-Star votes. So this year the two most popular players for the National League will be from the Central division."

Mike was going to make the All-Star team? He couldn't even play. Wasn't everyone aware of that?

Terrell and Mike high-fived each other, and Terrell turned to her, a grin like Mike's covering his face. "Daddy's going to be an All-Star again, Mom. Isn't that cool?"

"Yes. Cool." Life kept rolling for him, didn't it? She reached for her watered-down Coke and forced a sip past the lump in her throat. Oh, wonderful. Nice time to tear up. She grabbed napkins and trash from the table and stuffed them into delivery bags before bolting for the stairs.

Somehow she made it to Mike's kitchen with her tears in check. Not bothering with the lights, she dumped the bags in his trash, tying a knot in the top of the full bag.

Now what? She would not return to the Mike Connorfest downstairs.

She wandered across the kitchen to the deck doors and stared at the black sky broken by lights from scattered homes. It was a stupid All-Star Game. Why on earth was she crying?

"Meg?"

She jumped at Mike's voice behind her.

His hand settled on her shoulder, and she flinched again.

How did a man that big walk so quietly?

"Are you okay?" he asked in her ear.

"Yes. I'm fine." She blinked, hoping her eyelashes had caught the tears.

"Sure, you are. What's wrong?"

"Nothing. I said I'm fine," she insisted as he turned her around.

He flashed her a gimme-a-break look.

"I suppose it's not too early to congratulate you."

"For?"

"Making the All-Star team."

"Oh. Thanks."

She turned back to the window, hoping her back would dismiss him.

"You know, Meg, we haven't talked about last night."

And he thought that was an accident?

"I thought you'd be happy for me. There are things you wouldn't wish on your worst enemy, right?"

She shrugged, watching tiny headlights move along an invisible road.

"Are things that bad between us?" he joked.

She wiped her nose and looked higher in the window, surprised to see his reflection above hers. "What do you want from me, Mike?"

"What do I want?"

"Now that we're both Christians."

"Does that change things?"

Some people would think so.

He rubbed his chin. "Right now, I'd be happy with friendship."

No, he wouldn't. If she acted like a friend, he'd try to turn her into his girlfriend. And then… No, she wasn't going to be his friend. Not now.

He stayed behind her awhile. Then his reflection disappeared as he left the room.

Meg rested her forehead against the glass. *Remember me, God?*

What a life Mike led. He did what he liked, lived how he wanted, made the All-Star team without playing, then decided to try his hand at Christianity.

Doesn't what he did to me matter?

"Meg."

She whirled at Mike's voice. "Will you stop that?"

He approached her again, mouth straight, pupils large in the darkness. "I want you to know that what happened last night was real. All the weight I've carried—it's gone."

She had no doubt.

"Even though you haven't forgiven me, I know God has. I realize that doesn't negate the way I've lived or the way I treated you, but for the first time in years, I feel clean."

She remembered that feeling. How she wished she could feel it again.

He stood in front of her, studying her while toying with the edge of his cast. "I'd still like your forgiveness."

"I know," she whispered.

She stood still, and after several seconds, he left the room again.

This time she waited, making sure he didn't return, before giving in to her tears.

Chapter Forty-Nine

Meg's taillights faded into the darkness.

The euphoria Mike had felt for the past twenty-four hours had vanished as quickly as Meg's smile. While Clark made it clear that turning to God wouldn't create a perfect life, Mike never imagined Meg would be unhappy with his decision. Sure, one day was a little quick to expect a change in their relationship, but he'd hoped she'd at least stop turning brittle each time he looked at her.

He thought over last night's conversation in Clark's office. Clark had explained the commitment he was making, that he was giving control of his life and decisions and actions to God and that trying to take control back would result in hurt and increased trouble.

He'd had enough hurt and trouble.

God, if I'm going to do this right, you'll have to show me what to do about Meg. He wandered to the mailbox at the end of the drive. *Help me do it your way, whatever that is.*

Pulling a stack of envelopes from his mailbox, he tried to push away the depression that settled around him. He had so much to learn—what if he didn't figure it all out?

He shut the mailbox with his elbow and started back to the house. The mail was mostly junk—credit card applications, sales flyers, refinancing offers. He tapped their sides against his chest, forming a semi-orderly stack.

A large, square envelope stuck out.

A third letter.

Mike clenched his jaw. What would it be this time?

He jogged for the front door and, once inside, slammed and locked it before tossing the rest of the mail onto the console table. He tore open the envelope, his breath coming fast as he pulled out the folded paper.

It was a printout of the forty-man roster from the team's website. His gaze raced down the page until he found his name listed with the outfielders. A yellow highlighter lit his name, birthday, height, weight, and the symbol that showed he was on the disabled list.

But this time there was more. Beneath the highlighted line someone had printed, "Let's hope it isn't permanent."

Was that a joke? A threat? Anger flamed inside him. He couldn't take a chance. Whether the sender was Reynolds or some other pathetic joker, the letters concerned the police now.

Chapter Fifty

Heat built through the week, the high nineties and thick air leaving Meg sweating on the short walk between her house and mailbox. Every road promised a pond farther ahead, and as her central air ran, the reminder of the bill to come motivated her to work into the evenings.

Man, did she miss Dana. But at least she was safe and, from the sound of her texts, doing better.

While Meg worked, she kept the Wind's Tuesday and Wednesday home games on TV. Both days Mike called, ostensibly to talk to Terrell, but he tried to keep her on the phone too. She fought off a growing desire to tell him how sorry she was for the way she'd been acting, and each time that she successfully passed the phone to Terrell, the growing emptiness of her victory made her stomach ache.

How long could she hold this grudge? More importantly, how long would she have to for Mike to suffer enough?

And when he had, then what?

On Thursday, July Fourth, Mike took Terrell for the day, since the Wind were in Baltimore for a long weekend series. Meg slaved over details for the Ashburns' remodel. Tomorrow she and Jill were shopping for the final details for the room. Meg couldn't wait. The day would be a throwback to that wonderful decorating time in Texas.

Clark, always ready to try a new grilling recipe, invited her and Terrell for dinner on the Fourth, as had become tradition. The change this year would be Mike's presence.

Meg kept that in mind as she worked to the last possible minute. When she stepped outside, the smell of grilled meat wafted to her. Laughter—Terrell's, Mike's, and Clark's—called to her.

She slipped through the gap in the bushes, ready to fake enthusiasm. She greeted Jill and Clark, gave Terrell a hug, and tried her hardest to return Mike's smile. But the feeling of isolation grew, and her loneliness continued throughout dinner. Twice Mike tried to catch her eye, but each time she looked away, cutting Terrell's food or starting a conversation with Jill.

Misery swallowed her.

After the kitchen and deck were cleaned, Meg stood on the Ashburns' front steps and scanned the neighborhood. Like a handful of neighbors, Mike and Clark spread blankets across the front yard, preparing to watch the fireworks shot off at the nearby racetrack.

Meg seated herself on a cotton blanket farthest from Mike.

He sent her a smile as he spoke to Clark. "I can't remember the last time I watched fireworks from somewhere besides a stadium."

Memories of those rocket-lit nights returned, memories of Mike's arms around her as the sky lit up. She could hear his laughter in her ear, feel his breath stir her hair. She could feel their fingers link together and his lips on hers. The memory morphed into the kiss at her back door, and her skin warmed as she remembered how she'd kissed him back.

A tire skidded on the sidewalk. Three elementary boys on bikes stared at Mike. "Are you Mike Connor?" one asked.

Meg glanced Mike's way. Through the fading light, she caught the irritation that flickered across his face, irritation only she recognized, before he smiled and nodded.

The boys knelt around him while he signed one's Nikes and

another's Sox shirt. Amazingly, the third pulled from his pocket a Mike Connor rookie card. Mike signed it with a flourish. The boys asked him about his injury, and he answered their questions with a smile, but once he'd finished, he told them to enjoy the fireworks.

The boys took his hint and left.

"Think those shoes will be worth something?" Mike joked when they were out of earshot.

"Only if they get the stink out of them first," Clark said.

Before long, word spread that Mike Connor, baseball superstar, sat on the Ashburns' front lawn. A small crowd converged.

Mike balanced scraps of paper, baseball cards, and other objects on his knees as he scrawled his signature. Several sat next to him while Clark took pictures with their phones, Terrell grinning at Mike's shoulder.

From across the lawn, Meg watched him give up an evening of anonymity for strangers. In the dusk with his dark head bent while he autographed, the useless John Deere hat turned backwards on his head, he looked as young as the last time they'd loved each other.

She caught her breath as the memories swarmed her again, and by the time the first fireworks exploded across the sky, she imagined Mike's arms wrapped around her middle, her head nestled beneath his chin.

The lawn at last empty of strangers, Mike and Clark sat on either side of Terrell, who lay on his back and wondered what fireworks would look like upside down.

"Terrell, look." Mike oohed dramatically at a pink-and-green explosion before wiggling his eyebrows at Samuel, whose eyes were round. "Can you say 'aaaahhhh?'" he asked, then ahed with Clark at four big booms. Grinning, he glanced across the lawn to her.

Meg couldn't look away.

Mike held her gaze for several seconds, his grin fading.

Why couldn't she forget him? Why didn't the pull of him go away?

He pushed himself to his feet and darted around the back of the blankets. Her heart raced as he sat behind her and pulled her back to his chest.

"Mike, don't," she said loud enough for him to hear over the pop of fireworks.

"For old times' sake," he whispered in her hair.

His good arm, snug around her, told her he wasn't letting go. She allowed herself to relax, feeling his chin on top of her head, his fingers weaving with hers, his Adam's apple bobbing. She felt his contented sigh and released one of her own.

What could it hurt, this re-enactment of all they'd once shared?

For the rest of the night, she let her weight rest against him and relived, again, how wonderful it had all once been.

Chapter Fifty-One

Friday Meg woke feeling more rested than she had in weeks. When she looked in the mirror, she found a smile on her face and blamed it on the day's plans—shopping with Jill.

Mike had agreed to pick up Terrell for the day. Meg poured herself a cup of coffee and seated herself at the table.

Over his bowl of granola, Terrell grinned at her. "I have a secret," he sang.

"Really?" She couldn't keep back the playfulness. "What is it?"

With a shake of his head, he dug his spoon into the bowl and slurped milk and cereal. "I can't tell."

"You can tell your mom."

"Nope. Can't tell anyone."

For once, he managed to keep his secret, even through her light questioning. Meg sent him upstairs to brush his teeth while she rinsed his dishes and stacked them in the dishwasher.

Mike knocked at her back door before she finished.

She caught herself waving to him and dried her hands before hurrying around the peninsula to open the door.

He stepped inside, his scent and smile warming her. "You look nice," he said.

She glanced down at her beige shorts, lime green tank top, and white shirt opened over it. "Thanks. And thanks for taking Terrell today."

Mike pressed his lips together, looking past her. "Where is Terrell?"

"Upstairs, getting rid of his morning breath."

His footsteps sounded above them.

Mike leaned on the peninsula. "About that day with Jill—plans have changed."

Her shoulders slumped at his words. "You can't watch Terrell?"

"No, but Jill can."

Should she tell him he wasn't making sense? His mouth curved into a grin, and Meg crossed her arms. Something was up. "What's going on, Mike?"

"Nothing. Your day with Jill is really a day with me."

"With you?" As if.

"Yes."

He stretched to his full height, and Meg tipped her head back so he could see her glare.

It didn't seem to faze him. "Look. I knew you'd say no if—"

"Hi, Dad." Terrell barreled into the room, skidding to a stop between them and hugging Mike.

"You all set?" Mike asked.

Terrell nodded. "I'll see you tonight, right?"

Anger colored her voice. "You know about this?"

Terrell's smile faded. He looked back and forth between them. "It was my secret," he said. "You didn't guess, did you?"

"No, she didn't. You did a good job, Terrell. Why don't you head over to Jill's? I'll be there in a minute."

What was he doing, rearranging her plans, telling her son where to go and what to do? "Terrell, you wait outside. *I* will be there in a minute."

Meg waited until the kitchen door closed behind him before she shook her finger. "Michael Connor, I am not going *anywhere* with you—"

"Whoa." He laughed and backed up a step, hands up. "No one's called me Michael in years."

"You listen, Mike." She struggled to control her voice. "I have been looking forward to this day. You are dead wrong if you think I'm going anywhere with you."

"Calm down, Meg."

"Don't tell me to—"

"I have something for you. Will you listen?"

He would regret this. She crossed her arms and looked out the windows. He would so regret this.

"I knew if I asked, like a gentleman, you'd pull this. So yes, I'm resorting to kidnapping. You *are* going with me if I have to buckle your seatbelt myself, and if I have to go that far, Jill will be helping me."

"Jill is in on this?"

Mike nodded.

How could her best friend betray her like that? How had Mike convinced everybody that he was the good guy?

"Unbelievable." She snatched her purse from the counter. Shoving her way past him, she yanked open the back door, startling Terrell who jumped, tangled his feet, and fell to the ground.

Meg helped him up.

Behind her Mike closed the door.

She glowered over her shoulder. "Is there anything else I should know?"

"Nope. Wait and see. You'll like it."

That was highly doubtful. She marched toward Jill's yard, dragging Terrell beside her.

"Were you surprised, Mommy?" he asked.

"Very," she snapped.

Meg didn't calm down until they reached Aurora. The combination of sunshine and air conditioning made her drowsy and too tired to keep up her anger level.

Buildings flew by as they drove west on Interstate 88.

And Mike still refused to tell her where they were going.

"How much longer?" she asked again.

He glanced in his rearview mirror as if the light traffic was more important than she was. "You're worse than Terrell. Have patience."

"Kidnapping doesn't leave me in a good frame of mind."

"I'll remember that."

She'd make sure he would.

He tuned the radio to a sports station.

Fine. She could play bored too. She rested her head against the leather seat and let her drowsiness take over.

When she woke, the buildings of Aurora were gone. Farms dotted either side of the highway—silos rising behind barns and farmhouses and growing corn filling the landscape.

"Where are we?" She cleared her throat to get rid of the sleepy sound.

He ignored her question. "You slept awhile. Feel better?"

"You mean am I still angry? Yes. Are we almost there?"

A smile tugged at his mouth. "Almost."

"Still no hints?"

"Look around."

She studied the scenery. Farm after farm slipped by before she realized they looked familiar.

Then the toll sign flew past.

They were outside the town they'd met in.

"We're going to Dixon?" What did he hope to accomplish with this? Just because she'd let him hold her last night—

"Figure it out?"

Was he taking her back to that high school lab table they'd shared just to pass her another note? She could see it now. *Please forgive me*, it would read in some high school rhyme that would have been cute if she were sixteen. She shook her head. "The high school."

"Nope. Strike one."

"If I get three strikes, will you turn around and go home?"

He slowed through the IPASS lane. "Funny. Come on, Meg. Think."

"I am. My mind's still sleeping."

"Where else would we go?"

While Mike drove north, she tried to remember the places that had meant something to them. "That little restaurant where we all used to hang out. What was it called?"

"Phillip's? Wrong again."

She named a few more places with Mike shaking his head and smiling broader at each one.

Then he turned east.

Meg sat up in her seat. "The farm."

He grinned.

Former neighbors' farms flew by before the last hill, and her childhood home appeared, three silos rising behind it, the other buildings hidden from view. Meg stared as the house grew larger.

They were almost to the gravel drive before she could form a thought. "Why are we here?"

"I guess you could say I rented the farm. For you. For today."

She sat back to absorb the news. "Why?"

"Because you lost a lot because of me." Tires crunched on the gravel as he drove between cornfields. "I know this is probably too late to mean much, but I wanted to bring you back for a day so you could see it one more time."

The Range Rover rolled to a stop in front of the farmhouse, and Meg craned her neck to take it in. She'd never had a chance to say goodbye.

Coming back meant more than he knew.

She swallowed the emotion in her throat. "What are we going to do?"

"Whatever you want. Luke Wagner is the owner now. Remember him?"

She shook her head.

"I played high school ball with his younger brother. Luke will be around, working of course, but you can go in the barns and wherever else you want, reminisce as much as you'd like."

"And the fields?" She'd loved riding her bike along the dirt paths.

"We can't go in the fields. I promised him we wouldn't do that, but I did ask about the calves, since you liked them so much, and he said you could see them. His wife and kids are here so we won't go in the house. I hope that's okay."

"I don't think I'd want to see someone else's things in it anyway." The gray house looked the same on the outside.

"I brought lunch so we don't have to go into town. Just go explore, do whatever you want. I'll wait here until you're ready to leave."

Heat seeped into the Range Rover, but Meg's arms prickled in excitement. "Thank you, Mike. This means a lot."

"Aren't you glad you came?" he teased.

She flushed as it dawned on her how close she'd come to missing this. "You could have told me where we were going. I can be reasonable."

"And miss this look on your face?"

"Well, thank you."

He nodded, his smile saying he was pleased with himself. "You're welcome."

"I want you to come too," she blurted.

He studied her. "Meg..."

"As much as I want to, I can't separate you from the farm. We had too much fun here." She hesitated. She shouldn't say more. She should keep her mouth shut— "Despite… things, we were good together, once."

His voice was soft. "Yeah, we were."

"Maybe, today, we could remember that?"

"You're sure you want me with you?"

Perhaps it was a mistake, but it felt right. She sent him a smile as big as the one she'd woken with that morning. "I'm sure."

Chapter Fifty-Two

Gravel skittered down the slope as they walked toward the farm buildings. The original barn, the one her great-great-grandfather Caldwell had built, sat before the three silos, still gray, and beyond them sat the milking barn. To the left, cows milled across the pasture, and to the right of the buildings stood the large metal tractor shed her dad had built. Surrounding it all were green, healthy plants.

"It looks the same," she whispered. "It doesn't seem real."

"That's what I thought."

"You've been here already?"

"I didn't want to bring you if it had been run down."

There he went again, treating her so well. "Thank you." He might have come out here, seen the place in bad shape, and never said a word. She'd never have known how thoughtful he'd been.

His footsteps followed her to the old barn's first floor. Decades ago this had been where all the cows lived, but for as long as she could remember, it was home to the calves.

The door was open, and Meg stepped inside, stopping to let her eyes adjust to the dark interior. The smell told her the calves were still there.

Mike ducked beneath the doorframe. "I should have known you'd come here first."

"I miss these guys." She walked between the pens and counted the summer calves. Six. "They're like big, friendly dogs."

"Just dirtier. And stinkier."

"'Stinkier'?" she teased. She reached for the nearest calf and rubbed its nose. The calf's long pink tongue, rough and damp, licked her wrist. She rubbed its eager head some more and looked back to find Mike standing in the walkway, swinging at a fly.

She grinned at the calf.

She made friends with each calf while Mike walked around the room, apparently studying the barn's structure between trips outside for fresh air. She waited for him to urge her on, but he said nothing, eventually disappearing completely.

When she'd had her fill, she walked outside.

Mike leaned against the barn's white side and again waited for her to lead the way. She walked up the slope and around the barn to the second level.

On this side, an earthen ramp had been built for wagon access to the oversized double doors. The old tack room still stood inside the entrance, former horse stalls filled with hay bales. Above them, the three-sided loft was filled with more bales, as it had been years ago.

Mike moved past her to the open center of the floor. "This was my favorite part."

"I didn't know you liked anything about the farm."

"I liked our hay fights." He grinned at her. "You'd start it, thinking you'd get the best of me, but you always lost."

She contained her smile. "You were mean."

"I was flirting."

The hay fights *had* been fun. She meandered around the main floor, touching posts and walls, remembering rainy afternoons and cold winter days burrowed among the bales. She climbed the wooden ladder and explored the loft—only one batch of mewing kittens—before sitting on the edge and dangling her legs into open space as she'd done so often.

Below, Mike looked into the ancient tack room.

She watched him. What did this day mean? Was it a true change on his part, this gesture of giving back some of what he'd taken? Or was it another attempt to win her over?

And why again was that wrong?

She grabbed a handful of loose hay and watched it slide through her fingers to the main floor.

From the tack room doorway, Mike turned as if reading her thoughts. His gaze landed on her.

Meg fought back a smile. "Are you coming up?"

He shrugged. "I can."

He climbed the ladder, his progress slow with one arm. He took his time reaching her, then sat down beside her, surveying the room below. "I think the last time we came out here was around graduation."

She gave in to the impulse. "You mean it's been a dozen years since our last hay fight?"

A smile tugged at his mouth. "I may have one arm, but you'd still get the worst of it."

"Wouldn't it be awful if hay went down your cast?"

"I'd like to see you try."

She grinned back. "It's tempting."

He brushed a piece of hay from his shorts, his eyes still averted as if he were too shy to look at her. "And I'd feel terrible if your hair got messed up."

"Oh, really?" She laughed, and Mike faced her at last, surprise and humor in his brown eyes. "If I remember right, it seemed that the worse I looked, the happier you were."

"I wasn't a Christian then."

"Neither was I." She stuffed a handful of hay down his back.

"Meg!" He scrambled to his feet and shook his shirt. Hay fell to the ground. "You know you won't win."

Laughter bubbled from her.

Mike tried to scowl. "You're in trouble."

"But you have to let me win, Mike. You've won every single fight, and this will be the last time we'll do this. A real gentleman would let me win."

"You're asking me to throw a hay fight?"

"I'll never tell. It can be our secret."

He gave her the evil eye before sitting on the floor. "Don't you dare touch my cast."

With a grin, Meg circled him. "I may have to bury you just to get even." She dumped another handful on his head.

"Doesn't the Bible say"—he spit hay and rubbed his mouth with the back of his wrist—"something about not taking revenge?"

Not today. She bent to gather more hay. "It also says an eye for an eye, a tooth for a—"

Mike shot a load of hay in her face.

Meg sputtered at pieces on her tongue. Before she could react, he cornered her against a bale and shoved handfuls of hay down her back and dumped more on top of her, rubbing it into her hair.

She tried to fend him off, but laughter left her helpless.

When she freed herself from his grasp, she ran to the opposite end of the loft and threw hay in his direction. Mike tossed more her way, and before long hay covered both of them.

Minutes passed before Meg admitted another defeat. The particle cloud settled while she rested on a hay bale, trying to catch her breath.

A few feet away Mike sat on the floor and picked hay strands from his clothes.

Meg pretended to pout. "You said you'd let me win."

"No. I told you not to touch my cast." He dug hay from between his toes. "You should have known better than that."

"I go out with another loss. Poor Meg." She shook her hair,

watching hay pieces fall to the ground. "I'm a mess."

He scooted across the floor and pulled a piece from the end of her hair. "You look beautiful."

Her eyes darted to his, so close to her own, as he concentrated on a tangle. She took in his dark-brown eyes, long lashes, and a faded scar—new to her—an inch below his eye. She traced it with her fingernail, catching his flinch.

He tossed a piece of hay to the floor, his movement pulling him from her touch. Leaning farther back, he surveyed her hair. "That's as good as it gets. We'll be picking hay out all day."

"You mean I'll be picking it out all day. You look fine." She searched his face. What would he do if she responded to him the way he wanted?

"The advantages of short hair." He grinned and pulled her to her feet.

She returned his smile, waiting for him to draw her into a hug.

Instead he headed for the ladder. "You want to stay awhile or keep going?"

She frowned at the distance he put between them. "We can move on."

They descended the ladder and walked out of the barn into the sunshine.

Meg squinted against the sudden brightness. "Our hay fights always make me hungry. How about lunch?"

His stomach rumbled on cue. They laughed, and Mike draped his arm over her shoulder. "Sounds good. I forgot how hungry winning hay fights makes me."

She elbowed him away and marched toward the Range Rover, chin up but a smile on her face.

Mike chuckled behind her.

At the Range Rover, she waited while he pulled a cooler and navy-blue-and-orange Chicago Bears blanket from the back. He slammed the door, stuffed the blanket under his left arm, and held the cooler with his good hand. "Where to?"

"I know the perfect place, but it's a walk. Let me carry something."

He shifted the blanket out of her reach. "Nope. Lead the way."

She led them past the barns and followed the dirt path between the fields. The walk took five minutes, and by the time they reached the windbreak of trees at the edge of a cornfield, Meg held the blanket, which had refused to stay between Mike's cast and side.

She spread it beneath a tree's shade, and when the blanket lay flat and welcoming, Mike set the cooler down and leaned against the wide trunk. "This is nice," he said.

She stood beside him, soaking in the view of the farmhouse and buildings, the cows, and wide open fields of waving, green crops. She breathed in the smells of animals and earth and listened to the subtle noises of nature drowned out in the rush and closeness of the suburbs. "I used to come here when I wanted to read or be alone, especially when the corn was tall. You couldn't see anything else."

He sent her an amused smile. "How appealing."

"You never did catch the country bug, did you?"

"I tried my best to avoid them."

"It's all right." She sat down, watching him pop the lid off the cooler. "Were you up all night cooking?"

"You'd be surprised." With a flourish, he held up two bags. "Croissant sandwiches, made the way I hope you still like them."

She took the Ziploc bag he handed her and pulled out the large, soft croissant filled with sliced turkey breast, lettuce, and cheese. She sniffed it. The cheese was provolone, and there was Dijon mustard in there. Perfect.

"Hold on. I forgot the plates." From a blue plastic bag, he unwrapped a winter white china plate trimmed in sage and silver. He set it on the blanket before her.

"Our china," she breathed.

"I forgot until a couple days ago that I still had that, somehow." His smile was sheepish. His eyes focused on the plate. "I always liked your taste in decorating. Everything you touched turned out beautifully."

Her throat clogged. "Thank you."

She set her sandwich on her plate, cold from the cooler, and watched him separate silverware for them. She took hers and laid them on the linen napkin he set beside her plate. "This is too fancy for a farm picnic."

He grinned, holding up a china cup and saucer. "Drinking lemonade from this should tone it down."

Laughing, she took the cold china. "Mike, you've completely surprised me."

"Don't expect any more. I'm maxed out."

Mike passed out the rest of her meal—red grapes for him and cantaloupe for her, along with cheddar-and-sour-cream potato chips, an old high school favorite.

When they were ready to eat, Mike surprised her again by reaching for her hand and bowing his head. "God, thank you for this food," he said. "And thank you for Meg. Thank you that she didn't beat me up on the way here."

It had been tempting.

Nature accompanied them while they ate and talked. A breeze danced around them, and two butterflies flitted at the far edge of Mike's blanket, the only living things to crash the party. Meg imagined them as sentinels keeping ants and bees away.

Conversation flowed, the topics safe and familiar. High school friends, Mike's arm, Terrell's latest loose tooth, Meg's worst client, the rudest fan. By the time they finished eating, it was almost two o'clock. They let the few bits of leftovers sit before them.

"This is relaxing." From his lounging position at the base of the tree,

Mike looked across the waving stalks of corn. "Makes me want to buy a farm just for afternoons like this."

"This is *so* the farmer's life."

A smile wormed across his mouth, and, without looking at her, he plucked blades of grass and tossed them in her direction.

She batted them away, laughing.

"Thank you for coming, Meg."

"Thank you for doing this."

He nodded. "I didn't handle this morning the best. I should have asked you. I didn't think about how disappointed you'd be not having the day with Jill."

"That's all right. Just remember you owe me."

"That I do. You know what I've realized today?"

"What?"

"That I liked the farm more than I thought. I wish I'd come back with you more."

"But you did today. It means a lot, Mike."

"Good."

He studied her, squinting a little. A struggle appeared on his face, as if he wanted to ask something that might ruin the moment.

Instead, he plucked more grass.

"What, Mike?"

"Nothing. Just…" He blew out a deep breath and sat up, his arms across the tops of his knees. "I wonder what would have happened if I'd swallowed my pride and really looked for you."

"You'd have found me if you'd called my parents."

"I was sure they'd chew me out, then hang up."

"I told them to give you my number. There was a time when I hoped you'd call."

But what would have resulted? The reunion of two selfish people, their past problems unaddressed. What could follow but more heartbreak?

"It's probably best you didn't call then," she said. "Nothing about me had changed. I was so selfish."

Was? Who was she kidding?

She dropped her head to her knees. "I still am."

What if she told Mike what she'd done wrong in the marriage? What if she took the fall?

The breeze toyed with her hair as her selfish nature battled for control. The need to protect herself remained strong after so many years of blaming her fears and insecurities on Mike. *He* was always the enemy, despite how she longed for him.

But the real enemy was this desire to please herself and do right only when it worked in her interest.

Or what she believed was her best interest.

When she raised her head, Mike flicked ants off the orange bear-face in the blanket's center. She swallowed at the opportunity to let conviction pass beneath a joke.

"Mike."

He lifted the leftover grape cluster, cringing at the ants clinging to it. "Hmm?"

How could she let him go on carrying the weight of their failed marriage? "I'm sorry for the way I treated you."

Her words swung his head around.

Meg closed her eyes at the anguished look on his face.

"When?" he asked, his voice rough.

"Our whole marriage. I was—I was wrong." Many of their problems had been her own fault, and yet here sat Mike, trying to make up for things she'd invited into their home.

Why hadn't she realized what she'd been doing?

He slid next to her, pulled her to him.

Meg leaned against his chest while tears slid down her face. "I loved you for what you could do for me. The whole time, I was just focused on me. I'm so sorry."

She covered her face with her hands while the tears ran.

Mike held her tightly, the weight of his cast pushing on her ribs, and stroked her hair.

He deserved better than what she'd given him. No wonder he'd wandered—she'd been the one to leave first, really. Deep inside, he'd known how little she cared. "Everything that happened—it's my fault." She wiped her face and sat up. His damp eyes locked with hers. "Everything."

"No."

"Yes, it is. I don't blame you for what you did."

"*I* was the one who left the marriage. *I* abandoned you. Nothing you could do would make that right."

"But if I'd put you first, you wouldn't have felt alone. You wouldn't have left—"

"Meg—"

"Your child wouldn't have died. You and I would be together, and Terrell would have always had his dad. I brought it on myself, Mike."

"Stop it."

"No. I have to tell you—I forgive you." She hadn't expected to hear the phrase, yet once said, she knew she meant it, and the relief of letting go of Mike's painful wrongs confirmed her choice.

Why had she fought God?

Tears rolled down Mike's cheeks. Meg wiped them away with her fingers. He closed his eyes and held her hand against his face.

"Please forgive me?" she whispered.

He nodded, face crumpling, and pulled her into a bear hug.

She wrapped her arms around his neck and rested her head on his shoulder while his broad chest shook, the muscles beneath her arms convulsing from his fight to gain control. She closed her eyes, crying with him despite the smile on her lips.

Gradually her tears stopped. Her breathing returned to normal, and Mike's shoulders stilled. Meg sniffed and wiped moisture from her cheek.

He kissed her hair above her ear. "Thank you," he whispered.

She nodded. They stayed in each other's embrace, the sound of a distant tractor mingling with the rustling corn and leaves.

Mike finally broke the silence. "Meg?"

"Yes?"

"We need to move. I think this blanket's on an anthill."

Chapter Fifty-Three

The moon sat big and bright in the night sky when Mike turned onto his street. Today had gone so much better than he'd hoped. Not only had Meg forgiven him but she'd admitted her part in their problems and asked his forgiveness. And for the rest of the day she'd left herself open while they explored more of the farm before driving into Dixon for dinner at Phillip's, their old hangout. There, in the same corner booth in which they'd always sat, he'd asked her for a date. That slow smile he loved had said yes before her words did.

On the way home, she'd again fallen asleep. Her head had tilted in his direction, and her dark-blonde hair had spread around her shoulders and over the seat. Mike glanced now at the bits of hay in the empty passenger seat, proof that everything he'd wished for had happened.

He signaled for the turn into his driveway, turning the steering wheel slowly. No way would he be going to sleep any time soon. He might as well stay up and plan this second first date—

His headlights illuminated something on the garage door.

Mike touched the brakes. What was that? A piece of paper? He put the Range Rover in park and hurried out.

His silhouette from the headlights shrunk as he neared the garage. Plain white paper was held in place with duct tape. Centered in the middle of the page in small computer print was a message.

Have a good trip?

Mike gritted his teeth, his eyes locked onto the message. Somewhere this moron had to be watching him, waiting for some sign that he was mad or scared. Mike held still, even though everything in him longed to rip the paper from the door and tear it until it was confetti.

Yes, had a good trip. Thanks for ruining my night. Maybe he should write a reply. Curiosity would draw this scumbag from his hole, and Mike could beat him senseless with his cast.

Instead, he returned to the Range Rover and turned off the engine. He'd call the police and while they looked it over, he'd plan tomorrow night's date with Meg.

This creep wasn't going to ruin the most perfect day he'd had in years.

Chapter Fifty-Four

A date with Mike—how had this happened again?

Meg pulled back from her mirror as the doorbell rang. Either Mike was early, or she was late. She glanced at her clock and cringed. "Terrell," she called, "would you get the door?"

"Sure, Mom." Terrell's feet thudded against the foyer floor. The front door swooshed open, then Mike's voice carried up to her.

Anticipation slid over her.

She forced a bobby pin into the mass of curls on her head and arranged them until they rested in the casual knot she wanted. "If I'm late, I'll make it worth his wait," she told her reflection.

Her mind drifted back to the previous day. A wall that she hadn't realized existed had disintegrated after her confession. They'd spent the afternoon walking hand in hand around the farm, with Meg unable to shake the feeling that time had reversed itself and she was eighteen again.

The feeling lasted into the night. Dinner at Phillip's was her suggestion, but Mike jumped at the idea. Their old booth was empty, and Mike led her to it, handing her the same laminated menu from their high school years.

She couldn't get over the change in him. His eyes rarely left hers, and his smile lit every inch of his face. His laughter took her back to their early years, but the constant interruptions reminded her that time had passed. People she hadn't seen in a decade pulled up a chair to talk or ask Mike for an autograph. People neither of them knew also stopped by, wanting an autograph or a picture.

After half an hour of steady interruptions, Mike asked the waitress for a piece of paper. He folded it in half, wrote "Do Not Disturb" in bold letters, and stuck the paper in the menu clip on the aisle side of the table. Then he joined her on her side of the booth, his arm around the seatback behind her. He'd turned his back to the room and focused on her.

"Meg?" Mike's voice at the top of the stairs jolted her back to the present. "I'm taking Terrell next door."

"I'll be ready when you get back." She'd have to hurry to keep that from turning into a lie. She changed into lightweight black pants and a white shirt with three-quarter-length sleeves and pin-tuck detailing. She added a turquoise necklace and matching bracelet. Again she examined herself in the mirror. What would Mike think?

Downstairs, the front door shut. He was back already? She sprayed her hair, then pulled on black slingbacks. Their first date could begin.

She descended the stairs, her steps muffled on the stair runner.

Mike stood in the foyer and stared into the living room. He'd dressed up as well, wearing gray pants and a blue dress shirt that fit over his cast, the blue in the shirt bringing out the rich browns in his hair.

But he looked far away.

He wasn't regretting this, was he?

"Hello?" she said from the last step.

His distant look vanished. He turned, his eyebrows rising. "Wow." Smiling, he held out his hand.

Meg laid her hand in his palm. It felt right, their hands together again.

"Wow," he said again. "You look incredible."

As long as he thought so. "You do too."

"Not as good as you. No one's going to notice me tonight."

"They'll notice you, Mike."

"For all the wrong reasons." He winked at her and opened her front door, his mouth forming a tight smile. "I think we better go."

Mike drove to an Italian restaurant where a valet took his keys. The packed parking lot made her take a deep breath as they started up the sidewalk. What would it be like to date a star in public?

She reached for his hand.

Mike turned with a smile that changed to concern. "What's wrong?"

For once she felt relief at how easily he read her. She leaned into his arm. "How much privacy will we have?"

"Plenty. You'll see." He opened the restaurant's door.

People filled the entry. Those nearest the door glanced their way before doing a double-take and nudging companions who hadn't turned.

Meg tried not to show her doubt. They'd never be left alone.

Mike pressed his hand to the small of her back and guided her through the crowd, which parted for them. Some women checked Mike out. Several men patted him on the back and asked about his arm and when he'd be back in the lineup. Mike answered, still moving them forward until they reached the maitre d', who finished with the group ahead of them and then led Meg and Mike up a staircase that opened onto a quiet second floor.

They walked past banquet rooms and closed doors with voices behind them to French doors with delicate floral etchings in the frosted glass. The man opened the doors and moved aside.

Stepping inside, Meg forgot her discomfort. A warm gray colored the walls. The trim was a soft winter white, the hand-scraped floors a dark chocolate brown. In the room's center sat a small, round, rustic table with two pale, upholstered chairs. Ornate silver and cream china sat atop the table in two place settings. An upholstered chair and loveseat, both matching the table's chairs, formed a sitting area, and against a separate wall sat a mahogany sideboard decorated with fresh flowers and antique china.

By the time she'd absorbed her surroundings, Mike sat on the love seat, watching her, his arm across the back and an ankle resting on his knee. He patted the empty space. "Come sit with me."

He didn't have to ask, really. She seated herself beside him, crossing her legs.

His hand cupped her shoulder. "What do you think?"

"I can't say I've had a private dining room like this."

"I mean the room. As a designer, what do you think?"

"I like it. It has an elegant, restored-home look."

He surveyed the room. "It reminded me of you."

She almost didn't speak. But leaving questions unasked could be fatal later on. "You've been here before?"

"Last year. I came with Adam Destin and his wife. Remember him?"

Relief filled her. "Sure. You keep in touch?"

"I stay at his house when we travel to Texas."

"What's his wife like?"

"Shauni's nice—one of those women who doesn't care if people know she just wants to be a wife and mom. Did I tell you they have twins?"

"Adam?" She shook her head at the mental picture of Adam cradling two crying babies. "Can't think of anyone who deserves it more."

Mike chuckled. "He's staying at my house next week when Texas comes to town. I'll have to bring him over so Terrell can meet him."

Terrell still talked about meeting the other Wind players. Another all-star athlete, and he'd never recover. "It'll make his day."

"You know what else would make his day? Going to the All-Star Game."

She'd forgotten about the upcoming event. "You want to take him to San Francisco?"

"I want to take both of you. Terrell could sit with me on the field during the Home Run Derby. We could take him to Alcatraz, show him Al Capone's cell—"

She faked doubt, hiding her smile at his contagious excitement. "Where would we stay?"

"I'll get a room for you and Terrell. My whole family's coming." He wiggled his eyebrows. "We're renting a bunch of suites."

"Everyone will be there? Betsy? Linda?"

"Nieces, nephews, and grandniece."

Seeing Patty and Davis didn't appeal, but she missed Betsy and Linda. They'd been the big sisters she'd never had. "I'm sold. But who gets to tell Terrell?"

Mike gave her his best puppy-dog look. "Me? Please?"

She laughed. "I guess, since you are the all-star." She rested her head against his arm. His muscles pulled as he shifted toward her. "Thank you for doing this, Mike. I was nervous, dating you with people watching."

"I know. No normal dates for us." The distant look she'd seen at home returned. "Meg…"

She held her breath. What bomb would he throw at her? What woman or story—

"I should probably tell you I've been getting some strange mail."

Was that all? She let out her breath. No more imagining. She'd have to trust him. "What kind of mail?"

"Photo copies. Old articles about my injuries."

"Your arm?"

"No, my dislocated shoulder four years ago. It's somewhat mundane, but there's no return address, no message really."

She opened her mouth to dismiss his concern, then remembered how accurately he'd pinpointed Ben. "You seem nervous about them."

"I'm not nervous." He shot her a grin. "Uneasy. I found a note taped to my garage door last night."

"Someone was at your house?" She pictured a hooded man raising a crowbar over Mike as he stood outside his garage. "Mike, you have to tell the police."

"I did. They took the note."

If he'd already called the police, he was more concerned than he let on. "What did it say?"

He eyed her.

"You can't *not* tell me what the note said. I'll worry."

"You'll worry if I tell you."

"Now I'm officially worried."

He laughed.

She smacked his hand. "What did it say?"

"It said… It was a little personal this time."

Something about her? Or Terrell?

Mike raised his eyebrows. "Don't blow this out of proportion."

"Michael."

"All right. It asked if I'd had a good day."

A good day? Her mind drifted to Friday and the way they'd been alone in the open. Had someone been watching them?

"I knew you'd take this too seriously."

"Like you're not. What are you going to do?"

"What am I supposed to do? The police know. Nothing's going to happen anyway."

He was saying that for her sake. She wrapped her arms around herself. "The police had better find this stalker."

"They will." He tipped her chin his way until their eyes met. "No stalker's going to get the best of me, though. Or of my first date with you."

He was right. Tonight belonged to them. Whoever was hassling Mike—Ben, someone else—he wasn't here. She relaxed and returned his smile. Mike was capable of defending himself, despite having one arm.

"Do you know what I wanted to do?" he asked.

"What?"

"I wanted to write him back."

She leaned closer, whispering into his smile. "What would you have written?"

"That I had an incredible day with the most beautiful woman."

How she'd missed him, missed the way he made her feel special. Now it was time to make him feel special too. "I love that, Mike."

His eyes darkened with emotion. "Good."

Chapter Fifty-Five

To preserve the illusion of a true first date, Mike walked Meg to her front door and asked her to tell Terrell he'd see him at church in the morning. Tonight he wanted to relive how he'd felt thirteen years ago when he'd dropped Meg off that very first time.

He hadn't remembered the drive home then, and as he opened the garage door that led to the mudroom, he realized he didn't remember this drive, either. All he could think about was Meg curled up beside him, her face calm and happy with those green eyes that captured his attention. He could still feel the shape of her hand, slender and soft, in his. A faint trace of her perfume lingered on his right sleeve. What a perfect night, marred only by the fact that it had to end.

He caught himself whistling as he tossed his keys onto the kitchen counter. How long since he'd walked around his house, whistling?

His stomach rumbled.

He backtracked to the refrigerator. Well, it had been over two hours since his last bite of food. And he had been too distracted by the company to eat much. He scanned the contents. Nothing he could assemble in less than thirty seconds. Time to have Maria stock up again.

Or go back to Meg's. Eat there. With her.

He leaned over his phone. Should he call her? Yes, it was late, but—

The phone rang.

Mike jumped, a swear word launching from his mouth. He balled his hand into a fist and shook it. That was a habit he had to change. He raised his eyes to the ceiling. "Sorry."

The phone rang again, and Mike answered it. Meg must not have wanted the night to end, either. He could hear the grin in his voice. "Hey."

"Mike?"

His smile faded.

The woman sounded breathless as if she was surprised he'd answered. "Mike, this is—"

He pressed the end button and stared at the phone as if it was a traitor. Why had she called?

The phone rang again.

Not Meg's number.

Man, he should have looked at that the first time. He answered and spoke immediately. "Don't call me."

"Mike, listen—"

"I don't want to hear anything you have to say."

"One minute, please—"

"No, Brooke!" Her name felt like an explosion in the suddenly quiet room. He swallowed, his mouth dry. "Don't call me. Ever."

Again he ended the call, this time blocking her number.

There. That was done.

He set the phone back on the counter and looked around the empty kitchen.

He wasn't hungry anymore.

In his bedroom, he sat on the edge of his bed. The silence circled him while memories of his betrayal of Meg played, memories he would never be rid of. His stupidity would always be a part of who they were. They could never go back to what had been before.

Especially not with Brooke trying to butt her way back in.

He gave in to the old fear and guilt and let tears fall into his hands.

Chapter Fifty-Six

"Here. Catch."

From the bottom of his basement stairs, Mike tossed a bottled water to Adam Destin who was sprawled across the couch, texting on his phone. The Rangers had gotten in late the previous night. Like last year, Adam was staying in one of Mike's guestrooms for the four-day visit.

Adam set the bottle aside, still texting. "How'd the interview go?"

"Fine." Mike dropped into a chair and finished off his water. "I do a call-in interview with those guys every couple weeks so I know them pretty well. They don't give me much grief."

"That's cool. Hey, Shauni says hi."

"Oh. Tell her hi. What, do you guys just text when you're gone instead of talking?"

Adam looked up long enough to smirk at him. "No, she and some friends are at the zoo with the kids. So I just sent her a quick text. Speaking of women, what about Meg? I forgot to ask last night. How's that going?"

"We're good. Just went on our official first date."

"You're back together?"

"Since Friday. But so far, so good." As long as the past stayed out of their way.

"Shauni will be happy to hear that."

"Yeah. By the way…" Mike waited for Adam to look up from his phone.

He didn't.

"Dude, did you give my number to Brooke?"

Adam looked up. "Uh, yeah." A sheepish smile covered his face. "I guess she called?"

"Yeah, she called." What was Adam thinking? "What are you giving her my number for?"

"Well…" Adam set his phone aside, scratched his head. He gave Mike an apologetic look. "Did you talk to her?"

"Of course not. I blocked her number."

"Connor." Adam groaned. "Dude, you shouldn't have done that. You need to talk to her."

"Now you're on Brooke's side? You want me to get back with her?"

"No—"

"Then why are you giving her my number?"

"Mike, look. I got a call from her Saturday—"

"Because I wouldn't talk to her."

"Wait." Adam held up a hand, palm out. "She called me Saturday morning."

And must have given him quite a sob story to convince his friend to hand out his number. "She's using you, Adam. That's what Brooke does. She uses people."

"Hey, listen. I know that, okay? But she told me what it's about."

"I don't care what it's about. Do you know I had just gotten home from my first date with Meg when she called? Do you know what it would do to us if I talked to her?"

"You're not gonna have a choice, man. If you don't talk to her, she'll come find you."

Was he serious? "You're nuts, Destin." Brooke had done enough—Mike wasn't letting her ruin this chance with Meg too.

"Nothing she could say is that important."

"You might be wrong."

"Then you tell me."

"Mike…" Adam looked away. "I wish I could."

Mike groaned.

"Seriously, man. I told her I'd let her… talk to you. I know you and Meg are working things out, but consider that I'm asking you to listen to her. One last time."

No way would he talk to her. Mike shook his head. How could he? How *could* he do that? He picked up his empty bottle, shook it, watched droplets inside merge into one.

Nothing would be worth the risk.

Chapter Fifty-Seven

Meg's reunion with Mike's family took place in San Francisco's airport, outside of baggage claim.

"Meg!" Linda, Mike's oldest sister, wrapped her in a tight squeeze. "I've missed you, girl. Look at you, just as pretty as ever."

Chris, Linda's husband, hugged her as well. "At last, another in-law," he joked.

Meg returned his smile. "I hear you two are grandparents. Congratulations."

"Thanks. I'll pull out my stack of pictures in a minute." Linda let go of her arm to lean down to Terrell. "But first I'd like to meet this guy." She held out her arms. "Hi, Terrell. I'm your Aunt Linda."

Terrell gave her a tentative hug, looking up at Meg. "Does this mean I have cousins?"

Linda pulled back and winked at him. "If I'm a grandma, you'd have to have cousins, wouldn't you?"

He sent Meg a confused look.

"Your cousins are over there." Meg pointed past Linda and Chris to Mike with his niece Heather and her husband who pushed a stroller.

Terrell shook his head. "They're too old to be my cousins."

"Sounds like Mom when she found out she was pregnant with Mike." Linda laughed. "'Too old.' There's your other aunt, Terrell.

And the rest of your cousins. Are they young enough?"

Behind Mike and Heather, Betsy—Mike's other sister—walked with her two boys, thirteen and ten, and Linda's other son and daughter.

Meg caught her breath.

Betsy's face was lined, and her once blonde hair had faded to a grayish taupe. She looked years older than forty-five, years older than her big sister, the grandma.

Meg didn't wait for Betsy to reach them. She jogged past Mike and Heather to her former sister-in-law. "Betsy," she whispered, pulling her into a hug.

Betsy let go of her suitcase and wrapped her arms around Meg.

She couldn't cry. Meg closed her eyes. She wouldn't cry.

When they finally separated, they wiped damp eyes at the same time, then laughed together. Meg hugged her again. "Your boys have grown so much."

"Yours too." She nodded at Terrell, who stood with Mike and his grandparents. "There's no doubt he's a Connor, is there? Mom says Dad couldn't be happier."

"I'm glad." Maybe she'd been forgiven.

Betsy kept her arm around Meg's waist as they joined the rest of the family. She pointed to her boys, Erik and Gavin, who already had Terrell laughing. "No need to introduce them."

"I guess not." What had Betsy been through that had aged her so much? "Betsy, I'm sorry I never noticed."

"I made sure no one noticed, but thank you. And I'm sorry about my kid brother. Let me know if you want me to knock him around some."

Betsy's words formed a lump in Meg's throat, the ugly fear that Mike might someday repeat his affair ringing through her mind. She'd forgiven him—why couldn't she shake these thoughts and memories? What would it take for her to forget and move on?

Mike joined them. He raised his eyebrows at Betsy in mock alarm. "Forming alliances already?"

"He doesn't take me seriously, but he should," Betsy said. "I've learned some moves."

Mike tugged his sister into a hug which she returned. "How's your back?"

"Bearable. Thanks for the seat upgrades."

"You're welcome."

The three of them followed the rest of the Connors. Mike walked in the middle with an arm around Meg. People tried to stop him, but he refused. He lifted a finger from Meg's waist, pointing to the group ahead. "I'm with my family. Not now."

His family.

His finger fell back against her, and she tightened her hold on his waist as they walked. She'd forgotten how good family felt.

<hr />

Fans in the packed stadium cheered as a Seattle player launched another ball into the night sky. Terrell's eyes popped wide open as the ball sailed over fans beyond right field and into McCovey Cove.

From behind a screen, the pitcher tossed another ball. The batter swung, and the ball followed the previous one's path. The stadium noise rose another level. Little Katie Destin, sitting beside Mike with her dad, plugged her ears with her fingers.

Mike scanned the stadium from his grassy seat in front of his league's dugout. The biggest names in baseball sprawled around him with their children beside them dressed in miniature jerseys. Mike looked at Terrell, who sat between his legs, dressed in a matching Connor jersey. Tonight topped every other night, all because Terrell was here.

Mike craned his neck to look into the stands where his family sat. He'd managed some pretty amazing seats for them a little farther down the third baseline and could just see them. His three nephews huddled together, jaws slack as another bomb cleared the park. His parents sat together, as usual, with Linda deep in conversation with Mom. Meg sat sandwiched between his sisters, but her eyes were not on the home runs. They were locked on him.

He sat up a little straighter to get a better view of her.

She smiled at him, waved.

Mike winked back.

In his arms, Terrell leaned back, releasing an enormous yawn, his eyes drifting closed.

Mike chuckled. Terrell would fall asleep the second they left the park.

Their busy day had started with an early visit to Alcatraz, where Mike discovered how little of his Chicago heritage Terrell knew when he'd asked who Al Capone was, then a trip to Chinatown via cable car. Tomorrow, if they had time, they'd take in the Golden Gate Bridge—and make another stop for ice cream at Ghirardelli Square. Meg, Linda, and Betsy insisted.

By the time the Home Run Derby ended, Terrell's eyes were slits he struggled to keep open, and before their cab reached the hotel, he snored softly.

Mike carried him into the hotel's lobby.

"Mr. Connor." A man behind the registration desk held up an envelope. "For you, sir."

So much for checking in under an alias. Mike shifted Terrell's dead weight high on his shoulder so he could take the small gold envelope. Across the front, his name and the hotel's address were written in an unfamiliar script. "Thanks." He stuffed it in his pocket and returned to where Meg waited.

On their floor, Mike followed Meg to her suite and waited while she unlocked and opened the door. She stepped aside, and he walked through the living room to the bedroom and put Terrell on the bed Meg pointed to.

Still asleep, Terrell curled into a ball.

Mike tugged Terrell's tennis shoes off and dropped them beside the bed. "Where are his pajamas?"

Meg motioned for him to leave the room. He did, and she shut the bedroom door behind them. "I'll let him sleep in his clothes. He needs a bath tomorrow anyway."

"Fine with me." Mike pulled her close and leaned down for a kiss before she could speak. Her lips were soft and tempting. "I'm glad you came."

"Me too." Even though she smiled up at him, she pushed herself back a little, a bit stiff in his arms.

His gaze drifted back to her lips. He wanted to kiss her until she relaxed.

"Mike," she warned.

He smirked. "Is that a no?"

"You should probably go. This won't look good."

He glanced at her hotel room door. "No one can see in," he teased.

"Exactly. So you should go."

"All right." He released her, and she stepped back. "I'll see you in the morning."

She nodded. "I'll call you when we're up."

"I'll be waiting." He opened her door, wanting to go back for one more kiss. Instead he gripped the door handle. "Goodnight, Meg."

He shut her door behind himself and walked past his family's suites to his room. Inside, the living room was silent and dark. He left the lights off, pulling open the shades to look over the city. The night was clear, and the city lights rose and fell beneath him.

Mike left the shades open and turned on the TV. The Home Run Derby was replaying already. He sprawled across a chair, content to let baseball clear his mind.

The letter.

He sat upright as if it had jabbed him and pulled it out of his front pocket. The envelope was creased and wrinkled from his movements, thick between his fingers. Whatever was in here wasn't a single page.

"Okay, God. Let's see what this is." He slid his finger beneath the flap and pulled out a photograph covered by a folded piece of stationary.

What a pretty picture, the note read.

Mike looked at the photograph—a picture of himself and Meg walking through the airport.

Someone had taken the picture from behind them.

His heart pounded. Who'd sent this? Ben? Some stranger Mike would never recognize until it was too late? And why send this? What was the plan?

Meg.

He dropped the letter and picture, ran to Meg's room, and pounded on her door.

She opened immediately, forehead already creased with worry. "What's wrong?"

He slipped inside and shut the door behind him, whispering so his voice wouldn't carry. "I don't want you to open this door for anyone but me, okay?"

Meg opened her mouth to speak.

Mike raised his hand. "I don't want you or Terrell leaving this room by yourselves. Do you understand?"

Her face blanched. "You got another letter."

"Yes."

"What did it say?"

"Never mind—"

"Mike—"

"Listen to me. I don't want you to leave this room without me.

Not for room service, laundry, nothing. If someone's delivering something to your room, call me so I can be with you when you open that door. And make sure Terrell knows not to leave by himself."

"Did they threaten Terrell?"

"I don't think so."

"They threatened me."

Was that this stalker's plan? "Maybe."

She swallowed, her hand at her throat. "What are you going to do?"

"I'm going downstairs to talk to security." He pointed to the deadbolt on the door. "Use that."

Her eyes slid shut.

He pulled her close, her hair soft against his neck, her perfume filling his senses. He closed his eyes, refusing to be distracted. "Don't worry. Go to bed and sleep, all right?"

"I'll try."

"Good."

She stepped out of his arms, wrapped her own around herself.

Mike cracked open the door behind him. "Call if you need anything. Don't look at the clock. Just call."

"I will."

He left and shut her door, waiting until he heard the locks before jogging for the elevator. Who was sending these letters?

And what did they mean?

Chapter Fifty-Eight

When Meg opened her door Tuesday morning, Mike forced himself to look awake and cheerful, not easy with only a few hours of sleep.

He followed her into the living room. "How'd you sleep?"

"About as good as you. Is everyone ready to leave?" She picked up a mug of coffee—or maybe orange juice—and eyed him over the edge while she drank from it.

"Just about."

"You tell your parents?"

Of course not. They had no idea of the mail he'd gotten over the years, especially these latest ones. He winked at her, taking the mug from her and gulping a drink. Ouch, coffee—and hot. He wiped a few hot drops from his mouth.

Meg took the cup back, biting back an impish smile. "Can I get you some?"

Now this was more like it. "Are you flirting?"

"Doesn't take much for you, does it?" she teased.

He flicked his coffee-damp fingers at her, but she dodged him, eyes sparkling. He chased her, and with a shriek she ran behind the couch, her half-empty coffee cup held shoulder-high. He hurdled the ottoman, then rounded the couch and cut off her escape.

She halted, her hand palm out in front of his face, her expression serious. "Stop!"

He froze. "What?"

She lifted the mug like a weapon and tilted her chin enough to give the appearance of looking down her nose at him. "Don't make me hurt you."

He held up his hands, his tone sarcastic. "I surrender."

She considered him before nodding. "I accept."

He reached for her, but she turned her back and walked toward the window. "What's the morning's plan?"

He blinked at the abrupt change. "Everyone's in the lobby except for Betsy, who's still putting on makeup because her boys took too long in the shower, or so she says. What about Terrell?"

"Getting dressed." She drained the mug.

Mike winced. He'd be playing ball before his mouth healed.

She set the mug aside. "I'll be ready in ten minutes, if that's okay."

"Take your time." He'd send everyone else ahead, including Terrell, and the two of them could finish their game of chase. He wouldn't surrender this time.

The bedroom door opened, and Terrell came out. "Dad!" He ran to Mike and hugged him tightly.

Mike returned the hug. This never got old. "You ready to see the sights? We're going to have you go ahead with your grandparents and cousins."

"Okay." Terrell plopped onto the floor, putting on one sandal, then another. "Mom, can I leave?"

"Did you brush your teeth?"

"Yes."

"Put your dirty clothes away?"

He darted back into the bedroom, then reappeared in seconds. "Ready."

Mike high-fived him on their way to the door. "Be right back, Meg."

During the short elevator ride, Terrell jabbered about the home runs he'd witnessed last night. Mike listened, inserting the appropriate sounds when Terrell took a breath.

In the lobby, Mike led him to where everyone, Betsy included, waited near the revolving doors. Sunlight streamed through the glass and sparkled on the door's metal trim.

"Where's Meg?" Betsy asked.

"Almost ready. I'll wait for her, and when she's ready we'll join you. Hey." He leaned closer to his sister, to his parents, to his brother-in-law. "Make sure you keep Terrell close, okay?"

Mom sent him a patient, been-there-done-that nod. "Of course You know where we'll be?"

Mike named the restaurant where they'd decided to have breakfast.

Terrell waved goodbye before cramming into the rotating door with Erik and Gavin and pushing for all he was worth. On the sidewalk, Dad took Terrell's hand and Mom took the other. Terrell gave one last backwards grin, then disappeared with them around the corner.

Now for a few minutes with Meg.

But three teenage boys and two men moved in on him. "Mike, can we get an autograph?"

He tried not to sigh. Not now.

He took their pens and baseballs, anyway. He scribbled his name for each, aware of others approaching, phones raised at him.

"That's all." He handed back the last ball and pen. "Sorry. Gotta go." He jogged past them and turned down the hallway where the row of elevators stood. Each minute with Meg was precious. He could autograph at the ballpark. Right now—

Right now Brooke Jaeger stood between him and the elevator.

Chapter Fifty-Nine

As Brooke approached, Mike's feet seemed glued to the marble floor.

Her blonde hair, once long and shiny, stopped at her chin and swirled around her cheeks. Her skin looked worn, rough, almost yellow. Even the glint in her brown eyes was gone, and her flirtatious smile had transformed into straight lips that remained closed, even though she stood before him.

Behind her the elevator doors dinged.

Mike stiffened. If Meg had left her room and stepped out to see this—

The doors opened, and a gray-haired couple appeared.

Mike let out a gust of relief.

"You don't have anything to say?" Brooke asked.

How had this woman lured him from Meg? What had he been thinking?

"Give me a few minutes, Mike. Promise you'll listen, and I'll go away forever."

Adam had said Brooke would come to him. If Mike didn't talk to her now, she'd show up again, somewhere else. Like his wedding, maybe. "All right." He hated this. *Hated* it. "Over there, in the restaurant." He led her back the way he'd come to the restaurant's entrance, pointing out a well-hidden table.

Mike spoke as soon as they sat. "Make it quick. Meg's waiting for me."

"I'd heard you and Meg were together."

"I'm sure you did. What do you want?"

She glanced around the restaurant before leaning toward him. "There's something I've never told you."

He set his elbows on the table and balled his hands into one fist, his chin resting on top. If she was waiting for him to show interest, she'd have to keep waiting. Brooke was the biggest mistake he'd ever made. Living life that way had been more painful than being nailed by a crowbar.

"No guesses?" she asked with a hint of her old, seductive smile.

"No."

The smile faded. She reached into her purse and rummaged through it, finally pulling out a white envelope. She held it for several seconds as if what she was about to show him was precious.

"Can we hurry this up?" he asked.

"You promised to listen."

"I *am* listening. You're not talking."

"Please think over what I'm about to tell you."

"Then talk."

"All right." She lifted the envelope's flap and slid out a photograph. She laid it flat on the tablecloth, her hand covering the picture for a heartbeat, then slid it to him.

Mike lowered his fists as he looked at the photo. A younger and healthier Brooke and a blonde boy smiling at him, the boy hamming it up for the camera.

"This is my son, Noah."

So she had a kid. Poor guy. "Cute," he said.

"Mike." She wet her lips. "Do you notice anything?"

He was a kid, a blonde boy who looked like a handful. "What am I looking for?"

"A resemblance."

"He has your hair."

"You don't see it?"

"See *what*, Brooke?"

She leaned across the table again. "He's not just my son, Mike. He's yours."

⌒⚬⚬⌒

Outside the restaurant, Ben dashed for the elevators, Polaroid camera in hand. Connor had been so involved as he walked away with Brooke that he'd never noticed the camera's flash. Either that, or he was so used to people taking his picture that he hadn't paid attention.

DaVannon jogged behind him, prepared to intercept Connor if he'd gone after the picture. But Connor sat with that woman, not knowing the U-turn his life was about to take.

Ben pressed the elevator's call button. Connor had destroyed him in Dana's eyes. Now he would destroy Connor in Meg's eyes.

Running into that woman Brooke had been a huge bit of luck. Last night Ben had stationed himself at the hotel bar where he could see everyone who came and went from the elevators. The woman sniffing two seats down had gotten on his nerves until he realized she was glued to the television picture of Connor and his son sitting on the stadium grass.

Ben had slid down a stool. "He's quite a player."

Her smile was sad, and she dripped tears into her drink. "I used to know him."

"Really?"

She nodded, her movements exaggerated. "I ended his marriage."

"Really." Ben held still against the thrill that flooded him. "How's that?"

"It was a long time ago."

She drained her glass and lifted her hand for another, almost sliding off the stool.

Ben caught her by the elbow. "You still in love with him?"

"Could be, if he were interested. But I hear he's not. Too busy working things out with his ex."

"That's what I hear too."

She faced him for the first time. "You know him?"

"Yeah. Some."

She eyed him up and down before extending her hand. "I'm Brooke."

For the next twenty minutes, she spilled every detail of her relationship with Connor and what had brought her here to find him.

By the time she finished, the perfect revenge was in place. And it had just fallen into his lap. He leaned closer to her, voice low. "What if I get you some time with him?"

She rubbed away her tears, the mascara a dark smudge beneath her eyes. "How?'

He shrugged, even though the details were set in his head. "I have a friend here who can help. We just ask one thing."

"What's that?"

He'd told her.

The picture slid out of the camera as the elevator doors opened to the fifth floor. Ben held it up to the light. It showed Connor walking with Brooke into the restaurant, his head turned toward her as if he were captivated by her.

DaVannon grinned.

Ben smiled back. Perfect.

Following DaVannon down the hallway, Ben scanned the room numbers. In one of these rooms was a woman who would inflict in Connor the pain Connor had inflicted on him.

Ben couldn't wait to watch that happen.

Chapter Sixty

Meg glanced at the clock on the bathroom wall as she dried her hands. Mike was taking a long time dropping off Terrell. He'd probably been mobbed and was autographing his way to the elevator. She opened her lipstick tube. At least she had time to get ready.

A knock sounded on her door.

There he was. She finished applying the lipstick before jogging through the bedroom and into the living room.

Just in time to see a manila envelope slide partly beneath her door.

How odd. "Mike?" she called as she approached.

No answer.

She looked through the peep-hole.

The hallway seemed empty.

She picked up the envelope.

Meghan Connor.

Okay. She straightened her back, looked around the room, dropped her gaze back to the envelope. This couldn't be good.

She took a deep breath.

The flap wasn't sealed.

She reached down inside.

A picture. A piece of paper.

This had to be from whoever was sending Mike letters.

Now they'd sent her one.

She pulled it out, trying to make out the dark images, but the light by the door was poor. She walked to the window, where she'd opened the curtains, and held up the picture.

It was Mike, walking away from the photographer into a darker room. A much shorter person—a woman—walked beside him.

Unease crawled from her stomach to her spine and slithered up her back. "This is silly," she said out loud. There had to be a good reason for this.

But her fingers trembled as she pulled a piece of white stationary from the envelope. She took a deep breath and pushed her hair over her shoulder before reading the message.

Thought you should know your ex-husband is downstairs with Brooke Jaeger.

Her breath rushed from her. Brooke was here? And Mike was with her? Her gaze flew to the blonde in the photo. *This* was Brooke?

She searched the picture. Mike looked at the woman walking beside him, his mouth tight as if he were annoyed. On the other hand, as bad as the lighting in the picture was, maybe he was smiling.

No, he couldn't be smiling. Mike wouldn't—

She lowered the picture and closed her eyes. She needed to calm down. Maybe it was some groupie's demented joke.

Of course it was. Just a trick, some woman trying to worm her way between them. The picture was probably old.

But the note said downstairs. Downstairs—in the lobby? The bar? The restaurant—

She gasped as she recognized the entrance. And Mike's shirt—the same fitted, gray, long-sleeved T-shirt he'd worn in her hotel room minutes ago.

This picture was real.

She set her teeth together. If Mike was really there with Brooke, she'd know in a minute.

She grabbed her keycard from the coffee table. Her hand was on the doorknob before she remembered his warning.

Don't leave this room without me. Don't open this door for anyone but me.

Maybe the woman in the picture was a reporter. Maybe it was an innocent interview.

But who knew Brooke's name?

Maybe Mike had warned her to stay here to keep her from catching him.

No. She shook her head, her hair swirling around her. No way. Mike wouldn't do this again. Not now.

Would he?

Could Mike's stalker know Brooke's name?

Her hand shook on the doorknob. If that was the case, then she definitely couldn't wait for Mike's return. Because he might be in trouble—and not even know it yet.

She hurried out of her room, phone in hand as she ran for the elevator.

Chapter Sixty-One

Mike stared at Brooke. His... son?

No. He shook his head. No way was this happening again. "Nope." He pushed the photograph back. "What do you want from me? Money? You're not getting it. And I'm back with my wife. So—"

"I don't want your money. And I don't want you."

What then? He stared at her. Took in her yellowish skin. "Why are you here, trying to pawn off this kid as mine?"

"Because he *is* yours," she snapped. "Noah is five. He'll be six in November. Do the math." She dug into her purse again. Pulled out another envelope and pushed it across the table to him.

"What's this?"

"Paternity test. Proving Noah is yours."

What? Mike stared at her.

"Read. It."

"Where'd you get my DNA?"

"From Shauni. After you left their house."

"Shauni wouldn't do that."

She shoved her phone across the table. "You want to call her? I convinced her to let me see what I could find in your bathroom. She was with me the whole time. She said if I was going to do it, then she needed to be the one to bag it and mail it and get the results so there was no way I could mess with it. Call her."

No. He shoved the phone back, his hand shaking. Oh no.

He coughed into his fist, ran his hand down his throat. *Quit stalling, Connor. Read the thing.*

He did.

If she really had used his DNA...

Then he had another son.

Mike closed his eyes, pinched his nose. "I want my own test done."

"Fine. Won't change anything."

What was Meg going to say? He swallowed. His hands were sweating. This would ruin them. Again. *God, please...*

Please *what?*

"Why now? Why didn't you tell me before?"

"Because I didn't know." She looked away, then down to her lap. "I'd been with Damon longer than I'd told you."

Damon, the rising football star she'd left him for. Mike leaned back in his chair, blew out a deep breath. "How long have you known?"

"Only this year. Since March."

He nodded, even though none of it made sense. "How'd you find out?"

"Well..." She fiddled with her nails. "Damon and I didn't last real long. And I really *did* think he was the father. You and I... we were already drifting apart so..."

Mike closed his eyes. Rubbed his forehead.

"Anyway, I have cancer. And I'm not doing well. May not make it. Actually, probably won't." She flashed him a smile as if she found that ironic, in some way. "I'm getting my affairs in order."

He took in her skin color, her short hair. Was that hair even hers?

"Of course that means I need to make sure Noah is taken care of. And who better than his father, right? Except Damon hasn't seen Noah since we split up. So when I *finally* get in touch with Damon, he demands a paternity test. And lo and behold, he isn't Noah's father. You might not believe me, but that does leave only you." She shrugged. "The test proved it."

He watched her, trying to take it all in. Another son, raised by a woman he'd quickly known he never wanted children with. He looked down at the picture again, at a little boy with blond hair like Terrell. With all his baby teeth, like Terrell. With a wide smile that wasn't like Terrell's but was just like Brooke's.

His throat tightened. His chest shook. Not now, not in public. *Get a grip, Connor.* He sucked in a deep, loud breath. Covered his mouth with one hand.

Another child. Another son—and he wasn't Meg's. How on earth was he supposed to build a family with Meg now? What would she say?

He fought back the emotion, shaking once, twice, with the effort. He had to get out of here.

But where did he go for privacy in a city filled with diehard baseball fans? He wasn't taking Brooke to his room. That was for sure.

He sniffed, wiped his nose, picked up the picture.

A son. Noah, his son. Except… Mike could barely speak above a whisper. "What's his last name?"

Brooke sighed. "He has Damon's name."

Mike dropped the picture, buried his face in his hands. Lost control of those emotions he'd fought so hard.

"Mike."

He turned his face to the wall. Right now he needed Meg. Needed her badly, and yet… Telling her would break her heart all over again. She'd hurt just as much as he did.

Maybe worse.

There was no good solution, was there? No matter what he did— told Meg, took in his son by himself, told Brooke no—no matter what, someone would hurt.

Terribly.

And it would all start with Meg. He straightened, looked up at the ceiling, dried his face. He needed her right now. Needed to know it would be all right.

Even though it wouldn't be all right. *Couldn't* be all right.

He dug his phone out of his pocket.

"What are you doing?"

"I'm calling Meg. We need to find some place to work this out." He closed his eyes. *Meg, I'm so—*

His phone rang, Meg's picture appearing on the screen. He pressed Answer.

"Mike?" she said immediately.

"Hey. I, uh—" He couldn't speak, couldn't form another word without losing it. What a mess he'd made of everything.

"Mike, what's going on?"

"We need to talk." He hated how his voice shook. "I'm coming up. Someone will be with me."

"Brooke?"

How did she know?

"Mike, I'm outside the restaurant." Now her voice was shaking too. "Mike, *what* is going on?"

Chapter Sixty-Two

The last time Meg had heard Mike this way... She clutched her phone, the call gone. The last time had been when he'd come home for one night before going back to Brooke.

One night.

It couldn't be happening all over again, could it?

"Meg?"

She whirled at Mike's voice behind her.

He looked horrible. Had he been crying? She hurried the few steps to him. "What's wrong?"

He wouldn't look at her. His mouth trembled, and he pressed a fist against his lips.

Had something happened to Terrell? His family? "Mike, you're scaring me. What's happening?"

He finally looked at her, heartbreak all over his face. "We need to go upstairs."

"Fine. Let's go."

"Brooke needs to come too."

Brooke. So the picture was exactly as she'd been told.

The woman stepped around Mike. Nodded.

Meg stared at her. She was short, too thin, and clearly not well. There was nothing attractive about the woman, not in this condition anyway. Meg bit her lip. "Brooke."

The woman had the decency to look down at her hands.

Why was she back? What had she done that had Mike upset like this? Meg straightened her spine. "Let's go." Whatever was going on, they just needed to get it over with. And send Brooke on her way.

The elevator ride seemed never ending.

At her suite, Meg unlocked the door and led the way inside. She glanced at Brooke, then motioned toward the couch. "Have a seat."

Mike let the door close behind him.

Then stood there.

Meg waited for whatever nightmare Brooke had unleashed on them.

Mike looked at her. "Meg—" His face crumpled. He reached for her. Grabbed her and held her tightly.

God, what is happening? She clung to him while he cried against her neck. Her own tears trickled down her cheeks, tears for whatever pain Mike was going through. *God, help us,* she begged again. "Will you just tell me?" she whispered into his shoulder. "Just say it, Mike."

"Meg, I'm so sorry."

"I know." She pushed him up, watched him wipe the tears from his face.

He still wouldn't look at her.

She moved so he'd have to. "Please. Talk to me."

He nodded. Sniffed. Cleared his throat. Dug into his back pocket and pulled out a picture.

Meg took it.

Brooke and a little boy. A boy who looked so much like Terrell that...

"No." Her own moan startled her. "Oh, Mike."

They held each other again, the tears coming as if they'd never end. Meg clutched him tightly, her heart breaking with his. Another child. With a different woman.

How was this supposed to work?

Mike cupped her face with his hands, his red eyes locked with hers. "Meg, I can't even say—" He couldn't finish. "I'm making you go through it a second time."

She nodded. Yes, it was a staggering heartbreak, a horrible betrayal all over again.

Except that Mike was different. His remorse was real. He had sorrow—deep, gut-wrenching sorrow that somehow comforted her.

Here, in the midst of this awful pain, she felt safe. Secure with Mike.

This new Mike.

But there was still a little boy they needed to talk about. And a mother who would somehow have to fit into the picture.

How, God? Brooke couldn't be a part of their life. No way could she handle Mike travelling to Brooke's home to see his son. Couldn't handle Brooke dropping by every weekend to pick up her child. Couldn't handle this woman being around from now until another little boy was old enough to do the visiting on his own.

And yet this was Mike's son. His child. Part of him.

A huge part of him.

His words were quiet, his breath warm against her cheek. "What are you thinking?"

"I'm trying to solve it. And I can't."

He nodded, misery on his face.

Meg faced Brooke.

The woman sat on the couch, watching them, but when their eyes met, Brooke looked away.

Something about this wasn't right. Brooke wasn't here to win Mike back.

There had to be more.

Meg clutched Mike's hand and led him to the chairs opposite Brooke. "So…" She wasn't going to lash out at this woman. With

God's help, she'd be calm. Gracious. Even though everything in her longed to hurt Brooke. "I'm guessing there are things I need to hear. This little boy belongs to Mike?"

"Yes." Brooke bit her lip. "Meg, I want to apologize—"

"Thank you." Her name coming from Brooke made her sick. "But I can't hear that right now. Just tell me what's happened. Why are you here?"

Mike's voice was hushed. "She's got cancer."

The yellowed skin, the thin frame… "Are you…"

"Am I dying? Yes. That seems to be the case, barring a miracle."

Things began to fall into place. "And you decided it was time to tell Mike."

"Well, his father at least. Turns out, the man I thought was Noah's father, wasn't. That left Mike."

Noah. A name she'd loved. A name she'd considered for Terrell, based on the meaning.

Consolation.

She'd vacillated between the two names, finally choosing the one that gave way to her revenge. Terrell. Powerful.

But her power against Mike had backfired. She'd hurt him horribly, and watching him now, watching him agonize over a child he'd lost years with… *God, forgive me.* Fresh tears coursed down her cheeks. That power had only been used against them both. If she'd told Mike she was expecting their child, their whole history could have been rewritten.

But now, here, after all these years was consolation in Noah, a little boy who would, very soon, need a new mother.

Could she be it?

Meg squared her shoulders, grabbed Mike's hand.

He looked at her, his gaze cautious.

She squeezed his hand.

He squeezed back.

It was time to move forward. Whatever Mike needed, whatever Noah needed, she'd do it. No matter how it might hurt at times. "Why are we here, Brooke?"

She shrugged, but her lips pressed against each other, the first sign that maybe this was hard for her too. "I want Mike to take his son when I'm gone."

Meg closed her eyes. How awful to be forced into making such plans. To lie in bed at night, wondering who to give her precious child to.

She opened her eyes. Caught Mike's gaze. "Well?" she asked him.

He looked at Brooke, then back at Meg. "Brooke, can you give us some time?"

"Where do you want me to go?"

Meg pointed to the bedroom door.

When Brooke was behind the closed door, Meg let her shoulders slump.

"I'm so sorry, Meg." His voice was weak, broken. "Everything I did to you—it's come back to hurt you all over again."

Yes, it had. There was no denying that.

His grip on her hand tightened. "What are you going to do?" he asked.

"What do you mean?"

"I mean…" He faced her, agony etched across his features. "Am I going to lose you? I'd understand if you…" He lost control again and tried to hide his face in his hands.

"Mike." How badly he hurt—and how badly it hurt to watch him. She pulled him to his feet. "Mike, hold me. Please."

He crushed her in his arms.

His tight hold had never felt so good.

"I can't lose you again, Meg." His lips moved against her hair. "I can't do it. Please. You don't know how sorry—"

"Mike, I love you. I'm not going anywhere."

"How? How can you love me? After all of this?"

How? "The same way you can love me. Brooke didn't mean to keep your son from you. I did. What I did to you was awful. Wicked." Tears clogged her throat as the way she'd hurt Mike became far more clear to her than it ever had before. "That you could love *me*, Mike, after what I've done to you…"

"Meg, that's behind us."

"Then so is Brooke." She pushed him up, met his eyes. "I can't say it won't be hard to have a little boy around who doesn't belong to me. Because I'm pretty sure that it will be at first. But if you want to take him in…" *God, help me.* "If you want to make him part of our family—"

"Meg—"

"Then I'll do it."

He let out a sound that was half-laugh, half-cry.

"I mean it, Mike. He's yours. He's part of you. So he should be with you."

"That's what I want."

"Then that's what we'll do."

"Ah, Meg." He wrapped her in his arms again, this time his hold more gentle.

Meg rested against his chest, and Mike's cheek pressed against the top of her head.

He sniffed above her. "Meg Connor, will you marry me?"

Laughter broke through her tears.

"I'm serious. I want to marry you and have time with you and Terrell before we need to take in… before Noah. I want time for us before we have to make that adjustment. So I'm asking…" He pulled back and looked at her. "Man, I stink at proposals. First, Burger King. Now this. Why'd you ever say yes to begin with?"

Meg's laughter grew.

"What do you see in me?" The smile on his face faded. "Seriously.

Why do you love me?"

"Because you're Terrell's father. Because you're a good father. Because you're a good man now, Mike. You love God. Already you've let him change you. But most of all?" She breathed in slowly. Now was not when she wanted to break down. "Because you love me the way I've always wanted to be loved. You've been patient with me these few months when *I* was the one in the wrong. You've shown me true, unchanging love. How can I not respond to that?"

He closed his eyes, rested his forehead against hers. "Is that a yes?"

"It's definitely a yes."

"Thank you." His eyes opened, those warm eyes that usually sparked with laughter and teasing. "I love you, Meg."

"I love you, Mike. For the rest of my life, I will."

His mouth quivered. "I want to love you like I've never loved you before. I want you to never, ever be sorry again that you married me."

She stood on tiptoe and pressed her lips to his. "Quit talking and kiss me, Connor."

His mouth found hers before she'd finished his name, his lips warm against hers, gentle, tender yet strong. He kissed her again and again, kissed her thoroughly, and drove away any fear that their relationship wouldn't last.

No, this time they'd make it. This time, they were stronger than just the two of them. This time their home would stand.

The bedroom door clicked open.

Meg pulled away from Mike and sank back to her feet. How nice of Brooke to come out and ruin a moment.

But Mike stiffened, his focus beyond her shoulder. "Meg, get back." He tugged her behind him, shielding her with his body.

But not before she saw Ben Reynolds in the doorway, gun in one hand, Brooke's arm gripped tightly in the other.

Chapter Sixty-Three

Mike pressed his arms back, around Meg's body.

She shook against him.

Or maybe he was shaking.

Ben spoke, the gun aimed at Brooke's head. "Every time I think I've got you taken care of, Connor, somehow you manage to mess it up. Do you know how sickening you two are? Making up when you should be breaking up?"

So he'd been right—those letters had been from Raines. Which meant there was no telling what this deranged man would do. "What do you want?"

"To see you suffer like I've suffered. To have the woman you love ripped from you. To have the dreams you've had since childhood yanked from you. But no. DaVannon couldn't even hit you hard enough to bring on early retirement." He waved the gun toward them. "And now she doesn't care that you've got a kid with another woman. Come on, Meg. Think. What are the odds there aren't more Connor kids running around out there?"

"There aren't." The same thought had occurred to him during the last awful half hour. He'd mentally gone through his relationships, made sure he'd known each ex-girlfriend's status long enough after they'd broken up.

"Easy to say, Connor. Not so easy to believe after a morning like this."

Brooke jerked her arm, almost wrenching free of Ben's grasp.

The man managed to grip her arm again. He turned the gun her way. "That's enough."

Brooke stilled, fear clear in her eyes.

He had to get Meg out of there. Meg and Brooke. He had to make sure they were safe. "Why don't you let the women go, Ben? This isn't about them. It's between you and me."

Ben smiled at him.

"Right?" The crazy look in the guy's eye... Mike edged sideways, closer to the door, keeping Meg behind him. "Come on, man. I'll stay here. Just you and me. We can talk."

"No talking can fix this."

"Okay, but—"

Meg was slowly tugging his phone from his pocket.

Smart girl. He angled his body so Ben couldn't easily see that side of him. "Look, man. You can't hurt the girls. They've got kids to take care of. You wouldn't take—"

"Wouldn't I? I've had my own family ripped from me, Connor. Why shouldn't you? Why shouldn't your kid?"

There was no reasoning with the freak. No conscience Mike could reach. He swallowed. He needed to stall. Meg had his phone. Soon enough help would arrive.

"Okay." He held up his hands. "I get it. Life's not been fair. But how am I to blame for your family being taken away? How did I do that?"

"I've lost two mothers, Connor. Two. The first one—" Raines shrugged. "Nothing I could do there; I was a kid. But the second one..." He swallowed. "Baseball was gonna get her away from my dad. I could have provided for her. Could have taken care of her. But you made sure that didn't happen."

If only the girls were gone... Then he'd give in to his rising anger and rush the guy. Raines might not be a good shot. Sure, the guy had forty pounds on him, but they weren't forty pounds of muscle. Without the gun, Mike could take Ben. He knew it.

If he could just get close enough…

"What? You got nothing to say?" Raines snapped.

"What am I supposed to say? That I'm sorry? I didn't do anything."

Raines jammed the gun against Brooke's head.

Brooke cried out.

"Okay." Mike took a step closer, his hand stretched out. "Okay. Come on, man." He tried to force some sorrow onto his face. "Look, Ben, please. Really. You've got to let these girls go. You know what it's like to lose a mom. You'd do that to two little boys? Two boys who've never done anything to you?" He scrambled for something that would get through to Ben. "What about Dana?"

Raines lowered the gun a little. "What about Dana?"

Great. "You talked to her lately?"

"What do you think, Connor? You got the cops involved. Of course I haven't talked to Dana—"

"You love her?"

"Yes, I love—"

"Do you? What would she want you to do, Raines? What would she think if she knew you were holding us hostage, threatening two women who've done absolutely nothing to you?" He raised his hands in the air, just to show his helplessness. "What do you think she would say?"

Ben growled at him. "I don't care what she'd say. She's weak. But I'm not. I'm gonna do what needs to be done. I'm going to make it all even between us. Starting now."

The gun pointed his way before Mike could blink. The boom reverberated through the room, and something spun him around, knocked him backward over Meg.

They tumbled to the ground—arms, legs tangled.

Ears ringing, Mike scrambled off her. Was she okay?

Behind them, Brooke cried. She was alive at least. But Meg?

Her eyes met his, scanned him. "Are you hit?" she asked.

Was he? Where was the pain?

On his knees, he spun to face Ben—

To face the gun a foot away from his mouth.

So this was it.

Except Ben looked at the gun, the top of it slid back. Stuck. Jammed.

Mike's eyes met Ben's. Now *this* was it.

Mike knocked the gun away, lunged to his feet. Tackled Ben around the waist and fell on him. They tumbled against the corner of the couch, an edge banging Mike's ribs.

He shoved the pain away. Wrestled for control of Ben, fought to get on top of him.

And then hands grabbed him, hands stronger than Meg or Brooke, and hauled him back.

Mike fought them.

"Hey! Connor!" A face appeared in his vision. A badge. A uniform.

The fight left him.

The two cops who'd grabbed him kept him on his feet.

"Where's my—" She wasn't his wife yet. "Where's Meg?"

One of the cops pointed to the hallway where Meg and Brooke stood, officers surrounding them.

Meg was shaking, tears running down her face.

Mike shoved his way through the cops. Was she hurt?

She opened her arms to him, and he flung himself against her, crushing her to his chest.

But she fought against his hold, pushing against him until she could get a grip on his cast. "Are you hurt?" she asked, her voice demanding.

"Meg, I'm fine."

She dragged her finger down the notch on the surface of his cast. On the divot that hadn't been there before.

Meg looked up at him. "He hit you."

What did it matter? It was over. Mike looked back into the hotel room, where Raines lay on his stomach, hands cuffed behind him, three officers standing around him. "He won't hit anyone else, Meg."

She tugged him a few steps away from the growing crowd of security and police officers and pulled his face down to hers. Kissed him with an intensity he never thought he'd get from her again.

And just when it was all settling in his brain, just when he'd caught his breath, she pulled back from him—tears in her eyes, a grateful smile on her face. "You could have been killed."

Yeah, and he didn't want to think about it. "Just as long as you weren't, Meg. 'Cause it'd be hard to get married without you."

Chapter Sixty-Four

"Are they still asleep?"

From her spot in the bedroom doorway, Meg glanced over her shoulder at Mike as he came down the hallway. She nodded and looked back at the two boys in the twin bed, blonde hair standing out against dark pillowcases, mouths open in deep sleep.

Mike slipped his arms around her waist and settled his chin on her shoulder. "You going to watch them all night?"

She smiled, cocked her head. "Maybe?"

"Don't you think you'd rather watch me sleep?"

"Why? Are you planning on snoring again?"

He shook his head as she turned in his arms, his expression one of feigned hurt. "I told you. I don't snore."

She patted his chest. "Right."

He caught her left hand in his and played with the rings on her finger. "Why are you watching them? They've been asleep for a while."

"I know." She glanced back at two boys who owned her heart, even though one didn't call her Mommy, wouldn't yet open himself up to her. "This is the third night in a row that Noah went to sleep without crying. I just wanted to make sure…"

Mike brushed his lips against her temple. "Okay. We'll watch them awhile."

She settled back against his chest again. "How much longer are you home?"

"Five days. But I don't want to talk about spring training until I have to." His lips traveled to her ear. "I'm going to enjoy every second I have with you."

"I'd forgotten how fast these off-season months go."

"Me too."

She settled herself more snugly into his hold and closed her eyes. "Hey. Happy six-month anniversary."

He pressed his fingers into her side until she stifled a giggle. "Like I didn't tell you that first at breakfast, woman."

"I know. You're such a romantic," she teased.

"Don't forget it, either."

There was very little about the last year she wanted to forget. Ben's attack, yes. The pain of finding out that Mike had another son, sure.

But all of those losses had been redeemed. Mike and Meg had flown to Dallas the day after the All-Star Game to meet Noah. And while he'd definitely been the wild child she'd worried he might be, there was still a sweetness in him that pulled at her heart, partly because of what she knew he was about to face.

Losing a parent wasn't easy.

At any age.

Mike convinced her to marry him—after a game and before another off day like they'd done twelve years ago. So on a Sunday evening in early August, Meg married Mike in the church offices with just a few friends and Mike's family there to see it. He'd told her she could have a big wedding, but she hadn't wanted it. That would take too much time. And Mike was right—they needed time for themselves before Noah arrived.

Before September had ended, Meg asked Mike what he thought about moving Brooke and Noah up by them so Noah could get attached to Mike, at least, before his mother died. Mike had agreed, and so had Brooke who knew she wouldn't make it through the year. The move had been hard on her—had probably taken days from her—but it was the best thing for Noah.

He needed to know his dad well before that awful day came.

Not that Brooke's death was made any easier for the little boy. As much as they'd tried to prepare him, he hadn't fully understood. The nights of tears and tantrums and sobbing almost seemed like they'd never end.

Until finally Terrell began to climb in bed with Noah, talking to him while he whimpered for his mother. Or while Meg stroked his hair and cried silently with him. Or while Mike held the whimpering boy on his lap, Mike's own eyes closed as tears seeped from beneath his eyelids. Some nights it felt next to impossible to love this little boy who didn't want her, who wanted a woman who'd taken from her.

But tonight… Tonight there was hope.

That the worst was behind them.

That life would settle down.

That they could finally be a family of four.

Her stomach moved.

Make that five.

She grabbed Mike's hand and pressed it to her abdomen. "Feel that?"

"No."

She held her breath, waited. *Come on, baby. Do it for your daddy.*

There it was.

She pressed Mike's hand firmly against herself and looked up at him, biting her lip in excitement. "You feel it?"

His grin lit up his face, his eyes. He leaned down over her shoulder, their position a bit awkward, and kissed her. "I felt that." He ran his hand gently over her stomach. "First time. That was awesome."

Yeah, it was.

"And a little weird too, I gotta say."

She elbowed him in the stomach.

"Are you sure it's the baby? It's not gas?"

"Michael!"

"If you need to use the bathroom, Meg, just say so. Don't blame it on 'the baby.'"

She turned on him, swatted him on the arm.

He grabbed her wrist and pulled her close. His lips closed over hers, and she stilled beneath his hold, lost in the happiness of marriage to Mike.

He straightened, his smile warming her. "I wonder what this one will look like."

"Are you kidding?" She looked over her shoulder at the sleeping boys. "Have you seen how strong your DNA is?"

He chuckled. "You ready to let these guys sleep?"

She sent them one last look, her two little boys tucked together in one small bed.

Yes, she could let them sleep now.

Smiling, Mike took her hand and led her down the hall.

Dear Friend,

As always, I'm so grateful to meet you here. You've spent your time and money on my characters, and I hope you enjoyed every moment with Mike and Meg. They're the first in a series dealing with second chances, so watch for book two in the Chicago Wind series, *Shelf Life*, which will be coming out winter, 2016/17. If you'd like to be the first to know when the book is available, please subscribe to my newsletter. And do feel free to keep in touch! I thoroughly enjoy connecting with my readers.

If you're looking for another book to read, may I recommend *Kept*, my first book? Readers have compared it to Francine Rivers' *Redeeming Love*, and it's been very well received. It's about a woman who's fallen for every lie society preaches and a man who's given every bit of himself to God. So how could these two have a future together? I hope you enjoy this one while you wait for *Shelf Life*.

If you'd like to contact me, please visit me at my website, sallybradley.com, or my Facebook page, Sally Bradley, Writer. Until then, I pray you stay close to God and let His Word guide you every day.

Sincerely,
Sally Bradley

PS: Turn the page for a sneak peek at *Shelf Life*!

Prologue

October 18

Nothing good would come from this.

Kyla Burkholder eased onto her cream sofa. Why had they agreed to do this interview again?

As far as she could see, her home was in chaos. The crew from ESPN had covered half the living room with their equipment—wires, lights, cameras. They'd dragged the couch across her Brazilian hardwoods and positioned it several feet in front of the fireplace. As if the eyes in the back of their heads appreciated that view.

They'd need eyes in the back of their heads once the interview aired.

Of course, Brett didn't agree. He'd convinced her so well after ESPN first called, asking them to relive the nightmare for the entertainment of sports fans everywhere.

Kyla shivered.

"Cold?" someone asked.

She looked up.

Angelina, the make-up artist, stood in front of her.

Kyla shook her head. "Nervous."

"Don't be. You're made for TV. Let's do a last touch-up, and you'll be set."

Angelina held up her powder and brush, and Kyla closed her eyes. If the worst that came from this was a gouge in her floor or something knocked over and broken, she'd be ecstatic.

The brush swept across her cheek and nose.

Maybe whoever had sent the letter wouldn't see the interview. She'd pray nonstop that the writer would be at work when it aired. Or sick. Or—better yet—dead.

Dead would be great.

Angelina adjusted her hair. "All done. You can open your eyes."

The key lights had been turned on, momentarily blinding her. She looked away, toward the foyer doorway just as Brett entered.

He crossed in front of the couch and plopped down beside her, his face and shaved head touched up with just enough makeup for television. He took a deep breath and blew it out.

"Sure we should do this?" she asked.

"Of course." The look he shot her asked if she was stupid. "Nothing's going to happen."

"You don't know that."

"And you don't know anything will. It's been a year, Kyla. If they haven't done anything yet, they're not going to. Besides"—his smile felt cold—"this turns the tables on them. It shows if you pull stunts like that, people are coming after you. Ain't that right, Ryan?"

Kyla looked from Brett to Ryan, the producer, who'd walked up to them.

Ryan nodded. "I have no idea what you're talking about, but I'll side with the guy any day."

Brett lifted a fist, and Ryan bumped it with his own, then winked at her. "Brett, let's have you move right next to Kyla. And put your arm around her."

"Like we're in love?" Brett slid his arm around her shoulders, sending her his own bold wink as he did.

The three men on the crew chuckled, and Kyla rolled her eyes in pretend annoyance. Leave it to Brett to get all flirtatious with an audience present.

He started to pull away. "Now if we were an old married couple—"

She flicked his thigh. "We *are* an old married couple. We've got the kids to prove it."

He leaned in close, eyes sparking with a look she knew well after almost ten years together. "We are *not* an old married couple."

She held his gaze. His eyes snapped with a warmth she hadn't seen in months. Where had this come from?

A snicker sounded from one of the crew.

Of course. She lifted her chin. Just like Brett's pitching, his kids, his personal life, and his marriage had to be the best, and everyone within viewing distance needed to know it.

That had been fine when what he bragged about was true.

"That's great. Stay there." Ryan checked his clipboard. "We're going to tape the part where Kyla finds the death threat. Kyla—" He smiled at her. "Just talk to us. We'll stop you if necessary, but tell us what happened, what you did, all that stuff. Keep your eyes on me like we're talking. If you want to glance at Brett from time to time, go ahead. Just don't overdo it."

She nodded. An acidic flavor coated her throat, and she swallowed it away. She hated what this shadowy person had done to them. The threat might be old, but the fear came fresh every morning. If telling the story would end it, then she'd tell it. She was tired of living scared.

She folded her hands and tossed her head.

Angelina darted forward.

Kyla cringed. "Sorry," she said as Angelina toyed with a long strand.

Brett's callused fingers caressed the base of her neck, and she turned her eyes to him. What would she read on his face this time?

"You'll do fine," he whispered. His eyes drilled into her, encouraging her, supporting her.

Kyla willed her smile to be strong. Sometimes hope surprised her.

Chapter One

April 12, six months later

Only eight minutes from home.

Only eight minutes from chatter to silence.

Only eight minutes from life to death.

Kyla turned her Escalade onto the side street and drove beneath a chipped concrete trestle complete with a graffiti-covered train. She scanned the drab scene before her—a used car lot on one side, a black chain-link fence on the other, that overgrown evergreen, and then the sign for Lakeland Memorial Park. She flipped on her blinker. How fitting that the closer she got to the cemetery, the uglier the surroundings would be.

Above the cemetery's sign, treetops covered with infant buds and baby leaves announced that spring had arrived, that nasty season she'd learned brought only bad things. She drove through the gates. At least the grass was lush and green, thanks to a snowy Chicago winter. And overdue for its first mowing. She twisted her mouth at that. They should have looked for a better cemetery, but she'd liked that this one was so close to home. And two years ago no cemetery had seemed good enough to leave a child.

Halfway down the second curve, the marble tombstone appeared on her left. She parked and turned off the engine, then searched the grounds for Brett's gaudy red Alfa Romeo.

The tiny cemetery was empty.

She rested her head against the steering wheel and blew a deep breath into its center. Why she got her hopes up time and again made no sense. Brett had made himself clear—their loss was sad but over. The baby girl they never knew had little effect on him.

Kyla would never be the same.

She opened her door and stepped down. Robins chirped in the branches high above her. Maybe he'd come later—

No. She shook her head. Over breakfast, she'd told him her plans for the day. He'd nodded and stabbed another pancake from the pile as if she'd announced she was getting a pedicure.

Brett wasn't coming.

Other than the funeral, had he ever come? Had he ever loved their youngest child?

She crossed the paved, one-way road to the thick grass and stood before the gravestone.

Ashlyn Rose Burkholder
Received April 9, returned an angel April 12

Kyla closed her eyes, half embarrassed at the words she'd chosen two years earlier. But what had she known then about life after death? Unbidden, the Ashlyn she'd dreamed of rose in her mind, a curly-haired, blonde pixie with a dimple in each cheek, white bows holding her hair back.

But the Ashlyn she'd cried over, the Ashlyn attached to tubes and monitors in the NICU, bore no resemblance.

Kyla kneeled on the ground and ran her hand over the grass as she would have run it over Ashlyn's arm or leg, the way she ran her hand over Haleigh's hair when she slept. "Hi, Ashlyn."

She doubted Ashlyn heard in heaven, but up there she was alive and happy.

"Haleigh and Jax are in school or they'd be here. Haleigh asked me to give you a kiss." She swallowed the rock in her throat. "They might come later. We'll see."

Brett should be here.

"Your daddy's working hard these days. He hired a pitching coach to help him figure out what's wrong. He's happier now that he's busy." Which wasn't saying much. "Maybe he'll be back in the big leagues soon. It'd be nice, just to get him out of the house."

Her eyes slid shut at her words. She should be more understanding of what Brett was going through, but it wasn't that simple when he talked like he'd pitch in the majors forever. She'd never dreamed the Wind would release him two weeks before the season opener. He was completely unprepared for life after baseball.

What if he'd already pitched his last? If things were stressful now, what would they be like in a few months when his last check arrived?

A car door slammed behind her.

Kyla stiffened. She wouldn't look. It wasn't Brett. He hadn't come.

Still, she imagined his arm draped around her shoulders and his kneeling beside her. She could almost feel his sculpted chest as he held her against him. She wiped a rogue tear. She should be crying for her lost daughter, not her marriage.

Except Ashlyn wasn't lost. Ashlyn's departure had prompted Kyla's search into life after death. The woman she'd sobbed all over that first Sunday in church had told her about Ashlyn's new home. She'd shared how that home could be hers too, and finally Kyla accepted it—not for the reunion with Ashlyn, but for the meeting with the God who'd paid for her many, many sins.

Haleigh and Jax believed now. And Brett, well…

"You're my favorite, Ashlyn." Kyla laughed. "There. I've said it. And it's not because I never had to change your diapers. Without you—" She swallowed. "Without you, our family would never have a chance to be together. Forever." She stood and brushed bits of grass

from her jeans. "We'll see you someday, Ashlyn. All of us."
Eventually Brett would be persuaded. And they'd be a family of five
again, once they reached heaven.

Behind her a female voice sounded. "Kyla?"

Kyla turned, her throat tightening.

Her neighbor Lacey stood beside an SUV, plain brown hair
fluttering with the breeze. "I thought—I hope it's okay—"

"Of course it's okay." Kyla crossed the road, Lacey meeting her
halfway and wrapping her in a tight hug. How wonderful to feel arms
around her in this cemetery. "I'm glad you're here. I dread coming
alone, but I can't stay away either."

"As far as I'm concerned, you don't ever have to come alone. Call
me."

Somehow the words stung. "You shouldn't have to do my
husband's job."

"Then how about I do a friend's job?"

Kyla moaned. "Lacey, I'm sorry."

"For what?"

For letting her frustration out on the most selfless woman she
knew. "Thank you for coming. It means a lot. I just wish Brett was
here too." What was wrong with him? She unclenched the fist she
didn't know she'd made and motioned across the road. "Come with
me now?"

"Now is good."

They crossed the asphalt and grass until they stood before the
grave. "Lacey, this is…" Words vanished. Her throat swelled.

"You don't need to say anything, Kyla. I know how much Ashlyn
means to you."

The end of a physical life. The beginning of a handful of spiritual
lives.

For a few minutes, she stood there with Lacey, looking at the
tombstone, listening to the birds sing, feeling the crisp breezes dance

around them. Kyla inhaled the grassy scent and thought back to the day two years ago when the tiny casket had sat there. The pain then had been so sharp, as if it attacked her.

But today—even with her anger at Brett and the pain that threatened—today felt different. Somehow this place held more hope than the last time she'd come. And a little more than the time before that too. Maybe it was Lacey's presence.

Or maybe it was God's.

Beside her, Lacey sighed. "Sometimes I envy your having a grave to visit."

Kyla watched Lacey's profile. Despite the confession, her features stayed calm.

Lacey released a little laugh. "That lilac bush in the backyard is my spot to remember the baby. Maybe it's silly. I don't know."

"It's not silly." Lacey had miscarried a year ago, and Kyla—driving by—vividly remembered seeing Derek consoling Lacey in their backyard. His words had been impossible to hear, but, knowing Derek, Kyla had filled them in.

That he loved Lacey and would be there for her, whenever she needed him.

That God knew what he was doing, that he would help them through it.

That she could cry on his shoulder any time.

What Kyla wouldn't give for a husband who said those things to her. "It's not silly," she repeated.

Lacey gripped Kyla's hand as if she understood.

But she didn't. Kyla loved Lacey and Derek, but sometimes watching them just plain hurt. They were a constant reminder that there were men out there who loved God and who loved their wives for the right reasons. Men she'd missed. Had probably shunned.

Maybe… maybe that part of her life would change. She had to hold on to hope. For all she knew, everything could be about to change.

Lacey nudged her. "What are you smiling at?"

"Nothing. Hope. Dreams, I guess."

"Dreams are good."

"As long as they come to pass."

Lacey flushed. "Maybe."

Lacey with secret dreams? Kyla elbowed her. "Spill it."

"No way."

"Lacey! I thought we were buds."

Lacey shot her a glance, blushing again. "There are things I don't tell Derek, Kyla."

"And I don't tell Brett every deep, dark desire either."

"Then you understand."

Flashes of her own longings sprang before her, secrets she would never tell Brett. Or Lacey. "Well." She cleared her throat. "Okay."

If Lacey only knew...

But she didn't. Kyla rubbed her forearm, thoughts she refused to think making the silence uncomfortable. "We should head back."

Lacey nodded. "You okay then?"

"Better." Kyla forced a smile. "Thanks for coming."

They walked back to their cars, and Kyla cast one more glance around before opening her door. Yes, she was better than she'd been a year ago. Two years ago. Much better.

But was her marriage better?

No.

She eased onto her seat and from her rearview mirror watched Lacey turn her SUV around. Since the ESPN interview in October, the distance between her and Brett had slowly grown. Sometimes she thought it was Ashlyn's death. Sometimes she thought it was her new faith. Sometimes she thought it was just life.

Then, a month ago, Brett lost his job.

There was a chasm dividing them now.

She started the Escalade. She had to hold onto hope that Brett was home this spring for a reason. Maybe, for the first time in a few years, spring would finally bring something good into her life. Maybe this was when Brett would get it.

When that happened, everything about their marriage would be better.

Please, God.

Everything.

⁓⊰⊱⁓

"Haleigh, Jackson!" Kyla leaned around the doorframe of the kitchen stairs and called up to the second floor. "Time for dinner."

Above her the shuffle of footsteps sounded, then the arguing. Kyla closed her eyes and held up a hand. Seemed it was a day for arguing. She'd let this one go.

She'd returned from the cemetery to find Jackson and Haleigh in the kitchen eating a snack with Irina, her housekeeper. Brett was downstairs in the media room, Irina had said, analyzing pitching video with Miles Hamlin, his pitching coach.

Taking a deep breath, Kyla had pushed open the door to the basement media room.

"What do you want?" Brett asked without taking his eyes from the screen.

Maybe some manners? She forced calm into her voice. "I need to talk to you."

With a huff, he froze his image on the screen and stepped around Miles to walk up the side ramp of the theater. He stopped before her, the planes of his face especially taut. "What?"

"I mean a conversation. Can't you take a break?"

"No." He turned away. "We'll talk tonight."

"I have Bible study tonight."

He walked down the ramp. "So skip it."

"Do you know what today is?"

He sent her an angry look as he passed Miles in the front row. "Yes, Kyla. April twelfth. I know." He dropped into his seat and picked up the remote. The Brett frozen mid-delivery on the screen rewound smoothly.

She shut the door to the media room and stared at its dark wood veneer. "Do you care?"

The answer had been obvious.

A thud sounded as one of the kids banged into the stairway wall.

Now she and Brett wouldn't talk. In forty-five minutes, she and the kids would leave for church, and Brett was still downstairs working with Miles. By the time she returned and got the kids in bed, Brett would be asleep himself.

The anniversary of Ashlyn's death, and he'd said nothing except an irritated "I know."

Seven-year-old Haleigh emerged from the enclosed staircase, her six-year-old brother Jax behind her, wearing a smirk. "Don't push!" Haleigh snapped. "Mom, Jax won't—"

"Stop it, both of you. I'm not in the mood. Finish setting the table so we can eat."

Jax swung an invisible weapon at Haleigh's back. "I thought dinner was ready."

"It will be, as soon as you put napkins and salad dressings on."

"We're having salad?" He opened the refrigerator and stuck his head inside. "Irina never makes me eat salad."

"I'll talk to Irina in the morning."

"Aww, man."

Brett's and Mile's voices sounded from the basement stairway. Brett entered the kitchen first, Miles on his heels.

Kyla ignored Brett. "Hi, Miles."

As usual, Miles nodded back and stuffed his hands into his baggy shorts' pockets.

What was it about her presence that sent this man into his shell? Every time she entered a room, he withdrew, staring at the wall while she and Brett talked—or argued.

Miles pushed faded blond hair out of his eyes. He needed a haircut. His longish, wavy hair gave him the rumpled appearance of someone who'd just woken from a nap, and his shapeless, late-forties body and expressionless features made him look like a man lost.

"Feel free to stay for dinner, Miles," she said. "There's plenty."

"Thank you, but I've got dinner waiting at home." He glanced at her, then away. "Maybe another time."

Sure. Just like the other times he'd declined. She shrugged as the men left.

A glance into the dining room showed Haleigh tipping her chair back and Jax swinging his spoon like a baseball bat. "Jax, stop that. Haleigh, you too." Why couldn't the kids behave today?

"I'm hungry," Jax whined. "Can we eat without Dad?"

Kyla lifted the pan of lasagna from the warming drawer and carried it to the table where she set it on a trivet. Where had Brett disappeared to? She pointed to the pan as she backed from the table. "Don't touch that. It's hot."

Where was Brett? They always ate at six during the off season— he wanted it that way. She hurried through the living room and into the two-story, glass-encased foyer, pausing at the bottom of the main stairs. She leaned up them. "Brett, we need to eat."

Nothing.

"Now."

More nothing.

She climbed the stairs. The door to their bedroom stood shut, and she opened it. "Brett?"

He popped his head and bare shoulders out of the master bathroom. "What?"

"Time for dinner. We can't wait."

"Go ahead."

He disappeared back into the bathroom, and Kyla followed. He grabbed the T-shirt he'd changed out of and a damp washcloth and tossed them at the wicker hamper. They snagged on the outside, but he ignored them, digging through an open drawer.

Kyla ignored his actions too. Years of clubhouse attendants picking up after him had cemented his habits. She dreaded the day they couldn't afford Irina. "How was your workout?"

"Fine." He tugged a clean gray Yankees T-shirt over his head.

"Anything interesting?"

He shrugged as he picked up a tube of lotion and squeezed a dollop into his hand. "Taped pitches this morning, watched them this afternoon."

She waited for more while he rubbed lotion over his scalp.

Brett stayed silent.

"And?" she prodded.

"Really don't want to talk about it, Kyla." He slipped past her, into the bedroom, and grabbed his wedding ring from the dresser. He headed for the door, his face set as if he was walking to the pitcher's mound, the game on the line.

Did he think he was the only one in this house with problems? As he passed, she stretched her arm across his chest and tried to tug him close.

For an instant, his body tensed, as if to pull away. Then he stilled and looked at her, his eyes flat and unblinking.

Why was he so cold? She wrapped her arms around his waist and flashed a flirtatious smile. "Can't a girl hug her man?"

He gave her a token hug, the kind she'd come to expect. Where was he lately? Was it just his lack of a job? Or something else?

He pulled out of her embrace. "We should make sure the kids aren't having a food fight." He left and hurried down the stairs, as if he wanted to get away from her.

Slowly, Kyla followed. She shouldn't let him get to her. He was going through a difficult period. Baseball had always been his life, and to not have it now…

She lagged behind as they entered the dining room. The kids' faces lit up. Jax pointed his finger at Brett and started shooting, sound effects and all. Brett dipped and ducked as if evading bullets all the way to Jax's chair where he grabbed him in a bear hug and shook him gently.

Across the table, Haleigh squealed and put up her hands in pretend fear, a grin spreading across her pretty features. Brett growled around the table, taking exaggerated steps until he stood behind her. Haleigh curled into a ball on her chair, still squealing. Brett lowered his face closer, closer to hers, his mouth opening wide like a bear about to eat his dinner. At the last second, he puckered and covered her cheeks and blonde hair in kisses.

Jax wrinkled his nose. "Kisses—gross."

Never gross. Wonderful. How long since Brett had kissed her with feeling? Heat flooded her face, and Kyla escaped to the kitchen. Something beyond baseball had to be wrong for him to be cold one minute and so loving and open the next.

She tossed her hair and raised her chin, relieved that this time she'd contained her emotions. Still, she needed a moment to compose herself. She grabbed the basket with today's mail and flipped through it. Credit card applications, a Jewel grocery store flyer, the latest Restoration Hardware catalog, an envelope with Brett's name printed across it in funny type—

She picked it up and studied it, a vague memory fighting a film of time. She slid her finger beneath the sealed flap. A single piece of paper, covered in printed computer type, was folded inside.

Brett,
Are you sleeping well at night? Wondering where I am? If tonight's the night we meet?
I still owe some on those World Series games you

blew. The guy I owe is getting impatient. He's threatened my family. Because of you.

It's not fair what you did. I still keep the Glock by my bed. I keep it there because I might need it to protect my family. And I might need it for yours—

The paper fluttered from her hands. Her fingers chased it, clutching after it as it floated down, onto the floor, print side up. Kyla swallowed. Saliva stuck in her throat. She gagged and grabbed the edge of the quartz counter, her fingers slipping and sending her crashing to the floor.

"Kyla?"

Brett's voice sounded so far away.

A chair scraped the floor. "I'll see what your mom knocked over this time."

The paper lay an inch from her knee.

I still keep the Glock—

"Kyla?"

She jerked at his voice above her and looked up.

He frowned at her, a mix of bewilderment and annoyance.

She lifted a hand, watched it shake.

He stared at it, then her, before hauling her to her feet. "What's the matter with you?"

She couldn't keep her eyes off the letter.

Brett snatched it up, scowling as he scanned it.

Maybe she'd read it wrong. Maybe he'd look at her with that you're-crazy look she despised. Maybe—

He stiffened.

So it was real, it was true, she hadn't imagined it.

His eyes met hers over the paper. "Kyla."

A bitter laugh escaped. "I told you we shouldn't have done that interview. He's back."

"It's a copycat. It's just someone having fun—"

"How do you know it's a copycat?" She snatched the letter and glared at it. Shook it at him. "How do you know? They never caught whoever sent the first one. You *knew* that, Brett. You *knew* he might be watching. And guess what? He was!"

"Lower your voice," he snapped.

"Why? So the kids don't hear? I'm so…" She searched the room for the right words. "I'm sick of this."

"Of what?"

"Of everything being wrong. Of you being wrong."

"Don't you start blaming me for—"

"It *is* your fault!"

He flinched, his eyes narrowing in… in some emotion she didn't want to identify.

Yet she couldn't stop her words. Not after this bad choice of his. "I'm tired of living with a man who always gets it wrong. Look around, Brett. You're not the only one living here."

He drew in a breath, shoulders straightening. "Right back at you, Kyla. You act like you're the only one who knows what's right or wrong anymore."

She waved the letter in his face. "Evidently I am—"

"Mommy?"

Haleigh and Jax stood nearby, eyes wide.

Brett tossed her a glare. "Who's wrong now?"

She spun away from him. The closest exit was the basement stairs, and she took it, her words chasing her down.

That and the hurt that had flashed across Brett's face.

But she didn't care. She shook her hair. She couldn't care. It was time he realized what he was doing to this family. They were falling apart—in danger—and all the blame rested on him.

He'd promised her that nothing would happen. That they'd be safe. That the nightmare was over.

But he'd been wrong.

Scary wrong.

And she was tired of living with a man who got everything wrong.

Also from Sally Bradley

Kept

Miska Tomlinson knows there are no honorable men. Her womanizing brothers, her absentee father, and Mark—the married athlete who says he loves her—are all undependable. But Miska has life under control. She runs her editing business from her luxury condo, stays fit with jogs along Chicago's lakefront, and secretly blogs about life as a kept woman.

Enter neighbor Dillan Foster. Between his friendship and her father's reappearance, Miska loses control of her orderly life. When her relationship with Mark deteriorates, Miska compares him to Dillan. Dillan's religious views are foreign, yet the way he treats her is what she's longed for. But when he discovers exactly who she is and what she's done, she finds herself longing for a man who's determined to never look her way again.

When her blog receives national press, Miska is caught in a scandal about to break across the nation. Will the God Dillan talks about bother with a woman like her? A woman who's gone too far and done too much?

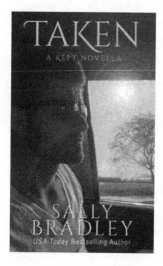

Taken, a Kept novella

Cam Winters is known as the guy who always dates the new women at church—and then ends the relationship quickly. He's never talked about his past, about his life before he became a Christian, but Jordan Foster has learned to look past the unknown part of him. To her, he's a strong, caring man—a man she can see herself with.

He's also a man who refuses to ask her out for fear of what her brother, one of his closest friends, might say.

So Jordan takes things into her own hands.

When Cam admits to sharing her feelings, the two quickly fall in love—just as that past that Cam won't talk about returns for him and those he loves... a group which now includes Jordan.

Acknowledgments

This is a book that's been a long time coming. Back in the last century—millennium?—I wrote my first contemporary adult fiction scene, the one where Mike autographs Terrell's baseball.

Meg and Mike are special to me because they spent a lot of time with me while I had two kids, figured out sleeping schedules (only to see it change the next week, right?), and endured the joys of teething and potty training. But even after the book was done, for the fifteenth time, and an agent had shopped it, no publisher gave my two favorite characters a home.

So getting back to this book all these years later, going over Mike and Meg's journey, updating and revising and making things just a little harder for them has been very, very sweet. Thank you, my reader friends, for welcoming these two into your world.

Two women were huge in the development of this book. Kerri Knox, Christian fiction reader extraordinaire, was as patient as any reader friend could be. Kerri, I think you read this thing about five or six times, right? You saw a number of variations on the story, and your feedback helped me get this book to where it is today. Thank you, thank you, thank you. Life has moved us away from each other, but I'm so grateful for all of your support, encouragement, and honesty.

Elizabeth Kramer became a friend while I was writing this and finally read it based on something Kerri said. But what Elizabeth got from reading it was all the "murder and mayhem" this seemingly quiet, normal, redheaded pastor's wife was writing. She gave me grief about that—and always in public! I'm sure you did it just to make me look tougher, right, Elizabeth? Thank you for sharing your medical knowledge as I worked to injure Mike in the right way. You've given me lots of feedback on medical situations in other projects, and I'm pretty certain there's more in our future. Thank you so much for your friendship outside of my writing.

I have to give a big thanks to Christina Tarabochia for her mad editing skills. One of the risks of editing for an indie author is that the author has the final say—because the author *is* the publisher. So any mistakes in the book belong to me alone. Christina, you're such a joy to work with, even though our conversations have just been via email so far. I always look forward to hearing your thoughts on the story, particularly your little side comments as you discover what happens. Those are, hands down, my favorite. Even above all those fun comma and paragraph break discussions. Thank you for all you've done to help my books look more professional.

This book caught me at a very hectic stage of life. I'm thankful for my husband and kids who put up with my getting lost in a book—it was the deadline's fault, honest—and love me enough to listen to my updates and even bravely ask on their own how the book is going. Steve, Ty, Alison, Luke—you guys are everything to me.

One more thing—this book debuted in the Whispers of Love box set along with eleven other authors. And we were blessed to see that set end up at #79 on the *USA Today* bestseller list! Much thanks goes out to Kimberly Rae Jordan, Leah Atwood, Valerie Comer, Christina Coryell, JoAnn Durgin, Autumn Macarthur, Lesley Ann McDaniel, Carol Moncado, Staci Stallings, Jan Thompson (our fearless leader) and Marion Ueckermann. Ladies, I learned a lot from you!

Lastly, thank you, God, for keeping this book on my computer and off the bookshelves so many years ago. The time gave me a chance to grow as a writer and create a stronger story than I ever could have then. And to see this book that filled so many years of my life now find readers and great success... well, I couldn't have even dreamed of that way back then. Thank you.

About the Author

 Sally Bradley has been a fiction lover for as long as she can remember—and has been fascinated by all things Chicago (except for the crime, politics, and traffic) for almost as long. A Chicagoan since age five, she now lives in the Kansas City area with her pastor/cop husband and their three children, but she and her family get back to Chicago when they can for good pizza and a White Sox game. A freelance editor and former president of her local writing chapter, Sally has won a handful of awards for her first book, *Kept,* and another, soon-to-be-released *Shelf Life*. Visit her online at sallybradley.com.

35769257R00220

Made in the USA
Middletown, DE
14 October 2016